KATE SCHUMACHER

ON THIS BROKEN EARTH

THE GRAIL CYCLE
3

ON THIS BROKEN EARTH, BOOK 3: THE GRAIL CYCLE

Copyright © 2025 Kate Schumacher

Paperback: 978-1-7636917-0-4

Hardcover: 978-1-7636917-1-1

Ebook: 978-1-7636917-2-8

First paperback edition: 2025

First hardcover edition: 2025

Edited by Henry Sinclair - https://authorsownpublishing.com

Cover design by Franziska Stern – https://www.coverdungeon.com

Map created by Rachael Ward - https://www.cartographybird.com

For more information, please visit https://www.kateschumacherauthor.com

For those who have been silenced.
Be loud.

TO THE READER

This story has been written for an adult audience. Within these pages you will find content that may be triggering, including physical assault and violence, death, emotional manipulation including grooming behaviours, torture, and discrimination against those from different backgrounds and those from LGBTQ+ communities. People who have suffered religious trauma may also find some of the story content distressing.

A NOTE FROM THE AUTHOR

Welcome back to Teyath and the penultimate book in *The Grail Cycle*. The waters are murky indeed! The Gods continue to meddle, and everyone continues to be tested as they untangle prophecies, their own emotions and try and survive the consequences of choice.

You will meet new characters, travel to new parts of the world of Teyath, and along with the characters, learn many things.

Strap in and enjoy *On this Broken Earth*.

PRONUNCIATION GUIDE

PEOPLE

Jenyfer - Jennifer
Ordes - Or/dez
Lamorna - Lar/morn/a
Jalen - Jar/len
Iouen - I/oh/an
Carbrey - Car/bray
Ulrian - Ol/re/ann
Bryn - Brin
Niniane - Nin/ee/aine
Aelle - Ay/la
Tahnet - Tar/net
Katarin - Kat/ar/en
Tregarthen - Tree/gar/then
Ankou - An/coo
Ophine - O-feen
Andromache - An/dro/ma/keh
Halymere - Hal/e/meer
Ethinne - E/thee/en
Morgause - Mor/gowz
Niniane - Nin/e/aine
Goerika - Gor/e/ka
Melhala - Mel/hal/ah
Ereshki - Ee/resh/key
Isolde - I/zol/duh

Elaine - Eh/lain
Medb - Meb

Sheleitari - Shay/leet/ar/ee
Syhren - siren

PLACES

Teyath - Tae/ath
Cruithea - Crew/i/the/a
Mahwenia - Mar/when/e/a
Kernou - Ker/know
Calledun - Cal/ee/dun
Sacellum - Sack/ell/um
Lyonesse - Lie/on/ess
Dinas Emyrs - Din/nass Emm/riss
Malist - Mal/iss/t
Kunis - Koo/ness
Ossuary - Oss/you/airy

THE LANDS OF
TEYATH
MAPPED
IN THE PRESENT AGE
CARINYA
CELIVALE GROVE
NEWLYN
THE FAIR WATERS
AVALON
VIDARRA FOREST
KERNOU
LYONESSE
BAY OF CALLEDUN
MAWHENIA
BANSTEIN RIVER
ABSHAW WOODS
ARCDON
PORT LEORE
SKOVER'S BAY
SEA OF ANDRED

GREENSTONE SEA
THE TEETH
THE MOON'S BITE
THE ROOST
THE DEAD WOODS
NIMUS ARBORES
HUNTER'S FOREST
CRUITHEA
KUNIS
THE CATIGERN SEA
FEY HIGHLANDS
CAMLANN PLAINS
DINAS EMRYS
LYSEIGN RIVER
NEMHAIN'S MOUNTAINS
MALIST
BAY AN ANAON
FAERY FOREST
VINIA
AVINIA RIVER
REDCANA FOREST
BAY OF SHADOWS
THE VALE
SKULL'S REST

CHAPTER 1

The curtains flew open and watery sunlight flooded the cabin. Another flick of the wrist and they snapped closed. Ordes did it again, his smile widening.

This new magic was actually pretty handy.

The curtains drew open once more.

'Will you stop that?'

Jenyfer lifted her head from the pillow and rubbed at her cheek, hair hanging around her face like a wild dark wave. The morning light caught on the scales at her wrist, painting the silvery-blue with flecks of gold.

'I'm tired,' she complained, shooting Ordes an accusing look.

'That's not my fault,' he said. 'I believe your words were, "don't stop, don't stop. Ordes, if you stop, I'm going to kill you".'

She blinked at him, stormy blue eyes narrowing. 'I did not say that.'

'You did,' he replied smugly. 'And by the way, I think half the ship heard you.'

Jenyfer scowled.

Laughing, Ordes pressed a kiss to her forehead. 'I don't mind,' he murmured, tucking her hair behind her ear, tracing the shell of it lightly, making her shudder. 'I kind of like it.'

'Of course you do.' Jenyfer rolled her eyes, giving him a lazy smile, before flopping onto her back with a dramatic sigh. 'Well, this is embarrassing. How am I going to show my face up there?' She gestured to the deck above them as she pulled away, climbing out of bed and stretching the kinks from her back. She peered out the porthole at the water with a grateful sigh.

Ordes had watched Jenyfer swimming every morning, and each time she returned from the water, her scales were more prominent, reminding Ordes more of the syhrens he'd seen in Lyonesse. Sometimes he swam with her, but most times he watched her from the deck, marvelling at how different she was, how changed since the time she'd jumped into the sea with him and sank like a stone. She was graceful and confident, as if she'd spent her whole life in the water.

He linked his hands behind his head, watching her hunt around for some clothing. Heat sparked in his chest and he rubbed at it absently. They were both still discovering how the heartfire worked. Niniane had told him it was a soulmate's bond, but more than that. The steady, pleasurable thrumming in his chest was always there, and quickened when Jenyfer was near. When she was unhappy, it flared with a sharp burst of heat. When she was happy, the heartfire's warmth spread through Ordes from head to toe, turning his muscles into liquid, like he'd been lazing in the sun for too long.

'Am I allowed to tell you I love you?'

Every time he said it, she became quiet and still. She still didn't believe she deserved his affections, no matter how many times he told her differently. He wished he could turn back time and crush that man she'd been forced to marry, make his head ring for the rest of his life.

Or kill him. That was still on the table. If Jenyfer wanted Bryn dead, Ordes would do it, and he'd find pleasure in it – the heartfire would demand it.

Part of him hoped they'd never see Bryn again. Everything he had done to Jenyfer haunted Ordes, the heartfire alight with vivid mental images so real, so visceral, he could smell blood he had not shed, could feel the heat of it on his hands, slicked over his fingers.

The images were omnipresent. Sometimes he couldn't shake them. Sometimes he wondered if he had killed Bryn already. Sometimes he wanted to go ashore and find the arsehole and get it over with.

But Jenyfer hadn't asked, so Ordes wouldn't.

She still had not turned around, Ordes' question hanging in the air.

'Yes.' It was a whisper, barely there, but it was enough.

'Good,' Ordes declared, throwing back the sheet and climbing out of bed. The corner of Jenyfer's mouth lifted. 'Because I'm going to tell you, several times a day, until you believe it.'

'I do believe it,' Jenyfer said, pulling one of his shirts on. She tossed some clothes at him, purposefully not looking at him. 'Please get dressed.'

His grin widened and he chuckled.

'Smugness is not your best trait, Ordes,' she said, laughing as he caught her arm and pulled her close, one hand gripping the back of her neck, the other pressed into her lower back.

'So what is my best trait then?'

'Definitely your humility,' Jenyfer murmured against his mouth. 'And there is your mouth, although that's not really a trait, is it? But it does say nice things to me. There's these, I suppose,' she said, running her hands down his arms. 'I like these because they make me feel safe.' Her hands grazed his hips; he bit his lip, feeling his blood warm and his muscles tighten as her fingers skimmed lower, then withdrew. 'I think that's about it.'

Ordes laughed. 'Your father told me that I wouldn't be enough.' He didn't know why he was telling her, why Melodias' words chose that moment to sneak into his head. Jenyfer pulled away, her face horrified.

'He said what?'

Ordes went to run his fingers through his hair before remembering he'd finally let Jenyfer cut it last night. He was yet to see his reflection, but he didn't care about hair, not at the moment. 'I'm going to do my best to prove him wrong.'

'Ordes—'

'I love you,' he said.

Jenyfer's face softened. 'I love you, too.' She stood on her tiptoes and kissed him gently, caressing his hair. 'It suits you.'

When Ordes went above deck, smiling at the world, he found Katarin with her arms folded, eyes locked on the coastline of Teyath in the distance. Brooding, as she had been since they left Cruithea. Her red hair was loose, the sea breeze tugging at it.

After greeting Carbrey and Kayrus, Ordes joined Kat. He leant against the railing with a blissful sigh. 'Life is good, isn't it, Captain?'

'I'm surprised you can walk,' Kat commented without looking at him. 'Where's Jenyfer? Still on her back?'

'Swimming. And if you must know, I'm the one who was on my back.'

'Thanks for the overshare,' Katarin said, then laughed. 'Nice hair.'

Ordes reached up to brush his hand over his head. 'Is it bad?'

Katarin chewed her lip, taking her time studying him. 'No,' she said eventually. 'Doesn't improve your face much, though.'

Ordes chuckled, his smile fading as he recalled the conversation he'd had with Jen before she took a pair of scissors to his head. 'You told her about us?'

'I sort of assumed you had already. Why didn't you?' Katarin asked.

He shrugged. 'I don't know. I wasn't trying to deceive her. I didn't think it was important.'

Katarin raised her eyebrows.

'That isn't what I meant. Look, can we start over?'

'Sure,' she said sweetly. 'Morning, Ordes. Have much sex last night?'

He burst out laughing. 'Thanks, Kat.'

'What for?'

'Making me laugh.'

The Excalibur and her crew were south of Kernou, tucked somewhere between Lyonesse and the mainland. Ordes fought the urge to glance over his shoulder and turn his gaze to the west, where the realm of the Master of Songs and Death resided. Many times he'd caught Jenyfer chewing her lip, eyes lost in the western horizon. Ophine had told Jenyfer that her father's syhrens would come for her, but so far, they hadn't seen a single one. That was probably for the best, although it left Ordes wondering what game Melodias was actually playing with them. He'd taken their map – a 'bargaining chip', he'd called it. Jenyfer was apprehensive about her father's motivations. She had her own thoughts to untangle about him and about Lyonesse, just as Ordes had about his parents.

The Myrddin and the Goddess of Magic.

In Cruithea, Goerika had told him his father's magic was also his, and she had told him Tymis Merlyni was not human. That Ordes was not human either. But he *felt* human – his heart beat, his lungs expanded when he took a breath. He ate because his stomach told him to, he slept because he was tired, and he felt that spark in his chest whenever Jen rolled in her sleep and curled herself against him.

But more than that, he *cared* about people. He had friends, and their wellbeing mattered to him. When Arthur gave the crew the option of getting off at the next port, part of Ordes had hoped they would, but not one man or woman had abandoned ship.

And that meant something – to Ordes, to Arthur, and to Katarin, even if she didn't let it show. There was a brittleness to Kat's smirk, when she didn't realise she was being watched. The look on Kat's face after the syhren attack on *The Queen* would stay with him forever. He had thought her unflappable, completely unable to be shaken. That had been what had drawn him to her all those years ago – her confidence, in who and what she was and what she wanted. Katarin's walls were well-fortified, though, and any offer of sympathy would be scowled at, or she'd flip her hair over her shoulder and turn away. Ordes and Jenyfer had each other, and Arthur had Jalen. But Katarin was alone.

She didn't cope with being alone, no matter how much she declared otherwise. So she kept busy, dragging them all into the captain's cabin at whatever hour of the day or night suited her, pouring over maps, over the words of the prophecy, rehashing what they had learnt, making plans only to discard them and construct new ones. They were sailing towards the Faery Forest, towards Arthur's Treasure. The Sword of the White Dragon was hidden somewhere in that ancient forest, if dreams and magical maps were to be believed. Katarin was sceptical – the map that had appeared on Jenyfer and Ordes' skin was the work of the shade of a long-dead human queen, Eseld, now bound to the Grail and its fate. If the Old Ones had been lying to them, could they really trust the words of a ghost that only Arthur saw in his dreams?

Nothing was as simple as it had once been; such was the nature of prophecies and long-lost destinies.

Ordes kept his eyes on the coast of Teyath. A few more days and they would be approaching Port Leore, and then Arcdon, before they weighed anchor at Skover's Bay. The weather had been good to them so far – clear skies and strong winds – so the journey had been swift.

'Kat,' Ordes began.

'You look like you're thinking terribly hard, Ordes,' she quipped. 'Should I be concerned your head will explode?'

He managed a small smile. 'Do you think we're doing the right thing?'

The light left Katarin's face, and he was sorry for his question. It wasn't that he ever forgot what they were doing – but sometimes he wished he could, that they could all live their lives without this pressure.

Katarin sighed, rubbing at her cheek. 'I don't know.'

'Did Niniane lie to us?' Ordes asked. 'You know her better than anybody, except perhaps my father, and he isn't here to ask. I want to know what you think.'

'I think she told us what she thought we needed to know,' Katarin said slowly. 'Is that a lie? Maybe. It's definitely omitting certain truths, and I'm unsure of how much trust I can put in her words. The storm demon would tell you she did not lie,' Kat added in a low voice.

'You don't trust him, do you?' Ordes asked her, lowering his voice. Neither Arthur nor Jalen were on deck.

Kat shook her head. 'I can't tell you why – call it a sense, or something, but he's not being honest with us, not completely. Which means he isn't being honest with Arthur, and if anything, that is worse.' She turned to face Ordes, drumming her fingers against the railing. 'Think about it. He was pulled from death by Ankou – because no one else can do that, given the powers he has – and then the God of the Otherworld ... what? Just let him leave? Let him attach himself to Niniane? Why? There is something I'm missing.' Kat sighed again, exasperated. 'But I can't prove anything, so I don't say anything. I don't want to upset my brother, not now, not when there is so much on his shoulders.'

'On mine as well,' Ordes murmured.

'Yes, but your shoulders are broad, Ordes,' she joked. Then, softer, 'I know you think you can't do it, that you can't be what you need to be to see this done. But we never see ourselves clearly, do we? That's a lesson for Jenyfer, too.'

Ordes nodded in agreement. 'Then I'm going to take this moment to tell you that you are not as scary and uncaring as you think you are. We all see through it, Kat,' he added, as she gave him a scowl. He didn't say any more – he'd let her brood over it for a while. 'Arthur has been quiet,' he offered.

'Let's see how chatty you are when we're about to walk into Malist and find your Treasure,' Kat snapped, then shook her head. 'I'm sorry.'

'You're worried about him. It's perfectly normal, Katarin,' Ordes replied.

Katarin didn't acknowledge the statement, instead slapping her hands on the railing. 'This ship ...'

'What about it?' Ordes asked, raising his eyebrows. 'You don't like her?'

'She doesn't like me,' Kat mumbled. 'I can't reach her. With *The Queen*, I could communicate with her – not talk to her, but *feel* her, and she could feel me. My magic and her magic were linked. But with *The Excalibur*, there's nothing.' She paused, glancing at Ordes before returning her gaze to the ocean. 'Maybe you should—'

'No, Kat. You're better at being Captain than me,' Ordes cut in.

She smiled. 'Of course I am. I was going to suggest you should use your new tricks to find your father and get him to tell this ship she's mine now.'

When Ordes didn't respond, she nudged his shoulder with hers. 'You haven't said much about it. Him, being the Prophet of the Gods and all that.'

'I'm not sure what I'm supposed to say about it,' Ordes answered, frowning.

'Well, his little prophecies have messed with all our lives,' Katarin said. 'I, for one, have things I'd like to say about it.'

'Like what?'

'Like why he waited, why he hid the truth – about who he was, about all of this,' she replied.

'What would you have done if he'd sat you down for a chat and told you your long-lost brother, who you had never met, was destined to be the King of Teyath, and soon you'd be risking your life to find the Treasures of the Gods?' Ordes asked. 'Would you have believed it?'

'No,' Kat said after a pause. 'I wouldn't have. But if I'd had some warning, then maybe when it did happen it wouldn't have come as such a surprise.'

'Maybe,' Ordes agreed. Jenyfer appeared in the water below them. She beckoned for him to join her. Ordes smiled, pulling his shirt off and handing it to Katarin, who made a noise of objection.

'Leave the rest on, please,' she muttered.

Ordes laughed, then threw himself into the water.

Chapter 2

In his mind's eye, Arthur could see the Sword of the White Dragon, the Treasure destined for his hands. When he looked down, his fingers were not curled around the hilt of a wooden sword, but a pommel glimmering silver, ornately decorated with a dragon. It was not the dull crack of wood on wood he heard when his sword clashed with Halymere's, but the ring of steel on steel, echoing through his ears and vibrating through his blood.

Nudging the hair out of his eyes, Arthur adjusted his grip on the sword, keeping his eyes low to avoid the glaring sunlight. He feinted left and swept his sword forward; the Cruithean countered easily, but Halymere was smiling beneath his beard.

'Good,' he said. 'That was faster than yesterday, Arthur. More instinct than thought.'

Arthur smiled in return. 'Let's go again,' he said.

They continued, dancing around one another, the ship's crew dancing around them. Arthur had been worried about practising on the deck, but there really was nowhere else. Katarin had assured him the crew would work around it, and they had. No one complained or grumbled whenever he got in their way. No one laughed when he dropped the sword, which wasn't as often now.

Not one person had jumped ship in Kernou when given the chance. He thought maybe they'd wait until Port Leore, but as far as he knew, no one was planning on leaving then, either. His heart swelled when he realised that these men and women were pledging themselves to this quest, to him and what he was destined to become.

It made everything a little brighter, a little easier for him to climb out of bed each day and face the world. These people trusted him, and as terrifying as that thought was, it sent a rush of heat flowing through him. He wished he knew what was going to happen, so he could give them some assurances.

As Arthur countered Halymere's strikes and forced the Cruithean to step back, he could feel Jalen watching them. He didn't have to look to know Jalen was standing on the quarterdeck with Kayrus. The helmsman had grown fond of the storm demon, who could read the weather and the waves better than any sailor.

Halymere lowered his sword. 'Enough for now,' he ordered, fetching a waterskin and sitting with his back against the main mast. Arthur joined him, sneaking a look at Jalen, who had his arms folded, face tight. His tension had lingered since that moment in Cruithea when Ordes had dropped the mysterious book into Arthur's lap and declared the Goddess of Magic a liar. Arthur wanted to think that was all it was, but something was chewing away at the back of his brain.

'Does Jalen seem alright to you?' Arthur asked Halymere, his voice low so only the Cruithean could hear him.

Halymere passed the waterskin to Arthur, wiping his mouth with the back of his hand. 'How should he be?'

'I don't know,' Arthur mumbled.

'We've all got a lot on our minds, Arthur,' Halymere said gently. 'I'm sure there is nothing to worry about.'

'You're probably right,' Arthur said. 'We should concentrate on our task.'

As he fiddled with the waterskin, he realised that his hands had grown stronger. He no longer woke with an ache in his wrist or stiff fingers. Learning to wield a sword was much the same as learning to scribe – both demanded strength of his body, be that of his muscles or of his mind. Scribing was definitely better on Arthur's shoulders, but even that ache was slowly slipping away.

'What do you think is guarding the Sword of the White Dragon?' he asked Halymere. 'Is the Faery Forest like the forest in Cruithea?'

Halymere rubbed his chin, fingers scratching in the thickness of his beard. 'No,' he said eventually. 'It's older and home to things I have never met. You'll need to be careful,' he added. 'The faeries in Cruithea are used to us – to humans. We live with them. They know us. We share their land and resources, and we respect them. The creatures in the Faery Forest are not likely to come across many humans, and those who do stumble into their trees often don't come out.'

Arthur nodded, pushing away the shiver of fear. 'The Sword is in there, so I'll have to hope nothing decides to eat me.'

Halymere grinned. 'There's a bit more muscle there, but not enough for a meal yet.'

Arthur laughed, and climbed to his feet.

'Enough for today,' Halymere said.

Arthur nodded, grateful. He flipped the sword in his hands, not dropping it this time. His smug smile slipped as his father's words crashed into his mind. *Pride is the worst of our sins, Arthur, for pride always comes before a fall.*

He had been dreaming about his father. The dream-Ulrian was so real that Arthur woke with a hammering heart, sheets sweat-soaked beneath him. He wasn't sure what it meant, that Ulrian was so prominent in his dreams. Perhaps it was the closeness to Kernou, and the knowledge that his father was not far away.

Goerika had told him he would have to face his father before the end.

Arthur was a different man to the one who had fled Kernou. He was stronger. His thoughts were his own, and he was proud of what he had done in Cruithea – what he had learnt about magic and the Sword and the world itself. And for the first time in his life he had friends, people he cared for and would do anything to protect. They had become his family, to his surprise. He'd always believed family was connected by blood only. But now, when he looked around at the crew of the ship – at Jenyfer and Ordes standing close and whispering about something; at Tahnet fixing sailcloth; Kayrus at the helm; Iouen dangling from the rigging; Melhala teaching Ethinne to use a dagger, the two of them laughing and happy; and at Halymere attempting to talk to Katarin – Arthur understood that family was what he allowed it to be. It wasn't about bloodlines or trees scribbled across pages of a book.

It was about trust, respect, and kindness.

Jalen slung his arm around Arthur's shoulders, making him jump before he relaxed and leant his cheek against Jalen's shoulder; they didn't speak for a while, both watching the water and the shoreline beyond.

'We'll drop anchor tomorrow,' Jalen announced. 'Skover's Bay is still a day away.'

'Ever thought of helping the ship along?' Arthur mumbled.

'I didn't know you were in a hurry to hunt for Treasure,' Jalen replied.

'I'm not, but this waiting is too much sometimes. We left Cruithea two moons ago,' Arthur said. He sighed, rubbing at his face. 'I need a wash.'

Jalen followed Arthur below deck, preparing the bath while Arthur peeled the sweat-soaked clothes from his body. He perched on the edge of the bed, watching Jalen, noting the stiffness in his shoulders. They didn't have a true bath, not like they'd had in their kibitka in Cruithea, or like the one Arthur had grown up with. It was a large basin, only big enough for Arthur if he tucked his legs up.

'It's cold, sorry,' Jalen said.

Arthur didn't mind – the air was thick and humid at this end of the continent, and a cold wash was a welcome thing. He glanced out the porthole. Teyath was a smudge of deep green on the horizon. Heat bounced off the surface of the water in a shimmering dance. Arthur sighed and stepped into the tub, remaining standing while Jalen took up a cloth.

Their eyes met.

'I'm worried about you,' Arthur said before he could stop himself.

'I'm fine,' Jalen insisted, fishing the soap from the water and lathering the cloth. 'I'll do your back first.'

Arthur closed his eyes as Jalen washed his back, running the cloth across his shoulders and down his spine, over the curve of his arse and the length of his thighs. When Arthur turned back around, Jalen was frowning.

'What is it?' Arthur asked, his hand finding Jalen's cheek. The storm demon closed his eyes and leant into Arthur's palm. He pressed a kiss there, then returned to the task of making sure Arthur was so clean his skin squeaked.

'Jalen,' Arthur said. 'I know something is wrong. You've had clouds hanging over your head since before we left Cruithea. Whatever it is, you can tell me.'

Jalen let the cloth drop into the water with a splash. Soap slid slowly down Arthur's chest, but he did not move, his eyes locked on Jalen.

The demi-god met Arthur's gaze. 'Ordes.'

'Are you still mad at him for criticising Niniane?' Arthur asked. 'It's not surprising. He had no idea she was his mother. He's bound to be angry with her about it, and anger can manifest as mistrust or fear – I should know.'

Jalen found Arthur a towel, then sat on the bed while Arthur dried off. 'I'm concerned Ordes' decision-making is going to be tainted by his anger towards his mother, and his father. Whatever Ordes decides, Jenyfer is likely to agree with him and that worries me. Because the prophecy is clear on what you need to do, Arthur.'

'Well, no,' Arthur said, wrapping the towel around his hips and sitting beside Jalen. 'It isn't. It doesn't say how we are meant to remake the world. It doesn't give us specific instructions. It doesn't give us any options to consider, leaving us with a decision to make that is going to affect everyone in the world, in some way.'

'I thought you wanted a world of magic?' Jalen asked.

'I want a better world,' Arthur corrected. 'But I don't know what that looks like. And it isn't just up to me, remember. I might be the one who will find the Grail, but I won't be the only one who will use it. Jenyfer, Ordes, and I have to agree on what we are going to do, or it won't work. At least, that's what I'm thinking.'

'Then you're going to need to convince them,' Jalen said.

'But convince them of what?' Arthur mused. 'I wish the Myrddin was here already. Maybe he can offer us some advice. I mean, if he's seen the future, surely he knows what we should do?'

Jalen slipped his hand in Arthur's. 'Maybe.'

Arthur lay back, staring at the ceiling. 'I wish I knew what guards the Sword, and what it will want from me. I'm not sure I can fight it. I've improved, I know that, but I'm not ready for an opponent who will actually try to kill me.' He rolled onto his side. The sun was starting to set; ribbons of deep gold and indigo had crept across the sky. Arthur closed his eyes, listening to the water stroke the hull of the ship. It was peaceful, that sound. There was something about the constant pull and shift of the ocean he found comforting, and after so much time aboard, he was beginning to understand a sailor's fascination with the sea. Yesterday, he had seen dolphins – a pod of them had followed the ship for a while. He had never seen a sea creature up close before, aside from the dead mermaid Bryn had dumped at his father's door.

Kernou belonged to another time, and definitely to another Arthur.

He had almost been pulled under the blanket of sleep when Jalen's lips touched his forehead, then his ear with a promise of dinner in bed.

Chapter 3

The further *The Excalibur* sailed from Kernou, the more agitated Jenyfer became. She never thought she'd be sorry to see the back of that place, but she needed to see her sister. As far as she knew, Tamora was still in Cruithea – surely she would not have left, not with the threat of death hanging over her head, the fate that awaited her and Keraine if they returned to Kernou. That meant Lamorna was alone, with the Chif, with Bryn. With Mordred.

It was not quite dawn. Ordes was still sleeping, and the deck was empty besides Jenyfer and the man on watch. She leant over the railing, the sea breeze tugging at her hair. She tried to keep her heart rate smooth and steady, not letting anxiety cause it to spike. The ocean was dark, but that wouldn't be a problem. As soon as the sailor on watch turned his back on her, Jenyfer dropped over the edge of the ship, hitting the water with barely a splash.

Beneath the surface, her lungs opened, and her skin pricked with scales. She shed her shirt and tied it to one of the lines. She wasn't sure this was a good idea, but she needed to know. Just a few minutes with her sister, and then, if Lamorna was safe and happy, or as happy as could be in Kernou, Jenyfer would leave.

She hesitated a moment longer, feeling Ordes' heart beating alongside hers, knowing he'd work it out, and fast. Kicking her legs, she shot through the water, leaving *The Excalibur* behind.

The swim to Kernou didn't take long. It wasn't far from the headland near the Sea of Andred to the Bay of Calledun, and Jenyfer paused out past the breakers, the top of her head and her eyes pulling free of the water. Kernou clustered with false innocence beyond the sweep of golden beach. Jenyfer ignored the warning of her song, and rode a wave in, keeping herself tucked firmly within its foaming crest, making for the rocks at the far end of the beach. The sun had not yet risen, but fear dug its claws into her belly, the familiar feeling of it making her want to vomit. Her old cottage was so close, up there on the cliff top. Lamorna would be there, surely. Jenyfer could not think of where else her sister would be.

She stuck close to the rocks, Kernou glaring at her nakedness and her scales, the mass of hair slicked to her body. Hurrying up the rocky path, the wind tugging at her body, Jenyfer slipped over the fence and crept to her bedroom window. It was wide open. Frowning, she heaved herself up, balancing on the sill, before dropping onto her old bed. Leaves crunched beneath her feet.

She bit her lip. Maybe she had been wrong? This room looked abandoned.

There were noises coming from the kitchen. As soundlessly as she could, Jenyfer pulled one of her dresses from the wardrobe and tugged it on, then crept to the door. The hall was dark, but light emanated from the kitchen. She took a deep breath and stepped in.

Lamorna was busy at the bench, humming to herself. Jenyfer blinked.

Her sister was *humming*.

She took another step, then cleared her throat.

Lamorna spun around, a bowl between her hands. A thin scream escaped her lips and the bowl dropped to the floor, shattering, ceramic and herbs spilling at her feet. Lamorna did not move, staring at Jenyfer with wide eyes. Her hair was loose around her shoulders, reaching to her waist.

Footsteps pounded down the hall and a man came charging into the room, wild-eyed and completely naked. Jenyfer gasped. Mordred met her eyes, and snatched up a knife from the bench, thrusting Lamorna behind him.

'No!' she cried, edging around him. She grabbed his arm, the one brandishing the knife, wincing. Jenyfer realised she must have stepped on the broken bowl and wanted to go to her, but she didn't move. Mordred was glaring at her, his eyes sharper than any weapon. Jenyfer darted to the other side of the table, dripping water all over the floor, while Mordred looked torn between lunging across the table and grabbing her, and trying to shield Lamorna with his body.

'Mordred, it's fine,' Lamorna whispered. Mordred's eyes moved to her briefly, before shooting back to Jenyfer, dark and filled with suspicion. Slowly, he lowered his arm, letting Lamorna take the knife, and urged her to sit. Jenyfer watched, amazed, as the Cruithean knelt at her sister's feet and inspected her bleeding foot. He frowned, taking up the cloth from the table and pressing it to her wound.

'It's fine,' Lamorna said again. 'Go and dress.' When he was gone, Lamorna sighed, setting the cloth aside and bending to collect the pieces of the broken bowl.

'Lamorna,' Jenyfer began, sinking into a seat. Her knees would not hold her any longer.

'You scared the life out of me, Jen,' Lamorna said. She dumped the pile of ceramic on the bench and turned to Jenyfer. Lamorna's cheeks were rosy, her lips plump, and Jenyfer was suddenly glad she had not arrived an hour earlier. Her sister was wearing one of their aunt's floral robes, belted tight at the middle, accentuating the swell of her breasts and the curve of her hips.

Mordred marched back in, dressed, and sat across the table from Jenyfer, folding his arms. 'What are you doing here?' he demanded.

'Mordred, don't be rude,' Lamorna scolded, but her tone was tight. She turned her eyes to Jenyfer. 'What *are* you doing here?'

'I wanted to see if you were alright,' Jenyfer answered faintly. Mordred had not stopped glowering at her, the force of his anger rushing across the table to slam into Jenyfer.

'She's fine,' he bit out.

'I wasn't asking you,' Jenyfer snapped.

Lamorna put her hand on Mordred's shoulder; his face relaxed a fraction. 'I'm perfectly fine, Jen.'

'You shouldn't be here – it isn't safe,' Jenyfer argued. 'Go back to Aunt Tamora.'

Lamorna's eyes became hard. 'You don't get to tell me what to do anymore, Jenyfer.'

'When have I ever told you what to do? You were always the one ordering me about.'

Lamorna said nothing. Jenyfer took a deep breath.

'I'm not here to fight with you.'

'You claim to care about your sister, but you've put her in danger by being here,' Mordred pointed out.

'And she's not in danger with you here, I take it?' Jenyfer asked tightly, while a different sort of fear suddenly clawed at her. She hadn't considered she'd be putting Lamorna at risk. Hastily, she stood, smoothing her hands over her dress. 'I'll go.'

'You just got here,' Lamorna protested. 'I'll make some tea.'

The air in the little kitchen suddenly rippled with magic as Ordes appeared; Lamorna shrieked and stepped back as Mordred leapt to his feet, but before the Inborn could draw a breath or a weapon, Ordes had slammed Mordred against the nearest wall, his hand around Mordred's throat.

'Did he hurt you?' Ordes demanded.

'No. Ordes, let him go,' Jenyfer said.

Ordes hesitated.

'I'd do what she says if you want to keep your pretty face in one piece,' Mordred said with soft menace. Ordes did not let go, and the next moment, Mordred had shoved him away and thrown the first punch. Jenyfer shouted at them to stop, but they were a mass of swinging arms and fists. The kitchen was not large enough for two grown men to brawl. They knocked over the table, the chairs scattering across the floor. Lamorna pressed herself against the bench, eyes wide. Jenyfer pulled her song to the surface and let her magic infuse her voice.

'Enough, both of you!'

Mordred froze, letting go of the front of Ordes' shirt. Ordes snarled and stepped away.

No one spoke for a terribly long moment, until Lamorna cleared her throat. 'I think you need to go, Jenyfer. If the Chif finds out you were here …'

'Lamorna,' Jenyfer whispered.

'I'm fine, truly,' her sister said. 'Just … it would be best if you left.' She surveyed the damaged kitchen and sighed, rubbing wearily at her forehead.

Ordes waved his hand and the table stood up again, the chairs righting and tucking themselves in neatly. He put his hand on Jenyfer's shoulder. 'Come on,' he said softly. She nodded sadly, and let him lead her to the front door. She could feel Lamorna and Mordred's eyes on her back.

Ordes opened the door a crack, then snapped it shut it again. 'We need to go,' he hissed. 'Now, Jen.'

Lamorna jolted violently as someone hammered on the door, and Jenyfer's magic swirled in response. The blood had drained from her sister's face – Lamorna looked utterly terrified. Mordred had moved to one of the windows in the living room, wrenching back the curtain, then letting it drop quickly.

'The Red Hand,' he hissed.

Lamorna gasped, looking at him in alarm. 'They can't find you here!' She turned to Jen and Ordes, eyes wide. 'Or you!'

The knocking continued and Jenyfer's throat constricted. Her magic readied itself. She'd sing the Red Hand into pieces if they tried to hurt Lamorna. That was if Mordred didn't get to them first. The Inborn was glowering at the door.

'Lamorna Astolat,' a voice called.

Jenyfer froze, every muscle coiling in on itself.

Bryn. It was Bryn.

'The Chif wants to see you,' Bryn called.

Jenyfer could not tear her eyes from the door. Her hands curled into fists, her heart stuttering and her mouth suddenly dry as a desert.

'The back – now!' Mordred snapped, keeping his voice low.

'Jen,' Ordes said. 'Come on.'

'Bryn is on the other side of that door,' she whispered. Her magic roared, her song deafening, almost suffocating her with the force of its anger – it climbed up her throat and sat on her tongue, waiting.

'Not now,' Ordes said softly, taking her hand.

'If the two of you don't move, I'll gut you where you stand,' Mordred threatened. 'Get out. Now.'

Jenyfer bristled, but Ordes tugged on her hand as Bryn knocked again. Lamorna threw an apron over her robe and quickly bound her hair at the base of her skull, shoving a white linen cap on her head. She turned to them, her voice a hissed whisper. 'For fuck's sake – the three of you need to get out of here *now*!'

Mordred kissed her cheek – Jenyfer blinked and swallowed at the action – then headed for the back door, Jen and Ordes on his heels. They heard Lamorna open the front door and greet Bryn as Mordred eased the back door open, avoiding the squeaky hinge.

'Done this before, have you?' Jenyfer accused in a whisper. Her magic was lashing at her insides – it wanted her to go back in there and rip Bryn to pieces.

Mordred's eyes were hard. 'Right now, we have a common enemy in my uncle, but if you put her in danger like that again, I'll kill you both,' he promised, then slunk away behind the cottage.

'Jen—' Ordes began.

'I'll be fine. Go,' she said. He frowned, then disappeared. Jenyfer lingered a moment longer, then tore off her dress, leaving it in a bundle at the back door. She raced across the backyard, ducking through the garden beds. She vaulted the wooden fence and did not look back, however much she wanted to, before she threw herself from the cliff top and into the sea.

When Jenyfer returned to *The Excalibur*, dripping and tired and dressed in the shirt she had left behind, Ordes was waiting. He ushered her below deck and down the dark and narrow passageway to their room, dragging her in and shutting the door firmly.

Jenyfer's teeth chattered, and she rubbed at her scaled arms, her head spinning. Without a word, Ordes bundled her in a towel, squeezing the water from her sodden hair, muttering to himself. She peeled her shirt off and tossed it on the floor with a sigh as Ordes rubbed her skin vigorously with the towel. He was frowning, his mouth a thin line.

'I'm dry now,' she muttered.

He nodded and slung the towel over his shoulder, staring at her, disapproval in every line of his face.

'Ordes—'

'What were you thinking?' he cut in furiously. 'What in the gods were you thinking?'

Jenyfer folded her arms, refusing to back away from his anger. 'I needed to see my sister.'

'So you thought sneaking off alone and going back to that pit of a place was a good idea?' Ordes fumed.

'Yes, because no one else was going to take me,' Jenyfer shot back. 'I'm sorry I worried you, but I'm not sorry I went.'

'Worried me? You didn't worry me, Jenyfer. You fucking *terrified* me! I thought my heart was going to turn to ashes! And then when I found you, and Mordred was there …' Ordes shook his head.

She reached out to touch his face, gently tracing the bruise that was forming on his jaw. 'You didn't need to start a fight with him.'

'What did you expect me to do?' Ordes answered, but his voice was softer. 'I couldn't control it. I saw you there, saw him, and it was like there was nothing more important in the world than making sure you were safe.'

'I'm sorry you got hurt,' Jenyfer whispered.

'I'm not hurt.'

'Ordes, your face is a mess.'

He shrugged. 'It was worth it. Did I manage to punch him once at least?'

Jenyfer smiled. 'You did. There might have been a drop of blood.'

'Liar,' Ordes murmured. He slipped his arms around her and pulled her close. 'Don't do that again.'

'I won't.'

He flipped her damp hair over her shoulder. 'I think you should kiss me better to make up for scaring me.'

'Do you? That might be difficult. You've got a busted lip,' Jenyfer pointed out.

Ordes grinned lazily. 'I didn't say anything about kissing my mouth.'

'Well, in that case,' she murmured, pressing a kiss to his neck. 'Is that sufficient?'

'No, I'm not sure that's enough to make me forgive you,' Ordes told her.

She kissed his earlobe; he shuddered but shook his head. She slowly undid the buttons on his shirt, kissing her way over his chest. Her fingers swept down his belly and lingered on the waistband of his trousers.

'You're getting closer to forgiveness,' he whispered. His breathing had deepened, and she watched the rise and fall of his chest before she let her eyes drop. She undid his pants and slipped her hand inside.

'I'm pretty sure this isn't healthy,' Jenyfer said. 'I mean, we should talk about our problems, don't you think?'

'Maybe, but I'm rather adrenalised right now,' Ordes said. 'And I'd prefer it if you used your mouth for something other than talking.'

'Oh?' Jenyfer closed her hand around the length of him; his groan speared through her, making her thighs clench. 'That doesn't sound like you, Ordes. Usually you love to talk.'

His face was a mixture of irritation and pleasure. She continued to stroke him, her touch light, teasing. He took her face in his hands, his expression tight. As always, she was awed by the power her touch had over him. 'Okay, okay. Promise me you'll never do anything like that again.'

Jenyfer pretended to consider it, chewing her lip. 'Say please.'

'Please.'

'I suppose so.'

A smile tugged at his lips. 'Good, that's settled. Now will you please, *please*, put your mouth to other uses?'

'Since you asked so nicely.' She kissed him, hard, forgetting about his wounded mouth, then pushed him onto the bed.

'I don't know how you did it,' Ordes murmured against her back.

'Did what?' Jenyfer asked lazily.

He gave her a sharp pinch on the arse, making her jump. 'You were supposed to be grovelling to me, and I'm the one who ended up begging. How did you do that?'

Jenyfer giggled as he pressed open-mouthed kisses along her arm. She stopped abruptly. 'Do you think he truly cares for her?'

'Who?' Ordes asked. Jenyfer shifted so she could see his face, taking note of the blissful smile.

'Mordred.'

'Well, he did threaten to remove our insides to protect her, so I'd take that as a yes.'

Jenyfer sighed. 'It doesn't make sense.'

'Why not?' Ordes argued. 'We can't control who we fall for.'

'I know they're sharing a bed, considering he was stark naked when I arrived,' she said.

Ordes' eyebrows lifted. 'Was he now?'

'And that's not the problem. I … can't picture it. Lamorna never wanted to get married – she never expressed any desire for a husband or a man in her life. She was going to become a Sister of the Sacellum,' Jenyfer said softly.

'Obviously she changed her mind,' Ordes replied. 'Look, I know Mordred is an arse, but as long as he isn't an arse to her, and she's safe, does it matter?'

Jenyfer frowned. 'Why are you defending him? He punched you in the face, Ordes.'

Ordes kissed her gently. 'I'm not. I just know that, sometimes, love can take you by surprise. You don't have to go looking for it – it will find you.'

Chapter 4

Mordred was sitting at the kitchen table when Lamorna returned from town. She refused to look at him as she unpacked her basket – fish, some cheese and bread, and some apples. Everything else she already had. The garden was thriving again, thanks to Mordred. He'd used magic, but Lamorna didn't care. At least she wouldn't go hungry, and if it came to it, she would have enough to sustain her without having to go into town more than once a week.

Jenyfer's surprise visit had rattled her, but not as much as the pirate exploding into reality out of thin air. Lamorna had seen Ordes do that before, in Cruithea, but there was something about that sort of magic that made her dreadfully nervous. Mordred's small acts, like lighting the fire or coaxing the garden to grow, she could deal with, but what Ordes could do was different. It was magic that should belong to … a god.

Lamorna's heart had stopped beating when Bryn had hammered on her door. Lamorna didn't want to think about what might have happened without Mordred being there, forcing Jen to leave. Bryn had taken her to the Chif, who hadn't wanted anything important at all, only to remind her she needed to start attending the women's prayer circle. It was the sort of thing he could have put in a note. Lamorna knew Bryn had enjoyed making her worry, how much the Chif had enjoyed being able to summon her and have her obey without question.

Her fists tightened, but she forced herself to unclench them. Mordred watched her as she checked the water level in the kettle, then set it to boil. Frowning, she rested her hand on the stove.

'The fire has gone out!' she said, giving Mordred an irritated look. 'You were supposed to keep it going.'

'I was, wasn't I?' he mused, then rose from his seat and went outside, returning with an armful of wood. Lamorna stepped aside and let him set the fire, lighting it with the click of his finger. 'How was the market?' Mordred resumed his seat. He was making what her Aunt Tamora would call 'small talk', but Lamorna had never understood the point of it. She turned from the stove and folded her arms.

'You don't care about the market,' she said simply.

Mordred held out his hand and beckoned. She hesitated, then placed her hand in his.

'You're cross.'

'I am cross,' she declared, letting him pull her into his lap. 'You're keeping things from me.' He left each morning to see the Chif, but had not told her why or what they talked about. He abandoned her to face the townspeople alone, to deal with their stares and the whispers, to clean and prepare meals and tend the garden. He did manage the bees, which she was thankful for, but it wasn't enough. 'Well?' she demanded.

'Yes, I am keeping things from you, but not for the reasons you think,' Mordred admitted, stroking the skin on her arm. Lamorna shivered and leant into his touch. She should have gotten up and made them some lunch, but she didn't want to move. Despite everything – the weight of eyes and the silence in the market and the shops that spoke volumes – she liked it when he touched her.

'Is this about those prophecies?' she asked.

'Yes.'

'I need to understand – why did you pretend to devote yourself to the One God? Why did you lie to me? Was it to gain my trust?' Lamorna watched his face carefully, but Mordred's expression was calm and smooth. She could not read him, not in the way she had been able to read her sister. Ordes had warned her Mordred could not be trusted. Arthur had implied the same thing, and sometimes, at night, when Mordred was asleep, she wondered if they had been right. There was so much she didn't know about him and sometimes, she wasn't sure if she truly trusted him.

But she didn't say anything. If he left, if one morning he got up and went to the Chif's house and never returned, she didn't know what she would do. She did not want to be alone. She did not know how to be alone.

Mordred continued to stroke her arm. 'We haven't talked about your sister and her untimely visit.'

'She won't come back,' Lamorna said. Her belly twisted a little at the thought. 'She wanted to know I was alright.'

'And are you?' Mordred asked.

Lamorna kissed him gently. 'Yes.'

He sighed, tucking his head in the curve of her neck. 'Have you ever questioned your faith, Lamorna? Truly questioned it. Where did the One God come from? Why did he come?' Mordred let the questions hang in the air, and she knew she wasn't supposed to answer – they were his questions for himself. 'The truth is, I turned from Inanna a long time ago, from the faith I had been born with.'

'The Blood magic?' Lamorna asked. The thought of it made her skin crawl. Mordred had not used it since that night he had shown her Jenyfer in the bowl of water, but sometimes she could feel the sting in her palm where he had cut her.

She did not want him to do it again, no matter how much she wanted to see her sister. It scared her, more than faeries and water horses that wanted to drown her. More than the thought of never seeing her family again. There was something dark and foreboding about it.

'That is part of it,' he answered. 'Blood magic is a gift of the Red One, Ereshki, the sister to Inanna. She was once worshipped by my people for many, many years, until my mother, in her wisdom, declared Ereshki should be cast out. Banished, if you will.'

Lamorna frowned. 'I don't understand – if your people banished her, why do you follow her? Why do the Red Sisters follow her?' Mordred had told her about the House of Bone, a wondrous place deep in the Dead Woods. He had said the Red Sisters were powerful. He had told Lamorna she would like them, but Lamorna wasn't sure about that. She did not like blood.

'The Red Sisters have devoted their lives to Ereshki, and even my mother's rule would not make them renounce their faith. As for me, what has Inanna ever done for me? Seen me born a man in a world that offers me no power?'

Lamorna's frown deepened. Mordred's insistence that being male granted him no power absolutely baffled her, and she could not understand why he thought the way he did. 'But you're the leader of the Inborn—'

'At my mother's beck and call,' he spat. 'Don't you see? Meeting you was fate. You gave me an opportunity to change things.'

'An opportunity?' she echoed. 'That is all I am to you?'

'No. You also gave me courage, Lamorna,' he murmured, kissing her throat. 'You see, when my people turned from Ereshki, she went in search of those who would listen, those who wanted what she had been denied – power. She was sick of living in the shadows.'

'And she found those people?'

'She found the men of this land,' Mordred said. 'People like my uncle. Easily manipulated, easily won. But things went wrong.' He paused, ran his fingers lightly down her cheek. 'I am not sure you are ready to hear the rest.'

'I am,' she declared. 'Didn't you tell me I needed to be strong? That I needed to stand up for myself? Well, I am. So you won't decide for me, Mordred. Tell me the rest of your story. I want to know.'

'Have you not started putting it together yourself?' he murmured in that tone he sometimes used, the one that made her feel like a child. 'The One God, Lamorna, is not what you have been taught to believe. When the Red One went in search of power, in search of men, she could not present herself to them as the Old One she was. She needed to be different. So, like a serpent, she shed her skin and became something new.' He paused. Lamorna climbed off his lap and sat facing him. She wanted to see his face clearly. He continued. 'As revenge for being cast out of Cruithea, as revenge on the other Old Ones turning their backs on her, Ereshki reinvented herself as the One God. Slowly, she began to turn the people of this land to *her*.'

Lamorna opened her mouth, but no sound came out.

The kettle shrieked in the background, but she ignored it, staring at Mordred's face. Waited for him to laugh or smile or tell her it was a lie. But he didn't. Mordred got up, taking the kettle off the heat and making tea. Lamorna did not move, not even when he placed a cup in front of her and the smell of chamomile wrapped around her head.

'Lamorna?'

She couldn't speak. She could barely breathe. Her heart felt like it had stopped beating. Heat washed over her; spots danced in her vision. She blinked, alarmed at the tears on her cheeks, wondering where they had come from.

'Ulrian lied to you. The Sacellum lied to him, caught him up like a fish in a net. He, along with so many others, lapped it up,' Mordred said. His voice was soft, regretful. He sat across from her, watching her closely.

'You lie,' she managed at last. 'You're a liar.'

Mordred sipped his tea. 'Somewhere in the back of your mind, you know this isn't a lie,' he said. 'I think you've known something was wrong here, in Kernou, for some time, Lamorna. Am I right? Your sister knew.'

Lamorna pushed her tea away and stood, smoothing back her hair, checking that all the pale strands were tucked away. 'I think I shall go and pray now,' she said, but her voice sounded strange to her ears. She headed outside into the garden and knelt in the dirt by the beans, staring at them until her eyes were watering, and the ocean wind had pulled her hair free of its binding.

Jenyfer knew the truth, or she had at least suspected. All those times when she told Lamorna the Word was wrong, that the Chif was wrong, that this whole thing was *wrong* – she had known. She had trusted her instincts, and Lamorna … Lamorna had no instincts. They had been stolen from her by a man who desired power over others. They had been stolen by his false god.

She took a gulp of sea air, wishing more than ever that her sister was here. Jenyfer had tried to tell her things, in Cruithea, but Lamorna had not listened, too caught up in what she was discovering about herself.

She glanced back at the cottage. Mordred had not come looking for her, and she was glad. She needed this moment alone. She needed this moment to … to … she wasn't sure. She needed to be alone. To think about all she had lost and not known about. Everything she had gained. All she stood to lose if she remained in this place with people like the Chif and Bryn, who revelled in the power they held over others. Over people like her.

Women. Slaves to a Word written by a goddess.

Lamorna thought about Cruithea, ruled by a woman, where women were warriors and healers and allowed to be whatever it was they wished.

She leapt to her feet and lunged for the beans, ripping and tearing the plants from their trellis, pulling their roots from the earth. It didn't make sense – why would a goddess do this? If the One God was Ereshki, why did she give men the power to control women's lives? Lamorna could barely see through her rage as she tossed the plants aside and reached for the wooden trellis, heaving it free. She stared at it, body on fire, then snapped it. A feeling of deep satisfaction rushed through her at the sensation of that thin timber breaking beneath her hands. Soon nothing remained but a pile of twigs at her feet. Lamorna glanced around, eyes wild, burning. Her gaze fell on the faery bush.

She hated that bush and everything it stood for. Enraged, she marched across the yard, but as she reached for the shrub, a little face appeared. The pisky. He stared at her, small beady eyes on her face, and she knew she could not destroy his home. They were alike, the pisky and her, both the victims of lies and betrayal. She backed away; the pisky smiled at her, and in that smile was understanding and cunning.

The Small Folk had survived Ulrian's lies – the One God's lies. They had survived and now, looking at the pisky peering out at her from his shrub, she had the overwhelming sense he had been waiting for this moment, and for all the moments that would come.

The One God was not what she had thought He was. It did not matter who He was. She did not have to believe. She had to think about things differently.

She needed answers.

Mordred was still in the kitchen when Lamorna swept back inside, hands and skirts covered in dirt and plant matter. Her head was filled with voices – her aunt's, Jenyfer's, the Chif's, even Keraine spoke in her thoughts, their words tumbling over each other.

Golden sunlight poured through the window, painting the side of Mordred's face. Lamorna wanted to touch him, wondering if he was even real. But she cleared her throat and indicated the stove.

'I'll make us lunch,' she said matter-of-factly.

'Lamorna,' he began.

She shook her head. 'Lunch first,' she ordered, washing her hands and tidying her clothes. She set about preparing the fish, but when she picked up the knife, her fingers were trembling so violently she could not cut into that dead white flesh. Mordred did it for her, telling her to sit.

She watched as he found the frying pan and cooked the fish, realising this was the first time he had made food for them – for her.

They ate, and when she was finished, Lamorna pushed her plate away.

'Did … Ereshki, the Red One, really write the Word?'

'She did.'

'I don't understand,' Lamorna said. Her hands curled into fists in her lap. 'Why did she want men to kill the Small Folk? The piskies? Why make people fear them? Hunt them? Why make someone like my sister a target? Why did she order them to take away our voices?'

'Whose voices?'

'Women's!' Lamorna shouted. Her voice echoed around the kitchen, angry and spiteful, full of truths that others had been speaking to her that she had refused to listen to. 'Why? Why would she make us cover our hair and our bodies and kneel for hours and pray for forgiveness for sins we had not yet committed? Why force us to marry men we did not love? To bear them children? To not complain, *never* complain, and to bear it all without a voice?'

Lamorna's chest heaved. Anger sizzled in her veins. She thought her insides might melt. She wound her fingers in the fabric of her dress so hard she heard the material tear.

'Ereshki did not do that,' Mordred said softly. 'The Word she wrote is not the Word that Ulrian has taught you.'

'He really lied to us?'

'Is it so hard to believe?'

'How could he do that?' she demanded. 'How could he change the word of a … a … divine being to suit himself?'

'Because a man will do what he must to hold on to power,' Mordred replied. 'When my uncle came to Cruithea all those years ago, he was sick and raving. He talked about the One God, but my Aunt Igraine thought it part of his madness. She treated his illness, saved his life, and fell in love with him. He was not like he is now. He was new to the One God and the world of power and authority. He was not yet the Chif.

When he had recovered from his illness, he left Cruithea and took my aunt and my cousin with him.'

'What happened to her?' Lamorna asked. 'No one ever talks about her.'

'She died, Lamorna. He could have saved her, but he didn't. Instead, he tied my cousin to a stake for the ocean to take as a sacrifice. And for that, I hate him,' Mordred said simply. 'And I hate him for what he has done here, what men all over this country have done – corrupted the Red One's words for their own gain, misused what She gave to the world of men for power. Men like my uncle and the men who rule the Sacellum are the worst sort of men.'

Lamorna's thoughts drifted to Bryn. 'There are worse,' she mumbled, then sat back, chewing her lip. Anger still tunnelled through her, but she let it simmer there. 'These prophecies that you believe in …' she began. 'What sort of world do you want? A world where magic runs wild?'

'You misunderstand me,' he said. 'I want a world of control, a world where magic resumes its rightful place. But all power needs a hand to guide it.'

'And you want to be the hand?' she asked shrewdly.

'Perhaps.'

'Don't lie to me,' Lamorna said, with deadly softness. She was not going to sit here and be compliant, not with him. 'I see your ambitions on your face, Mordred.'

He held her gaze for a long moment. 'Yes. I want to be the hand of power.'

'And the Chif?'

'A pawn, like the Magistrar and the Sacellum are pawns,' he replied.

Lamorna swallowed. 'And me? Am I a pawn in your games?' She waited, scarcely able to believe she had asked such a question, afraid of what she would do if he said yes. 'You lied to me.'

'You were,' he admitted, and her heart seized. 'But,' he said. 'Not anymore. I don't want to use you in my games, Lamorna. I want to play them *with* you.'

Her belly dropped, heavy with satisfaction. 'Does the Chif know the truth about the One God?'

'You believe me, then?'

'Does he know?' she asked again.

'No,' Mordred said eventually.

Lamorna nodded. Something squirmed inside her chest, something deep and dark and powerful. 'I want to be the one to tell him.'

Mordred smiled, a slow smile that made her want to kiss him. 'Then you can be. But not yet.'

'When?' she demanded.

He stood, cupping her cheek, fingers curling around her ear. 'Soon. There is power in knowing something others do not. Remember that.'

'Mordred, will you try and take away my voice?' she asked. 'Because I won't let you.'

'Never.'

He kissed her deeply; need for him rose in her belly, and she was certain there were still sins she had not yet committed.

'Do you promise?' she whispered, brushing his lips with hers.

Mordred spun her chair around, the legs squeaking in protest, and knelt at her feet. 'Lamorna, I promise. I want your voice alongside mine, and whatever I do from this moment on, you shall do it with me. My power shall be your power.'

'Good,' she said.

CHAPTER 5

Jenyfer glanced up at the cloudless sky. The endless blue was oddly disconcerting. At this time of year in Kernou, she would wake each morning to dark grey clouds with purple undersides and heavy storm-charged air. To have not seen a cloud for weeks left her strangely on edge, like she was waiting for something other than rain to happen.

'What sort of world should we build?' Ordes mused, smiling lazily. Jenyfer, Ordes and Arthur were sitting on the deck near the main mast. Ordes rested against a barrel; his face was relaxed, cropped curls catching the sunlight. His legs were stretched out, feet crossed at the ankles. 'I want a world where I can sleep all day if I wish.'

'You already do that,' Jenyfer reminded him, making Arthur chuckle.

Ordes shrugged. 'True. What do you want then?' he asked her.

The answer was automatic. 'What I have always wanted – the freedom to choose.'

Arthur gave her a reassuring smile, pushing his hair from his eyes. 'That's a given, Jen.'

She nodded. 'But what will it look like, Arthur? For the women of this world? We've been forced to conform, to make ourselves fit the world around us. To not speak out of turn. To hold our tongues—'

'I can hold your tongue for you,' Ordes murmured. She rolled her eyes and swatted him.

'I'm being serious,' Jenyfer said quietly. 'How do we give freedom to people who don't know what it looks like? Who have never sought it because they never knew they were being denied it?'

Arthur was chewing on his bottom lip. 'I'm not sure,' he said eventually. 'It will be an adjustment. It was for me.'

'For me also,' Jenyfer agreed.

'Your sister seems to be coping,' Ordes pointed out.

Jenyfer shook her head, exasperated. 'Lamorna is playing a dangerous game, and I'm concerned about her, more than I was before.'

'Wait, you saw her?' Arthur cut in. Jenyfer told him quickly about her visit to Kernou. 'Mordred is still there?'

Jenyfer sighed. 'I wish I knew why.'

'He's with my father,' Arthur mumbled.

'He was with Lamorna,' Jenyfer corrected, scowling.

'I know you're frightened for her, but I'd be more concerned with what my cousin is up to,' Arthur said. 'Every conversation I had with him in Cruithea always came back to the idea of power. Mordred's given up a position of power in exchange for what? I can't imagine my father and the Konsel welcoming him with open arms.' Arthur's frown deepened.

'It all comes back to power, doesn't it?' Ordes said. 'I mean, once we claim the Treasures and then the Grail, we will, essentially, be the most powerful people in the world.' He paused and rubbed at his jaw, his eyes troubled. 'I, for one, have never gone looking for power. In any form. I was born with my magic, which is power in itself I guess, but beyond that … it's not something I've ever wanted.'

Arthur's laugh was brittle. 'My father was preparing me to rule a town, which I never wanted either. I've seen what power does to people. What it did to my father.'

'You don't want it because you're both men,' Jenyfer put in. 'As a mere woman, a little bit of power was all I wanted. Power over myself, not others. I don't want to be telling people what to do, ever.'

'You tell me what to do all the time,' Ordes pointed out.

'That's different. And anyway, you don't have to do what I say,' Jenyfer said.

Ordes' lips quirked. 'But I like taking orders from you. Especially when you say—'

Arthur cleared his throat meaningfully. Ordes gave Jen a wink and slipped his arm around her, pulling her into him, and the moment he touched her, the heartfire purred. She wondered if it would always be like this between them – would her belly always tighten when he was near, her blood always burn, her breaths deepen? Would she always be filled with wanting?

She hoped so. It was the best feeling in the world.

'I think it's safe to assume that whatever we're going to have to do to claim the Treasures isn't going to be pleasant,' Arthur said quietly.

'Possibly not, but it will be achievable,' Jenyfer said. 'We're meant to have them, so why would anyone make these … trials, or tests or whatever, so difficult we couldn't complete them?'

'When it comes to my father's prophecy, and Old Ones and magical Treasures, I think it's safe to say that anything goes,' Ordes replied. 'I don't think we can make any assumptions.'

'Alright, let's say we've collected our Treasures already,' Jenyfer said thoughtfully. 'Then it's time for the Grail. Where is it? How do we find it? Will it appear when we need it?'

Arthur sighed. 'I have no idea. Whenever I've seen it, it's been in the Fisher Queen's lap. I couldn't tell you if it was really there, though. It was only a dream.' He paused. 'I think. Jalen told me they weren't really dreams, but if not, then what are they?'

'Have you ever heard of dreamwalking?' Ordes asked Arthur.

'No. What is it?' Arthur leant forward, curious.

'The power to travel in your dreams,' Ordes told him. 'Different places, different times.'

'Do you think that's what I'm doing?' Arthur asked, excitement colouring his voice.

Ordes shrugged. 'I don't know. I'm no expert in that type of magic.'

Arthur sat back, tapping his fingers on his thighs. 'But you two share dreams, right?'

Jenyfer shook her head. 'We haven't shared a dream since the location of the Treasures was revealed to the three of us.'

A wooden sword suddenly landed on the deck near Arthur, making the three of them jump. Halymere's shadow was fast behind it.

'Apparently you're all terrible sailors, and if we weren't on a mission to save the world, our good Captain would throw you all off her ship at the next port,' he said. Jenyfer peered around the Cruithean to see Katarin across the deck, arms folded, eyes narrowed. She was tapping her foot impatiently.

'So,' Halymere continued, nudging Arthur with his boot, 'on your feet, future King.'

Grinning, Arthur stood and stretched, picked up the sword and followed Halymere.

'We'd better find something to do,' Ordes said. He stood, offering Jen his hand, pulling her upright so he could slide his arms around her. 'Whatever world we decide to build, it doesn't matter what it looks like, as long as you're in it with me.' He leant down to kiss her, but before he could, he yelped and jumped away, rubbing at the back of his head.

Katarin was standing nearby, a smirking Iouen at her shoulder. The quartermaster had two buckets of soapy water at his feet, and a scrubbing brush in one hand. The other was lying on the deck at Ordes' feet.

'I outrank you now, sailor,' Iouen said, his grin widening. He indicated the buckets. 'And there's a deck that needs scrubbing.'

'You've got to be kidding,' Ordes said.

Kat tapped her chin thoughtfully, her red hair brilliant in the sunlight, eyes sparkling. 'I'm feeling the need for a cabin boy,' she said. 'Would you rather get your hands dirty, Ordes, or use them to cater to my every whim?'

'I'm learning she does change her mind rather frequently,' Iouen pointed out.

Ordes groaned. 'We'll take the deck.'

'That's what I thought,' Kat said smugly.

The Cruithean Priestess, Ethinne, had been sneaking glances at Katarin all morning. She'd tried to ignore it, keeping her eyes on her crew and the tasks they were engaged in – Arthur and Halymere sword fighting and getting in the way; some of the crew repairing sailcloth, some checking the rigging. She scowled as she watched Jenyfer and Ordes flick water at one another, supposedly scrubbing the deck.

Kat shifted her weight, leaning back against the door to her cabin while she watched Iouen. She had to admit he was a good quartermaster. When she told him to jump, he asked 'how high?', and he ran a tight ship. She appreciated it. They were a crew of almost fifty, the largest Kat had ever commanded. She carried those fifty people with her wherever she went and through whatever she did. They were her responsibility, and they'd stuck with her, with Ordes and Arthur and Jen. She was not without her worries, but her quartermaster eased the burden.

There had been no sign of Merlin, and Katarin had not had a message from Niniane. She'd not heard from her since she'd stormed away from Avalon, leaving Ordes in Lyonesse. Kat could not help but feel oddly abandoned by the Goddess of Magic, and wonder what it meant. Had

Niniane decided she couldn't trust Kat anymore? Had she decided she didn't care?

Katarin swallowed. Had Niniane ever truly cared?

'How far from the Faery Forest are we? I find it difficult to tell how far we've travelled on a ship,' said a voice at Kat's elbow.

Katarin jolted to see the Cruithean Priestess standing beside her. Kat had found herself wondering why Ethinne was here at all, until she remembered the High Priestess had sent her. Katarin might not put much faith in Inanna anymore, but she did have faith in her aunt's judgement. Ethinne was dressed like a Cruithean warrior, her sleeveless shirt revealing the markings inked on her light brown skin. Not warrior tattoos like Halymere and Melhala wore, but symbols of the elements.

Her skin was practically covered in them, a reminder that Ethinne was a powerful Magic Wielder.

Priestesses of Inanna spent their lives in service to the Goddess, marking their bodies with elemental glyphs as a symbol of their knowledge and their magical achievements. Kat studied Ethinne's glyphs as covertly as she could.

The Priestess' lips curled into a smile. 'Air, if you're wondering. That's the element I am most proficient in. If you'd have gone into the Temple, yours would have been water, but you know that,' she said simply.

Kat stared at her. 'How do you know that?'

'Inanna tells us many things.'

A shiver skidded the length of Katarin's spine. The idea that a Goddess was talking about her behind her back made her blood run cold. 'And what else did she say?'

Ethinne turned soft brown eyes on Katarin. 'I know who you really are.'

Fear gripped Kat's insides. She licked dry lips and forced a laugh. 'Most people know who I am. My reputation—'

'You hide behind your mask, but I can see your true face, Morgaine Tintagel,' Ethinne said, lowering her voice. 'You're yet to claim what is yours.'

'Stop,' Kat demanded.

'You will claim your heritage, in the end,' the Priestess said, and walked away.

Kat pressed herself against the door. Her heart was thundering, her palms sweaty, and a desert lived in her mouth. She closed her eyes – trees were suddenly imprinted behind her lids. With a gasp, her eyes flew open. She looked about for Ethinne, but the Priestess was nowhere to be seen.

CHAPTER 6

The Excalibur dropped anchor. Skover's Bay sat to their left, Arcdon behind it, while Skulls Rest clustered around the headland to their right. They had run into a brief tropical storm overnight, slowing them down, and now Katarin had decided it was too close to sunset to leave the ship. Some of the crew would head into Arcdon for supplies, some would remain onboard. But there was little time to waste — the rest of them were to go ashore to find the Sword of the White Dragon.

Ordes slipped his arm around Jenyfer's middle. The Faery Forest lay directly ahead, a dark green stain on the otherwise flat and harvested landscape. She spied nearby spice groves, and in the distance, the Nemhain Mountains cast a shadow on the land. The ship was as close as they could get her. A coral reef lay between them and the beach; the water was clear as crystals, the reef a splash of fractured colour beneath the surface.

Everything was about to change. Jenyfer wasn't sure if she wanted the days to move slower, to keep them bound to the ship for a little longer, firmly inside this bubble they had created for themselves, or if she wanted to fling herself into the water and get moving, charging headlong into whatever was coming.

But she also knew that rashness often meant poor decisions. She had lived through that already.

Katarin was barking orders. She called those who would be journeying into the Faery Forest into her cabin again, no doubt with another change in plan. If Katarin kept changing her mind about things, nothing would happen. Since leaving Cruithea, Katarin had become strategist and leader of this whole expedition. Jenyfer could understand it – Kat was used to being in control, to being the one who made the decisions. For now, no one said anything, following her command without question.

Jenyfer suspected that Kat knew that the moment they left this ship, the moment Arthur claimed his Treasure, control would slip from her fingers.

Jenyfer and Ordes followed Halymere's broad shoulders into Kat's cabin, finding Iouen, Tahnet and Melhala already waiting. Katarin was pacing behind her desk, a glass of rum in one hand, the other fiddling with the beads threaded through the ends of her hair.

'Where's Arthur?' she demanded, glancing around.

'Here,' Arthur muttered, stepping in, Jalen on his heels. Apprehension was clear as the sky outside on both their faces.

'Right,' Katarin began. 'We'll go over this again.' She glared at Iouen before he could utter a grumble. The quartermaster tactfully remained silent. 'We'll leave before dawn. I have no idea how long we will be gone. Let's assume there is nothing that we can, or should, eat in that forest, so we carry enough food for a few days at least. Rationed,' she added harshly. 'No hunting, either. I don't want anyone to accidentally kill something we shouldn't and upset the locals. No eating pretty coloured fruits unless we know what they are. No—'

'Katarin,' Arthur cut in gently. 'We know. Everything is organised. Tahnet has the food prepared and ready to go. Iouen has the maps. We've got blankets and clothing and all the potable water we can carry.'

She folded her arms, a scowl on her face, then turned her attention to Jenyfer and Ordes. 'The two of you need to get your heads in the game.'

'What's your problem?' Ordes bristled. 'I get that you're nervous, Kat, but—'

Kat narrowed her eyes. 'My problem? You've got to collect your Treasures and—'

'Katarin,' Halymere said. 'Leave them be.'

She glared at him, then promptly ordered them all out of her cabin.

Arthur rubbed at his face. 'We should all get a good night's rest. You too, Kat,' he added as everyone filed out and went in search of their beds. Jenyfer and Ordes remained above deck. Halymere was still with Katarin, and Jenyfer could hear them bickering.

'She's right,' Jenyfer said eventually. 'And,' she went on before Ordes could argue, 'she's worried. About Arthur. About all of us. She just doesn't know how to show it.'

'I heard that,' Katarin shouted from behind her door.

'I know,' Ordes murmured.

Jenyfer gazed at Katarin's door, then up at the stars scattered across the sky. 'Are you worried?'

'I am. But not about the Treasures,' Ordes answered. 'More about what we're going to do with them once we have them. What if we do what Niniane wants and create a world where magic rules again? What will happen to all those without magic? People like those on this ship. Will we be setting them up for a life they cannot control?'

'What's the alternative, though?' Jenyfer asked. 'Leave things as they are? We can't do that either. I guess it needs to be somewhere in the middle, but I don't know what that will look like. Do you?'

'No,' he admitted, then glanced at her. 'My life was pretty simple before I met you. But,' he added, leaning over to rest his forehead against hers. 'I wouldn't change a thing. None of it, because if I'd never gone into that town, bored and looking for a bottle of rum, I'd never have found you.'

'I think we would have found each other regardless,' Jenyfer whispered. 'You saved me, Ordes, in more ways than one.'

'But I wasn't quick enough about it, was I?' he murmured.

'It doesn't matter,' Jenyfer managed. 'You came back for me.'

Later, in the safety of their bed, moonlight crept in through the porthole, the air thick and heavy. Jenyfer sighed, resting her head on Ordes' chest, drawing little circles on his stomach. 'We need to focus on our task.' Her instincts were telling her to lift her head and kiss him, or put her tongue on his flesh. She made herself stay where she was. 'I'm apprehensive,' she said. 'About all of this – this quest. And regardless of what she says, I am worried about Lamorna. I can't help her when she's in that place.'

'Jen, maybe you can't,' Ordes said. 'Maybe she's where she wants to be. In fact, I would say she is exactly where she wants to be, or with whom, at least.'

'I know,' Jenyfer replied, although her stomach twisted at the thought. 'But she's my family, and I'm …'

'The heir to your father's magic, as I am to mine,' Ordes finished. It wasn't what Jenyfer was going to say, and it hadn't been what she was thinking, but he was right. *That* bothered her more than anything. 'I think we both need to face what that means,' Ordes went on softly.

'Your father isn't a sociopath,' she mumbled. 'Mostly.'

Ordes chuckled, his laugh vibrating through his chest and into Jenyfer's cheek. 'I know you're scared about using your magic because you don't want to be like him, and maybe that's valid, but Melodias is an Old One. He's powerful, like my mother, like my father, and his magic is your magic, Jen.'

'Maybe you're right,' she said. 'Maybe it is time I accept it, accept who and what I am.'

'You are yourself,' Ordes told her, fingers trailing down her arm.

Jenyfer smiled against his chest. 'As are you.'

They didn't speak for a while. The ship rocked gently, small waves brushing against the hull.

'I don't feel like I've spent enough time with my magic, though,' Jenyfer said. 'My elemental magic is stronger, thanks to Melhala – more within my control anyway – but my syhren song? How do I truly learn to use that?'

She knew the answer; part of her had known all along. It was instinct, like Andromache had said, and no matter what she did, she couldn't avoid it forever. She knew the lyrics – they were branded on her brain and heart. Jenyfer had thought she'd never learn them all, but it was as if some part of her had always known them. When she first read the lyrics, they were strangely familiar.

She needed to move past the fear of using her voice.

She did not share Andromache's thoughts about power – destructive power – being a gift, and, surely, her syhren song was more than a tool for destruction and death. Why couldn't she create with her voice instead? Why were all of the songs designed to control and manipulate?

Jenyfer knew the answer to that.

Her father's desire for control lay at the heart of syhren magic.

Jenyfer had to learn her own form of control if she was going to be different. And she could not do that when she was frightened of herself.

She took a deep breath, and sat up.

'Ordes, will you let me practise on you?'

His eyebrows lifted. 'Are you going to make me stand on my head?'

'Maybe. I don't know yet,' she answered.

He sat up, tucking a length of her hair behind her ear. His fingers lingered on her cheek, before sliding down to curl beneath her jaw; she tilted her face into his palm. 'I trust you, Jenyfer. I've always trusted you. So yes, you can practise on me.'

She frowned. 'Will my magic still work on you? I mean, you're *you* now.'

Ordes shrugged. 'There's only one way to find out.'

'Now?'

'Why not?' he said. 'Besides, I like hearing you sing.'

'Alright,' Jenyfer said, shifting so she could sit cross-legged, the sheets bundled around her. 'Let's see if I can put you to sleep to start with.'

'What was it like?'

'Strange. I could feel the magic in your voice and I knew what was happening, but there was also nothing I could do to keep my eyes open,' Ordes said. He yawned and stretched, linking his hands behind his head and looking at her thoughtfully. 'It was like there was another voice in my head – your voice, but different to when you're talking to me through the heartfire.'

Jenyfer frowned. 'What do you mean?'

'Your voice was deeper, cool, like the depths of the ocean,' Ordes said. 'But gentle. You told me to sleep, that it was okay, that I would be okay.'

She blinked at him. 'You heard that?'

He nodded.

'That's what I was thinking as I sang to you,' Jenyfer said, amazed.

'So the magic in your voice is connected to not only what you sing, but what you're thinking?' Ordes asked.

'I don't know. Maybe,' Jenyfer said. She pulled her bottom lip between her teeth. This was something new, something her father or Andromache had not mentioned, but it made a strange sort of sense. She hadn't wanted to hurt Ordes in any way, hadn't even wanted to coerce him. She'd wanted him to sleep, nothing more.

'Try a different song,' he suggested.

'Like what?' she asked. Part of her was growing excited at this new discovery. If she could keep her inner voice, the one he heard in his head, calm and gentle, then maybe there would be no danger she would hurt him, or anyone.

Ordes smiled. 'Make me forget you put me to sleep.'

All the doubts came flooding back. 'What if I mess up and take away *all* your memories?' Jenyfer shook her head. 'No.'

'You won't,' he insisted.

'How do you know?'

'Because I trust you,' he said. 'And you need to start trusting yourself with this.'

She exhaled a tight breath, then nodded. He was right. 'Okay,' she whispered. 'Let's try it, but Ordes, if I make a mistake ...' *I won't*, she thought. *Not with him.* The idea that he could end up forgetting her was too much to bear. She used that, kept it at the front of her mind as she called up the song for forgetting. Before she opened her mouth, she leant forward and kissed him. 'Just in case,' she whispered, and then sang.

His eyes glazed over immediately, then slipped closed. She made sure not to sing for long, not to let the magic sink too deeply.

Please don't forget me, she thought desperately, watching his face carefully, and when she stopped and his eyes opened, she searched for any signs that she had destroyed his memories.

Slowly, he sat up. Jenyfer couldn't breathe. He said nothing for a long time, a small frown between his eyes and her heart leapt into her mouth.

'Ordes? How do you feel?'

He frowned. 'I feel like I've slept, but the last thing I remember is being on deck. Katarin had the shits with us again,' he added. Jenyfer knocked him back onto the pillows as she threw her arms around him.

'What's going on?' he asked, and she laughed and kissed him.

CHAPTER 7

A black bird had been following them through the Faery Forest all morning. It had appeared overhead not long after they had landed on the beach, ducking and weaving through the canopy as they walked. Sometimes, it perched in a high branch ahead of them, and Ordes had the unmistakable feeling he knew that bird.

Jalen's shoulder brushed his as the storm demon stepped past him. He glanced up at the bird, then shook his head and continued walking. He wasn't sure what to think about Jalen and his mood, not yet, not when there were other more important things to focus on.

The black bird cried out harshly, then took to the air again, sunlight catching on its wings. Ordes lost sight of it; a smile crawled over his lips.

Yeah, that bird was definitely familiar.

Jenyfer waited for him to draw level with her, then slipped her hand in his with a smile. Ordes knew they were like a pair of love-sick fools, but he didn't care. Even something as simple as holding hands made his heart sing.

The trees thickened, trunks standing like sentinels to this ancient place. Ordes could feel the magic of this forest all around him, like he could in Avalon; the hum and swell of the air, the small snatches of light that winked between the trees that were not sunlight, but the fey of the forest, so tiny the human eye would not notice them. Squirrels danced through the branches, and a family of spotted deer poked their heads around the tree trunks, watching them pass with dark, solemn eyes. Jenyfer marvelled at the brightly coloured butterflies, as large as dinner plates, and floating around them, so close they could feel the beat of those delicate wings against their skin.

Beneath the tranquil beauty of the place, the forest had eyes. Their path was being tracked. Whispers floated through the air around them. Did those fey creatures who dwelt in this place know who they were, and what they were there for?

Deeper in, granite boulders dotted the landscape beneath the trees, their grey faces cloaked in pale lichen. Moss carpeted the trunks and branches of trees, and wildflowers poked gloriously coloured heads from the sides of the path. Leaves carpeted the ground, green and vibrant, the occasional splash of autumn gold or orange woven throughout.

The black bird lingered above. Ordes could sense it, even if he couldn't see it. He slowed his steps – Jenyfer tugged on his hand.

'I'll catch up,' he told her. She nodded, puzzled, but hurried to join the others. Ordes glanced up at the trees. There was no sign of the bird at first, and then he spotted it, sitting high in the branches, preening itself. He chuckled; the bird stopped and glared at him. Ordes sank to the ground beneath the tree, resting his back against the trunk. In the tree opposite, dainty faeries were flitting about, their gossamer wings catching pieces of sunlight.

He could see the rest of the group up ahead, could hear Iouen moaning about being hungry. Ordes watched them share their meal, Tahnet counting each piece of fruit that left the bag. They kept walking, eating as they went.

Ordes snuck a look at the bird. It sat directly above him, watching him. Now, instead of irritated, he thought it looked smug. He sighed, plucking at strands of grass absently. 'I can't believe, even as a bird, you manage to give me a headache.'

This time, a laugh answered.

There was a flash of light, feathers drifting on the air, and then his father was sitting in the grass beside him. Ordes' heart swelled at the sight of him – ruffled white shirt, red sash around his middle, his long coat and cutlass, hair loosely tied back, beads glittering in the light.

It was one of the sights he was most familiar with in the world.

'You're in a mood,' Tymis declared, removing a feather from his mouth. 'Are you not getting any?'

'My sex life is fine, not that it's any of your business,' Ordes said, biting back his laugh. 'Mother gave you back your magic, I take it?'

Tymis scoffed. 'She can't say no to me. I can be very persuasive.'

'Keep the details to yourself, Tymis, please,' Ordes said. Then, 'It's good to see you.'

Tymis ran his eyes over his son. 'You're different, and I don't mean the hair. Who did that to you, anyway?'

Ordes laughed and got to his feet, offering his father a hand. Tymis took it and let Ordes pull him upright. He groaned dramatically, rubbing at his back and shoulders.

'It's been a long time since I've been a bird. I forgot how much work it was on the arms,' he said with a grin. Laughter bounced back to them through the forest. Tymis' face shifted – it became expectant, excited. 'I think there is someone I need to finally meet.'

Ordes nodded. 'Come on then, great and powerful one.'

Tymis was smiling. Ordes led the way through the trees. The others were seated in a small clearing. Katarin was on her feet, hands on her hips, ordering everyone about, but when Ordes and Tymis approached, she stopped mid-sentence.

Everyone froze. An apple dangled from Arthur's hand.

Ordes cleared his throat. 'This is my father, the …' He hesitated, then, 'Merlin.' He felt his father look at him in surprise. 'And this,' Ordes said, indicating Arthur, 'is—'

'The Once and Future King,' Merlin said, and it was Ordes' turn to be surprised as his father bowed to Arthur Tregarthen, who blushed. 'You are as I saw, all those years ago – exactly as you are meant to be.'

Merlin's voice was softer than Ordes had ever heard it, different somehow. There was power and magic in it. Only then did he realise that the air around his father was moving.

Arthur drifted closer. He hesitated, then held out his hand. When Merlin took it, a broad, relieved smile lit Arthur's face. 'I'm so glad you're here.'

'You might regret saying that,' Katarin grumbled.

Merlin's eyes remained on Arthur and when he spoke, his voice was pitched low. 'When the battle is waged in the skies, in the sea and on the land, darkness and blood will come for you,' he murmured. Arthur jolted but did not pull his hand free. 'You will fall into the darkness, but there cannot be darkness without light, Arthur, and the light that will shine will be your light, as bright and glorious as you choose to let it be.'

Nobody moved; even the forest around them was silent. The breeze that had been skimming through the trees was gone. Arthur's eyes were wide. Jalen moved, a whirlwind of storm clouds and lightning. He disappeared, only to reappear next to Arthur.

'Enough, Merlin,' he demanded, pulling Arthur's hand free. 'What were you thinking?'

'Jalen,' Arthur murmured. 'It's fine.'

'You think I can control it, demi-god?' Merlin asked. 'Tell me – how would it feel to have your magic caged inside your body for years, never being able to reach it, always aware of it beneath the surface of you, to suddenly have everything back, every part of you filled with power? With magic and music and the scent of the earth, the touch of the wind and the rain, the taste of fresh water, and a raging flame curling in your blood?'

Ordes sucked in a sharp breath. His father had put into words all the things he had been feeling since leaving the temple, since Goerika had helped him unlock what was hidden inside him – things he was still hiding, unwilling to let it all out. Now maybe, with his father here, that might change.

Merlin blinked, then took a step back, running his hand over his face. 'Forgive me. I've been a bird for four days. Has anyone got any food?'

Melhala hurried over, handing over an apple. The Cruithean Magic Wielder's face was glowing with awe. 'I can't believe it's you.'

As the Prophet of the Gods casually munched on an apple, the Once and Future King approached him again, shyly. 'Perhaps, when you're ready, we can talk?'

Merlin magicked his apple core away and wiped his hands on his shirt. 'Of course, but I'd like to talk to my son first.' Without waiting for anyone to reply, he closed his fingers around Ordes' wrist, and the world dissolved into mist and blinding, white light as they vanished.

'A bit of warning might have been nice,' Ordes managed. He was bent-double, hands on his knees, struggling to keep his breakfast in his stomach. Slowly, he straightened, frowning as he looked around.

They were in the captain's cabin on *The Excalibur*.

As he watched, his father strode across the room, plonking down into his usual seat with a grateful sigh. He put his feet up on the desk, then glanced at Ordes. 'Don't tell our dear Ms Le Fey I sat in her seat, will you?'

'I take it that means you don't want your ship back?' Ordes asked.

Merlin shook his head. 'I didn't come back to ruffle Katarin's feathers, as amusing as it would be.' He gestured to the seat opposite him. Ordes sat, like he had a hundred times before, and the familiarity of it was oddly soothing. 'Ask your questions,' his father said simply. 'I know you saw Goerika. What illuminating things did she have to tell you?'

'Are you a demon?' Ordes blurted. It was the first thing that came out. 'Am I?'

'Neither of us are demons,' Merlin said gently. 'I don't know what I am, exactly, other than a man who can't quit this blasted world and who knows a little too much of what is going to happen, or a version of it, in any case. You, my boy, did not come crawling out of the Pit Melodias has on his doorstep.'

Ordes swallowed, fidgeting. 'They spoke to me.'

'They tend to do that,' his father said. 'You saw the Pit?'

Ordes nodded.

'Hot, isn't it?' Merlin mused, linking his hands behind his head and stretching back in the seat until his bones cracked. 'But that's all it is – a hole in the ground filled with fire and smoke and misery. Nothing to worry about. So, you met Melodias. I can only guess what the God of the Seas had to say about me.'

'You do realise not everything in this world is about you, right?' Ordes said, grinning. His smile slipped. 'It's not, is it?'

His father laughed. 'No, but, a lot of it is, I suppose.' He rubbed at the back of his neck, the beads in his hair chiming gently. 'The problem with prophecy, Ordes, is there is never a straight answer, and words are open to interpretation. I'm here to guide, not to define.'

Ordes sat back and sighed. 'Still as cryptic as ever, thanks.'

'I wish I could do more,' Merlin replied. 'But, enough of that. Have you got a handle on what you can do?' He narrowed his eyes. 'What can you do?'

'Scared I won't live up to your fabulous legacy?' Ordes quipped. 'The elements are as simple as breathing, which I've learnt I don't actually need to do. I can summon and conjure, click my fingers and turn a mouse into a cat, move through time and space. I haven't shifted my shape yet, so don't ask. I—'

'Still have no idea what you are capable of,' Merlin said.

Ordes folded his arms. 'Then teach me.'

'Some things cannot be taught, Ordes – they need to be felt, experienced. But you won't be able to do anything if you hold back, if you let the fear of what you are stop you from being what you are,' his father explained. 'But yes, I will teach you what I can. Be warned – I had no one to teach me, so don't complain about my methods like you usually do.' He stood, stretched, then reached for Ordes' wrist. 'We better get back.'

Ordes shook his head. 'I'll do it myself, thanks. I'd like to keep my stomach.'

Merlin laughed, and vanished in a whirl of light.

CHAPTER 8

'Everything is about to change,' Jalen stated. He and Arthur had left the others at their makeshift camp. They'd not long finished a dinner of fruit and bread, with some salted meat and cheese. The sun had set, and the only light came from the fireflies dancing around their heads.

Arthur indicated their joined hands with a smile. 'But not this.'

'No,' Jalen agreed. 'Not this.'

They continued walking, moving deeper into the trees of the Faery Forest. They didn't speak, but Arthur didn't mind. He liked these quiet moments with Jalen, moments that, since they had left Cruithea, had been fleeting. Apart from when they were locked away in their cabin, they hadn't been alone in months.

Arthur missed that. Even in Kernou, with fear of an omnipresent shadow, they had managed to find moments for only them.

Back then, they hadn't been what they were now. But the spark had been there and, once kindled, it had smouldered away in Arthur's belly and he hadn't been able to extinguish it. He'd tried, desperately so, knowing that spark would turn into a raging fire, and if that happened, he wouldn't have a hope of stamping it out.

And he was glad he hadn't.

He stole a glance at Jalen, watching the way the orange glow of the fireflies danced over the lines of his face; the sharp jawline, the strong nose and brow, the sculpted cheekbones and the generous mouth.

'I remember the first day I saw you,' he said.

Jalen's lips curled into a smile. 'Oh?'

'You'd just returned from the water. It was early, and I was where I wasn't supposed to be. You didn't see me – you were busy with the nets – but I could see you from where I was hiding in the trees.'

Jalen squeezed his hand, an encouragement, so Arthur went on.

'I watched you for what felt like hours, but it was probably only a few minutes. There were others with you, but my eyes kept returning to you, like I didn't have a say in it at all. Then you were alone, the others gone. You sat on the sand and watched the water. I wanted to go down and sit with you, but I was too frightened. You wouldn't have even known who I was then,' Arthur added with a laugh.

'I would have,' Jalen murmured in response, then, 'I remember that day. I'd not long arrived in Kernou, and it was my first day on the water – well, my first day that my workmates knew of, anyway.' He gave Arthur a smile. 'I've been a fisherman my whole life, in some way or another. It was soothing to return to that life, even if it was pretend. Do you remember when we met? You ran into me, too busy looking at your feet while out with your father.'

Arthur nodded, smiling. 'I thought I'd run into a wall,' he said, reaching over to run his hand across the breadth of Jalen's chest.

They stopped walking, the trees thick around them. The fireflies floated in the air like tiny sparks, waiting to touch down and blaze away, like Arthur's heart did whenever Jalen looked at him – whenever he was reminded that Jalen was his.

'Niniane sent you to find me,' Arthur said. It wasn't a question. Jalen nodded. 'How did you know I was the one you were looking for?'

'We knew your name, Arthur. Merlin had spoken it,' Jalen replied. He brushed a curl from Arthur's cheek, tucking it behind his ear. 'But I think I'd have found you anyway.'

'Did you always know you were … well … that you preferred men to women?' Arthur asked. He'd wondered about it, especially when that part of himself was waking up. For a long time, he'd thought he was losing his mind. Then, when the thoughts, the want, did not go away and instead grew roots and anchored him, the fear set in.

Jalen nodded. 'As a young man, I had dalliances with women as well as men. It wasn't frowned upon. Who you loved, who you allowed close to you, did not change who you were as a human being. There was a man that I loved, not long before I died. I don't even remember his name now.'

'Can we sit?' Arthur asked.

They lowered themselves to the ground, sitting opposite one another. For a long moment, they stared at each other.

'Will the Sword change me?' Arthur asked eventually.

'Maybe,' Jalen answered, and Arthur's heart skipped a beat. 'It's a weapon of war, Arthur, and as much as the idea of you on a battlefield terrifies me, I fear this is where everything is leading.'

'Only on Camlann field,' Arthur murmured. Jalen took Arthur's hands in his, his calloused thumbs brushing over Arthur's fingers.

'I won't let anything or anyone hurt you, you understand?' Jalen said, his voice low and fierce.

Arthur nodded.

'As the Inborn are the shield of the world, I shall be your shield, Arthur,' Jalen promised.

Arthur swallowed. 'I know.'

They lay down on the forest floor. The canopy was so thick Arthur couldn't see any stars, but he knew they would be out there. Before he had left Kernou, he'd never seen the night sky except from his bedroom window, a tiny slice of it, the view caged like he was.

He sighed, resting his head on Jalen's shoulder, his arm around Jalen's middle. The demi-god kissed him on the top of the head, his hand pressed into Arthur's lower back.

'Promise me that when I'm King we can still do this,' Arthur whispered.

'Hold each other? Of course.'

Arthur smiled. 'I was thinking sneak away and lie beneath the trees and the night sky.' He twisted so he could see Jalen's face. Their eyes met, held, and broke apart when Arthur leant over and pressed his lips to Jalen's.

'I promise,' Jalen murmured against Arthur's mouth.

Chapter 9

Katarin was agitated, more than usual. She didn't like change, because when things changed, things went wrong. Merlin's arrival had stirred her up. He'd always been capable of that, with that superior smirk of his, but now, it was different. The man she had spent years playing games with on the water, whose ship she had threatened to send to the bottom of the sea, whose crew she had threatened to drown, was the Prophet of the Gods.

She had been kept in the dark. She knew she should let it go, focus on the task at hand, like she had demanded everyone else do, but it was one of the only things she could hold on to. One of the only things she had to be mad at that made sense, because nothing else did.

Niniane had lied to her and deserted her. Merlin had brought no message from the Goddess, no words of comfort, and no explanation for the silence. Katarin could read people, men in particular, who usually wore their thoughts clear on their faces. She thought she was a good judge of character. But her faith in Niniane had been thrown back in her face.

She was entitled to be angry.

With a sigh, Katarin lifted her pack higher and hurried to catch up with the others. Lagging behind was not usually her style, but she needed a moment. It had been Aelle who had convinced her that taking a moment for herself was not a sign of weakness, but a sign of strength. And Katarin was trying desperately to be strong, for her brother, for everyone.

Niniane had said that Arthur needed her. It felt like the only true thing she had ever said.

Arthur and Merlin were up ahead, walking close together, talking in low voices. She wished she could hear what they were saying. Jalen hung back, and Katarin could practically see the annoyance rolling off him. Melhala and Halymere had embarrassed themselves by sucking up to Merlin, but Iouen treated him like he had never left, like he was still the captain of *The Excalibur*. A ripple of worry ran through Katarin – would she lose the ship now that he was back?

Jenyfer and Ordes strolled along hand in hand, glued to one another like they had been since they left Cruithea.

Katarin sighed. She was jealous. She knew the feeling, the way it burnt in her belly. It wasn't to do with Ordes at all – she had that opportunity and she let it go, and had no regrets about it – but simply that they had each other. She had caught herself many times looking for Aelle, looking for that one person who knew her better than anyone.

Halymere glanced at her over his shoulder. Katarin gave him her best scowl and he turned away. On a whim, she caught up to Jalen and took hold of his arm. The storm demon went still in surprise, but waited until the others had drawn ahead before he spoke.

'If you're about to—'

'I don't trust you,' Katarin said bluntly. 'But that doesn't matter, not at the moment. We both love Arthur and don't want to see him hurt.' She paused, released Jalen's arm and resumed walking, keeping her pace slow. 'I saw your face when Merlin arrived,' she pointed out. 'I thought you'd be pleased to see him, considering who he is and who he's attached to.'

'If you think I have any say in the affairs of a goddess, you're sorely mistaken,' Jalen mumbled.

'But you don't like him?' Kat pressed.

'I don't trust him.'

'Why?' she asked.

Jalen gave her an irritated look. 'You couldn't possibly begin to understand.'

'I thought he told you it was your duty to serve Arthur,' Katarin said, ignoring the insult, letting it go like Aelle would tell her to. 'And now you are. So what's the problem?'

'Are you saying you care about my feelings?' Jalen snorted and shook his head.

'Not at all,' Katarin replied. 'But if your feelings are going to cause trouble for Arthur, then I'll have a very vested interest in them.'

Jalen laughed, a low and bitter laugh. 'Why is it so difficult for you to see him with me? Why can't you let him be happy?'

She blinked, taken aback. 'That's not—'

'Isn't it?' Jalen asked. 'Look, I understand. He's your family. You love him. But I love him too, and I don't want to see him hurt. Yes, Merlin told me it was my destiny to serve Arthur, but that isn't why I'm here.' He paused, running his hand over his face wearily. 'At first, I was supposed to help him. Guide him towards his path. But even a demi-god can fall in love, Katarin.'

'You truly love him?' she asked quietly.

'Yes, I do, which is why I'm nervous,' Jalen replied. 'I'm worried about who and what this guardian will be and what they will want him to do. I'm concerned that Arthur will try and carry the weight of the Grail and the prophecy on his own, because he seems to think that is what he has to do to be strong, to be a leader. And I'm worried I won't be able to help him, in the end.'

Katarin fell silent and let Jalen move away from her. She watched him rejoin Arthur, watched Arthur turn to him, and saw the smile they shared.

Perhaps she had it wrong? Maybe there was nothing to worry about at all.

'We should stop,' she called out. 'And take a break.' She hurried to catch up to the rest of the group. 'I can hear water — there must be a stream up ahead. We can stop near there.'

Her request was met with nods of agreement. It was hot in the south of Teyath, hotter than any of them were used to. It wasn't the bite of the sun, but the way the air hung moisture on their skin. Katarin was tired, and she needed a wash. She hadn't been sleeping well, and didn't know how that was going to change unless she could coax her brain into some sort of order, even if it meant shoving some of them away to deal with later.

They went deeper into the trees, where the shade draped itself around them like a sigh. Katarin dropped her pack, grateful, and knelt to rummage through it for spare clothes. The others were sharing the last of the bread. Katarin's waterskin was empty; she'd fill it at the stream.

'I'm going to wash,' she announced, standing, her clean clothes tucked beneath her arm.

'You probably shouldn't go alone,' Halymere said. She raised her eyebrows at him. 'Katarin, we don't know what's lurking around in this forest.'

'I don't need a babysitter,' she snapped, stalking away from the group, heading into the trees, following the gentle sound of water. She kept going, even when she heard Jenyfer tell the others she'd go. Kat didn't want the syhren with her — she didn't want anybody — but she slowed her steps, allowing Jen to catch up with her. They didn't speak, picking their way through the forest in silence until the stream came into view.

A gasp escaped Jenyfer's lips and they both stood and stared.

The water sparkled with dappled light; willows crowded the banks, their branches falling like a bridal veil to tickle the surface of the water. Every colour was unnaturally saturated, from the verdant green of the leaves to the crystal-flecked granite that bordered the stream and the textured moth-grey of the willows trunks. Teal and magenta butterflies, sparkling like jewels, drifted through the air. Birds sang from the trees. Clusters of pink and purple flowers bowed their heads towards the water, dark green foliage shining as if it had been kissed with rain.

'Alright,' Kat admitted. 'It's beautiful. I know you're going to say it, so there. I beat you to it.'

Jenyfer grinned and began tugging off her clothes, leaving them in a pile on the ground. Before Kat could tell her to wait, she plunged into the water.

'That's better,' she sighed, ducking under. While she waited for Jenyfer to surface, Kat removed her clothes and balanced on the rocks at the edge of the stream. 'Just water, nothing nasty,' the syhren announced, gliding on her back, her expression blissful, before she dropped back under.

Katarin lowered herself onto the rocks and dipped her legs in, sighing in relief as the water stroked her skin with cool fingers. She splashed her arms and face while Jenyfer did whatever syhrens do underwater. When Jenyfer emerged again, Kat gave her a curious look.

'Is it different from the sea?' she asked.

'Yes,' Jenyfer said. 'But it's still water, so it's good. And it flows into the sea, eventually.'

Kat nodded, leaning forward to reach for her feet. Days in boots without a wash. She shuddered, reaching forward to scrub at her toes with her hands.

Jenyfer made a startled noise.

Kat froze, but did not sit back. Her hair had fallen forward, and her back was exposed. She let Jenyfer see it all, every tortured and puckered strip of flesh.

'What happened?' Jenyfer whispered at last.

Katarin's first instinct was to tell her to mind her own business, but instead she sighed. She wasn't ashamed of what had happened to her body, by the marks it had left behind. Aelle had known, of course, and Ordes had been smart enough not to ask about it, and Halymere …

There was something cathartic in letting her past be seen on her flesh, in not having to hide. In the freedom of being able to choose to talk about it. 'I made a mistake. I was young, barely eighteen. I thought I knew what I was doing. It was in Malist. My arrogance got the best of me, and the girl I was trying to save was burned anyway.'

'I'm sorry,' Jenyfer said awkwardly.

'From my cell I could see them building my pyre. They whipped me – I thought they wanted information, but they just did it because they could. Had they worked out my connection to Niniane, it might have been different,' Katarin said quietly; that moment was stamped on her brain and she knew that, no matter what happened, it would never leave her. 'Obviously, I didn't have my fearsome reputation then, or I'd be dead.'

She did not tell Jenyfer how one of them had enjoyed the sight of her blood, had enjoyed hurting her. He hadn't violated her, but had threatened he would. Katarin had not forgotten the savage pleasure in his eyes when he dragged the lash across her flesh like a caress before he slashed her with it.

'How did you escape?' Jenyfer asked. She shifted closer, laying half in and half out of the water. The scales on her long legs glittered, her hair floating around her back like a dark cloud.

'Did your aunt ever tell you stories about princesses being rescued by a man on a horse?' Kat asked, poking at the water angrily. This part she did not want to talk about.

'Halymere,' Jenyfer guessed.

'It took me a long time to forgive him. I was so angry—'

'You were angry at him for saving your life?' Jenyfer cut in, incredulous.

Kat nodded. 'I know it doesn't make sense, but I was angry because he got involved. Because he interfered in my problem – a problem I should have been able to fix. But the moment they tied me to that stake, I was a child again on the beach in Kernou. I froze.'

'Katarin ...' Jenyfer swallowed. 'They tried to burn you.'

Kat closed her eyes. She could still feel it, the heat building beneath her feet. Could still imagine what would have been left of her if Halymere hadn't arrived when he did. 'They'd lit the pyre when Haly appeared out of nowhere. He killed two Witchfinders, several others – it all happened so quickly. All I remember is his blade, moving with such precision, such skill. There was a moment where the sunlight caught on the blade and it glowed, and he with it and …' she paused, rubbing at her face. 'Don't repeat that,' she warned. 'I sound like a—'

'You sound like someone who was about to die, and didn't,' Jenyfer said. 'I know what that feels like. There is nothing wrong with being grateful. There is no weakness in it.'

Kat glared at her a moment, then felt her face relax. 'No, I guess not. But I still don't like to think about it, about what I owe him.'

'He wouldn't see it that way,' Jenyfer said. 'What happened between you two?'

'I don't even know how it started. I was so confused afterwards, so hurt and so angry at myself for letting it happen. He took me back to Avalon to heal – I refused to let him take me to Cruithea. I was afraid of going back there, in that state. My aunt wouldn't have let me leave again and Cruithea was not home, not anymore,' Katarin said. 'Haly stayed in Avalon with me, until I was well, and everything was fine as long as no one talked about what happened, or about what was happening between us. But there is only so long you can do that for. You know that,' Kat added.

Jenyfer's smile was brief. 'I do.'

'We were together for a while, close to half a year, I guess. For a long time, I didn't feel like I could be back on the water. The failure was so strong, so biting. It ate away at me. He helped me understand that I could still be me, be who I wanted to be. I hated him for that, too, because why couldn't I see that myself? Why did I need someone else to show it to me?' Kat asked. 'And then, I walked away from him.'

Jenyfer hesitated. 'Why?' she asked.

'Because he had seen me at my weakest, and I couldn't deal with that.' Kat reached for the washcloth. They finished bathing in silence.

The crew camped close to the stream, and Katarin lay awake most of the night, eventually falling asleep to the sound of flowing water. It was comforting. It wasn't the ocean, the rhythmic slapping of waves against the hull of her ship, but it was familiar, and in a world that had been turned upside down, that was important.

Halymere woke her not long after dawn, his large hand resting on her shoulder.

'I know you're not a morning person, so I'll keep this brief,' he said. 'Whatever happened, happened in the past, Katarin … I am here to support Arthur. To do whatever he needs to succeed. The High Priestess has set me this task. So as much as it might pain you to have to put up with me, I am not leaving, no matter how much you snap your teeth at me.'

Shame curled in her stomach. But instead of an apology, she sat up swiftly, almost knocking him in the teeth with her forehead. 'You're right. It's too early for this.' She pulled her boots on and went in search of her brother, spying him with Merlin at the edge of their hastily arranged camp.

The others were still asleep. Annoyed, Kat picked her way through bodies until she found Ordes and Jenyfer. She watched them for a moment, then jabbed Ordes in the ribs with the toe of her boot.

He jumped, silver eyes snapping open in alarm. 'Fuck, Kat,' he groaned as Jenyfer woke and rubbed at her eyes.

'Something's going on,' Kat said. 'Get up.'

Ordes stopped mid-yawn and jumped to his feet, Jenyfer following him, blinking and bleary-eyed. The three of them hurried over to where Arthur and Merlin stood beneath the trees. From this distance, the

Nemhain Mountains were draped in low-hanging clouds, the sky heavy with haze and heat.

'Early morning stroll?' Katarin asked.

'I'm retrieving the Sword,' Arthur answered, nerves threaded through his voice. 'It's close – I can feel it.'

'We'll come with you,' Kat said.

Arthur shook his head. 'You can't. This is for me to do, alone,' he added as Jalen caught up to them, his face tight. Arthur took his hands. 'I'll be fine.'

Katarin folded her arms. This was Arthur's task; it didn't mean any of them had to like the fact that he was going off, alone, to retrieve the Sword.

The look on Jalen's face told her he agreed.

Chapter 10

'There will be a test,' Merlin told Arthur. The trees arched over them like a cage, leaves trickling down in quick bursts. 'Before she lets you have the Sword, you will need to pass her test.'

'What sort of test?' Arthur asked.

'She will ask you to face your fears,' Merlin answered. A small, winged faery darted from the nearest tree to perch on his shoulder. He smiled, reaching up to touch her gently. 'But what that will look like, only you know.'

'I have faced many fears since leaving Kernou,' Arthur said. The little faery was watching him. She had green skin and twigs for hair, her features sharp and pointed. 'I honestly don't know what there is left.'

'You are afraid of power,' Merlin said simply. 'But you don't need to be, for there are two types of power in the world, Arthur. The power created from fear, and the power created from kindness and love. Each is a construct you can master. But you first need to decide the form your power will take, for there is a thin line between the two. It is often hard for people to see the difference.'

'My father's power is rooted in fear, and I've suffered its consequences,' Arthur said. 'I don't want power like that.'

They walked in silence until Merlin stopped, laying his hand on Arthur's arm. 'Beyond the treeline ahead is a veil of leaves,' Merlin told him. 'Part that veil, and you will find your way to the Sword and She who guards it.'

Arthur's throat tightened, his mouth suddenly dry, but he nodded. He did not glance back the way they had come.

This was his task.

He set off, focusing on breathing, on staying calm. Merlin had not told him what guarded the Sword of the White Dragon, only that it was a faery, and Arthur had learnt enough about faeries to know that he needed to be careful.

It was warm beneath the trees, the air thick and damp. He could hear a waterfall in the distance, and as he followed the river, the trees grew right up to the bank, their network of ancient roots tumbling into the water as though suspended between two worlds.

Much like he was. Part of him was still in Kernou, stuck in what his life had been. The newer, fresher part of him was here, daring to confront an ancient and powerful faery and ask her to hand over a magical relic that Merlin had decided was his.

The trees thickened, their trunks coated in moss and lichen. The air cooled, the canopy so thick barely a slice of sky could be seen. Up ahead, Arthur could see light, and he quickened his pace, the rushing river urging him forward. He could feel the energy of this place, the power of these ancient trees. Magic was in the air, light and warm, but beneath that, he could sense discontent. The trees were angry, he realised. This forest was angry. And in pain. Arthur recalled the map he had seen in his dream, before the location of the Sword was revealed. On that map, there were no human settlements, except for Dinas Emrys, and the Teyath of old had been shrouded in forests, stretching from one end of the continent to the other. He had always thought the land must have always been like it is now – settled, *conquered*, by men, but the Faery Forest told a different tale. Whispers floated through his brain, words he could not decipher, but could sense in the deepest part of him.

He continued walking, paying more attention to the trees, to what he could feel from them. Longing for what was, fear at what would be. Arthur licked his lips, pausing for a moment to rest his hand on the trunk of a tree. He wanted to tell it he was sorry, that he would fix it, but he didn't know how, or if it was a false promise. He gave the tree a gentle pat, hoping that it could sense his thoughts.

The forest floor was woven with ancient tree roots, shrouded in leaf litter. Sunlight eased through the trees, stretching like fingers, reaching closer until Arthur felt it touch his feet and, for a moment, he was rooted to the spot, part of the landscape. He gazed up, searching the canopy for birds, pulling a great breath into his lungs. He could taste the forest, the earthy tang of it, the sweetness that settled on his tongue. Each breath was like water, cleansing and pure.

The roar of the waterfall increased and then, everything paused, and Arthur was encased in a thick silence. There, beyond the treeline, he could see it – the veil of leaves. Nothing held it in place, the leaves hanging like a curtain in the air before him. Slowly, Arthur approached, reaching out and touching one of the leaves – it shimmered in the light, and then pulled back. He stepped away, heart in his throat, as the leaf curtain parted, wide enough for him to pass through. Arthur took a deep breath. He could feel the Sword now, could hear it calling him the way it did in his dreams.

He stepped through the curtain.

Like a semi-molten mirror, a lake glimmered in the sunlight; a waterfall thundered into it with enough force to crush a person's skull. It was beautiful and terrifying all at once, and the sound of it settled inside Arthur's chest like thunder. The peaks of the Nemhain Mountains rose into a cloudless sky.

In the middle of the lake was an island of rock, one lone tree growing solitary from the stone. Beneath that tree was a woman. Arthur approached the lake, his steps quickening as he neared the water. A series of stepping stones lead to the island. Arthur traversed them slowly, not wanting to fall in.

When he stepped onto the island, he breathed a sigh of relief.

'You can hear it, can't you?' the faery said. Her voice was like the summer sun, warm and golden. There was no sign of the Sword, but Arthur nodded. 'Come closer, King who Shall Be.'

He did, eyes locked on her. Her gown of leaves and bark floated around her body like a cloud, touching her and not touching her at the same time. Her hair reminded him of tree roots, dark and flecked with pale gold. A pair of antlers rose from her head; tiny white flowers sprouted from the vines wrapped around them. Her eyes were large and doe-like, and in them, Arthur could sense the age of the earth, just as he had when he met the Green Knight. The faery smiled and warmth spread through him, like the pulse of his fledgling magic.

'What are you?' he asked her, as politely as he could.

'I am a dryad,' she told him. 'One of the last, for when the forests fell to the cities and towns of men, we were banished from our homes. I have watched my kin fade and die. I have watched their life forces flicker out as the trees toppled. I watched this world change, and I have seen what is coming.'

Arthur swallowed. Her words triggered a memory – Mordred, speaking of the destruction of the earth and the waterways, the pollution and poison and man's desire for what the land could give him, rather than what he could give it. 'I am sorry,' Arthur told the dryad, knowing it meant nothing. 'If I could fix it, I would.'

'Perhaps you can,' she said. The air around her shimmered, and suddenly she was holding the Sword of the White Dragon. Her fingers, Arthur noted absently, had an extra knuckle. His heart raced at the sight of the weapon. Before he could say a word, the dryad turned and drove the Sword directly into the rocks at her feet.

'No!' he cried.

'It is yours to take,' she said.

Arthur did not move, even though the Sword was calling him.

'You do not want it?' the dryad asked.

'I don't know,' he replied. 'If I take it, this whole thing becomes … real. I don't want to be a king, not really. But the world is so full of hate and pain. I can't abandon it to that fate.'

She nodded. 'Then you will not be able to take the Sword – not until you can prove to me, and to yourself, that you are worthy of your destiny.'

'Destiny,' Arthur echoed. 'My father always believed it was my destiny to serve the One God and spread the Word. Merlin believes my destiny is to be a king, but me … how can I accept a destiny I have no choice in?'

'You think you have no choice?' the dryad asked. 'There is always choice, Arthur Tregarthen. You can choose to walk away from this path and return to your life, or you can choose to accept what is being given to you.'

'And what is that?' he asked. 'The chance to remake a world I am only beginning to understand? I'm being asked to make decisions that will affect all living things in Teyath. How is that fair? Do the people of this land have a say in their fate?'

'That is what it means to wield power,' a voice said.

A deep, male voice, one that Arthur knew. He swallowed, and slowly turned around.

His father stood behind him, dressed as he was the last time Arthur had seen him, in his rich, red cloak trimmed with gold. One side of his face was scarred, the skin puckered and angry. Arthur fought back the urge to vomit at the cruel reminder of what he had done.

'You're not here,' he whispered, the courage he had garnered since he'd crept aboard his sister's ship slowly withering and turning to dust. 'You can't be here.'

Ulrian ignored him, moving past him to stand by the Sword. He did not touch it, just stared at it. The dryad had vanished. Ulrian Tregarthen's form flickered out of focus and back again, and Arthur suddenly understood.

This would be his test, his trial for the Treasure. His greatest fear.

Ulrian looked at him, eyes dark and filled with the bitter disappointment Arthur was so achingly familiar with. 'You're going to fail.'

'No.'

'You are, Arthur.'

Arthur shook his head; his fists curled.

'You're a sinner. You need to be punished.' His father came closer. Arthur wanted to step away, but to do so was to show weakness. He fixed his feet firmly and kept his eyes on his father's face. Ulrian expected him to back down, not to fight, and for a moment, Arthur wondered if that would be the sensible decision. Maybe his father was right. He wasn't cut out for this – he wasn't anyone important. He … could hear the Sword calling to him. He could hear Jalen's voice in his head, reminding him that this was his path, that he had been chosen for this. Arthur would not run away, not this time.

Ulrian took another step towards him. 'The Word—'

'The Word says our sins will be forgiven, if only we ask it of Him,' Arthur cut in, the words rushing from him, words he had forgotten until this moment.

Ulrian's face was coated in anger. 'Where did you read that?'

'You lied to us, didn't you?' Arthur murmured.

'I told people what they needed to know,' his father answered.

'No, you told them what you needed so you could control them,' Arthur said. He took a step closer. His father stepped back. 'You lied to them. Exploited their ignorance. Abused them in the name of power. I finally see it. You terrified our people into submission to control them.'

'You have no concept of what it means to be a leader, Arthur,' Ulrian said, his lips curling cruelly.

'I know that manipulating people through fear is not how a leader should behave,' Arthur argued. 'A true leader respects his people, leads them with honesty. He does not rule through deceit.'

His father laughed. 'You think people would follow someone like you? You're a weakling who lacks courage.'

Arthur felt the Sword tugging at his insides. He shook his head. 'I had the courage to leave Kernou, to leave you, because I knew what you were doing was wrong.'

'You know nothing!' Ulrian's eyes flashed with rage and a terrible eldritch wind ripped across the world, throwing waves against the shore of the rocky island, tugging on Arthur's hair and clothes.

'I know more than you think. But you never saw me, Father, for the man I was. But others do – they believe in me,' Arthur said firmly. The wind pushed and shoved at him, but he held steady, the way he did when he was holding the wooden practice sword. The poise of a warrior, Halymere had said.

'Weak and cowardly, a sinner, a blasphemer, and a heathen, like your mother,' Ulrian spat.

'Do not speak of her,' Arthur growled. 'I know the truth of what happened. How she died, how you did nothing to save her, how you tied my sister to the stake for the sea to claim. You turned your back on Morgaine and my mother, when you could have saved them both. You're the coward, Ulrian – you let the whispers of the One God dictate your existence, your life little more than attempts to gain the Sacellum's favour. You seek power, but you do not know how to wield it.' Arthur did not stop, stepping closer to his father and the Sword. 'A true leader cares for his people over himself. You are not a leader. You're a shell of a man, battling insecurities so strong that you had to take them out on your own son, to justify the weakness of your decisions, to purge yourself of the *guilt* of them.'

Arthur's chest heaved, his blood burnt. The Sword sang, and the words continued to flow, each sentence healing, soothing the hurt he had carried his whole life.

'I am not hiding who I am anymore because if people cannot accept me for who I am, for who I love and what I believe, then that is their problem, not mine. If people will allow their prejudice to shape their opinions of me, that is their problem, not mine,' he said. 'Just as you have allowed your prejudice, insecurities, and cowardice to shape your opinion of me. I'm your son, yet you have never truly seen me.'

The figure of Ulrian Tregarthen began to fade.

'I will not follow your lead again. I will make my own decisions. And the first decision I make, as my own man, my own true self, is to stop your poison from spreading across the world,' Arthur said. 'To make the world a better place, I will sacrifice myself – if that is what needs to be done.'

He took another step towards his father. Ulrian flickered again. 'I will be true to myself,' Arthur declared.

Ulrian vanished.

Arthur stared at the place where his father had stood. Slowly, he smiled. He felt lighter, unburdened, *good*.

But he did not approach the Sword, not yet. From where he stood, he could see the intricate dragon design on the hilt, the strange words inscribed on the blade. His fingers twitched. He ached to hold it.

'Will you take it?' The dryad had returned. She circled him slowly, and he could smell the rich earthy scent of her magic. 'You cannot claim this sword until you believe in who you are and what you're meant to be,' the dryad said. 'Until you have drawn the Sword from the Stone and embraced your destiny.'

Arthur took a deep breath and nodded. He approached the Sword, wishing the others were here to witness this – he wished Jalen was here – but at the same time, he was glad they weren't, in case it didn't work.

In case he failed.

'I know what it is like to be voiceless, to be powerless in a world ruled by power. I know what it is like to lack courage, to have to hide who you are. I know what it is to lose your agency, but I also know what it's like to gain it,' Arthur said. He paused, glancing at the faery, her eyes filled with an intense curiosity that made Arthur's cheeks flush. 'I don't know how to be a king, but I know what I don't want: people who are afraid to follow their dreams or speak up when they suffer an injustice. I want a world where no one is a slave to anything. I want to give people the power of choice.'

'Then be who you were born to be,' the dryad told him.

'I will be true to myself.' Arthur closed his hand around the hilt of the Sword, and pulled.

As the Sword of the White Dragon slid free of the stone, a voice, low and breathless, whispered to him.

Home at last.

CHAPTER 11

'What do you and the Chif talk about?' Lamorna asked, stroking the hair back from Mordred's forehead, droplets of sweat lingering on her fingertips.

Mordred sighed. 'Nothing.'

'If I am to help you, I need to know,' Lamorna said. His eyes cut to hers, golden and dark in the light sliding into the room through the sheer curtains; she held her breath, until eventually, he smiled.

'You are right, you do. So, you will come with me to speak with Ulrian.'

'I will?'

Mordred rolled over so they were lying face to face. 'Don't you think it is time the Chif saw your worth? That he listened to the things you have to say?'

'And what could I possibly say to him?' Lamorna breathed. The idea of it – of being able to speak her mind to the Chif after so many years …

'That is up to you, my love,' Mordred said, his voice soft. 'What would you like to tell him? This is about your voice, remember. The one you had stolen from you.'

Lamorna chewed her lip. She thought finding her word would be difficult, but they came easily. 'I would tell him that I know the One God's love as he does. I would tell him he is not as wise as he believes, because he does not see what is in front of him.'

'And what is that?'

'Me,' she said. 'He does not see me. But you do,' she added, leaning over to press a kiss to his mouth. He kissed her back, lightly at first, and then harder, rolling to pin her beneath the bulk of his body. She curled one leg around his hip; he made a noise in the back of his throat and pressed himself firmly against her, and the core of her body began thrumming and aching.

'I do, do I?' he murmured, his hand creeping up her thigh.

'Yes,' she whispered against his lips. 'I think you do.'

Lamorna was securing her linen cap over her hair when Mordred's hands rested on her shoulders.

'Leave it off,' he said.

'But—'

He kissed her neck, below the ear.

'We were told that our bodies were for our husbands' eyes only.'

Mordred chuckled. 'I am not your husband, and you allow me to see you.'

Lamorna stood still as Mordred ran his hands slowly down her sides, tracing the curve of her body, the curve he had told her caused a fire to surge to life beneath his skin.

She did not know what to do about the cap. Her fingers had frozen on the straps. 'I should wear it, but …'

Gently, Mordred took her hands from her face. 'Let them see you,' he murmured, his fingers stroking the line of her throat.

Lamorna took a deep breath. 'No,' she said, quickly tying the straps of her cap. 'Not yet.'

Mordred would not allow her to follow behind him, so they walked side by side towards town. To Lamorna, the world was brighter, more alive. There was secret knowledge living inside her, and although it had been difficult to accept, it all made sense, in some strange way. Perhaps she had always known something was wrong. Perhaps not, but now, in the knowing of it, she felt closer to her sister.

The market square was full of people going about their morning business. Lamorna hesitated at the edge, but Mordred smiled at her, so she ignored the whispers, ignoring the heated glances, wondering whether this was how Jenyfer had felt whenever she had broken the rules: wicked and wild and free.

Mordred was not her husband.

She did not walk behind him.

She smiled, and kept that smile in place until they reached the Chif's house and found Bryn waiting for them. He ordered them to follow him, and led them into the hall, where he made them wait while he fetched the Chif. Lamorna's throat was tight, her mouth dry. When the Chif arrived, he frowned at her and everything fell away – all her bravery, all her purpose – her mind becoming as smooth as glass, thoughts sliding from it like water.

'Lamorna —'

'She is here because I want her to be here,' Mordred cut in. 'And if you want me to be here, and you want these conversations to continue, you will allow Lamorna a seat at your table.'

For a horrible moment, she thought it had not worked, that the Chif would send her away. Instead, Ulrian simply nodded and led the way down the dark hallway into his formal room. Mordred gestured she was to go first, so she did, her chin lifted proudly, remembering why she was here. Before they entered the room, Mordred stopped her, leaning close to whisper in her ear.

'Do you see?' he asked. 'Do you see the power I have?'

'Yes,' she whispered back.

'Is that something you would like?' Mordred continued.

She hesitated for the briefest moment. 'Yes.'

'Then we shall get it for you.'

He turned from her and strode into the room, but did not sit. This was the room where Lamorna had been taken after her return from the sea. She shuddered and pushed those memories away. The Chif was already seated. As Lamorna approached the table, he watched her intently, and she could feel his displeasure, could feel the words he wanted to say to her. He opened his mouth, but Mordred spoke before him.

'I thought it was rude to seat yourself before your guests.' He stood with his hands on the back of one of the chairs. He pulled it out, then gestured that Lamorna was to sit there, closest to the head of the table, where the Chif had not risen from his seat. His expression was dark, but he said nothing in response to Mordred's polite scolding.

'Thank you,' Lamorna found herself saying, taking her seat and busying herself with arranging her skirt around her legs, feeling the Chif's eyes on her. Mordred sat himself on her other side, an obvious statement that the Chif could not fail to understand.

Lamorna hid her smile, composing her face, making sure the expression she showed the Chif was the right one – one that said she knew what this was, that she understood the game, that she was not a tool for him to use, as he used everyone.

The Chif cleared his throat, but he did not speak. Something sparked in Lamorna's chest. Her presence was making him uncomfortable.

Ulrian turned to Mordred. 'What is it you want, nephew?' he asked bluntly.

'The answer to that is simple – I want to know the power of the One God,' Mordred said.

'Power is never a simple thing,' Ulrian said. His eyes moved over Lamorna briefly, before returning to Mordred. He chuckled, as if the meeting amused him.

'I didn't say it was,' Mordred replied, his voice low and calm. Lamorna snuck a look at Bryn, who had followed them in and was standing behind the Chif. His face was tight and watchful, his hand resting on his dagger.

Ulrian was watching Mordred closely. 'You think someone is going to hand power over to you?'

Mordred shook his head. 'To insinuate such reveals your lack of understanding of what power truly is, Uncle. No man hands another man power – power is a thing to be earned.'

Ulrian's face remained calm and still. 'I'll ask again – what is it you want? And no more of your games, Mordred. I'm tired of them. I've been a gracious host, and I've entertained you for long enough.'

'That you have, and I am grateful for it,' Mordred said. 'I'll speak plainly, then. For a long time, I wanted an end to the Sacellum. I wanted an end to the hatred of magic – the hatred you were helping to spread. I wanted to see magic rule this world once more.'

'And now?' Ulrian asked.

'Now, I see things differently,' Mordred said. 'You sent Lamorna to Cruithea to convert the people – my mother's people. She may not have brought them all into the fold, but she did show me the Light. She can be very convincing,' he added, throwing Lamorna a warm smile.

'I remember you as a boy. Always lingering on the outside, looking in. Is that where this has come from? You lacked control then, so you want it now?' the Chif mused.

'Perhaps I am simply tired of wasted potential,' Mordred said. 'And I am a boy no longer, Uncle. I want more. I am tired of spending my days patrolling the forest in Cruithea looking for an enemy that isn't there. Lamorna has taught me that the One God is not my enemy. He only wants to love me, and share His Word with me.' He sighed. 'But perhaps you are right – perhaps this is a dream of mine that will never be. Perhaps

I cannot be saved. But, I would like to stay here a while and learn from you. You're a powerful man.'

Ulrian narrowed his eyes. 'Do you think I am so stupid as to let a viper into the nest I have built myself here?'

'Snakes shed their skin,' Mordred told him. 'Perhaps I need to shed mine.'

'You will need to prove yourself to me,' the Chif said firmly. 'You will come to the men's prayer circle. You will come to me every day to study the Word. You will—'

'I would like Lamorna to continue to teach me,' Mordred cut in.

'Is that so?' Ulrian's voice was hard, filled with suspicion.

'She has lived in Cruithea. She understands me, and how hard it can be sometimes to let go of the life that I used to lead,' Mordred said. 'She is a good teacher,' he added. 'Loyal to the One God and the Word.'

Lamorna held her breath. She kept her eyes lowered as the Chif stared at her. She could feel the weight of his gaze burning a hole in the side of her head, but she waited, pulling on the mask, showing him the supplicant woman devoted to her faith. Showing him who she used to be before Mordred.

'No,' the Chif said eventually. Lamorna's heart sank.

Mordred cleared his throat. 'You don't trust me, and I can't blame you for that. But, surely, you trust Lamorna? You sent her to Cruithea. You trusted her then to do the One God's work, but now you have decided she is not worthy of the task? I don't understand, Uncle.'

He was so good at it, Lamorna thought, listening to the way his voice remained compliant, how he appeared genuinely puzzled at Ulrian's lack of faith.

So she would play along.

'It's alright, Mordred,' she said demurely. 'Thank you for trying. Your uncle, our Chif, knows that I am not up for this task, not truly. I am a woman. This is not meant for me. And I failed him in Cruithea. I failed the One God. I was only able to share the Word with you. Perhaps

I should not have left so soon. Maybe I was too hasty. That was my mistake. I will pray on it,' she added, lifting her gaze briefly to the Chif. He was watching her, dark eyes narrowed. 'I am sorry to speak out of turn,' she said, dropping her eyes again. 'I only want to serve the One God, and you are His voice, so I shall follow your orders.'

She hoped she had sounded contrite enough.

They waited. The only sound was the crackling of the fire and Lamorna's tortured heartbeat, Mordred's steady breathing and the Chif's fingers, drumming rhythmically against the table top.

Eventually, Ulrian sighed. 'I will allow it,' he said. 'But your lessons will happen here, in this room, with a member of the Konsel present. And afterwards, Mordred, you will report to me and tell me what you have learned.'

'Thank you, Uncle,' Mordred said politely.

'You will stay with me,' Ulrian said. 'I should have insisted the moment you arrived, but truthfully, I was not expecting to see you, even after your letters. I imagined you would return to Cruithea, but you are still here. Maybe there is some truth to this, after all.'

Lamorna sensed Mordred's nod. Her heart sank, but maybe it was for the best.

'I know you have been staying with Lamorna,' the Chif began and Lamorna's stomach rose to coat the back of her throat. The scars on her knees began to throb.

'Surely you think better of me than that, Uncle?' Mordred said smoothly. 'I was concerned for her. A young woman on her own is not proper.'

'And a man who is not her husband staying in her home is also not proper,' Ulrian bit out.

'I have respected her,' Mordred said. 'I have not dishonoured her.'

Lamorna squirmed in her seat. She had the horrible notion the Chif would want proof, and she knew there was no way she would let that happen. She knew what the Konsel did after a marriage ceremony. She knew about the bloodied sheets. She would kick and scream and fight before she allowed the Chif or any of those men to touch her.

And Mordred would not let them touch her either.

'It appears I have no choice but to trust you both,' Ulrian said. Lamorna heard Bryn shift his weight from one foot to the other. She frowned, wondering. It had been too easy. Ulrian had accepted Mordred's word, even though Lamorna suspected the Chif knew Mordred was lying. But why? If Mordred was any other man in Kernou …

But he wasn't.

And Lamorna realised one other thing. The Chif was afraid of his nephew.

She cleared her throat. 'I will not disappoint you,' she said piously.

The Chif excused them, allowing Mordred to walk Lamorna home. They did not speak on the way, remaining a respectful distance from one another, but when Mordred opened the door, he reached back to pull her inside, slamming the door and pressing her against it, his hands beneath her skirt, his mouth on her throat, lifting her and folding her legs around his middle. She clung to him, trying not to weep at the horrible sense of loss she knew she would feel when he was gone.

Chapter 12

The Sword of the White Dragon sang, its voice a sharp cry as it cleaved the air. It hacked and slashed, mournful whispers to a foe it could never fell, no matter how fiercely it yearned. Forged for this singular purpose, it thirsted for blood, but with every swing was denied its due.

It sang the melody of steel on steel, glorious and treacherous and dripping with purpose.

The Sword of the White Dragon was more than a weapon.

It was Death itself.

It was a destroyer of worlds.

The hands that held the Sword were strong. They did not tire or show weakness.

And they held against the forest maiden's blade. Ancient, her antlers a crown beneath which the earth swayed, she struck with a grace that made the trees hum, the kiss of steel reverberating through its timeless limbs.

'You don't know what you do, brother,' the woman said.

The Sword and the one who wielded it embraced the melody and twisted the notes into a shape it knew – a shape it yearned for.

Arthur blinked.

He looked down at his hands.

'Not yet,' Eseld told him.

The Fisher Queen's cave dissolved and the vision shifted.

Stars wheeled overhead.

The edge of the world opened.

The skin of the world peeled back.

Things with wings were a streak across the broad expanse of the sky as—

'Too far,' Eseld said. 'You walk too far.'

'Wait!' Arthur cried. 'Let me see.'

The Fisher Queen shook her head. 'You do not understand what it is you carry.'

Arthur felt something heavy drop into his lap. He glanced down.

The Sword of the White Dragon lay there.

It wanted to be held.

He stroked it like a kitten and it purred in his mind, content.

'It likes me touching it,' he observed, unable to take his eyes off it. 'Is it really here?'

'Yes and no,' Eseld said. 'The Sword was crafted from the earth, from the magic of the world. Like all the Treasures were, and it is your burden to carry, Arthur. It is this magic you will use when the Grail is unleashed.'

Arthur trailed his fingers along the blade of the Sword. He could hear it singing, the melody delicate yet strong, promising. It filled him with the fire of hope and ambition. How was that a burden?

'Eseld,' he asked, glancing at the shade of a queen long passed. 'Why hasn't my magic strengthened? Why is it so hard to use it? I can feel it there, inside me, but I cannot access it.'

'Your magic is tied to the Sword now, Future King,' she told him. Her voice was low, rough, like the wind through the leaves. It echoed through the air around him and sank into his chest.

'I don't understand,' Arthur admitted.

She smiled then, a curving of dead-pale lips. He imagined she must have been beautiful in life. 'Your gift was given only to guide you to your destiny. Think of what would never have come to pass if you did not—'

'Almost kill my father,' Arthur finished. A vision, a memory, of Ulrian's broken face.

'Yes,' the Fisher Queen said.

Arthur's fingers danced along the blade of the Sword. He pushed his father from his mind as his fingers traced the dragon wound around the hilt.

'You had to experience magic before you would be able to choose. How can we decide to relinquish something if we do not understand the sacrifice?' She paused, then, 'There is still much for you to witness. Magic has two sides, Arthur. Two faces. There is darkness to come.'

He swallowed. 'And I'm assuming it cannot be avoided?'

'It shouldn't be avoided,' the Fisher Queen said gravely.

Arthur emerged from below deck, his head swimming with visions, the Sword at his hip. In truth, he had barely let it out of his sight since he had claimed it as his own. It should be heavy, but he could barely feel the weight of it. His fingers stroked the hilt absently. Arthur found Jalen leaning against the main mast, who eyed him with a discerning stare.

'It wants to be held,' Jalen murmured.

'I know,' Arthur agreed. 'I can hear it in my mind. I can see it in my dreams.'

'You were restless last night,' Jalen commented. 'Does it trouble you? The Sword?'

'No. It feels … right. Like a piece of me that was missing has been returned, only I wasn't aware it was missing, if that makes sense.'

'The Treasures are sentient,' Jalen reminded him.

'I know. She gave me a choice, the guardian of the Sword. I could have left it, but I chose not to. I guess this means I've absolutely embraced the role Merlin set for me?'

Jalen nodded. 'I suppose it does. And once Ordes and Jenyfer claim their Treasures, you will be able to find the Grail and reshape the world. My King,' he added, his voice low. A smile tugged at his mouth, but didn't quite make itself known.

Jalen still appeared troubled. More often than not, there was a small frown pulling at his brow, and his smiles were fleeting. Arthur had thought that after he had the Sword, the storm demon might relax a little, but if anything, Jalen was more tense than before. Arthur wanted to ask him what was wrong, because he was certain it was more than Jalen being cross with Ordes. He wanted to know what he could do to fix it, whatever it was. He wanted Jalen to know that he would share the burden that weighed on him.

But he said none of those things.

Instead, he said something he had been wanting to say for a long time. 'I love you, you know that. Prophecies, destinies, all of that … I can deal with it all, because it gave me you.'

For a long, heart-pounding moment, Jalen said nothing, did nothing, and Arthur felt the courage building inside him begin to slink away. He wanted to drop his eyes, but didn't, holding fast to what he felt inside – love. There was no other word for it, and although he still had nothing to compare it to, he knew that was what he was feeling, what he had been feeling since they were in Cruithea.

Before he could do or say anything more, Jalen caught his face between his hands and kissed him, in full view of everyone. For a brief moment, Arthur froze, that old familiar fear reaching for him, trying to dig its claws in, but it could not find purchase. There was nothing to be afraid of, not anymore, not when it came to Jalen. There may be something swirling around the storm demon's head, but Arthur knew it was nothing for him to worry about. He could feel it in the kiss, in the way Jalen's lips met his and the way the demi-god pulled him close, one hand on his lower back, the other on the back of Arthur's head, fingers tangled in his hair.

'Get a room,' Katarin shouted from the quarterdeck, breaking the spell; beside her, Iouen chuckled. 'Or I promise, I'll find you two things to do that you won't enjoy.'

Arthur laughed.

Chapter 13

They weighed anchor in the Sea of Andred. There were several other ships nearby, a mixture of frigates and sloops. None were as large as *The Excalibur*, though. Jenyfer glanced across the water to the glowing lights of Skulls Rest, remembering the last time she'd been here, that moment when Ordes had told her what he suspected she was. So much had happened since then.

'Oh goody,' Katarin said, gesturing to the ship to their left. 'Marsh is here.' She sighed, checking her daggers were secure. 'Well, let's go and let our hair down or whatever.'

'Katarin, you need to learn how to relax,' Iouen drawled, slinging his arm around Tahnet's shoulders as Jenyfer grinned.

'I'll relax your face for you in a moment, Iouen,' Kat rejoined, but a smile tugged at her mouth. The boats were lowered into the water and everyone scrambled over the railing. Jenyfer went to climb down, but Ordes touched her arm, telling her to wait.

'Are you coming?' He called to his father. Below, Carbrey was waiting in the last of the boats. The old sailor grunted impatiently.

Merlin was standing by the door to Katarin's cabin. He hesitated. 'No. I'll stay with the Sword.'

'I'd like to have a drink with you,' Ordes said.

'We'll have one when you get back,' his father said.

'I'm sure the Sword will be fine,' Jenyfer said gently. Merlin, like Arthur, had barely taken his eyes off it since Arthur had walked out of the Faery Forest with the Treasure strapped to his hip.

'You don't understand the power of the Treasures of the Gods,' Merlin replied. 'The Sword is not an ordinary sword. You can't hear it calling because you're fey, but every human on this ship will hear it.'

Jenyfer frowned, climbing down from the railing. 'What is it saying to them?'

'It sings to them. Like a syhren song,' Merlin said, glancing at her meaningfully. 'It's a compulsion. The Sword of the White Dragon *wants* to be held. It wants to be drawn, it wants to be used. Its magic is strong, and the last thing I want is for anyone on this ship to draw it.'

'Everyone has gone ashore,' Ordes reminded him.

Merlin nodded. 'And every person in Skulls Rest will hear the Sword.'

'Will our Treasures be the same?' Jenyfer asked. 'Will they want people to use them?'

'No. The Sword is different. War is all it knows,' Merlin said. 'I will stay here. Go and enjoy your night. Get drunk, listen to someone butcher a piano, sing – not you,' he added to Jenyfer, who laughed. She slipped her hand in Ordes'.

'Come on,' she said. 'Let's go and have some fun.'

Music spilled out of the tavern and into the street. Jenyfer gripped Ordes' hand, practically dragging him down the cobbled street. He laughed, sidestepping a drunk stumbling towards them.

The tavern was packed. Someone was, as Merlin had said, attempting to play the piano in the corner of the room. Jenyfer's song squirmed in protest. The piano was out of tune and the dissonance hurt. Ordes followed her inside; they watched Katarin elbow her way through the men gathered at the bar, passing mugs back to Iouen and Kayrus, who ferried them away.

Their crew had managed to claim several tables along the far side of the room.

Ordes went to get them drinks, so Jenyfer made her way across the tavern, joining Tahnet and some of the men. The skin on the back of her neck prickled; they were being watched. She glanced over her shoulder, meeting the eyes of a large man sitting across the room. He held a tankard in one hand, and a girl in his lap with the other.

The girl was pretty, with deep brown curls falling to brush her cheeks. As Jenyfer watched, the man slipped his hand over her breast. The girl's cheeks flamed and she squirmed, trying to get away from him, but he laughed loudly, like it was all a joke, and held her firmly against him.

Fire spread through Jenyfer, fast and hot. She gasped and closed her eyes against a memory she thought she had buried, of hands and lips that she did not want. Of his weight pinning her down, his breath in her ear.

She turned away then changed seats, sitting so she could see the man and the girl.

Katarin joined them, putting her feet up on the table and pulling her pipe from her pocket. Tahnet had not noticed the girl on the other side of the room; nobody had, all nursing their drinks and laughing. Relaxing.

But Jenyfer couldn't relax. Her song was swirling around in protest, full of anger, fire in her blood. Ordes returned. He slid her a drink and she clutched it so hard her knuckles turned white.

The girl with the brown curls had her head hung low. She wasn't fighting.

'If no one else is going to do anything about it,' Jenyfer muttered. She pushed her mug away, but before she could get to her feet, Ordes draped his arm around her shoulders and pulled her close.

'Your face is like a thundercloud, Jen,' he murmured. 'We're supposed to be relaxing. Fun, remember?'

'Over there,' she muttered. 'That man with the girl. Who is that?'

'That's Marsh, the Captain of *The Black Rose*,' Ordes told her, pressing a kiss to her temple. 'Ignore him.'

'Like that girl in his lap is trying to ignore him?' Jenyfer snapped, and Ordes pulled back, looking at her in concern. 'She's terrified,' Jenyfer said. 'It's not right, that he thinks he can take whatever he wants.'

'No,' Ordes agreed. 'It isn't.' He removed his arm from Jenyfer's shoulder and stood. 'I'll talk to him, but I can't promise it'll do anything.' He touched her cheek gently and made his way towards Marsh.

'Where's he going?' Kat demanded.

Jenyfer folded her arms, not taking her eyes off Marsh and the girl. Katarin twisted in her seat, and, seeing where Jenyfer's gaze lay, she scowled. 'It's not like I was relaxed anyway,' Kat said, repositioning herself on her seat so she could watch Ordes and Marsh. Her fingers abandoned her pipe, stroking the hilt of her dagger instead, her expression dark with loathing.

Marsh's face shifted from smug to unveiled annoyance as Ordes approached him, and then, after Ordes spoke to him, he laughed. Jenyfer shot to her feet, striding across the room to plant herself in front of Marsh. The girl glanced at her, and Jenyfer was struck by the look in her eyes – the defeat, the acceptance of her fate, and her powerlessness in this horrid situation.

Marsh's smile was like an oil slick on water; his grip on the girl tightened and she whimpered. Jenyfer clenched her fists. 'Let her go,' she demanded.

'Care to take her place, syhren?' Marsh turned his gaze to Ordes. 'He doesn't look like he's willing to share, though. Pity. You're rather becoming, for a halfbreed.'

'Let the girl go,' Jenyfer said again. She could feel her magic slithering beneath her skin, her song straining to get out. She could no longer hear the piano or the off-key singing; there was only her heartbeat, and Ordes', and her magic gathering power in her veins.

'Marsh,' Ordes said. 'Do as she says.'

'Or what?' The Captain grinned. 'Tell me, Ordes – does she taste like fish?'

Ordes moved quicker than Marsh anticipated. His hand shot out, silver light dancing from his skin. His fingers curled around the Captain's throat; the girl tumbled from Marsh's lap, hitting the floor. Jenyfer hurried to help her up, pulling her close. She couldn't be more than sixteen.

'Get out of here,' Jenyfer whispered.

The girl nodded and scurried off.

'You cost me my evening, cunt,' Marsh bit out.

Ordes' fingers tightened; the Captain made a choking sound. The whole tavern had gone silent. Those of Marsh's crew who were able to stand were on their feet, drinks forgotten, daggers drawn.

'Ordes,' Jenyfer warned. She heard chairs being pushed back, legs scraping against the rough stone floor. Most people were on their feet, including Katarin and *The Excalibur's* crew. Kat, dagger in hand, began making her way across the room.

This was not what Jenyfer had wanted. She had only wanted to help the girl. Now, they were two heartbeats away from a tavern brawl.

Slowly, Ordes released Marsh, stepping away. 'Enjoy the rest of your evening,' he said. His magic still danced over his knuckles, and Jenyfer held her breath as Marsh stood. She swallowed. The Captain of *The Black Rose* was tall, his chest broad. The grin beneath his thick beard was cruel.

'How about you get fucked?' he snarled, and then smashed his fist into Ordes' face.

Jenyfer gasped, and for a moment, nobody moved. Ordes kept his feet, and when he wiped the back of his hand beneath his nose, his fingers came away bloody. Marsh was laughing; his men were laughing as well.

Ordes' face was like stone.

Slowly, he wiped his hand on his shirt, then threw himself at Marsh. The room erupted. Jenyfer was elbowed out of the way, crashing into the nearest table. She lost sight of Ordes as people converged on them, shoving and shouting, fists pummelling faces. Glasses smashed as tables were tipped over.

'Ordes!' Jenyfer shouted.

She drew her dagger, trying to push her way through the crowd. A fist glanced off the side of her head. She blinked, tightening her grip on her weapon. A pistol discharged somewhere in the room, but the fighting did not stop. Every person in the place was on their feet. The discordant melody of fists thumping into flesh, furniture snapping and glass shattering was painful.

A man with cropped, dark hair stepped in front of Jenyfer. He grinned. She shoved at him, trying to get past, but he grabbed her, hauling her off her feet and slinging her over his shoulder so quickly she dropped her dagger. She slammed her fists into the broad spread of his back, but it was like hitting a wall of stone. With alarm, she realised she was being taken towards the main doors. She opened her mouth – she'd sing her way free – but she'd only managed a few notes before the man dropped her, pulling her into his body, back to chest, and slamming his hand over her lips. She could smell old sweat, ale and menace, and her stomach rebelled.

Suddenly, Katarin was there, Iouen with her, a broken bottle in one hand, dagger in the other. Katarin spun her blades between dexterous fingers, her smile lethal. 'Going somewhere, Johnny boy?'

With a snarl, Johnny let Jenyfer go, shoving her towards Iouen as he lunged for Kat. Her blades slashed – one sliced across his cheek, the other narrowly missing his stomach. He swung a massive fist at her; she danced out of his reach, while Iouen pulled Jenyfer away.

'She's got it,' he shouted, rushing across the room, jumping over a table on the way. Jenyfer hesitated. A laughing Kat smashed her fist into Johnny's face, so she followed Iouen, ducking as a glass was hurled across the room. A discarded dagger lay on the floor near her feet, so she snatched it up.

She could see Arthur and Jalen on the other side of the room. Arthur was bleeding from a cut on his forehead and as she watched, Jalen's unnatural strength sent a man flying out the nearest window. Another man rushed at him; the storm demon's fist put him on the ground, then Jalen drove his knee into the man's face. Halymere and Melhala had their weapons drawn and a pile of unconscious men at their feet.

Jenyfer pushed her way through bodies, trying to get to Ordes, punching a man in the nose so hard her wrist stung and blood dribbled down his face. He grabbed at her, but she brandished her dagger purposefully. He held up his hands and stumbled away.

'Good choice,' she mumbled. She could feel her song swirling and pushing at her, desperate to be free, but she pushed it away. Her friends were in this tavern, and she did not want to hurt them with her magic.

Ordes and Marsh were still fighting. She watched Ordes drive his knuckles into Marsh's ribs, once, twice, before another man grabbed Ordes around the middle and hauled him away from the Captain, tossing him against a table lying on its side. Ordes got to his feet as Marsh, bleeding from the forehead, one eye swollen and a cut on his lip, drew his pistol and pointed it at Ordes.

Jenyfer froze. The heartfire surged in her chest and as she opened her mouth, her song pouring out of her without warning, unchecked, completely unbound. Ordes spun to look at her, eyes wide.

'Jen—'

She ignored him, her attention focused wholly on Marsh. His arm lowered as his eyes glazed over. Every man in the tavern had stilled. Bottles dropped from fingers, daggers clattered to the floor. Faces turned towards her. She was aware of Katarin and Tahnet, and the girl she had rescued from Marsh's lap, the barmaid and the whores huddled in the corner, all of them completely unaffected by her magic.

And she was aware of her voice, the power in it as she sang. She could feel the men in that room, feel their insignificant little lives wrapped up in her music. Marsh's jaw slackened, his arms hanging useless at his sides.

Without letting her song falter, Jenyfer tightened her grip on her dagger. It would be so easy. He couldn't fight her, not like this.

'Jenyfer, stop.' Ordes slid an arm around her middle. 'Stop.'

She shook him off as her vision, and her power, narrowed to the Captain of *The Black Rose*.

'Jen, you don't want to do this.'

'I think maybe she does.' Katarin's voice. 'I won't stop her.'

Jenyfer's song changed; Marsh lifted his pistol. Ordes sucked in a breath as the Captain turned the weapon towards his own chest. Ordes shook her, hard enough that her magic slipped, and then his voice was in her head, urging her to stop.

She swallowed, gasped, and her song faded.

Marsh had not moved. The spell still held him and every man in the tavern.

She pulled out of Ordes' grip, turning to him, her throat tight, her song waiting, ready to strike again. 'He deserves this. I want him to know what it's like to drown in his own blood. Men like him think they can do whatever they want, take whatever they want. They think because they're big and strong and menacing, they can scare people into doing their bidding.'

'Jen,' Ordes whispered. 'He isn't Bryn.'

'I know that,' Jenyfer snapped. 'But he's still a bastard.'

The Captain blinked as Jenyfer's song finally released him. He saw the pistol resting against his chest and dropped his arm, his fury finding Jenyfer as comprehension dawned. 'I'll slit you from cunt to sternum and remove your tongue, you syhren bitch,' Marsh growled. He pointed his pistol at Jenyfer, but before he could even think about firing, Ordes snapped it from his hand. Marsh snarled as Ordes coaxed the lead from the barrel with magic, before tossing the weapon on the ground and pocketing the bullet.

'You're not powerful, Marsh, and you don't scare me,' Jenyfer said. The Captain's face was as red as an open wound. 'You're pathetic and weak. You think any man in this tavern, any one of your crew, would mourn you if I made you slit your own throat?'

'Marsh,' Ordes said. 'Get out of here.'

Jenyfer shook her head, tossing the dagger at the Captain's feet. Without another word, she marched towards the door, stepping over bodies and broken furniture. No one said anything, the silence in the tavern thick and heavy. Jenyfer shoved the doors open and stumbled into the street, pulling gasps of fresh sea air into her lungs.

She had held a tavern full of men in thrall with her voice. And it had been easy, so easy. She shivered, but she wasn't cold. Slowly, a smile spread over her lips.

Ordes flung open the tavern doors, his voice urgent. 'Jen, wait.'

'I'm going back to the ship,' she managed, then spun to face him. 'Why didn't my magic work on you in there? It worked the other night. Or were you pretending?'

He shook his head. 'No, I wasn't pretending. I'm not sure what happened in there either – I could feel your magic pulling at me, compelling me, but I …' He paused, glancing down at his chest. 'The heartfire,' he breathed. 'You were in danger.'

'But … are you saying our soulmate's bond is stronger than my syhren magic?'

'What other explanation is there?' he said.

Jenyfer stared at his chest in wonder.

Ordes pulled her close and kissed her deeply. She could taste the metallic tang of blood on his lips. 'You saved my life – again,' he whispered, resting his forehead against hers.

She wound her arms around his middle. 'You could have saved your own life.'

'I could, yes, but to be honest, I like you doing it. It's an incredible aphrodisiac,' he murmured, her laughter resounding through the street as he pinned her against the nearest wall, kissing her again. She pulled him close, fingers digging into his back, her song purring contentedly as his hand reached beneath her shirt, her groan escaping into his mouth. She scraped her nails down his flesh. Desire pooled in her belly, as smooth as water and as potent as the open sea – wild and rough, reckless.

She felt powerful and strong, in control, and no longer afraid of what lived inside her.

Ordes pulled back. His lips brushed hers teasingly, his mouth a blazing brand on hers. 'Are you alright?'

She nodded. 'Yes. I knew what I was doing this time. I could control it. It's not the same as Alric – I'd have let Marsh shoot himself and not felt any guilt whatsoever if you hadn't gotten involved.'

Ordes chuckled. 'I'll let him shoot himself next time, but right now, I have wounds that need attending to.'

'Are you asking me to patch you up?'

'There's one part of me that's particularly painful.'

Jenyfer slid her fingers into what was left of his hair and kissed him. Her whole body liquefied beneath the warmth of his mouth, his fingers digging into her flesh as he pressed against her.

The tavern doors opened, followed by voices.

'Hey, this is a respectable place and a respectable establishment,' Katarin drawled.

Ordes laughed, adjusting his clothing while Jenyfer peered around him, relieved to see her friends were in one piece, except for a few bloody noses and bruises. Some of the men glanced at her, but it wasn't fear on their faces this time – it was awe.

Kat slapped Ordes on the back as she passed. 'Thanks you two. *Now* I'm relaxed.'

Iouen grinned, holding up two bottles of rum. 'On the house. Actually, it was more of a 'get the fuck out of my tavern and never come back' parting gift, but I'm not going to complain.'

Katarin snatched a bottle from him. 'We'll need music. I hope some of you can actually dance.'

Laughing, Jenyfer and Ordes followed them back to the ship.

CHAPTER 14

When Lamorna woke, it was still dark, the sun yet to climb over the Nemhain mountains and strike Kernou. She got up, not bothering to light a lantern, leaving Mordred asleep. She should wake him – he liked to be gone before sunrise. She knew he climbed back into the Chif's house via a window, and each time he left, she experienced a little thrill of fear that he would be caught. It was always followed by another thrill – not of fear but anticipation. She knew she'd see him again soon, as he returned every evening once he had dined with his uncle.

Lamorna hummed to herself as she made breakfast. Eggs. It was Mordred's favourite, and she knew how he liked them – fluffy and scrambled. When she turned from the stove to slice the bread for toast, a pisky was standing on the table.

'Oh!' she said, clutching her chest in fright. 'What are you doing here?'

The little faery grinned, showing off his pointed teeth. He tipped an imaginary hat as Mordred emerged, yawning.

Mordred blinked. 'Lamorna, there's a pisky on your table.'

'Yes, I know.' she said, turning back to the stove. ' It's the one that lives in the garden. Jenyfer used to see him all the time.'

'And you didn't?'

'Well, I did, but …' When she looked, the pisky had gone, no doubt remembering all the times Lamorna had pretended he didn't exist.

Mordred ate his eggs and was soon gone, out the back door as usual, leaving her to clean the kitchen and sweep the floors. She had changed out of her nightdress when a brisk knock echoed through the house.

Lamorna froze, her hand reaching for her hair. Quickly, she snatched one of her caps from the table and shoved it on, tying the straps as she opened the door.

Bryn was standing on her doorstep. Lamorna's heart skipped a beat. She lowered her eyes, not liking it for one moment. She did not want to take her eyes off him, but fear was a burning brand sizzling in her blood. She kept her hands behind her back; her fists curled where he could not see them.

He cleared his throat, then told her the Chif had sent for her. Bryn waited while Lamorna returned to her room and fixed her hair properly, breathing deep, forcing the tremble from her fingers as she tucked flyaway strands of hair beneath her cap.

Lamorna only dared raise her eyes when they reached the town proper, wondering if he could feel the heat of her glare between his shoulder blades. They passed down the main thoroughfare, straight through the market and past the shops, taking an indirect route to the Chif's home.

Lamorna knew exactly why. He was parading her, showing the people of Kernou his power, the Chif's power. Lamorna's mouth pulled into a scowl, but she didn't raise her eyes again.

Bryn led her all the way to the Chif's front door. She was met by a servant and brought to the Chif in his formal room.

A fire was blazing, and the room was too hot. Lamorna shifted her weight from one foot to the other, waiting, feeling the Chif's eyes moving over her, assessing and probing. She grit her teeth.

At last, the Chif spoke. 'Be seated, Lamorna.'

Lamorna sat at the grand table, her spine straight. She fought to control the furious beating of her heart as Ulrian took his seat at the head of the table. She did not look at him.

'We need to talk about Mordred,' the Chif announced.

'Oh?'

The Chif cleared his throat; his fingers fluttered over the ruined half of his face, before they fell to the tabletop. He had short, stubby fingers, Lamorna noticed. He chewed his fingernails.

He was nervous.

She bit her lip and kept her face lowered, but not out of worry or contrition. She could not help the smile rising to her lips, the satisfaction that spiked in her blood.

'There is talk, in town,' Ulrian began. 'Although my nephew has been instructed to stay here, he has been seen visiting your cottage.'

'He is my friend,' Lamorna said.

'He has been seen visiting your cottage *at night*, Lamorna,' the Chif said, voice tight. 'Is he visiting your bed?'

Lamorna's head shot up then. 'That isn't your business.' The words left her lips without thought, and for a moment, burning fear replaced the satisfaction. She forced it away, keeping her eyes on Ulrian, reminding herself that she knew things he did not, and that, like Mordred had told her, held its own power.

'The One God—'

'If the One God sees all, then He already knows the truth, doesn't He?' Lamorna said. 'But you don't, and that's why you're asking me.'

The Chif's cheeks coloured, but with outrage or embarrassment, she could not tell.

She decided she didn't care.

'You will marry him,' Ulrian bit out furiously.

'I will do no such thing.' Beneath the table, she clenched her fists above the place where Mordred had his mouth in the middle of the night.

She liked what they did together. No one had ever talked about how it felt. No one had ever mentioned what it felt like for a woman. They had spoken only of the sin, the damage it wrought on a woman's virtue. Any talk had always been about the man's pleasure, about what pleased him. Lamorna wanted to talk to someone about it. She especially wanted to talk about last night, when she had done something she didn't even know people could do. When she had taken him in her mouth and enjoyed it, the rush of power when she met his eyes, how she hadn't looked away, watching as he came undone.

Lamorna wished Jenyfer was here. She could talk to her.

The Chif was watching her through narrowed eyes.

'If that's all,' she said, getting to her feet. 'I have things to do.'

'What things?' he demanded.

She smiled. 'If you'll excuse me.'

As she sauntered out of the Chif's house, she was trembling. The scars on her knees screamed in protest, wanting her to turn around and throw herself at her Chif's feet, to beg forgiveness for her wicked mouth, but instead, her smile was broad.

Her victory soon fell away.

Bryn was waiting for her, and with him, was Mordred. Lamorna froze on the threshold of the Chif's home. She could not hear the conversation, but Mordred was doing most of the talking. Byrn's arms were folded, his expression suspicious, eyes narrowed and mouth tight, but he was nodding along with whatever Mordred was saying. Mordred's eyes found her. He gave a slight nod before approaching. For one wild moment, she thought he was going to sweep her into his arms and kiss her, but he didn't. He passed her and went into the house, leaving Lamorna alone with Bryn.

She lifted her chin and walked slowly down the path. His red coat glowed in the sunlight. He opened the iron gate for her.

'I'm to escort you home,' he told her. She nodded, and followed him. Bryn did not speak to her all the way home. It wasn't until she had her hand on the door to the cottage that he cleared his throat meaningfully. Lamorna swallowed and turned to face him. She hadn't realised he had followed her up the path and was alarmed at how close he was.

All her earlier bravery fled as his hand brushed the dagger at his hip.

'It's an interesting thing, change,' Bryn mused, his voice low. 'You think you know a person, know what they are truly capable of, and then something happens that you didn't expect.'

Lamorna wanted to tell him how right he was, but she didn't. His boots were so polished she could see his reflection in them, see the hardness to his face.

'Your aunt remained in Cruithea, but you came back,' he said. 'Why did you do that, Lamorna?'

She swallowed. 'Because Kernou is my home.'

'Is it?' Bryn asked. She said nothing. He repeated his question, voice sharp.

'Yes,' she whispered.

'We shall see.' And then he was gone. Lamorna hurried inside and bolted the door, snatching up the sharp knife for cutting herbs and sat herself at the kitchen table, heart pounding, staring at the door. She did not move until someone knocked on the doors, hours later, long after the sun had set. The cottage was dark and cold – she realised she had sat there all day.

'Lamorna?'

It was Mordred. Relief coursed through her. She leapt to her feet and rushed to open the door. Mordred's eyes widened when he saw the knife clutched between her fingers. She shook her head, returning to the kitchen and setting the kettle to boil. The chair scraped as he pulled it free of the table and sat down. When she had made them both tea, and he had finished his cup, Mordred looked at her curiously.

'What did my uncle want with you?'

'He …' Lamorna paused, unsure if she should say it, but she took a deep breath. 'He knows about us. He knows you've been coming here at night. He told me I needed to marry you.'

'Did he?' Mordred murmured.

She nodded, toying with her tea cup.

'And is that what you want?'

Her head shot up. 'No,' she said. When a frown crossed Mordred's face, she went on quickly. 'Not because I don't care for you, but because I have decided that if I am to marry anyone, I will do it because *I* want it, not because someone is telling me I must.' She had not decided anything until she spoke the words, but once they were out and filling the space between them, Lamorna knew it was the truth. 'It will be my choice.'

As it should have been Jenyfer's, she thought guiltily.

Mordred nodded. 'I can respect that.'

Lamorna tapped her fingers against her cup. 'Why were you talking to Bryn?'

'He intrigues me,' Mordred answered, sitting back. 'I don't think I've ever met someone so angry, so hungry for it.'

'For what?' Lamorna frowned.

'For revenge. He hates that your sister rejected him, that she left him. He cannot understand why she did that, and it is driving him mad.'

'I don't want you to talk to him,' Lamorna said firmly.

Mordred raised his eyebrows.

'I don't trust him,' she added.

'Neither do I,' Mordred agreed. He leant forward, reaching across the table to take her hands in his, his thumbs moving gently over her fingers. 'There is a saying – keep your friends close and your enemies closer. I know you do not like him, and I am not going to tell you that is wrong. But I am going to say that, sometimes, it is better to draw those you dislike close to you, so that you can watch them, so that you can use them – control them.'

Lamorna said nothing, watching Mordred carefully.

'Bryn of the Red Hand could end up being rather useful to me. If I can find a way to use that anger of his, that is. A man like Bryn likes to be useful. He likes to feel he is contributing and that his contribution will be rewarded. I am not sure my uncle can offer him what he needs.'

'And what is that?' Lamorna asked.

'His chance for revenge.'

She pulled her hands away. 'I won't let him hurt Jenyfer again.'

Mordred chuckled. 'He won't. But he needs to think he will be able to. Do you understand?'

She nodded, uncertainty spiralling through her. Mordred didn't know Bryn like she did.

Chapter 15

Malist loomed on the horizon, smoke haze from thousands of chimneys hanging over the capital. Katarin folded her arms and gave the city her best glare. The small relief she'd garnered after the tavern brawl in Skulls Rest had lasted two days before it slipped away, leaving her shoulders tense and her temper short. And now, seeing the city before her, memories pushed their way to the front of her brain.

The smell of smoke.

The smell of burning leather as her boots caught alight.

The stench of charred flesh that hung over the main square like a cloud.

The taste of the bile as it rose in her throat and the feeling of helplessness that swept through her.

The smiling face of the man who had wielded the whip. He had been the one to light the pyre, she remembered suddenly. And he had been the first to fall under Halymere's blade.

She jumped when Halymere touched her shoulder. Their eyes met briefly, before she turned away.

'This is probably not the best time to talk about it,' he began.

'What happened after Skulls Rest can't happen again, Halymere,' she said.

'That wasn't what I was referring to, but yes, I already guessed that.'

Katarin sighed. Maybe she'd had too much rum that night, or maybe it was the adrenalin of the fight, but when everyone had left for their beds not long before sunrise, and it was her and Halymere in her cabin, it had happened. She wasn't even sure who had started it, but she'd ended it, curling on her side and pretending he wasn't there.

They hadn't spoken since.

She'd been avoiding him, not because she was ashamed of what had happened, but because she was ashamed of her weakness, her need to *feel* something, even when it wasn't a good idea.

Kat turned her back on Malist and leaned against the railing. 'Then what do you want, Halymere?'

'I was going to say that the ghosts of the past are thick in his place, Katarin,' he said. 'But Inanna would not have sent you back here if she didn't want you to face them.'

Kat closed her eyes briefly.

Smoke and heat.

'Thanks for the reminder.' She gave Halymere a scowl and turned towards the deck.

Ordes and Jenyfer were standing with Iouen, Tahnet, and Arthur. They were all smiling, although Ordes looked tense. There was more danger here than they needed, but they didn't have any other choice. Maybe it wouldn't be so bad — Arthur had retrieved the Sword easily enough, and all Katarin could do was hope that Ordes' experience would be similar. She snuck a look at Jenyfer. The syhren's smile was tight, her spine rigid, and for a brief moment, Katarin felt sorry for her.

This was what came from caring about people. Fear and worry.

Merlin came above deck, looking to Katarin as he approached. She wondered what was really swirling around his head. He hadn't asked for his ship back. He hadn't even mentioned that she was now *The Excalibur's* captain. He spent most of his time with Arthur or Ordes, and when it wasn't them, it was his old crew, where, for a brief moment, he was the man Katarin used to know.

Now, she wasn't sure who he was.

Mystical and powerful.

Still annoying.

'Right,' Katarin called when Melhala, Ethinne, and Jalen arrived. 'My cabin. Let's go.'

She expected a collective groan, but none came, and it wasn't just Ordes looking tense now.

When they were all gathered in her cabin, she gestured to the city, visible through the wide windows. Night fell rapidly on this side of the continent, and once the sun slipped behind the Nemhain Mountains, it would be pitch black on the water. If anyone was going ashore, it needed to be soon.

'Firstly, we're sitting ducks out here. It won't be long until someone notices us, if they haven't already. Pirates are one thing, Magic Wielders are another. We should pull the anchor and—'

'No.' Merlin closed his eyes, and all the air in the cabin was pulled towards him; a breeze ruffled Katarin's hair as the world outside became strangely grey. She hurried to peer out the window.

Thick mist was quickly rising from the ocean, cloaking the ship and shrouding the harbour. Soon, Malist was barely able to be seen – only the tallest buildings poked above the mist desperately. Katarin smiled. It looked completely natural, a blanket of fog rolling in from the ocean.

'Neat trick.' She turned back to Merlin, unable to avoid the sharp spike of envy. 'How long will it last?'

'As long as I want it to,' he answered.

Ordes had his arms folded. 'I can feel the Bow,' he said, glancing at Arthur. 'Was that how you found the Sword?'

'Sort of,' Arthur said. 'Merlin told me where I needed to go, but once there, it was like I was being pulled towards it. But I wasn't looking in a city full of buildings and people.'

'I've never been here,' Ordes said. 'At least, I've never been ashore. I wouldn't know where to start looking.'

'That's where I come in,' Iouen announced. He pushed himself off the bulkhead where he had been leaning and slapped Ordes on the back. 'Happy to go ashore, speak with a few people, see what I can find out.'

'You're going to ask around after a magical artefact, are you?' Halymere said.

Iouen shrugged. 'If you know the right people to ask, sure.'

'Well, I'll come with you,' Ordes said, but Iouen shook his head, saying it was better he went alone, which no one liked the sound of.

'I can't take any of you, not if I'm going to be poking my nose in places. We don't know who might be watching and, in a place like this, there is always someone watching,' Iouen said, turning to Ordes. 'No idea what you're meant to be now, but a Witchfinder would sniff you out in seconds.' He nodded at Jenyfer. 'Scales,' before turning to Arthur, 'definitely not.' Iouen pointed at Melhala and Ethinne. 'Magic Wielders,' then to Halymere. 'Obviously not from around here.' He glanced at Merlin. 'Probably not a good idea. If they don't know who you are now, they'll know who you used to be.' Iouen flashed Katarin a grin. 'And everyone knows your face, so—'

'Are you coming, Iouen?' Ordes was at the door. He yanked it open and left before anyone could stop him.

Kat shared a look with Jenyfer, who hurried after Ordes. Slowly, the others peeled out, leaving Halymere lingering. 'What?' Katarin bit out.

His smile was knowing, and it made her want to punch him. 'You need to stop biting people's heads off,' he said, closing the door and leaning against it. 'And you need to stop worrying.'

'I can't help that,' she shot back before she could stop herself. She sighed and plopped into the chair, putting her feet up on the desk. 'Everything is … upside down. My whole world has been turned upside down, Haly, so forgive me if I'm having a little trouble dealing with that.'

'Perhaps you should speak to someone about it,' he said, coming to sit opposite her.

'Like you?'

He rolled his eyes, such an uncharacteristic thing for him to do that she wasn't sure how to react. 'I wouldn't dream of asking you to unburden your soul to me, Katarin Le Fey, but perhaps you could unburden it to Inanna.'

'No.' The response was automatic, sharp and hard.

Halymere's expression became soft. 'She has not deserted you.'

'She left me on a beach to die,' Kat snapped. 'She left me tied to a smoking pyre, and if you're about to tell me your arrival was goddess sent, I will knock your teeth out.'

'You've been away from Cruithea too long. It's your home, Katarin,' he said. Before she could argue, he continued, 'Inanna does not forsake us. She is there when we need her, as she will be for you, but you need to ask it of her.'

'Want me to build a little shrine in the corner of my cabin for her, do you?' Kat asked bitterly. 'And do not tell me that all that has happened to me has happened for a reason. Do not, Halymere. You might have given your life to the Goddess, but I have chosen differently.'

He stood, looking down at her as he shook his head, pushing whatever words were on his tongue back behind his teeth. He was at the door before he spoke again. 'If you want to talk about what's going on with you, I'm willing to listen, Katarin.'

'Nothing is going on with me.'

'When you're sick of trying to convince yourself, you know where to find me,' he said, and left. Katarin stared at the closed door until her eyes blurred. With a snarl, she snatched up a mug and hurled it at the door, taking no satisfaction from watching it shatter and scatter itself all over the floor.

She sat until she couldn't any longer, hurrying out onto the deck, crunching shards of ceramic beneath her boots. Some of the men were lowering one of the boats to the water. Tahnet waited nearby. Katarin stopped, her heart in her throat as she suddenly remembered the day she had found Tahnet floating in the sea, not far from here.

Katarin had never sailed that far north before, but something had driven her to push *The Queen* past Malist, towards Kunis.

Halymere would probably tell her it was fate or some such garbage.

Ethinne was talking softly with Tahnet. Tahnet wore an amulet of Inanna around her neck, but she never spoke of the Goddess at all. Even though Tahnet was not going into Malist, Katarin could not shake off the fear that clawed at her.

'I'm coming,' Kat announced as Iouen began the climb down to the boat. Ordes raised his eyebrows at her, but said nothing. She watched him plant a kiss on Jenyfer's waiting mouth, before following Iouen. Kat raced back to her cabin, picking up an extra dagger and adding it to her belt, before hurrying back out. Ever since they had arrived, Katarin had fought the urge to jump in a boat and row herself over to the city. The place pulled at her, and she couldn't just sit around – she needed to get off this ship for a while. She needed to *do* something other than wait while others risked themselves.

Halymere was waiting for her. 'Need some company?'

She snorted.

'Listen, it might help for us to scope the place out while Iouen is tracking down his contact,' Halymere argued. 'I don't want to linger in Malist any longer than you do, but—'

'Go on then,' Kat said, nodding. 'I'll be right behind you.'

He looked like he was about to argue, but swung himself over the railing and into the waiting boat. Kat swallowed, glancing towards the city, but before she could climb down into the boat, someone touched her arm – Ethinne.

'You're worried.'

'Of course I am,' Kat found herself saying.

'I dreamt of you,' Ethinne said.

'Won't your girlfriend be jealous?'

The Priestess smiled. 'You don't belong here, not really. You want to, but this isn't your place. It isn't your destiny. I saw you surrounded by trees.'

Something cold skittered down Katarin's spine. 'Whatever you dreamt was wrong. I belong on the water,' she added firmly. 'Inanna is wrong.'

'Is she?' Ethinne asked. Her voice was lilting. She met Katarin's eyes then walked away. Kat frowned, watching the Priestess' retreating back, until Iouen yelled at her to hurry up.

The journey across the water was slow without magic. Halymere rowed. Kat glanced over her shoulder – *The Excalibur* was hidden in Merlin's magic mist and as the boat bumped against the jetty, she had to bite down on her unease. They didn't speak, climbing out and waiting while Iouen tied the bowline to the piling. She scrutinised how many loops, how tight the knots. He met her eyes, but said nothing. Their getaway secure, the crew made their way towards the centre of town, passing by large storehouses and shabby cottages.

Kat kept her eyes on Ordes' back. She hadn't felt this nervous when Arthur was collecting his Treasure, but the Faery Forest was not Malist. She had the right to be anxious about this, considering how hospitable the city had been the last time she visited.

Hard-packed earthen streets slowly gave way to cobblestones. They had a few hours at most before it was dark, and lingering on the streets after nightfall was not a good idea. They passed a tavern, its windows dark, and then the guild houses – the blacksmith and tannery, the butchers and the fishmonger. The only people they saw were on their way home from work, and soon, they had come to the edge of the main square. Shops lined the streets, facing towards a decorative water fountain, and, Katarin scowled deeply, an imposing cross of the One God.

'Right,' Iouen said. 'We'll be off.'

Halymere nodded. 'We'll wait here.'

Before they left, Katarin grabbed Iouen's arm, keeping her voice low. 'If anything happens to him—'

'You'll kill me and wear my skin as a coat, yes, got it,' Iouen said. 'Nothing will go wrong, Katarin. You need to relax.'

She glared at his back as he and Ordes crossed the street.

CHAPTER 16

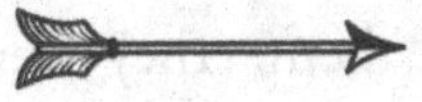

'Have you noticed our good Captain is becoming a bit of a mother hen?' Iouen commented.

'She threatened you, didn't she?' Ordes asked.

'She did, yes. I'm rather offended.'

Ordes smiled ruefully. 'She doesn't really mean it, Iouen. Kat's a good person, beneath all the rough edges. She's scared. Losing *The Queen*, her crew, Aelle … it's left a hole in her that she doesn't know how to fill,' he said. 'And now all this waiting. Kat isn't good at it. She's all action.'

'Yeah, I know,' Iouen said. They lapsed into silence, moving further away from the shops and the fountain and that horrible cross. Malist was a rabbit warren of side streets and alleys beneath a darkening sky.

'Do you know where you're going?' Ordes asked.

Iouen scoffed. 'Please. I know these streets. This city was my playground. I was a king in this place.'

'You told me you had your arse kicked,' Ordes pointed out.

Iouen shrugged. 'Nonetheless, you need to stick with me.'

Ordes sidestepped a couple of young boys chasing a mangy dog and raised his eyebrows at his friend.

Iouen's grin was broad. 'Look, if I don't return with you … well, I won't. Those women on that ship would murder me.'

Ordes laughed, which fell away as four figures in black appeared up ahead. Iouen quickly stepped to the side, flattening himself against a wall to allow the black-clad figures to pass. They were masked; a caricature of a man's face, his serene expression frozen in plaster artistry. Ordes joined Iouen as the figures passed them. They were armed, he noticed, with daggers and shining swords tucked against their backs. There was a simple insignia on their outfits – a red serpent coiled around a cross emblazoned over their chests. Ordes sucked in a sharp breath as he realised what he was looking at.

The Warriors of the Light. The Sacellum's fighting arm. He had never seen them before, had never seen them fight, but rumours of their prowess had reached even those out on the waves. The Warriors were deadly, incredibly skilled. They trained since childhood, and rarely left Malist. Their job, as far as Ordes knew, was to protect the Sacellum and help maintain order in the city. Once though, it had been different. He had heard stories of the Warriors travelling to outlying towns, places so small they were not on the maps, helping to spread the Word of the One God.

Once they were gone, Iouen visibly relaxed, although his face was folded into a scowl. 'I can't stand those bastards. They often had nothing better to do than rough up street rats like myself.'

Ordes was still watching the Warriors, taking note of how they moved, the way they held themselves, the shape of them, as if they —

'They're women, Iouen,' Ordes said.

'Who are?'

'The Warriors.'

Iouen's head whipped around to stare at the black-clad Warriors, so quickly Ordes was surprised he didn't snap his neck. 'Are you sure?'

Ordes nodded. 'The way they stand. The way they move. The Warriors are women.'

'What the fuck does that mean?' Iouen said in a low voice.

'The One God is actually Ereshki, which means that there is definitely more to this than an Old One with a grudge,' Ordes replied. 'But this? I have no idea what this means.'

With another look at the Warriors on the other side of the street, Iouen turned away. Ordes fell into step beside him, and they walked in silence until Iouen groaned. 'You know what this means? It means I had my arse handed to me all those years ago by a bunch of girls!'

Ordes chuckled. 'You want to go pick a fight, see if you recover your dignity?'

Iouen sighed dramatically. 'As much as I would love to, we have places to be,' he said. 'I'm taking you to see, well, not necessarily a friend, but someone who will be able to help us. He might not be too happy to see me, actually,' he added thoughtfully.

'What makes you so sure he'll know where the Bow is?'

Iouen smiled. 'Because he's the sort of man who knows everything. You want a new watch? He'll get it for you. A crate of the best rum? Not a problem.'

Ordes grinned. 'So he's a crook?'

'You're a pirate, don't be judgy,' Iouen shot back. 'And anyway, Voss has no love for the Sacellum. He's not going to turn us over.'

'Voss?' Ordes asked. They had left the shops and the city centre behind. The streets had become thinner, dustier; warehouses could be seen poking their heads above houses. A tired-looking grey horse drawing a wagon full of crates trundled past – the man holding the reins didn't spare them a glance. Iouen led Ordes past another tavern, customers outside smoking pipes and thin cigars while they waited for the place to open; a group of ragged children chased each other around the legs of tired-looking women.

Iouen chewed his lip. 'Voss is … alright you'll work it out in a heartbeat, anyway, so I may as well tell you. Voss is a therian, a shifter.'

A memory tugged at Ordes – Goerika, telling him to change his shape. Ordes pushed it aside. He'd watched his father do it, but he'd watched his father do a lot of things since he'd gotten his magic back. Merlin made it look effortless, as simple as breathing. Ordes had no desire to attempt it himself. He wasn't even sure how someone learnt to shift their shape, and he was perfectly content to keep all his body parts as they were.

'There aren't any shifters anymore,' he said with a shake of his head.

Iouen shrugged. 'Tell Voss that, then. Come on. He's this way. He calls his place the den.'

The den was a large warehouse with a townhouse facade, located at the end of a narrow alley, overlooked by an emporium on one side and a Sacellum-owned apothecary on the other. The cobblestones outside the apothecary were swept free of dust and rubbish. Ordes recognised text from the Word beneath a painting in the window, depicting a man holding a sword. In a strange way, he thought the man looked like Arthur, as he would be in the years to come.

Iouen called for him to hurry up and Ordes turned from the apothecary, joining his friend at the end of the alley. He chewed his lip as Iouen knocked on the door. Shifters were supposed to be extinct, but apparently there was one living right under the nose of the Witchfinders and the Sacellum. As a kid, Ordes has been fascinated by the idea of being able to become something else, to shed your skin and transform. One of the oldest fey races, a shifter was not faery or human but something in between. Their magic was innate, and as far as Ordes knew, changing their form was the only power they possessed.

Iouen rapped on the door again. They waited, and it eventually eased open a crack, then swung wide for them once the man who answered saw who stood outside in the growing dark.

'You're either incredibly brave or incredibly stupid,' the man told a grinning Iouen, who followed the man inside. The air in the den was thick with smoke, a smell not much better than outside. Ordes wrinkled his nose, walking through the large living area, picking his way through bodies reclined on moth-eaten cushions. The faint sound of a violin floated through the air, the music eerily mournful.

Ordes leant close to his friend. 'What did you do, Iouen?'

Iouen rubbed the back of his neck. 'Ah. Voss may have loaned me some coin that I was supposed to pay back, but since I didn't have any coin, I jumped onboard a ship and left.'

Ordes shook his head.

In the far corner of the room, at a polished wooden table, sat a large man. He wore a black coat, his shoulders broad enough to belong to two men. His long and shaggy hair was as golden as a sunrise, and his eyes gleamed orange in the semi-darkness.

'Voss!' Iouen called. Beneath the cheerful charm, Ordes could sense his friend's fear.

The man inclined his golden head. 'Iouen, you little street rat,' he said, lifting his glass in greeting. 'Come to settle your debt?'

Iouen rubbed the back of his neck again. 'Umm … about that.'

'It's been five years,' Voss reminded him. 'I charge interest now,' he added, laughing at the look of horror on Iouen's face. His orange eyes swung to Ordes. 'And who do we have here, then? Or should I say, what?'

'He's a friend,' Iouen said.

Voss gestured at the vacant seats across from him and grinned, revealing elongated canines. 'Alright, Iouen and friend. What do you want?'

'I'd like to know how a shifter manages to survive in Malist,' Ordes said as he sat. Iouen did the same, muttering under his breath about subtlety and social graces. 'I can't imagine it's easy.'

The shifter's answering laugh was bitter. His face was smooth beneath the wild hair, his eyes bright and alert. Flecks of fur crept down his neck, golden with black spots – the sign of the great cat he would become when he changed form. Ordes sat back as a woman with a glorious mane of dark hair threaded with feathers placed a drink in front of him. Another shifter.

'How many of you are there?' he asked.

'Not many now. Once our numbers were mighty, but the Queen of The Teeth ended that a long time ago. When we would not bow to her whims, well …' Voss replied after a pause. The big man tapped his fingers on the edge of his glass. 'You remind me of someone. Don't tell me, I'll work it out. Something about the eyes …'

'Wait, you said the Queen of The Teeth,' Ordes said, a sinking feeling in his stomach.

'Her name is Medb,' Voss said. 'And she's a bitch, and that was before she and her bunch of fey bastards were locked in The Teeth for eternity. But you're not here to talk about Medb, are you?'

Iouen and Ordes exchanged a look.

'Where else have you been, boys?' the shifter demanded.

'The Faery Forest,' Ordes answered, not taking his eyes from Voss' golden ones.

'Ah,' Voss said, golden eyes narrowed. 'Now it makes sense.'

'Do you know where the Bow of Mists is?' Ordes asked bluntly. Beside him, Iouen shook his head and sighed.

Voss folded his arms. 'Who's asking?'

'I already told you—' Iouen began.

'I want to hear it from him,' the shifter said.

'Three sets of hands upon the Stone,' Ordes replied, keeping his voice low. He held up his hands. 'You're looking at one set. My mother is the Goddess of Magic, and my father is the Myrddin. He's here. I can get him, if you wish.'

'Now it makes sense,' Voss murmured. 'Told you it was the eyes.'

'You know my father?' Ordes asked.

'We've met,' the shifter answered. 'If you want this thing, you will have to earn it. The Bow of Mists won't just do what you want. This is one Treasure you might not find so easy to collect.'

Ordes blinked. 'Any chance you could be more vague?'

'Do you want this thing or not?' the shifter asked.

Ordes and Iouen exchanged a look. 'What do I have to do?'

Voss' cat-like, golden eyes crawled over Ordes' face. Ordes got the sense the shifter wasn't looking at him, but inside him. 'There will be a test, but you already know that. It might be the making of you, that is, if you're ready.' He called for another drink, raising his glass in a strange sort of toast. 'Come back here tomorrow, at dusk.' Voss glanced at Iouen. 'You can bring him, I suppose.'

Chapter 17

Lamorna and Mordred were studying the Word in the Chif's house, as he'd instructed. They sat next to one another at the long table in the Chif's dining room, close enough that they did not need to raise their voices to speak to one another, but not close enough that Lamorna could touch him.

She desperately wanted to touch him. She felt like her bones were about to crawl from her skin and leave her a puddle of blood and guts on the Chif's fancy carpet.

A member of the Konsel sat in the corner of the room. Lamorna could feel his eyes on them and could hear his starched red robes rustle whenever he crossed and uncrossed his legs, which was often. She grit her teeth.

This was the third morning she and Mordred had met here, under the watchful eye of the Konsel, and it was the third morning she had woken aching for his touch. Her bed was too large without him in it, and cold. She missed being able to curl up against him for warmth. She missed the way he often slept curled up against her, one large arm draped over her, his fingers splayed on her lower belly. She missed the smell of him, the way he would kiss her in those hours before dawn, like he could not get enough of her.

She missed *him*.

She shot the Konsel man a foul look.

Mordred was reading aloud from the Decalogue, his deep voice smooth and clear. Lamorna chimed in, explaining what the verse meant, even though he already knew. The morning dragged on, and Lamorna was twitchy. She knew that, after this, Mordred would accompany the Chif on his errands around town, where he would check in on people. She remembered Arthur following his father around, uncomfortable and unhappy. She wondered what sort of expression Mordred wore when he was out with Ulrian. She had never seen him and the Chif together anywhere except this house, but she imagined it would be a carefully constructed facade. Mordred knew what his uncle needed to see, and hear, and was able to provide exactly that.

She wondered if the Chif missed his son. She wondered whether he hoped Mordred could fill that space. She knew that was what Mordred wanted, if only as pretence. Keep your friends close and your enemies closer, she thought.

He was smart, and cunning. He would work out how they could get out of this.

Lamorna's gaze kept returning to the Konsel man, who sat in his red robes like he was a king or something, watching them with his beady eyes. No doubt he had been told he was not to leave them alone for one second.

She decided to test that command. She could be smart and cunning.

On the table was a jug and two mugs. She stood, reaching for the jug, and as she poured some water into one of the mugs, she slipped. Water splashed over the table, spreading across the tablecloth like a dark stain. She gasped dramatically.

'Oh! Oh no,' she said, frantically searching for something to mop up the water. The Konsel man was on his feet.

'The Word!' he cried, and Lamorna gasped again, snatching up her copy of the Decalogue and holding it free of the water. 'Foolish girl!' He came over, glaring at her. He was a small man, nervous and, she suspected, keen on keeping his job.

'I'm sorry, I'll clean it up,' she said breathlessly, rubbing her eyes contritely. 'I need some cloth. There would be some in the kitchen—' She pushed her chair back and hurried towards the door, but the Konsel man was there before her. He shook his head, his hand firmly on the door handle. Lamorna snatched her hand away, noticing with a strange sort of pleasure that there was a nervous tick to the man's left eye.

'You are to stay here. The Chif does not want you wandering around his home. I will fetch the cloth,' he said furiously. He gave them both a hard glare, and hurried out, locking the door behind him.

Mordred started laughing. 'So devious, my love,' he said. 'How long—'

He did not finish his sentence before Lamorna threw herself on him, pressing her lips to his so hard she thought she could taste blood. He sighed into her mouth, his hand gripping the back of her neck and pulled her close, so close she could feel the firm line of his body.

'This is torture,' he whispered against her mouth. 'I want nothing more than to lay you out on this blasted table and bury myself inside you.'

Lamorna moaned. She kissed him again, her hand sliding down his chest, fingers stroking the length of him. 'I miss you,' she managed. 'My bed is cold and lonely.'

Mordred sighed and set her away from him gently. He cupped her cheek, ran his thumb across her lips. 'I miss you as well.'

He pulled away as the Konsel man unlocked the door and flung it open. He glanced around suspiciously, narrowing his eyes, finding nothing but Mordred in his seat and Lamorna in hers. She rose when he came in, holding out her hand for the cloth, keeping her face lowered so he could not see her kissed lips. He watched her mop up the mess. She got her sleeves wet in the process, but it had been worth it.

Lamorna stopped at the bakery on the way back to the cottage, making sure to get enough bread for one person. Mordred liked the bread they made here, but she did not want to raise any suspicions. Everyone knew that Tamora had not returned to Kernou and that Jenyfer was gone.

As she stepped out of the bakery, Lamorna ran head-first into a body.

'Oh,' she exclaimed, her basket slipping from her arm and tumbling to the ground. Her bread rolled free. She bit back on the sudden spurt of anger as a young female voice cried out an apology. 'It's alright,' Lamorna said, but the woman dropped to the ground and scooped up Lamorna's basket and bread before she could stop her.

She stood, holding the basket out for Lamorna, apologising again. The woman had dark hair tucked beneath her linen cap and deep brown eyes. She was taller than Lamorna, and thin, like Jenyfer was. Her face was all sharp lines, cheeks pink from the ocean wind. Lamorna realised suddenly she couldn't place her, but that was no surprise. Kernou was not a large town, but before everything had happened, before everything had changed, Lamorna had barely looked at anyone who shared the prayer circle with her. All her attention had been on the Decalogue, on reciting the Word perfectly. Her time had been for the One God only.

But now, that too, was different.

The woman hurried off, and Lamorna began the walk to her cottage. She didn't mind the walk – she never had. It allowed her a moment to simply think. But today, all she was able to think about was Mordred. She touched her lips, fingers trembling. Only when she was unpacking her basket did she discover the note. It was folded in half, the paper nondescript. Curious, she unfolded it.

See you at the next prayer circle.

Lamorna frowned, wondering who could have written it. The dark-haired woman from outside the bakery. Had she slipped the note into the basket when Lamorna had dropped it and she was helping her collect her goods?

Calla, Lamorna remembered suddenly. That was the woman's name.

Lamorna had not begun attending prayer circle again, and since learning the truth about the One God, she had no desire to sit in a stuffy, dimly lit room and read the Word with a bunch of women she cared nothing for. But Mordred had asked her to go, and she wanted to help him.

Jenyfer had never liked going, attending only enough to stop people asking unwanted questions. Lamorna wondered what sort of questions they were asking about her now. Maybe if she went, she'd find out. Or maybe not. If there was one thing the women of Kernou were good at, it was the ability to talk behind someone's back without ever revealing what was said. Lamorna should know. She had engaged in nasty conversations in the past, as a way of fitting in, but quickly found she preferred to listen and store the information away to pass on to her aunt and sister.

She picked up Calla's note again. Calla, if it had been her who wrote it, had neat handwriting. Lamorna wasn't sure what to make of the note, though. Was it genuine? Did Calla really want her to go? And for what reason?

She set the note aside. It didn't matter right now who wrote it. She would go to prayer circle.

Chapter 18

'They're taking too long,' Kat muttered. Malist's main square was slowly emptying – the shops were all closed for the night, more than one shopkeeper looking their way as he packed up his displays and locked his doors. She didn't blame him. She was obviously a pirate, and Halymere was obviously not a local. She ground her teeth. Perhaps they should have waited somewhere else. She'd almost had a heart attack when the Warriors of the Light had marched across the square. They'd not even glanced in her and Haly's direction, but Kat's fingers had been brushing the hilt of her dagger ever since.

'Stop pacing,' Halymere told her, motioning across the square. On the other side of the cross of the One God was a wooden bench. 'Let's sit down.'

She shot him an irritated look. 'Don't tell me what to do.'

He sighed, but his eyes were amused. 'You want to draw attention to us, Katarin, then keep going. At least ten people have noticed you stalking about like a caged beast. And keep your weapons out of sight.'

Realising he was right, she marched across the square, cursing under her breath at the cross, and sat herself on the bench, shifting over to keep some distance between them as Halymere joined her. They didn't speak for a while, until Halymere exhaled a gentle sigh.

'I still remember the first time I saw you,' he said. 'As a woman, that is.'

'If you're about to get all mushy—'

'I wouldn't dream of it,' he muttered.

'So, what? You want to drag up what happened here, Halymere?' Kat challenged. Memories pressed against the back of her eyes. She shoved them away.

He shook his head. 'This wasn't the first place I saw you again,' he said. 'It was in Cruithea. I'd heard about you from your aunt and your charming cousin. When you showed up that day, your ship emerging from the water in the Moon's Bite, Mordred thought he'd seen a ghost.'

Kat blinked. 'You were there that day? I don't remember you.'

'Why would you? You'd just returned from the dead. You were busy.'

She laughed, then choked on it when a young man plonked himself onto the bench beside her. Katarin tensed, hand dropping to her hip, but the look of utter relief on the man's face made her pause.

'It's you,' he whispered, staring at her with wide, blue eyes. He had brown hair shorn close to his scalp, and was wearing the simple clothes of a guildsman. His face was smooth – young, or not someone who had laboured outside his whole life.

Katarin narrowed her eyes. 'Do I know you?'

He shook his head. 'You've got to help me.'

'I do, do I?' Kat arched her brow.

'Please,' the man begged. 'They'll burn her!'

Kat froze. 'Who?'

'Isolde,' the man said. When he lifted his arm to run his hand over his head, his sleeve fell back, revealing a branded scar on his forearm. Kat stared at it, trying to work out where she had seen that sign before – a cross and a serpent. 'They've taken her. I've been watching them carry wood across this square all day. The pyre they're building with it? I think it's for her.'

Kat sighed in understanding. 'Look, I'd love—'

The man closed his fingers around Kat's wrist; she tensed, as did Halymere. 'I thought if anyone could help her, it would be you. I couldn't believe it when I saw you – it was like my prayers had been answered.' His voice dropped, and he released her wrist, glancing around nervously. 'Please. I don't know what else to do.'

Katarin exchanged a glance with Halymere, who shook his head. 'Who is she to you? A lover?'

The man nodded, dropping his eyes. 'Yes.'

'Why did they take her?' Kat asked.

'You aren't considering this,' Halymere mumbled. 'Katarin, we have a job to do here.'

Kat glared at him, a warning to keep quiet, then turned back to the terrified man. 'Your name?'

'Tristan,' he breathed. 'I'm Tristan.'

'Do you know when she is—'

'Tomorrow, after sundown,' he cut in.

Kat rubbed at her cheek in concern. 'That doesn't leave me much time. What else do I need to know?'

Tristan hesitated and then, quietly, 'Her husband is high up in the ranks of the Sacellum.'

'No,' Halymere said firmly. 'We are not doing this!'

Kat ignored him. 'Meet me here, at sunset tomorrow,' she told Tristan. 'I'll save your girl for you.'

He hurried off, and by the time Ordes and Iouen arrived, Katarin had never been so grateful to see them. Haly had not stopped muttering and cursing under his breath. Perhaps she'd been too hasty, agreeing to help Tristan, but it was done now. She'd pledged her support and she wasn't going to go back on it. No matter the danger, Katarin would do this, and Halymere knew her well enough to know it. Just because she was hunting for Treasure did not mean she had forgotten what she had vowed all those years ago. *The Night Queen* may be gone, but Katarin was not.

The sun had vanished, and the city was cloaked in darkness. Kat went to reprimand Ordes and Iouen for taking so long, but the look on Ordes' face stopped her.

'Did you find it?' she demanded, keeping her voice low.

Iouen nodded. 'Well, sort of.'

'Either you did or you didn't,' Halymere said, folding his huge arms.

'You're as friendly as she is,' Iouen said, motioning to Katarin. 'Honestly, a man does you a favour and—'

'We found it,' Ordes cut in. 'But I have to come back for it, tomorrow night.'

'And?' Katarin insisted.

'And I don't know,' Ordes answered.

'Can this Voss be trusted?' Arthur asked as Iouen relayed what had happened. They were in the galley, plates full, but no one was eating much. Jenyfer was poking at her food, a frown on her face.

'Shifters are notoriously duplicitous,' Jalen added.

'Voss can be trusted, if there is something in it for him,' Iouen answered.

Katarin folded her arms. 'So what does he want? If he's a guardian of the Bow, he shouldn't want anything, except to do what he was told.'

'Yeah, he's not that sort of guy, and, well, here's the thing,' Iouen said. 'We didn't part on great terms you see, and as for trusting him – I wouldn't trust him as far as I could throw him, which wouldn't be far. But this is how Ordes gets his Treasure.'

'Something about this makes me uneasy,' Arthur said, shaking his head. 'Maybe we need to spend some more time looking for it ourselves.'

'I mean, sure, we could go back, but Malist isn't Kernou, Arthur. It's not the sort of place where you should be caught asking questions,' Iouen said simply.

'Kernou isn't either,' Jenyfer mumbled.

Iouen shifted in his seat. 'I don't plan on letting anything happen to Ordes.'

'Touching,' Katarin muttered. She sighed. 'Fine.'

'It's not up to you, Katarin,' Ordes reminded her. 'Why don't you tell Arthur what you agreed to do?'

Arthur watched his sister glare at Ordes and then, as calm as ever, she recounted her meeting with Tristan. 'I told him I'd help.'

'Of course you did. Can you do it?' Arthur asked. His heart was thundering. He liked this idea less than putting their faith in a fey they knew nothing about. The irony of it wasn't lost on Arthur – he'd stepped through a magical curtain and asked a dryad to hand over a sword, but this felt different. Maybe it was Malist and what it represented to him, what it had always represented – more of a prison than Kernou. This was the place his father had wanted to send him.

Katarin nodded. 'Yes.'

'Can you do it *without* putting yourself in danger?' Arthur corrected.

'Yes,' Kat said, rolling her eyes. Halymere mumbled something under his breath, and she turned to him, furious. 'What's your problem?'

'Did you fail to notice who your new friend is, Katarin?' Halymere spat. 'He belongs to the Sacellum – he's Sheletari! He wears their mark on his skin, the cross and the serpent. You saw it.'

Arthur's heart sank.

'This whole thing could be a trap,' Haly said.

Ordes nodded in agreement. 'Kat, as much as I would love to help this girl, Haly has a point here,' he said.

'This is what we will do. I'll rescue the girl, and while I'm doing that, you,' she said, nodding at Halymere, 'will be holding a blade to Tristan's throat. If he looks in the wrong direction—'

'I'll slit his throat, and before he's finished bleeding out, I'll come and save your arse,' Halymere snapped.

'Fine,' Kat snarled.

Ordes rolled his eyes. 'Get a room and get it over with,' he muttered.

Katarin snarled at him, then turned to Jenyfer. 'You're with me. I saw what you did in the tavern in Skulls Rest. You held a whole room of men in thrall with your voice. If you can do that, you can help me.'.

As Jenyfer nodded, her face set into determined lines, Arthur could not help but feel something was about to go terribly wrong.

CHAPTER 19

Malist at dusk wore a cloak of mist and a perfume of charred wood and smoke. Darkened windows tracked Jenyfer's steps as she followed Katarin through the winding streets. She had never thought she would see Teyath's capital, and had spent half her life terrified of the place. Yet here she was, a Magic Wielder and a faery, the daughter of an Old One, willingly marching into the One God's city.

The Excalibur was anchored as far out in the harbour as was possible, Merlin's magic protecting the ship. As they had rowed, she, Kat and Halymere in one boat, Iouen and Ordes in the other, Jen had glanced back at the ship, and found it had vanished. She only hoped the glamour would be strong enough to keep them hidden from Witchfinders and not so strong that the Sheletari could sniff it out from the Sacellum.

They had left the boats at the wharf, walking together to the edge of the warehouse district. Ordes had been distracted, frowning, leaving Jenyfer deeply bothered. The heartfire burnt in her chest, and she wasn't sure whether it was a warning or not.

He would be alright, she told herself, as Ordes and Iouen broke away from the group. He was meant to have the Bow.

The outer living quarter of Malist reminded Jenyfer of Kernou – small houses with thatched roofs and few windows, the streets wide and clean, but as they moved nearer to the centre of the city, the buildings stood shoulder to shoulder, not enough space between them for even a cat to fit. It made Jenyfer wary – there was nowhere to hide if they needed to. Kat had told her one hundred times already that nothing would go wrong. Jenyfer desperately wanted to believe her and usually, she would. But when Katarin thought no one was watching, a frown pulled at her face and she chewed her lip – a sign that she, too, was concerned about being here.

The lamps were lit along the main thoroughfare that led towards the heart of the city. Iouen had told Jenyfer about the city – the harbour and the bustling wharves became warehouses and then brothels and dark-windowed taverns. For such a large place, Malist was practically silent as night approached. Iouen had not mentioned the curfew. It made Jenyfer want to smile – sneaking around after curfew was something she was well practised in.

Katarin set a brisk pace, avoiding the halos of lamplight cast on the paved streets. Halymere walked behind Jen and Kat, and Jen felt a little better with the Cruithean at her back. She had watched the Inborn sparring with Arthur – he knew how to handle a weapon. Her daggers were concealed beneath her clothes and she could feel the cool kiss of the steel against her stomach, but it was the weapon in her voice Katarin was planning to use.

Jenyfer was no longer afraid of the power of her voice. Something about that night in Skulls Rest had changed her. The control she'd had, so easily manipulating that room full of people – that was the sort of power her father and Andromache had spoken about. Jenyfer's song seethed beneath her skin, anticipating what was to come.

Malist's taverns became shops and a town square, paved, with a water fountain in the centre. Beyond the town square were the homes of the wealthy, grand buildings that Jenyfer could only guess at. Towering over them all was the Sacellum, a silhouette of dark stone against the setting sun.

They did not burn Magic Wielders in the main square in Malist. There was a special place designed for such an event – an amphitheatre with seats and a stage, where the only performances were that of burning flesh, death, and the One God's retribution.

Katarin led them across the square. The people they encountered ignored them; they were dressed like ordinary city-dwellers. Katarin had left behind her long coat and cutlass, and her daggers were hidden beneath her clothes, as were Jenyfer's. Only Halymere could carry weapons in plain sight. His Cruithean braids were hidden beneath a peaked cap, and he was dressed in ordinary dark pants, a grey shirt and vest. He still stood out, though not as much.

As they neared the edge of the square, a man stepped from the shadows of a hat shop. His dark hair was cropped short, his clothes plain. His face was a pale orb in the growing darkness, tense with worry and, beneath it, relief.

'You came,' he breathed.

'I said I would,' Katarin answered, while Halymere grumbled under his breath.

'You're Tristan?' Jenyfer guessed.

He nodded. 'Thank the One God you've all come.'

'Don't thank him yet,' Kat warned. 'I said I'd try.' She paused and ran her eyes over Tristan. 'Can we trust you, Sheletari?'

'I'm not a Witchfinder yet. I guess now, I never will be,' Tristan said firmly. 'But that doesn't matter. We have to hurry – they've moved it along. I thought you'd have more time, but they're taking her out now!'

'Now? Shit,' Katarin moaned.

Halymere approached Tristan, patting the dagger at his hip. 'You're staying with me, while these two save your girl. If I think for half a second you're about to betray us, you die, understand?'

Tristan nodded. There was no fear on his face, just bleak despair mingled with urgency. 'I'll do whatever needs to be done.'

Halymere vanished into the shadows, dragging Tristan with him. The plan was they would wait at the edge of the first row of warehouses. Jenyfer knew that if she and Kat failed to show up, with or without Isolde, Tristan would die.

Jenyfer and Katarin headed for the amphitheatre. A group of people, mostly men, walked ahead, talking in whispered voices. One glanced over his shoulder. Jenyfer met grey eyes and dropped hers quickly. She did not need anyone remembering her or Kat after this.

'How do you usually do this?' Jenyfer asked as quietly as she could.

'I'm not usually pulling people off stakes in Malist,' Katarin answered. 'We'll have to go about this differently, which is where you come in, Jen. There will be a crowd to witness this – she's the wife of a senior member of the Sacellum. It'll be the show of the year.'

'Fantastic,' Jenyfer muttered.

'Hold them,' Kat said. 'All of them. I don't care what you sing, just give me enough time to get Isolde away. I was hoping to grab her before they took her out and only have to worry about her guards, but that's no longer an option.'

Jenyfer chewed the inside of her cheek. 'The women in the crowd?'

'They'll realise we're helping one of their own,' Kat said.

Jenyfer wasn't so sure about that. In Kernou, distrust in her and her difference had come from women as much as it had from the men of the village, and this woman – Isolde – was more important than Jenyfer had been. *Katarin doesn't understand that*, Jenyfer thought, *and I don't have the time to make her understand.*

Katarin paused on the edge of the amphitheatre. Jenyfer felt eyes comb over their bodies and silently cursed herself. They should have an escort. In Kernou, two young women out alone, even to witness the burning of a witch, would raise suspicions, but it was too late. No one said anything as they moved down the stone stairs, finding seats close to the stage. Jenyfer had never felt more vulnerable in her whole life, sitting with her back to Malist's finest. What sort of people considered the death of a woman entertainment?

She surveyed the crowd as covertly as possible, taking in the number of people sitting in the sunset-tinged darkness. She swallowed. She could do this. She had to, or else an innocent woman would be burnt, she and Kat alongside her because Katarin was not leaving this amphitheatre without Isolde. After what Katarin had told Jenyfer in the Faery Forest, she understood this was about more than an unknown woman and her lover.

'Right, she's not out yet,' Katarin said. 'If we're quick, we might be able to—'

A woman's pleading voice rang out, and Jenyfer's heart sank as a young woman, blonde hair loose and messy around her shoulders, face streaked with tears, was dragged across the stage towards the stake.

'Fuck,' Kat hissed.

'Now what?' Jenyfer asked. She clenched her fists, her magic swirling in her veins as Kat's eyes scanned the area. 'Arthur said not to put ourselves in danger,' Jenyfer reminded her.

'I am *not* letting this girl burn.' Kat's whisper was tight.

Jenyfer lay her hand on Kat's arm. 'Kat,' she said softly. The Captain shook her off. Isolde was being tied to the stake. Her pleas and sobs washed over the apathetic crowd, and Jenyfer could only think of how different yet similar this moment was to that morning on the beach in Kernou when Lamorna was left for the sea.

A man dressed in deep red made his way onto the stage. His words inspired a sickening feeling in Jenyfer's stomach – he was Isolde's husband and was perfectly content to watch his wife burn. Pleased, even, by the tone of his voice and the expression he wore, like a conquering hero making this sacrifice to prove to all the depths of his devotion to the One God. People clapped when he spoke. A voice lifted in gratitude to the One God for sending them Mark, and Jenyfer realised that was the man's name.

Bryn hadn't come for Jenyfer when she was locked up and waiting to die. He had done nothing to help her, just as no one except Jenyfer had tried to help Lamorna. If it hadn't been for Ordes, Jenyfer would have been tied to a stake atop a pyre in this cursed place.

Her heart burnt in agreement. She licked her lips. Isolde pleaded with her husband, who wouldn't even look at her. *At least*, Jenyfer thought, *I had Ordes.* A man with the power and the means to rescue her. With the courage to do what was right. It didn't matter who asked him to do it, or why, only that he had.

Isolde had no one. Tristan could not help her, so he had done the only thing he could.

Found Katarin.

'Alright,' Jenyfer said resolutely. 'Screw the consequences. Let's do it.'

Chapter 20

Ordes heard the echo of Jenyfer's heartbeat in his ears and wondered where she was. She was safe, he knew that. He'd feel it if she wasn't. *And then what?* A little voice asked him. *Would you forget what you were here for? Would you rush off and save her?*

Something shifted beneath Ordes' skin, moving and pulsing through his blood; if he wished it, it would crawl free. Irritated, he rubbed at the back of his neck.

'Come on,' Iouen called. A single lantern hung above the gaping mouth of Voss' den. The same dark-haired man who met them before let them in without a word. Feathers dropped from his hair as they walked. A bird, Ordes realised, taking in the powerful arms that would support equally powerful wings, the broad back and narrow waist of the shifter as he led them deeper into the den. The air was drenched with a strange, quiet sort of anticipation. Bodies spread out on the cushions, more than there had been last night, and this time they were awake. Some shifters were half-transformed, tails and fur visible amongst the skin and clothes.

Ordes saw the fluffy tail of a fox and the delicately pointed ears of a cat. He wondered if they chose their shifting skin, or if they were bound to the skin of the animal they were born with.

The dark-haired shifter led them through a small kitchen – food was scattered over the benches, as if a whole pack of ravenous dogs had raided the pantry, which they possibly had – and into an adjoining room where Voss was waiting for them. He was sprawled on a red velvet lounge, long muscular legs stretched out, bare feet crossed at the ankles. A plate of food sat on the low table, within reach of his large hands. His golden eyes assessed them as they approached; he waved them to the matching armchairs on the other side of the table. In the far corner of the room was a bed piled with cushions and blankets. It was occupied; a muscular, black-spotted leg poked out the side.

Ordes sat, realising they were in Voss' bedroom, and gestured at the bed. 'Umm …'

'Don't worry about Negrao. Once he falls asleep, it'd take an explosion to wake him.' Voss glanced over his shoulder, his face soft for a moment, before turning back to Ordes and Iouen with a sigh. 'What do you know about this Treasure?'

'I know it was my mother's,' Ordes said. 'But that's all.'

'It's a weapon of war,' the shifter said. 'Is it war you're seeking?'

'No,' Ordes said. 'It isn't. I'm not a warrior and I don't want to be one.'

Voss' eyes glowed in the lantern light. 'Sometimes we have to be what we thought we could not. You want the Bow? You do what you have to do.'

Arthur had confronted his father, but Ulrian Tregarthen had been a shade, nothing more. Ordes licked dry lips, pulling his hand through his cropped hair and finding nothing to grab hold of. Arthur had confronted his fears, and the Sword of the White Dragon was in his possession. The skin on the back of Ordes' neck tingled, and he reached up to rub at it absent-mindedly.

'How are you involved in all of this?' he asked.

'Someone asked for my help, long ago, and I gave it,' Voss answered. The big shifter sat back, tapping his fingers on his thigh. His fingernails were more like claws. 'Let me tell you a story, from when the world was last going to shit. The Old Ones were about to rip the place to pieces because they're a temperamental bunch. It isn't my story to tell, so I won't, but I will tell you that the fey creatures of the world were never asked what we wanted, and neither were the humans who inhabited this place. You need to understand – Teyath was the Old Ones' playground, and they did what they wanted with it.'

Ordes frowned. More questions that needed answers, but he didn't ask Voss to explain. The back of his neck itched like crazy; he scratched at it absently.

'You got fleas, boy?' Voss asked with a grin.

'Just a little unsettled,' Ordes shot back.

The conversation turned to shifter magic, a distraction while Ordes tried to work out what he would have to do to get this Bow. Face his fears, obviously, but which ones?

'The fey races were created from the magic that created this world – your mother's magic, mostly. While the Green Knight shaped the mountains and the valleys, and Melodias crafted the seas and everything in it, Niniane set her power loose on the world, and from that power came the fey,' Voss explained.

Iouen leant forward, interested. 'So you're as old as the earth?'

Voss surprised them by shaking his head. 'We came later. Before us garden variety shifters, there was another race, mostly extinct now. Not to be trusted. They're more animal than human, and unlike us, they can take whatever form they choose. We call them Skin Roamers. They're cousins of ours, I guess, but you can't choose your family, can you?'

Ordes had never heard of Skin Roamers. 'How does it work? How do you change your shape?'

'The same way you breathe,' Voss told him. 'The other part of us, the part you currently can't see, is always there, beneath our human facade.

This shape you see now is the one I was born into, but my other shape has always been there. I exist in two worlds, Ordes, a foot in each. I suppose you'd understand that, but unlike you, I embrace what I am.'

Ordes froze.

'You fear what you are and what you could be,' Voss said.

'Of course I do,' Ordes replied. 'I spent my life thinking I was human, a normal Magic Wielder, but I'm not. I don't know how to deal with that, not fully.' He sighed, rubbing at his cheek. 'Are you human or are you an animal?' he asked Voss.

'I'm both,' the shifter answered. 'I move in both worlds. Am I part of them equally? Of course not. This face I wear is a mask, but it allows me freedom. As long as the people of this city, of this world, think I'm human, I'm safe. We're all safe. Yes, they look at us and they know something isn't right, but the world of magic has been lost to them for so long they can't put their finger on it. I would bet they look at you the same way.' Before Ordes could ask more questions, Voss stood. 'I can't explain how it works – how shifters change their form. I only know it's part of who and what we are. Come on then.'

Ordes and Iouen exchanged a look, then followed the shifter wordlessly. They left through a concealed door at the back of the room, finding themselves outside beneath the night sky. Iouen demanded to know where they were going, but Voss told him to shut up and follow. A man emerged from the darkness, his face cloaked in shadows. The man whispered to Voss, who nodded, and then the man was gone. The shifter made them wait in the shadows in an alley that smelt like garbage and stale water, before he moved off again, not bothering to check that they were following him.

Backstreets led into more backstreets until they found themselves standing in front of a nondescript door, tucked into a building that stretched into the sky, all dark grey stone and sharply angled shadows. A warning screamed through Ordes' mind, but at the same time, that pulling sensation he'd been feeling since they dropped anchor near Malist increased. The Bow was close.

'Where are we?' Iouen demanded again.

The shifter sighed. 'Does it matter? We're getting your friend's Treasure, as you wanted.' Without waiting for a response, Voss rapped large knuckles on the door. Footsteps approached, and the door eased open. Ordes caught a flash of a woman's face. She spoke with Voss, her eyes finding Ordes, and like he had with Voss, Ordes had the sensation that she was looking inside him, not at him. He could sense her magic, strange and dark, different to anything he had encountered before. Not fey, but something else.

The woman said nothing, motioning for them to follow.

The woman walked ahead, raising a lantern against the dark. She was wearing robes that brushed along the ground behind her, and in the darkness, Ordes couldn't tell their colour. She led them through a narrow passageway, around multiple bends, the walls close. Ordes touched one – stone, damp and cold. Were they beneath the ground?

The woman eased open a door at the end of the passageway, a slice of light flooding Ordes' senses. They emerged into a large room, torches lit along the walls. A deep red carpet graced the floor, and decorative arched windows framed the night sky outside. Each window was a mosaic of brilliant colour, noticeable even in the dim light. The symbol from the uniform of the Warriors of the Light was visible on the banners that hung ceiling to floor. His stomach twisted.

At the end of the room was an ornately carved wooden chair, throne-like, sitting on a raised dais, and in that chair was an elderly man, white hair cropped close to his scalp. He was dressed in white robes with a familiar cross embroidered in red on his chest.

Tension dug into Ordes' muscles as, slowly, he realised where they were.

The shifter had led them into the Sacellum, straight to the feet of the Magistrar.

Chapter 21

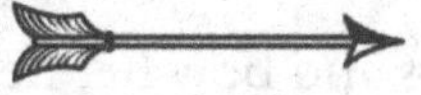

Jenyfer and Kat both had unfinished business with the men of the Sacellum, those tyrants who tied women to stakes, who made rules stripping people of freedoms in the name of a god they did not truly know. The horrible scars on Katarin's back reminded Jenyfer that no matter how well you thought you knew someone, a monster may lurk beneath the surface of them. She wasn't so naive to believe she'd known everything there was to know about Katarin, but when she'd seen those whip marks, it was a testament to the fact that even the strongest women suffered at the hands of men. But he who wielded the lash had not broken Katarin Le Fey. Jenyfer had always admired Kat's strength, but now she was a symbol of hope, of power, of resilience. Kat could have let her experience bury her, but she didn't.

Jenyfer could only hope that this woman, Isolde, would be the same. That she would be able to bury the hurt and betrayal handed to her, and use it to survive this world. Until they found the Grail and could give everyone a better world.

Mark's lofty speech had ended. Jenyfer had not paid attention – she had heard it before, the same words from a different mouthpiece. The same condemnation and shaming. The same lies.

The same death sentence.

A man in shining red robes approached Isolde's pyre, a flaming torch in his hand. In the firelight, Jenyfer could see the tears rushing down Isolde's face. She struggled, screamed – there was no acceptance of her death. She fought hard.

She did not close her eyes and bow her head and wait for the end, like Lamorna had.

'And the witch dies, as is proper,' Mark called.

The torch was touched to the pyre. The wood caught, then went out, a thin stream of smoke trailing into the air. A murmur trickled through the watching crowd.

Twice more they tried to light the pyre, and twice more it went out.

Kat's lips moved soundlessly, her fingers hidden in her lap, working quickly.

Mark faced the crowd, and Jenyfer's heart leapt into her throat as his dark eyes swung over them. She knew what was coming. Two Witchfinders in red robes stood at either end of the stage, their hoods covering their heads, eyes shifting through the crowd, hunting.

'Witchcraft,' Mark shouted, his voice booming, echoing off the stone and shooting into the night. 'A witch works her sorcery, come to try and save her own!'

'That's your cue,' Katarin whispered, reaching beneath her clothing for her blades. Magic curled around her hands as Jenyfer took a deep breath.

She had done this in Skulls Rest, her song rushing out of her. This time, it hesitated, unsure, and the heartfire surged through her.

'Ordes,' she whispered, rubbing at her burning chest.

'Jen,' Kat hissed. 'Now.'

Melodias had told Jenyfer her syhren magic was tied to her emotions. She'd been furious in Skulls Rest, and furious when she destroyed Andromache's water-Bryn. She needed that fury once more.

She couldn't think about Ordes right now. She made herself focus, reaching inside for all the memories she had pushed aside.

Bryn. Betrayal, the hard look in his eyes. The tone of voice, cold and chilled. Her aunt, having to hide who and what she was. Lamorna and the Decalogue, her sister's mind twisted into shapes that Jenyfer did not recognise, the child Lamorna was completely swallowed by the One God's Word.

The Chif, eyes blazing with fire.

The dead mermaid.

The *fear*, so constant and omnipresent.

The choice and control that had been stolen from her life.

The powerlessness that invaded not just her life, but the lives of everyone in Kernou, man or woman.

Jenyfer's song rushed up her throat. She opened her mouth, and sang.

It was not death she sang, but sleep and forgetting, two songs in unison. She filled her voice with urgency, her power washing over the crowd. She barely registered that Katarin was climbing onto the stage. The Witchfinders, Jenyfer noted, had not been as affected by her magic as the men around her, but they were no match for Katarin, who cut them down with magic and blade, before climbing the smoking pyre.

Around Jenyfer, men slept, their chins on their chests or their heads fallen onto their neighbour's shoulder. The few women in the audience were frozen in shock or fear – Jenyfer could not tell which. They said nothing as she stood, still singing, and none tried to stop her as she hurried to join Katarin as she helped a terrified Isolde down from the stage. The woman was still weeping, her eyes streaming and rimmed in red.

'Let's go,' Kat ordered. 'How long do we have?'

Jenyfer stopped singing; her voice echoed around the amphitheatre. 'I don't know. It didn't take Marsh long to come back to himself.'

'Who are you?' Isolde whispered, gazing up at them. Her face was streaked with tears and grime, and the fingers that grasped Jenyfer's hands were trembling. Isolde made no protests when Katarin took her by the arm and hauled her away. She grabbed the hem of her dress and ran, following Kat into a narrow street that led to the edge of the town square. They didn't pause for breath. Jenyfer's ears were straining, and she gripped her daggers tightly, her magic pushing through her blood. Her song sat on her tongue, ready to be unleashed again.

It was happy with what she had done, and, she acknowledged, so was she. She hadn't been able to save her sister. She hadn't been able to save herself. But today, she had helped save another.

By the time they had reached Halymere and Tristan, Jenyfer's magic had faded. Alarm bells rang out, loud and distraught, and voices could be heard shouting in outrage. Tristan caught Isolde in his arms, holding her close.

'Haly, can we make it to the water?' Kat asked.

He nodded, flipping his blade in his hands. 'I'd like to see them stop us.'

'The Witchfinders will follow the magic,' Tristan said with certainty. Isolde clung to him, her face pressed against his neck.

'Then let's move before it leads them here,' Kat said.

They hurried from the city, trusting Tristan to lead them down sidestreets towards the water, racing down the jetty to the boat. Jenyfer glanced at the second boat, bobbing alongside theirs. 'Ordes and Iouen aren't here.'

Kat's face was conflicted. 'We can't go back,' she said. 'Shit shit shit.'

'He'll be alright,' Halymere said, jumping into the boat and reaching up to help Isolde down. 'He can look after himself – they both can.'

Jenyfer bit her lip, glancing back at the city.

'Get in, Jenyfer,' Kat demanded. Swallowing, Jenyfer did what she was told, and as soon as she was settled, Halymere pulled on the oars. With Kat's magic helping him along, they hurried back to the ship.

CHAPTER 22

Magic curled in Ordes' hands before he knew what he was doing. Standing either side of the Magistrar were two figures in red cloaks. Their heads were bowed, eyes cast to the floor, their faces hidden. Like the woman who had led them into this room, Ordes could sense dangerous magic coming from them. Iouen sucked in a breath. 'What the fuck are the Red Sisters doing here?'

Ordes jolted, his eyes swinging between the impassive red-robed women. They had not moved, nor given any indication they were aware of other people in the room. The Magistrar's blank face was as still and unnerving as the sentries either side of him. They weren't guarding him, however. Ordes could see the shapes of magic they wove around the man, the thin threads, as red as blood.

Before Ordes could demand answers, their guide stepped past the Magistrar and disappeared, wraith-like, into the shadows at the back of the room.

Iouen stared at the Magistrar with narrowed eyes. 'What's wrong with him?'

'Would you like him to snap out of it?' Voss demanded. He gestured to the Red Sisters. 'Their magic is what's wrong with him. Come on. We've got a Bow to collect.' Voss stepped past the Magistrar, slumped in his seat. Ordes and Iouen exchanged a glance, then Iouen shrugged, following Voss. Ordes remained behind, his eyes on the Magistrar of the Sacellum, even as the Bow of Mists called him from somewhere within the building.

Voss growled a command, so Ordes left the Magistrar and the Red Sisters. Their guide was waiting near an unassuming door, cut into the wooden panelling behind the Magistrar's seat. From the folds of her cloak, she withdrew a large golden key and unlocked the door. The woman stepped through, not checking to see if anyone was following her into the thick darkness.

Ordes met Voss' eyes.

'After you,' the big shifter said simply.

Swallowing, Ordes descended into darkness, that tugging sensation behind his navel growing stronger. His fey senses revealed roughly cut stone walls, the smell the must and damp earth of a long-forgotten ancient space. The floor pulsated beneath his feet. Behind him, Iouen cursed as he stumbled. The stairs ended in a long and narrow chamber, empty as far as Ordes could tell. The Red Sister waited for them at the far end, a ball of glowing blood-red light hovering in the air above her head.

This place reminded Ordes of Goerika's Temple, and that made him uneasy. He'd learnt things in that place that had rocked the foundations of his world, and that had been more than enough for one lifetime. There was magic here; it thrummed through the air, breathing with him.

Beside him, Voss made an impatient noise.

'If you're the Guardian …' Ordes began.

The shifter chuckled. 'Who said I was the Guardian?'

Ordes blinked. 'But …'

'It's easy to believe what we want to believe, isn't it?' Voss mumbled. He nodded at the Red Sister standing in the darkness. 'There's your Guardian.'

'The Bow of Mists has been under the watchful eye of the Red Sisters for a long time, Ordes,' the woman said, her voice, rough, ill-used, but powerful. Ordes wondered how she knew his name. 'Are you ready to become yourself?'

'What do you mean?' he asked, a chill sliding down his spine.

She didn't reply.

Voss joined her. Behind them lay a simple wooden chest on a stone table. Ordes could feel the magic surrounding it – spells and wards, charms, and the Bow of Mists itself, calling his name from within its prison.

He took a step forward. He could feel Iouen's eyes on him, could sense the Red Sister watching him closely.

'Open the chest,' Voss told him, his gravelly voice low and rumbling. 'If this truly belongs to you, no spell, no matter how strong, will keep you from it. Open it,' he repeated.

Ordes took a deep breath, stepped forward, and placed his hand on the chest.

For a moment, nothing happened. Then he could feel it – the magic giving way to him, shifting like a tide. The click of a magical lock echoed through the room. Ordes felt the protective spells snap and vanish. He held his breath as the lid opened on its own.

'The Bow of Mists,' Voss announced, 'it's yours. Take it,' he added, watching Ordes with a strange look on his face. 'It's what you came here for, isn't it?'

The Bow lay cradled in the bottom of the chest. It shifted in and out of focus, a curving of silver mist.

Slowly, Ordes reached inside.

His hand passed straight through it.

He frowned, and tried again, but no matter what he did, he could not grasp the Treasure. He looked at the Red Sister in alarm.

'If you want it, you need to claim it,' she said. Her lips curled. 'And you need to claim who you are. Tricks will not suffice, not this time.'

'What the fuck does that mean?' Iouen asked.

Ordes ignored him. Goerika's words echoed in his head.

Do you truly know who you are?

He didn't. He had no idea. Since learning the truth of what he was, there had been a tautness living in the depths of him, something Ordes had tried desperately to push away: a cord of shimmering light, calling him, urging him to do *something*, but he didn't know what. Opening curtains with a flick of his wrist, summoning a mug when he was too lazy to get up, juggling a ball of water, or even moving through time and space – they were nothing, small magics that squandered his talent, an insult to the truth he must embrace.

But he had not followed that cord. And if he didn't, Ordes knew the Bow would be lost to them.

He wasn't human. So what was he?

Time slowed as he took a deep breath. He could feel the magic of this place, the magic of the Treasure, buffering him, surrounding him like a breeze. It curled around his body, searching for a way inside him, and Ordes understood what he needed to do – surrender himself. Hand over what he thought he was, what he had always believed he was, the thing he'd been stubbornly clinging to – his human self.

The magic of the Bow of Mists flowed over him and the magic under his skin shifted in response.

The form you wear is the form you choose to wear.

Ordes met Voss' eyes.

You fear what you are …

Heat washed through Ordes, and as he let go, let the barriers around him crumble, something tore from his back.

He caught sight of his shadow as red light flickered around them – his body was engulfed by a pair of wings, rising above his shoulders in a graceful arc. Ordes froze, then reached over his shoulder to touch one.

He had *wings*. Like the Bow, his fingers passed right through them.

The back of Ordes' neck burnt; insects scurried across his flesh. He stepped back, his giant wings opening. The Red Sister watched him with eager eyes; somewhere behind him, Ordes heard Iouen swear.

'Claim what you are,' the woman whispered.

Ordes closed his eyes. The world shifted, stretched and reformed. His senses, everything that he was, every blood vessel and scrap of flesh, every bone and organ, became something else, something foreign and alien and so far from who he was he felt himself slipping away. Panicked, he reached deep inside, held on to that kernel of himself. The heartfire tore through him anew, reshaping itself.

When Ordes opened his eyes, everything was sharper. His feet were no longer on the ground – and they were no longer feet. He had claws, and wings flapping by instinct. He hovered in the air a moment, before dropping to the damp stones. He could hear everything – Iouen's sharp, disbelieving breaths; three heartbeats, two human, one not quite human; the dripping of water somewhere in the darkness and the far-off shriek of a siren.

His eyes narrowed in on the wooden crate – he could hear the Bow, calling his name, urging him to claim it.

Ordes snapped back into himself so suddenly it made him want to vomit. Human once again, he dropped to his knees, gasping. Slowly, he lifted his head. The Red Sister was smiling. She gestured to the box that held the Bow.

Ordes got to his feet, squashing his panic, his wonder – he had become something else, if only for a short time. He had felt his body *change*. His muscles and nerve-endings were on fire, but as he approached the Bow, that fire cooled and washed away. The blood in his veins slowed, thickened and pulsed. His magic swirled in response, his heart a thundering drumbeat in his ears, his eyes filled with mist and light. His ears were overwhelmed by the sound of the wind through the trees. His lungs were choked with smoke, the taste of it in his mouth. Ash coated his tongue, and when he took a breath, he breathed fire. He could smell the earth after rain, hear the crash of waves on a far-off shore.

Ordes reached for the Bow once more.

The moment his fingers brushed that silver mist, the Bow became corporeal, filling him with harmony, and balance. A piece of a puzzle that had been yearning to be whole, only Ordes had never known it. As his hand closed around the grip, heat rushed through him from head to toe. He gasped, and lifted the Bow free, staring at it with a thundering heart as wings uncurled from his back once more.

'And the rest,' Voss ordered reverently.

In the chest was a quiver of arrows. Ordes took it. Voss grunted, and the spell broke, the shifter turning abruptly to follow the Red Sister. Ordes and Iouen hurried to catch them. They ascended the stone stairs in silence, passed the dull-eyed puppet Magistrar. No one spoke until they were back at the plain wooden door opening into the back alley.

'You … holy fuck … Ordes, you turned into a fucking *bird*,' Iouen stuttered. 'A bird. With wings and feathers and a bloody beak.'

Ordes swallowed. The Red Sister reached up and removed her hood, revealing a face much younger than Ordes had been expecting. Her skin was dark, eyes full of shadows and mystery, her hair shorn. 'You're in charge of the Sacellum, aren't you?' he said.

She inclined her head.

Iouen cleared his throat, and the Red Sister turned to him.

'I know you question your purpose in all of this, but your role was written long ago. Long has Kunis stood beside us, and long has Kunis promised to be there when the day finally came. You will go home sooner than you think.'

The blood drained from Iouen's face.

'The Red One thanks you,' the woman said.

'Yeah, yeah,' Voss answered. 'Tell your mistress to get fucked. She could have made things easy, at least. And tell her I thank her for all the years of non-communication while I kept watch for this one to come and get his toy. Tell her I'm done – I won't get involved with Old Ones and their bullshit again.'

The Red Sister shut the door on them without another word.

'Ungrateful bitch,' Voss mumbled darkly, and Ordes wasn't sure if he meant the Red Sister or the Goddess she served. Beside him, Iouen made a noise. His face was corpse-pale, his lips a thin line.

'What the actual fuck just happened?' His voice teetered on the edge of panic.

Voss ignored him, his eyes locked on Ordes. 'It bothers you.'

'Of course it bothers me – I turned into a bird,' Ordes shot back.

Voss grinned. 'You'll get used to it.'

'The shifters serve Ereshki,' Ordes stated. Voss wouldn't confirm nor deny anything. Ordes shook his head, turning to Iouen. 'We need to leave.'

'Yes, we do,' his friend managed. 'Nice seeing you again, Voss.'

'Fuck off, Iouen. Don't come back here, understand?' Voss growled. 'If she said you need to go home, take the long way. I don't want to see you unless you're returning my money, with interest.'

Iouen mumbled something under his breath.

Ordes could not take his eyes off the Bow of Mists, cradled in his hands.

Malist was in lockdown. Ordes and Iouen made it to the docks, but could not make it to their boat. A group of Witchfinders lingered around the end of the jetty.

'Now what?' Iouen hissed.

'We get wet,' Ordes said. He slung the Bow of Mists and the quiver over his shoulders. They passed right through the wings. He shuddered, wishing he knew how to get rid of them, at least for now. He and Iouen crept further away from the Witchfinders and slipped into the water. It was cold, and a long swim back to *The Excalibur*; Ordes didn't dare use magic, not with Witchfinders lurking so close. By the time the ship appeared, Iouen's teeth were chattering and Ordes' head was going to explode.

Forget the Bow of Mists.

He had fucking *wings*. He'd turned into a bird.

But he'd come away from this with more than a Treasure – the knowledge that the Sacellum was under the control of the Red Sisters made his head spin, and with the shifters aligned with them … Ordes pushed the questions aside, reaching for the Jacob's ladder. As his fingers closed over the first rung, Arthur's voice floated down to him.

'Ordes? You're okay?'

'Sort of,' Ordes managed. He paused, turning back. 'Iouen, you go up. You're freezing.'

His friend did not object.

'You got it?' Katarin's voice.

'We got it,' Iouen answered as he began to climb the ladder onto the deck. Ordes made sure the Bow of Mists was still securely over his arm, and followed Iouen, the taste of dread in his mouth, his stomach churning. The moment he clamoured onto the deck and stepped into the lantern light, a hush fell over the deck; even Katarin, who usually had something to say about everything, was silent.

Jenyfer shoved Arthur aside to get to him, her eyes widening as she took in his wings. She raced forward and threw her arms around his neck, not caring he was dripping wet. Or winged. He closed his arms around her gratefully. Ordes could feel the furious rhythm of her heart beating alongside his.

'It's okay, it's okay,' she whispered against his neck. 'You're safe.'

No one else moved until his father pushed his way between Kat and Tahnet, coming to a halt. 'Oh!' Merlin exclaimed, clapping his hands in excitement. 'Like the ones your mother used to have, only hers were prettier.'

'Get rid of them,' Ordes ordered.

Merlin shook his head. 'I can't.'

'What do you mean you can't?' Ordes shouted, making Jenyfer jump. 'You're the gods-damned power of the world, aren't you?'

'I can't get rid of them because it was your magic that called them into being,' Merlin explained. 'You want them gone, you get rid of them.'

'How do I do that?' Ordes asked from between clenched teeth. It was approaching dawn and he was exhausted. He needed to sleep, but his blood was still burning.

'There is something you all need to know,' Iouen began, as Katarin began ordering the crew to prepare to set sail.

She stopped shouting. A ripple of magic shifted in the air.

Ordes felt it, as did Kat and Jen. They all turned to look at the city. Jen gasped as a plume of red smoke shot from Malist's wharf and into the air. It spun and wove around itself, diving straight for them.

Katarin snarled a warning, her magic pooling in her hands and swirling around her body. Her face promised violence as the smoke landed on the deck of *The Excalibur*. Swiftly, without thinking, Ordes freed the Bow of Mists from his shoulder, notching an arrow as the smoke coalesced into human form.

A figure in a red cloak.

Chapter 23

The figure in red stared them down. Arthur could not see their face, but could feel their eyes. Katarin's magic swirled around her body, silvery-blue light coiled like a spring about to snap. The red-robed person sighed.

'Well, I guess I shouldn't have expected a warm welcome,' a low, female voice said.

Katarin let her magic loose as Ordes fired an arrow. Before either could find purchase, the mystery woman dissolved into red smoke again, reappearing so close to Arthur that he took a hasty step back, fingers fumbling for a sword that was not strapped to his hip. He caught a flash of brown eyes and a smirk before the woman was gone again, materialising behind Ordes, who vanished and reappeared a few feet away, arrow already notched.

Magic rippled across the deck, deep and thick, and the mystery woman froze. Merlin, hands held before him, wandered over to her, his expression deeply curious. He waved his hand and the woman could move her face but nothing more.

'And who might you be?' he asked pleasantly.

She struggled against his magic, her eyes darting between them, until they stopped on Iouen. Her face registered her shock and then, a smile.

'Hello, Iouen,' she managed.

Iouen, dagger still held firm, approached the woman warily. His eyes narrowed, and then widened. 'Olwen?' he breathed.

'Nice to see you,' she said.

'You know her?' Katarin demanded of the quartermaster.

Iouen nodded, face blank with shock. 'She's my sister. I thought she was dead.' He turned to Merlin. 'Let her go. She won't hurt you.'

'I don't know about that,' Katarin said firmly, but Merlin released his hold on the woman. Iouen rushed forward and threw his arms around her. She patted his back soothingly, her dark eyes finding Arthur, and then Katarin.

Kat gestured at the main mast. 'Tie her up.'

Iouen made a noise of protest but said nothing, and his *sister* allowed herself to be secured to the mast by Kayrus, Kat lending a magical hand. Arthur did not take his eyes from the woman, this Olwen. Katarin guarded her, dagger in one hand and magic in the other. If this woman so much as breathed wrong, Arthur knew she would end her, Iouen's long-lost sister or not.

Katarin's face was pale but determined, and Arthur wondered what she was thinking. His sister looked *scared*, and that scared him. He had never seen anyone turn into smoke before. Ordes retained a firm grip on the Bow of Mists, an arrow trained on Olwen.

Arthur jumped as Jalen rested his hand on his shoulder.

It was Iouen who broke the tableau. 'What are you doing here, Olwen?' he asked, his face conflicted, and a spark of pity wormed its way into Arthur's stomach. 'Why aren't you in the Ossuary?'

Halymere's voice rang across the deck, full of authority and disgust. 'Slit her throat and throw her overboard,' he said, folding his arms.

Kat shook her head. 'Questions first,' she said firmly. 'But let's get moving. We've been here long enough and with our new friends below deck, we need to get out of here.'

'You probably should,' Olwen said. 'I mean, I would.'

'What do you know?' Kat demanded.

Olwen shrugged. 'They'll be after you in a few hours. They're preparing the ships. Best get a head start.'

Kat narrowed her eyes. 'How—'

'She sees things that are yet to happen,' Iouen cut in. 'At least, she did.'

'Magic isn't how I know this,' Olwen said quickly. 'The Sacellum is preparing to launch their armada, so unless you all want to end up dead or prisoners of the Sheletari, I'd fill those sails and get out of here. You think you've been undetected out here?'

'Let's go,' Kat said. She turned back to Olwen. 'We will talk later.'

'Can't wait,' the Red Sister said, throwing Kat a wink.

'Watch her,' Kat told Iouen, and then in a low voice to Ordes, 'and you watch him.'

She strode away to the quarterdeck, keeping her eyes on the horizon as Arthur's head spun out of control. A *Red Sister*, a worshipper of Ereshki, was tied to the main mast on their ship. Ordes had wings. Kat and Jenyfer had rescued a woman from a pyre and brought her and her Witchfinder-in-training boyfriend back with them. They had two of the Treasures of the Gods, and now, the Sacellum was coming for them.

He wasn't sure whether to laugh or cry.

At dawn the following morning, the call echoed across the deck, and Arthur's heart sank.

'Sails! Six ships!'

Olwen glanced out to sea, back towards Malist. The Red Sister's soft brown hair hung in wild curls around her shoulders, matching her deep brown eyes. The more Arthur looked, the more he could see Iouen in her face – they shared the same nose and strong brows, but where Iouen's jaw was strong and sharp, Olwen's was softer, decidedly feminine.

Olwen's cold glare, however, held nothing of Iouen's positivity.

She was troubled, her bottom lip between her teeth. She glanced back to sea, her eyes swinging back to his as he cleared his throat and approached her. Olwen had spent the night tied to the mast. When Arthur had sought his bed, Iouen was sitting with her, the siblings not speaking, just staring at one another. Arthur remembered he did a lot of staring at Katarin when he found out who she was to him. He could understand how Iouen must be feeling.

Around them, *The Excalibur's* crew prepared the ship. Arthur glanced up as the sails snapped in the breeze. Iouen was shouting at the men to get the cannons ready.

'The Once and Future King,' Olwen said, her voice low. Arthur raised his eyebrows.

'You know who I am?'

She rolled her eyes. 'You have it written across your face.'

'I'm sorry you had to stay here all night,' Arthur said apologetically. Olwen lifted her eyebrows. 'You knew they were coming, and we thank you for the warning, but why are they following us?'

'Because you stole something important, perhaps?' Olwen said. 'Look, I can help you.'

Katarin scoffed, and Arthur jumped, not realising his sister was standing beside him. 'Unless you want to be sent to the bottom of the sea, shut up,' Kat said.

'If I wanted any of you dead, if the Red One wanted any of you dead, you'd be dead by now. We knew you were here ever since you arrived.' She stopped, her eyes finding her brother. 'Except I didn't know he was here.'

Sensing his sister's gaze, Iouen hurried over, but it was Kat he addressed.

'Can't this ship go any faster?' His expression was troubled, and it looked like he hadn't slept at all. Arthur supposed no one had.

Katarin scowled. 'We fight.'

Arthur raised his eyebrows. 'We do?'

Kat nodded. 'I'm sick of these bastards. We make a stand, and we send them to the depths. Here and now, right on their own fucking doorstep.'

No one said anything, until Iouen pulled at his hair.

'We're one ship against six,' he shouted.

'I can count, thanks,' Katarin said, patting him on the shoulder. 'We've got some of the most powerful Magic Wielders in Teyath on this ship.'

Arthur nodded, although his stomach squirmed with fear. 'Alright. We need a plan.'

'No, you are not involved, little brother,' Katarin said.

'Kat—'

She shook her head. 'Not happening.'

Arthur ran his hand through his hair, aware that the Red Sister was watching them with interest. 'You can't expect me to hide while others fight for me.'

'That's exactly what I expect,' Katarin declared.

'I can fight,' Arthur protested, loud enough that Halymere heard him.

The Inborn shook his head, coming over. 'You heard what Merlin said. Once you draw the Sword of the White Dragon, you will not be able to stop.'

'Oh, you've got the Sword, too,' Olwen commented.

'Shut it,' Kat hissed. The Red Sister shrugged, completely unfazed by Katarin's threats. Kat kept her eyes on the approaching ships, then called Ordes and the others over. With a suspicious glance at Olwen, she motioned them away from the Red Sister.

'Right. We let them get close enough to board us—' Kat began, to a chorus of objection. She jammed her hands on her hips and raised her eyebrows. 'I have done this before,' she said. 'We let them close, and then we sink them.'

Stunned silence met her words. Arthur cleared his throat, but before he could speak, Iouen made a choking sound.

'How?' he spluttered.

Kat nodded at Jen and Ordes. 'With them. Syhrens destroyed *The Queen*. You can do that to those ships out there, Jenyfer,' Kat said.

Jenyfer swallowed audibly, but nodded, her lips a thin, determined line.

'Ordes, get that pretty head of yours focused. Yes, I know you're freaked out by those things sticking out of your back – I am too, to be honest – but I've seen what you could do before you had any idea of what you were. So, you're our defence when – *if* –the cannons fail,' Katarin said.

Arthur watched his sister, the way she lit up as she took command, as she pulled them back from the chaos of the previous night. Katarin's face was bright, her eyes shining, even as they faced their possible doom. He couldn't help but share Iouen's sentiments.

'Hello, powerful Magic Wielder here,' Olwen sang.

'Shut. Up,' Katarin snarled. 'Iouen, take your *sister* below deck and tie her up.'

'Kat,' Arthur objected. 'Surely—'

'Do it!'

Olwen grinned. 'No need. I'll behave,' she added, holding up her hands in surrender.

The hands that had been bound tightly to the mast, with both rope and magic.

They all gaped at her, until Jalen chuckled. 'She can come with me.'

'A demi-god,' Olwen said in mock awe; she sketched a bow. 'I've never met one of you before.'

'Keep watch on the others, demon,' Kat ordered. 'And where the fuck did Merlin go?'

'Others? What sort of ship is this?' Olwen asked.

Jalen rolled his eyes, striding across the deck to grab her around the upper arm. As she was being led away, she winked at Kat, who turned away, gritting her teeth. When she turned back around, everyone was watching her expectantly.

'Let's do this,' she said. She met Arthur's eyes. 'You want to fight? Keep that sword of yours under control, then.'

Arthur nodded, his heart jumping. 'I won't draw it,' he said; in the depths of his mind, he could hear the Sword, as if it knew what was coming. It urged him to release it, but he pushed the compulsion away with effort. 'But I'll keep it with me, just in case.'

Katarin raised her eyebrows at the unspoken suggestion this could all go wrong, and then hurried off to prepare her ship for a one against six sea-battle. Arthur watched his sister go, the confidence in her bearing as she marched across the deck, shouting at people. He snuck a glance at Ordes. Those wings were still there. The other man sensed Arthur's gaze; their eyes met briefly, before Ordes turned away.

On the horizon, moving steadily closer, was the Sacellum's armada.

CHAPTER 24

It was Mordred who came to collect her that morning, not Bryn. Lamorna breathed a sigh of relief when she opened the door to his face. He swept inside and kissed her, and she wound her arms around him, pressing herself as close as possible.

'We don't have time for that,' he murmured against her mouth. 'My uncle wishes to test me on the Word, and I want you there.'

'Oh?' she said. 'Why?'

'Because he expects me to fail, and I want you to see his face when he realises I know his blasted book inside and out,' Mordred said. 'I told you I wanted to play my games *with* you, Lamorna, and this is truly the start of them.'

Lamorna pulled away from him, going to fetch her cap from the table. 'Has he invited me?'

'No,' Mordred said.

She swallowed, securing the cap over her hair, but Mordred shook his head. She held still as he removed the cap, followed by the pins that held her hair in place. Unleashed, it flowed freely down her back, and as Mordred arranged it around her shoulders for her, his touch gentle, something inside her slithered away, leaving her feeling bold and full of courage. She had the sudden desire to see her reflection, to see whether this new Lamorna looked the way she imagined she did. But there was no mirror, so she had to trust the feeling in her chest instead.

He kissed her gently. 'I'll meet you there,' he said, and then he was gone, leaving her to make the walk through town alone. She wished they didn't have to hide, but she also knew that it was dangerous not to. She had already been tied to a stake once, and did not want to repeat the experience anytime soon – her sister would not be here to save her.

Would Mordred save me instead? she wondered, then cursed herself, mentally stomping on the little worm of doubt that worked its way into her belly. Of course he would.

He loved her. Didn't he? He'd never actually said the words, but she felt it each time he kissed her. But she also had nothing to compare it to, so maybe she was wrong.

By the time she reached the Chif's house, Lamorna was frowning and tied up in knots, all her earlier happiness and confidence gone. People had stared at her as she'd crossed the town square. She had kept her chin lifted, her gaze straight ahead, but still had felt their eyes like a flame on her back as she passed, trailing the sway of her loose hair.

She was met at the door by a member of the Red Hand, a man she didn't know and didn't care to know, but she could sense his judgement and wished she had not been so brave, or so foolish, to think she could do this.

It's just hair, she reminded herself. *Just hair. Why should it matter?*

But it did matter, and when the Chif saw her, his lips pursed and his eyes darkened with anger. However, he held his tongue, perhaps because Mordred was already there. Lamorna took comfort in that, some of her anxiety easing. The Chif ushered her into the formal room, where a chair was waiting for her. Mordred did not sit until she did.

Lamorna watched the Chif from beneath her lashes as she arranged her skirts. His spine was rigid, and his fingers flexed against his rich, red coat. He hesitated, and then sat at the head of the table, clearing his throat.

Lamorna tensed, waiting for him to reprimand her, but when he spoke, it was not to her, but to Mordred.

He was pretending she wasn't there. Like Jenyfer used to do, when they were younger and their aunt forced her and Bryn to take Lamorna with them on their adventures around town. Lamorna remembered what that felt like, and she did not like it one bit.

The Chif asked after Mordred's lessons. He quizzed Mordred on the Word, and Mordred answered each question correctly. He had been hoping she would fail. She could tell by the way his eyes narrowed. Ulrian shot Lamorna a quick look, his gaze lingering on her hair.

Lamorna smoothed her hands over the table-top and as the Chif opened his mouth again, she spoke over him. 'Do you know where your son is?' She made sure her voice was steady and clear, that her tone left no space for him to chastise her for speaking out of turn.

'No,' he answered, his tone short. He would not look at her.

Lamorna smiled. 'Mordred can help you find him.'

The silence was thick and heavy and dripping with the man's conflicted emotions.

'With magic,' the Chif growled.

'Yes,' she said. 'With magic.'

The Chif turned to Mordred, displeasure written all over his face. 'You are not here to work your sorcery. You are here to learn, and then you will help me in the One God's work. That is what we agreed.'

'I won't hunt my own kind,' Mordred said bluntly; the Chif's face tightened to hear his ambitions spoken so plainly. 'If there are Magic Wielders here and you want them, find them yourself.'

'Then what use are you to me?' the Chif demanded.

'The good people of this town look to you for answers, Uncle. For the moment, at least,' Mordred said.

'Are you threatening me, Mordred?' Ulrian asked after a pause.

'Not at all,' Mordred said, leaving the truth of the matter unsaid – *I don't have to.*

Both Lamorna and Mordred knew the Chif was wary of him, of his reasons for being here. Despite Mordred doing all the Chif had asked, Ulrian did not trust him.

Ulrian's frown was deep. 'The people of this town respect me. They know I look out for them, and they know it will be me who delivers them into something greater.'

Mordred tapped his fingers on the tabletop. 'Perhaps. But your enemies are out there. The enemies of the One God are out there. Your son, for instance.'

'Arthur is no enemy of mine,' Ulrian began.

'Arthur is the prophesied King of the heathen Cruitheans, and all those left in Teyath who still believe in the Old Ones,' Lamorna said. The Chif fought to contain his shock. 'You didn't know? I assumed a man as learned as yourself would have heard of the Myrddin's prophecy.'

'Perhaps, it is time you asked for *my* help, Uncle,' Mordred said.

'I don't need your help,' Ulrian managed. 'I don't believe a word of this.'

'It's true,' Lamorna said pleasantly. 'Arthur told me himself. In Cruithea.'

'He was there?' Ulrian breathed. 'With … her?'

'If you mean my mother, then yes, with her,' Mordred said. 'She liked him. Treated him like a son,' he added, the words dripping with bitterness. Lamorna touched Mordred's leg under the table; he flashed her a look, a tiny smile dancing across his lips so quickly she thought she had imagined it.

Mordred shook his head. 'My relationship with my mother is complicated, but the things Lamorna has taught me, about the One God, have made me view the world differently. I am prepared to renounce my mother and the land of my birth – for you, Uncle. You have your Konsel and your Red Hand, but they are not warriors, and you may need warriors. We need to know what those who are helping Arthur are planning. We need to be able to see what is coming for us before it arrives.'

Ulrian was silent, his eyes turned towards the table, but he was listening.

'I will not abandon you, Uncle. You're family. I will stay here, and continue to help you with your good work, and perhaps, one day, you will trust me,' Mordred said. 'At least, that is what I wish.' When the Chif did not respond, he stood. 'If that is all, I shall walk Lamorna home. I will return later,' he added. Lamorna placed her hand in his and let him guide her to her feet. The Chif's face was downcast.

He did not say another word.

'The knowledge of Arthur being the prophesied King will be enough for the moment,' Mordred said. 'Let him stew on that for a while.'

'Will it really bother him that much?' Lamorna asked. It was the middle of the day. She should be out tending the garden, but she did not want to move and wondered if it was possible to stay where she was for the rest of her days. Her heartbeat was slowly retreating, the sweat drying on her skin.

Mordred rolled onto his side, facing her. His expression was soft, but his eyes were determined. 'Ulrian has spent his life shaping Arthur into the future leader of this place, and now he has discovered his legacy is about to end. I don't know if that means anything for you, but I know that for a man like Ulrian, the knowledge that his only son is now lost to him will sink inside him like a poison, eating away at him until there is nothing left.'

Lamorna frowned. 'Are you sure?'

'Trust me,' Mordred said, running his fingers down her bare arm. 'Legacy is something I understand all too well.'

'Mordred,' Lamorna said. She was unsure if she should ask. 'If you are not going to be the future leader of Cruithea, then who is?'

'My cousin,' he said eventually. 'Morgaine. She doesn't want it, but she did, once.' He shifted onto his back and stared at the ceiling. She had the sudden urge to ask him whether he liked her cottage, or if he preferred his kibitka. If he missed anything about Cruithea at all. 'It became a point of tension between us, and I sometimes wish that it hadn't. She was taken from our home by Ulrian before I could apologise for being cruel to her, for being jealous.'

'He brought her here?' Lamorna asked. She sat up so she could see his face when he spoke. His eyes met hers. 'So how did she end up being a pirate? How had I never met her before Cruithea?'

'Because Ulrian tied her to the stake, like he did you.'

Lamorna sucked in a breath and her heart began to race again. It was not pleasure that drove that furious rhythm this time, but fear and anger combined, a swirling mass rushing through her.

'She was a child,' Mordred continued.

Lamorna did not ask any more questions. She recalled Mordred telling her this story before, how the Chif sacrificed the girl for his dying wife, feeding her to the sea. She sat there, fuelled by anger, thinking of the woman she had met in Cruithea, of her bold smile and her fierce eyes. She recalled everything she had ever heard of Katarin Le Fey, every story Jenyfer had ever told her of the pirate Captain's bravery and her daring, her fortitude and strength.

Ulrian had tried to kill a child.

And that child had grown into a powerful woman.

At that moment, Lamorna decided that she would be a woman like Katarin Le Fey. She might not be a pirate, nor did she want to be, but Lamorna could still be brave – braver than she had already been. She would play whatever games Mordred asked of her, and she would play them with one outcome in mind.

The end of Ulrian Tregarthen's lies.

Chapter 25

Jenyfer pulled her lip between her teeth and gnawed on it. Katarin expected her to *sink ships with her voice*. She had no idea how to do that, but while part of her panicked, another part, the part that had emerged in Skulls Rest and again in the amphitheatre in Malist, was bouncing beneath her skin in anticipation.

She could do this.

She wasn't sure how, but she could.

The Sacellum's ships were within firing range. Ordes, hands held out before him, had conjured a shield of magic around the starboard side of the ship. Jenyfer had seen him do it before, but this time, the magic was stronger. She could feel it threaded through the air, like a vibration, a hum that sank into her blood.

Ordes had wings. They weren't feathered like a bird, but were made of what looked like silver mist. Jenyfer could see the shock of it still branded on his face, even as he did what Katarin asked and protected the ship. She studied the wings, noting the way the sunlight passed straight through them. When she'd touched them, it had been like touching air. Ordes had told her in a quiet voice he'd shifted his shape, and she knew that scared him more than wings or sea battles ever could.

The boom from the closest of the enemy ships' cannons echoed across the water, pulling Jenyfer back to the present. Ordes' shield took the impact; he rocked on his heels, but the magic held. Jenyfer scurried back from the railing as another round was fired in their direction, crashing into the shield. Smoke from the cannons drifted across the water. They'd been exchanging fire for twenty minutes already, and despite Katarin's plan, the Sacellum's ships did not come any closer, waiting until they were out of ammunition and magic to launch their final assault. Kat had ordered the gunners to aim for the enemy ships' rigging and sails; one ship was disabled, dead in the water, but another had quickly taken its place and was continuing to return fire.

'Orders?' Iouen shouted, as chain shot collided with the shield of silver light. Jenyfer wasn't sure how much longer Ordes could hold. She could see the tension in his shoulders and jaw, but his expression was determined.

'I am sick of this shit,' Katarin growled. 'Drown the bastards – and *where the fuck is Merlin?*'

Iouen nodded. 'Aye aye, Captain.' The quartermaster turned to the waiting crew. Jenyfer took note of the men's faces – she did not find fear there, but resolution. This ship was their home, and now it was under threat.

It was Jenyfer's home too. Anger was a blinding white flash in her veins. That night on *The Queen* crashed into her head. Her magic crooned in response to the memory.

'Cannons!' Iouen shouted.

Before another shot could be fired, before the fuses could be lit, Merlin materialised between Jenyfer and Ordes. She jumped, but Ordes kept his hands steady and held the shield in place.

'Where have you been?' he demanded, but Jenyfer could hear the relief in his voice.

His father ran a critical eye over the magical shield. 'Dig deeper – solidify it. Round shot would get through that, unless you've made it heatproof. It needs to be stronger.'

'Why don't you do something, then?' Jenyfer snapped.

'I'm not supposed to interfere anymore than I already have, but fine,' Merlin said. He waved his hand lazily. The nearest ship was engulfed in a wall of water – the distraught shouts of the crew rang out as the ship rocked dangerously, before it toppled and was eaten by the ocean.

'About fucking time!' Kat's voice rang out as a cheer went up amongst the crew.

The Sacellum's remaining five ships took Merlin's action as a signal to increase their own attack. They moved closer with alarming speed, their sails catching a wind that was stronger than the one that filled *The Excalibur's* sails.

'They've got a wind-slinger with them, the bastards,' Melhala called, lowering a spyglass. The Cruithean was standing on the quarterdeck with Kayrus, whose face was set in hard lines.

Katarin groaned. 'Just what we need – an air elemental with that sort of power working for the Sacellum.'

'We need to get into open water,' Merlin called to her. 'If we can make them chase us, we—'

'How?' Iouen gestured at the sails, hanging limp. Arthur was at his side, eyes wide, brown curls dangling in his eyes.

Merlin nodded at Ordes. 'He can do it.'

'I'm a little busy!' Ordes yelled.

Merlin put his hand on Ordes' shoulder. 'Forget the sails. Forget the shield. Move the ship.'

Ordes turned to his father in disbelief. 'Are you serious? We're under attack, and you want to teach me to use my magic *now*? What if it doesn't work?'

Merlin's expression was stern. 'Move. The. Ship. You can do this,' he added, gentler now. 'Pull the magic from the air around you – it's saturated with it. Use the power of Melodias' realm.'

Jenyfer frowned. 'What do you mean?'

The Excalibur's cannons exploded around them.

'Your father rules the sea – it's his domain, but not his alone. Ordes, Goerika told you what I am. She told you what *you* are. You can control the elements. *All* of them. Move the ship,' Merlin repeated.

Ordes glanced at Jenyfer; she nodded. It seemed impossible, but all that had happened since she'd left Kernou seemed impossible, and if that could be real, then so could this. 'Can I help?' she asked Merlin. 'Melodias' magic is my magic, right?'

Merlin tapped his chin. 'We want a tempest to distract them, and we need to be out there,' he added, gesturing at the open ocean. 'You could sing us a storm, but …'

She nodded and lay her hand on Ordes' forearm, sensing the magic flowing through him – it shifted beneath his skin like a living thing. 'Ordes, you can do this.'

Ordes let out a breath, then lowered his hands. The magical shield dissolved immediately; Katarin's head whipped around, hair swinging wildly.

'What the fuck, Ordes?' She conjured a wave and sent it hurtling towards the nearest ship as *The Excalibur*, no longer protected, took a hit. Splintering timber echoed across the deck. The Sacellum's ships were close, aided by the Witchfinders, the air and water elementals snatched from Cruithea.

Melhala called out as another cannon was fired. *The Excalibur* returned fire.

'Ordes!' Katarin shouted.

For a long time, nothing happened. The world was smoke and water and explosions. Shattered timber and shouting. Adrenalin pooled in Jenyfer's mouth. She kept her eyes on Ordes, her song poised to fight, to protect, to rip the world to pieces. Around them, Melhala, Ethinne, and Kat protected the ship with magic, while the crew manned the cannons.

The Excalibur suddenly shuddered.

The hair stood up on Jenyfer's arms.

Magic undulated through the air. It raced across the water like a wave, flowing over the sides of the ship to coil around Ordes like a snake, before it slipped beneath his skin. The sky darkened, storm clouds rolling in from nowhere.

The ship shifted.

Jenyfer took a step back as the air around Ordes became a swirling mass of silver mist. His wings curled around him, now dark like storm clouds, veined with lightning. Wind tore at her clothes and hair; she glanced up at the snap of sailcloth. The sails filled, *The Excalibur* groaned, then they were moving. A wall of water soared into the air from the ocean behind them. It hovered there and then began to break. *The Excalibur* shot forward. Distantly, cannon fire echoed across the ocean, but they were well out of range.

Jenyfer pushed the hair out of her eyes. Storm clouds cloaked the sky above them and the sails were pulled taut with the ferocity of the wind. Rain pelted their faces as *The Excalibur* suddenly stopped, timbers groaning. The wave collapsed behind them, hitting the face of the ocean like a punch. Water surged over the sides, sweeping people off their feet. Jenyfer found herself laughing as the storm clouds vanished, and the wind died to a gentle breeze.

Ordes opened his eyes. He met Jenyfer's astonished gaze and smiled, before he turned to face his father. 'Happy now?' he asked, his wings folding away. The ship dripped with water and dumbfounded silence.

Merlin's smile was broad, and Jenyfer realised she had never seen him truly smile – she'd seen smirks and a crooked grin, but never true happiness, swelled with pride. For a moment, he was a man proud of his son, nothing more.

Katarin rushed over, pushing her sopping hair from her face and almost tripping on one of the sailors as she went. She was saturated, and as Jenyfer looked around, she realised everyone was dripping wet. Some people were picking themselves up off the sodden deck.

'That was brilliant. Absolutely fucking brilliant,' Kat shouted.

'Is that a compliment?' Ordes asked, making her laugh.

'It's whatever you want it to be,' Kat said. She glanced back at the Witchfinders' ships; the Sacellum's armada had not given up, but they were behind them now. 'You bought us some time, at least. Iouen,' she called. The quartermaster hurried over, eyes wide. 'Damage?' Kat asked.

'We'll need to patch it up, but we're not taking on water yet,' Iouen answered.

Katarin nodded, turning to Jenyfer. 'Are you ready? Because once they get here, we sink them, understand? We don't want them following us all the way to The Teeth. Witchfinders don't give up, so we'll take the choice out of their hands.'

She moved away, checking in on those who manned the cannons.

Ordes had not conjured his shield again. Jenyfer slipped her hand in his.

'That was impressive, but I still like your flower better,' she said. He laughed.

The crew scrambled about, checking the rigging, rolling cannons to their exposed port side. Some of the men cried out as Merlin transformed into a bird and took flight, soaring towards the Sacellum's ships. Jenyfer kept her eyes on him until she lost sight of him in the sunlight, and she wasn't sure she took another breath until he returned.

'At least five Witchfinders per ship,' he announced, brushing feathers from his sleeves.

'You'd think they were worried about something,' Kat replied, pushing her damp hair off her neck. 'That's a lot of magic. Alright, same plan as before. Drop the sails and let them get close. Let them think we're dead in the water.'

There was no objection this time. Iouen immediately began shouting at the crew.

'I think he likes his job,' Ordes commented.

Merlin was standing with his hands on his hips, long coat flapping in the breeze. He glanced over his shoulder and met Jenyfer's eyes. 'It's your turn, Daughter of the Sea. Unleash yourself, and show us what you can do. Don't hold back, Jenyfer. Let it all go.'

Jenyfer nodded and made her way onto the quarterdeck, heart pounding, adrenaline coating the back of her throat. From the quarterdeck, she could see the other ships spread out across the water. She felt Kayrus glance at her.

Ordes had resumed his position in the middle of the deck, ready to reform their shield as the Sacellum's ships sailed within range. The gunners were waiting, fuses ready, but Katarin did not give the order to fire.

'Captain?' Iouen called, but she held up her hand, a signal to wait.

The Sacellum's ships drew closer.

'Stand down the cannons!' Katarin shouted, then, 'It's your show, syhren.'

The crew dropped what they were doing and slammed their hands over their ears.

Kayrus had not let go of the wheel. Jenyfer placed her hands over his, lifted them free. 'I don't want to hurt you,' she said. 'I won't let them take the ship, I promise.'

The old man nodded and put his hands over his ears.

Jenyfer turned to face the Sacellum's ships.

The sea fell silent, the waves calm, as still and smooth as glass. Wind tugged at their hair and the sails, but *The Excalibur* did not move.

When Jenyfer opened her mouth, the world exploded into music.

Melodies tumbled over one another as timber splintered and sailcloth tore. She didn't think about what she sang, allowing instinct to control her magic. Dark grey clouds with purple underbellies swooped in to eclipse the sun once more. Waves like mountains crashed onto decks and ripped their way through bodies. Screams rent the air, the sound another layer to the song Jenyfer sung as her power surged through her, deep and dark and raw with emotion.

This ship was her home. These people were her family and she would not let them be taken. If the Witchfinders did not succumb to her voice, they would succumb to the waves as Katarin, Ethinne, and Melhala unleashed their magic, silver and blue light streaking through the sky, wrapping itself around the magic in Jenyfer's song. She could see the notes in the air, watching them hovering before they soared into the sky and smashed their way through ships and men like they were made of sand.

Jenyfer was the storm. She was the soaring crescendo and the hypnotic silence that slipped into the minute spaces between notes. She sang until her throat was raw, and the last man was embraced by the water.

'See what's in the hold we can claim as a prize,' Katarin instructed, landing beside Jenyfer on the deck. The ship was the one – it had been the furthest away, at the back of the pack, which saved her from sinking but not from damage.

Kayrus had guided *The Excalibur* through the wreckage strewn across the face of the ocean, pulling up alongside *The Angel*. Her sails were limp, dangling from the masts like wet sheets. The ship was silent, eerie in the haze of destruction that hung over the ocean.

No one challenged them as they boarded, its crew all face-down in the sea, having flung themselves from the deck of their ship as Jenyfer's song washed over them.

She could still feel her magic ploughing through her, stronger and more powerful than it had been in Malist. She had begun to understand something else about her voice – whenever she used her syhren magic, it came back stronger, more precise. She could control it, aim it, like a weapon.

Like the weapon Andromache told her it was. Jenyfer swallowed. Did the syhrens who drowned men and destroyed ships for sport ever think about the people they'd killed? She already knew the answer – they were her father's puppets, and Melodias cared nothing for the human realm.

The door to the captain's cabin hung from one hinge. Barrels and crates were scattered across the deck. Jenyfer ducked beneath shredded sailcloth, avoiding the dangling rigging that swayed gently. The timbers of the deck looked like they had been lifted and dropped back down – there were gaps revealing the flooded belly of the ship, bodies floating there amongst the debris. Jenyfer swallowed and stepped away.

Her magic had done this.

Iouen had drawn his pistol and moved off into the shadows that draped themselves across the deck. Jenyfer held her breath, waiting, but there was no sign of life except for those of their crew who had begun boarding the ship.

Ordes materialised beside her – his wings had vanished.

'I saw you cover your ears,' she said.

'Not at first,' he replied, indignant. 'But then, your magic made me want to jump in the sea. It wasn't like Skulls Rest. I knew you were fine, you were safe, and the heartfire knew it, so I was as vulnerable as the rest of them.' He paused, running his eyes over her face searchingly. 'Are you alright?'

She nodded, taking a deep breath. 'I know what I've done, Ordes. Perhaps, in ending their lives, I've saved more than ours today.'

He kissed her cheek; she leant against him, suddenly exhausted.

'Over here!' Iouen's voice cut through the gloom.

Jenyfer and Ordes hurried across the deck, following the sound of Iouen's voice, and found him standing over a dazed and confused man, the ship's captain. His chest rose and fell, but was still enthralled by Jenyfer's magic. He wore a blissful smile, and was tied to the main mast, fingers bloody with rope burn.

'What do we do with him?' Iouen asked.

Ordes crouched to stare into the Captain's face. 'Untie him. Leave him enough food and water for at least a week. Disable the helm. He'll drift back to shore, or somewhere.' He glanced up at the torn sails. 'If he's lucky, that is. She won't sail, but she'll float.'

'Ordes,' Iouen objected.

'Look at him,' Ordes mumbled. He waved his hand in front of the man's face. His expression did not shift. 'It would be like shooting him in the back.'

'Plus,' Katarin put in, coming up behind them, 'he gets to return home and tell the tale of how we kicked their arses.'

'I don't think that's the song he'll sing,' Jenyfer mumbled. 'He'll find some way to make this a victory of the One God's.' Katarin raised her eyebrows in disbelief and Jenyfer shrugged. 'All I can say is that every bad thing that happened in Kernou was because of the One God and Ulrian Tregarthen, but that man still made it seem like it was a blessing.' She nodded at the captain of *The Angel*. 'He'll do the same, or if not him, someone else will twist what happened here today.'

They could hear the men below deck. The dazed captain did not so much as blink, and the smile never slipped from his lips. Ordes withdrew his dagger and sliced through the rope that held the man securely to the mast. The crew made their way back to *The Excalibur*, a few boxes and crates carried between them. There wasn't much to salvage.

'Cut us loose,' Katarin ordered, leaping onto the gangplank. The sun was setting, the sky a glorious mix of gold and red, the light bleeding to blue and violet at the edges, and suddenly all Jenyfer wanted was to sleep.

She headed for the gangplank, feet stumbling. Ordes scooped her into his arms. Jenyfer closed her eyes and when she opened them again, she was on the deck of *The Excalibur*.

Chapter 26

There hadn't been any time for Katarin to process that they'd taken on six armed ships and won. The wreckage of the Sacellum's armada was behind them, and *The Excalibur* was headed north, drawing closer to The Teeth.

She shuddered. She'd heard stories about the creatures in The Teeth her whole life. She wished she could offer Jenyfer some encouragement, some relief about what she would find there, but there was nothing Katarin could say. Worry crawled over her skin like insects.

If the inhabitants of The Teeth were human, that worry would be unfounded, but she knew, as Jenyfer did, that her magic was unlikely to affect the creatures who called those rocky islands home.

They had at least a week of sailing in the Catigern Sea before The Teeth came into sight. A week for Jenyfer to sit and think and prepare for the unknown. The syhren was sleeping still, which Katarin did not find surprising. The magic that Jenyfer had unleashed would have put Katarin on her back for days. Magic was not an unending well. It was part of who and what a Magic Wielder was, and it needed to rest and recover. Using so much magic at once took a toll, especially for one not used to it.

Kat glanced across the deck to where Ordes and Arthur stood, deep in conversation. Ordes should be sleeping, she thought, but his eyes were alert. She shook her head, barely able to believe what had happened. Ordes had moved *The Excalibur* through the water like it was a child's toy. And then Jenyfer had opened her mouth and destroyed four ships with her voice.

The Night Queen had never stood a chance.

But she could not dwell on what had passed, only what was to come. She would start with the prisoners in the hold.

Katarin went to find Iouen, asking him to bring his sister to her cabin. He gave her a suspicious look, before hurrying off, while Katarin collected Ordes, her brother, and Merlin.

'I miss this place,' Merlin commented, glancing around the cabin. He met Kat's eyes. 'But I'm happy where I am.'

'Where do you sleep?' she asked him. They stood side by side, looking out the window at the ocean. Stars winked overhead, and moonlight painted the water a shimmering silver.

'I don't,' he replied. 'Like our demi-god, I don't need to.'

Katarin glanced over her shoulder. She hadn't invited Jalen into her cabin, but the storm demon was there anyway, a brooding presence lingering near her brother's shoulder. She turned away, frowning. 'Something's not right with him,' she murmured.

Merlin's reply was quiet. 'He's bound to Niniane, Kat. Like you are. But it's different for him. You had the freedom to choose. Jalen doesn't. Remember that.'

She narrowed her eyes. 'What aren't you saying?'

Before Merlin could respond, the door opened and Iouen ushered his sister in. Olwen's eyes soaked up every detail, her red robes so reminiscent of blood that it made Katarin uneasy. She knew next to nothing about the Red Sisters and their worship of Ereshki.

'Well,' Olwen said. 'This is fancy.'

'Sit.' Kat pointed at the seat on the other side of the desk. The Red Sister did what she was told, Iouen remaining at her side. Merlin stood behind Katarin, and she was oddly comforted by his support. Olwen's magic was unknown to Katarin, and that made her nervous. What the Red Sisters learnt in the House of Bone was never spoken of in Cruithea, and from what Katarin had witnessed, Merlin was the only one of them powerful enough to subdue Olwen if necessary.

The Red Sister was watching Katarin.

'What?' Katarin demanded.

'Nothing,' Olwen said. 'It's only, you're prettier in real life.'

Kat snorted to cover her surprise. 'Oh, so you've heard of me in the House of Bone, have you?'

'I haven't been in the House of Bone for a long time,' Olwen said, her voice low.

'So, where have you been, then?' Iouen asked. He had his arms folded, a frown on his face. Now that the battle with the Witchfinders was over, Kat could only imagine what was going through his mind.

'Malist. For years now.'

'Why?' Kat demanded. The door to her cabin eased open. She was about to reprimand whoever it was for their interruption, but when she saw Halymere, the darkness on his face and the look in his eyes as they settled on Olwen, she didn't tell him to leave.

Another support she hadn't realised she needed.

Halymere joined Arthur, siting on the edge of Katarin's bed. Ordes, the show-off, had conjured himself a chair.

'I want to speak to my sister first,' Iouen said suddenly.

'Fine, but you do it in front of the rest of us,' Katarin replied. Iouen looked like he'd argue, but then he sighed and turned his attention to Olwen.

'Father?' he asked tightly.

'Dead,' she replied.

Iouen's swallow was audible in the hollow silence of the cabin.

Olwen smiled. 'I was told I wasn't to interfere, but I've never been good at doing what I'm told, have I? I went to visit him. He thought I was there to bless him, that the Red One had sent me. He'd taken a new wife, you know. She did nothing as I ripped the blood from his veins and left him lying in a pool of it. I don't think she minded. She had the same look you used to have, brother.'

Ordes made a noise in the back of his throat. 'He beat his children?'

'He beat Iouen,' Olwen corrected. 'He wouldn't lay a hand on me. My brother didn't tell you that, I assume?'

'No,' Ordes said quietly.

Iouen was looking at his hands, clasped tightly at his chest.

'We always said we'd kill him, didn't we?' Olwen said.

'Yes,' he whispered.

'None of this explains why you're here,' Katarin cut in. *Ripped the blood from his veins?* What had she let on her ship?

'We know about the prophecy,' Olwen said. 'My mistress was there when it was spoken, after all.'

'She stole the Treasures before this, though, didn't she?' Arthur asked. Next to him, Jalen tensed, the storm demon's jaw so tight Kat thought it might shatter.

'Stole is a strong word,' Olwen muttered.

Halymere was eying Olwen with open distaste. 'We can't listen to a word it says.'

'It?' Olwen laughed. 'Do you know how easy it would be for me to snuff out your existence, Inborn?'

'Do you know how easy it would be for me to slit your throat?' Kat rejoined.

'Enough,' Arthur ordered. 'This isn't helping. We need to focus on what comes next.'

'No, you need to listen to me first,' the Red Sister said bluntly. 'Because you need to know exactly what you're going to do once you have all the

Treasures and find the Grail. But before you can decide that, there are things you must understand.'

'Like what?' Ordes said.

Olwen did not look at him. She turned her sharp, brown gaze on Merlin, standing behind Katarin. 'Like exactly what you're walking into and exactly who you're walking into it for.'

A shiver crawled down Katarin's spine.

Merlin's chuckle was soft. 'Is there something you want to ask me?'

'It depends,' Olwen said, just as soft, just as smooth, 'on how much you've bothered to tell them.'

All eyes swung to Merlin. 'Send my regards to your mistress,' was all he said.

Kat could feel the argument brewing, and she wasn't sure she wanted the strongest Magic Wielder in Teyath and a powerful Red Sister to come to blows in her cabin. Whatever Merlin was hiding, she would find out later, but there were other things that needed to be sorted out. She gave the Prophet of the Gods a warning look over her shoulder, then folded her arms. 'Enough. We need to focus on The Teeth. And we need to work out what to do with the other two,' she added. 'Iouen, can you bring them up for me? I want to ask some questions.'

He nodded, and hurried from the cabin.

Kat shared a quick look with Ordes. His lips curled in acknowledgement of what she had done – given the quartermaster time to collect his thoughts. Kat knew what it was like to suddenly discover a family she thought were long gone.

Olwen was watching her again.

'You,' Kat barked. 'Move.'

'Does that mean you won't be throwing me to the sharks?' the woman asked.

'Not today,' Kat replied.

'Oh, thank you, fearsome Captain,' Olwen breathed, dramatically wiping her brow in sarcastic relief. Ordes chuckled as Olwen stood and gave Kat a mock curtsy, before stepping away to examine the bottles on the top of one of Kat's cupboards. Kat half expected the woman to pour herself a glass of rum.

No one spoke while waiting for Iouen to return. Once the novice Witchfinder and his girlfriend were standing on the other side of Katarin's desk, she indicated the empty chair. Isolde sat, pushing her blonde hair over her shoulder, her blue eyes darting nervously around the room before settling on Katarin.

'Talk,' Kat demanded. 'Explain to me why I risked my life to rescue the wife of a Sacellum official from the pyre he had built in her honour?'

Isolde lifted her chin. 'There was no love between us, but my husband was a powerful man with connections. That was enough for my mother. My happiness meant nothing to her. I endured because what other choice did I have? And then,' her voice softened as Tristan's hand came to rest on her shoulder, 'I met Tristan. I did not plan any of it, but how do you plan for love?'

The question was met with silence; the only sound was Olwen rifling through the contents of Kat's bookshelf. Katarin ground her teeth. Isolde resumed her story. 'We were careful,' she said, 'but not careful enough. When we were discovered, Mark ordered my execution to cover up the shame of having a faithless wife – and for refusing to give up my lover's identity.'

Tristan's face was hard. 'Once they came for her, that was it – I didn't care if they caught me. I wanted to save her. And then you were there, an answer to my prayers.'

Kat scoffed. 'I hardly think the One God sent me.'

Olwen was thumbing through a book she'd pilfered from Katarin's shelf when she piped up. 'The Red One sent you.'

'Shut up,' Kat snapped. 'Do I have to gag you?'

'It depends on what you use,' Olwen replied. 'Rope is harsh and scratchy. Got any silk?' Olwen shifted her attention to Tristan before

Kat could respond, tossing the book on the bed near where Arthur was sitting. 'So it was you two they were after?' Olwen asked.

'I'm sorry, but who gave you permission to question my prisoners?' Kat demanded, folding her arms.

Olwen shrugged. Kat bit the inside of her cheek and clenched her fingers in the fabric of her shirt to stop herself from flying across the room and ramming her fist down the Red Sister's throat.

'I know you,' Iouen said suddenly, nodding at Tristan. Olwen glanced over, interested. 'You're from Kunis, aren't you? Your family were poor farmers, but Mark was your uncle, wasn't he?'

Tristan nodded as Olwen chuckled.

'The Sacellum pay well for their Sheletari slaves,' she said. 'More money than a farmer from Kunis would ever see in ten generations.'

'So your parents get rich, you get trained as a Witchfinder, steal your uncle's bride – what are we meant to do with you?' Kat asked Tristan.

'We could come with you,' Isolde suggested quickly. 'Please don't send us back.'

Kat shook her head. 'I'm not going to send you back, but you can't come with us.'

'Kat,' Arthur began. He came over to stand beside her, resting his hand on her shoulder. 'It's not a terrible idea. Another Magic Wielder, and a Witchfinder, at that.'

'Exactly,' Kat growled. 'He cannot be trusted.'

'The moment they took Isolde was the moment I renounced any vows that I had taken,' Tristan said firmly. 'I never wanted to be a Witchfinder. I wanted to be a farmer, but my father … once the gold was put on the table, I had no choice anymore.' He stood a little straighter, his chin lifted. 'I want to choose my own path. I want to help you, and when this is done—'

'Do you know what "this" is?' Ordes cut in, not unkindly.

'No,' Tristan admitted after a pause.

'They're on a Treasure hunt,' Olwen announced. Before Kat could even scowl at her, she closed her mouth dramatically.

Tristan frowned. 'The Treasures of the Gods? So this is about the prophecy?'

'What do you know about it?' Arthur asked.

'Or, more importantly, what does the Sacellum know about it?' Ordes added.

'Mark would talk about it often,' Isolde said. 'There were always meetings. The Magistrar came once. I was not invited, of course, but I overheard them. Mark wanted to send out a force to stop you, but the Magistrar didn't agree. They argued, and then the Magistrar left. Mark was in a terrible mood afterwards.'

'Why would the Magistrar not want to stop us?' Arthur asked.

Olwen sighed loudly. 'This is what I was trying to tell you,' she said. 'The Sacellum is not what you think it is. The Red Sisters are not in Malist for decoration.' She looked around at them all, rolling her eyes when no one reacted. 'The Witchfinders are their own creatures – the Magistrar lost control of them years ago. We tried regaining it, but some of those men are powerful Magic Wielders, and our magic doesn't work on them.'

Nobody said anything – everyone was looking at Olwen with deep suspicion.

She rolled her eyes. 'Who do you think has been whispering in the ear of the Magistrar for years?'

The suspicion morphed into stunned silence.

'It's true,' Ordes said eventually. 'The Guardian of the Bow was not the shifter, but a Red Sister. We took the Bow from beneath the Sacellum, but the question is – why? If the Red Sisters are the ones pulling the strings and the Magistrar is nothing but a puppet, why let men do what they do? Why let them hunt the Small Folk? Why let them torture and kill and—'

'Take that snarl off your face, whatever-you-are, and let me explain,' Olwen cut in. 'Things got out of hand. Men are too willing to abuse and oppress others for their power. Once they got a taste of it, they wanted to keep it.' She waved at Merlin. 'He knows this.' Then she turned to Arthur. 'And you know this. The Word was rewritten, Arthur, changed to suit those with the power to wield it. The Word you have been taught is not the Word the Red One first wrote.'

Arthur frowned. 'Then why did Ereshki not intervene until now, when it's nearly too late?'

'It isn't too late,' Olwen said. 'Things are happening exactly as they were supposed to.'

'What are you saying?' Ordes asked.

Olwen smiled. 'I'm saying the Red One is on your side. She always has been.'

Chapter 27

Olwen, Tristan, and Isolde had been taken back to the hold while Katarin worked out what to do with them. Arthur had argued for them to be released. While Ordes could appreciate their future King's desire to have no prisoners, he could also appreciate Katarin's need to keep their three new guests under close watch, especially Iouen's sister. Ordes wasn't sure what to do about Olwen – she was a powerful Magic Wielder who had already shown she could escape if she wanted. For now, they had to hope that whatever reason the Red Sister had for being here was important enough for her not to slaughter them all in their sleep. Olwen had claimed Ereshki was on their side. They couldn't dismiss what she had said. The more he learnt about the Old Ones, the more Ordes' head hurt trying to puzzle it out.

Jenyfer was still sleeping. Ordes had checked on her, finding her curled on her side. He was tempted to join her, to rest. He hadn't taken the time to dwell on what had happened in Malist, or the fact that he had grown wings, or on what Jenyfer's magic had done to the Sacellum's ships.

Melodias' words swam around his head. The God of the Seas had hinted at Jenyfer's powers. While what Jenyfer had done had been necessary, and she had told him she was alright, he was concerned that once she recovered, she'd look at the whole event differently.

He left Jenyfer to her rest and went in search of his father. Merlin had barely taken his eyes from their mysterious Red Sister throughout the whole meeting (Kat would call it an interrogation). Ordes wanted to know what his father was thinking, what he knew. And, if he was being truthful, he needed the distraction.

He found his father in the galley, nursing a mug of steaming tea. Merlin's face was thoughtful, eyebrows drawn together. He tapped tattooed fingers against the mug, a gesture Ordes was familiar with and that, for a moment, tugged at his heart.

He took a seat across the long table from his father. Merlin glanced up, and smiled.

'What a day,' he commented pleasantly, like they hadn't fought off six ships and Olwen hadn't confirmed the Red Sisters were controlling the Sacellum. 'Tea?'

Ordes nodded faintly, and before he could get up to find himself a cup, his father had conjured one for him. They sat in silence for a while, until Ordes asked, 'Is Olwen telling the truth?'

'Do you think she's telling the truth?' Merlin replied.

'For once, can you answer the question!' The wings exploded from Ordes' back, a familiar exasperation shooting through him at his father's habit of answering a question with a question.

'Don't unfurl your wings at me,' Merlin said, a grin tugging at his mouth. 'Always dramatic, aren't you, Ordes?'

'Wonder where I get that from?' Ordes muttered.

'You know, you could make them look however you wish?' his father said. 'Feathers are always nice. See?' A pair of blue-black wings burst from Merlin's back. He blinked, and they were white. 'You're doing it the hard way, though. It's much easier to become a whole thing than part of it. Try it,' he prompted.

'I already did.' Ordes took satisfaction in the look that crossed his father's face. 'In Malist. I couldn't get the Bow until I changed my shape.'

Merlin's smile was broad. 'What did you become?'

'A bird, an ordinary, boring bird according to Iouen. Sorry to disappoint. So,' Ordes said, 'if it will shut you up.' He closed his eyes and concentrated, imagining his wings transforming from shadowy mist to shining black feathers. He felt a tingle, a tug on the senses, and then nothing. When he opened his eyes, his father gave him a nod.

'They'll do,' Merlin said.

Ordes reached over his shoulder. Feathers. Silky and smooth. A little thrill shot through him, but it faded as he remembered why he had gone looking for his father in the first place. 'How do you know Olwen?'

'I don't.'

'Alright. How long has the Sacellum been under the control of the Red Sisters?' Ordes asked.

'It's always been under their control, in some way or another,' Merlin answered.

Ordes took a deep breath, held it, then pushed it out violently. They had known already that Ereshki was the One God, and it shouldn't be surprising, but it still was, and he was yet to wrap his head around it, around *anything* that had happened in the last forty-eight hours.

He looked his father in the eye. 'Should we collect this last Treasure and find the Grail?'

'Yes, you should.' Merlin sat back, drummed his fingers on the table. 'The world is out of balance. You need to set it right.' Ordes opened his mouth, but his father cut him off. 'I can't tell you what to do,' he said. 'Except listen, learn, ask the right questions, and trust your instincts, Ordes.'

'So, Ereshki's involvement in all of this is much more than we thought?' Ordes said. 'Which also means Melodias was right. He told us there was more to it, and I didn't really believe him. I didn't want to believe him.'

'Melodias has the potential to destroy everything with his choices, which he will not make until he is certain he will benefit from it,' Merlin explained.

'And what are the choices?' Ordes mused. 'A world where magic, in all its colours and shades, has absolute control. This is the world my mother wants, isn't it?'

Merlin nodded, though his face was troubled.

Ordes took a deep breath. 'Or a world without magic.'

'Or a world in the middle of those things,' Merlin said. 'Magic is part of the fabric of this world – it was created from magic, and to remove magic from it … I can't say what would happen if you did that.'

'Can't, or won't?'

'Can't. Of the myriad of future possibilities I have seen, that is not one of them. Whoever gave me this power has, for whatever reasons, decided I am not to know that,' Merlin replied. 'I saw a world on the brink of change. A world suspended between two realities. A world out of balance.'

'Alright. So a world in the middle,' Ordes said. 'What would that look like?' He stopped, chewing his lip thoughtfully. 'There is a difference between magic and power, isn't there? The magic a common Magic Wielder has is not the same as the magic of a faery, is it?'

'No.'

'Or a god.' Ordes sighed. 'Whenever I talk to you, I come away with more questions than answers,' he mumbled. 'I shouldn't be surprised. You've never been overly forthright, have you?' He picked up his tea; it had gone cold, but he drained the cup anyway and set it down, drumming his fingers on the rim, before standing. He needed to sleep. 'I wish I knew what was going to happen. I mean, I've got a life to live after all this, I guess.'

He was at the door before his father spoke. 'Ordes, whatever happens …' Merlin's voice trailed off. Unease skimmed the length of Ordes' spine. He made himself turn around, made himself look at his father, anticipation prickling at his skin.

Merlin ran a hand over his face. 'Know that I am proud of you.'

Ordes could not sleep. He watched the ocean from the porthole, the play of moonlight on the water, that timeless dance of light and dark that he had witnessed his whole life. Usually, the sight calmed him, but tonight the flicking tongues of silver light were dull.

He couldn't shake the feeling his father was keeping secrets, a sensation he was terribly familiar with, but now it seemed more important than ever that he deciphered Tymis' cryptic words. He had the overwhelming sense time was going to run out, but for what, he couldn't say. He'd retrieved the Bow of Mists. Did his mother know he had her Treasure? Was she still connected to it? She'd claimed the Old Ones weren't, which was why they hadn't been able to find their own Treasures, but Ordes didn't know if that was the truth. Niniane had, as far as he was concerned, proven she couldn't be trusted.

The back of Ordes' neck tingled, that scurrying insect feeling he now understood was his magic shifting beneath his skin. He shrugged his shoulders and felt his wings take form. He smiled, focusing his attention on his hand. Heat rushed over his fingers as they lengthened – he had claws. Ordes huffed a laugh; the claws and the wings vanished.

He glanced over his shoulder. Jenyfer was lying on her side, the blankets half-covering her, one pale leg dangling free. He could see the scales on her thigh. She couldn't hide them anymore, not that he would ever ask her to, but what sort of life would the two of them have when all this was over? A normal life – marriage, a home, and a family – didn't seem like a future that was within their grasp, unless magic and magical beings were free to be what they were without fear of persecution.

Would they spend their lives hiding what they were?

He turned back to the window.

'Ordes?' Jenyfer's voice was soft from sleep. He watched her climb out of bed and pad across the floor, her shirt – his shirt – slipping off one skinny, scale-flecked shoulder. She slipped her arms around him and leant against his back.

'How are you feeling?' he asked.

'I'm fine,' she replied. 'You're brooding.'

'I'm thinking. There's a difference,' he replied.

'What are you thinking about?'

'The future – ours. After all this is done.' Ordes twisted so he could slide his arm around her. 'What sort of life do you want?'

She chewed on her bottom lip. 'I honestly don't know. What are the options?'

'I think that will depend on what we all decide to do once we have the Grail,' Ordes replied. 'But we still have your Treasure to collect before we can find the Grail. My father thinks we should be considering a world in balance.'

'What does that mean?'

'I don't know, hence the thinking.'

'Brooding.' Jenyfer chuckled, standing on her tiptoes so she could press her mouth to his throat. 'Come back to bed. You can *think* tomorrow.'

Ordes shook his head. 'I can't sleep.'

'Who said anything about sleep?' Jenyfer nipped at his skin. When he didn't respond, she pulled away, squeezing her body between him and the window, reaching up to run her hands over his shoulders, then his arms. She laced her fingers through his, pale skin against his honey-brown. She squeezed, then let go and drifted away. His eyes followed her. She slowly shed her clothes until she was bare before him, perfect and flecked with moonlight and *his*.

'You need to feel, not think.'

An echo of the words he had spoken to her the first night they were together. Ordes managed a smile. 'I do, don't I?'

Jenyfer smiled, stepping forward to kiss him, closing her teeth gently over his bottom lip. He let her peel the shirt from his body, slide his pants over his hips. She dropped to her knees to free them from his feet, then kissed her way back up his legs, torturously slow, yet not slow enough, lips dropping stars and fire on his skin.

'You know, I believe Katarin thinks we spend too much time in bed,' he murmured.

'She's only saying that because there is no one in her bed,' Jenyfer replied, teeth nipping at his hip. She glanced up at him, mischief dancing in her sea-storm eyes.

'You going to tell her that?' Ordes quipped.

Jenyfer chuckled, then closed her hand around the length of him and took him into her mouth. Ordes gasped at the suddenness of it, the pleasure so intense it was painful. The air fled his lungs as his knees buckled. His hands wove into her hair and the sight of her, naked and on her knees, lantern light gilding her skin, was nearly enough to undo him. The warmth of her mouth, the teasing of him with lips and tongue and teeth, her eyes sparkling as she met his gaze ...

With a groan, he moved her away, let her rise to her feet and push him towards the bed. He caught her before they fell, spinning her around. Their eyes met, held, before their mouths crashed together, fingers digging into flesh hard enough to leave bruises. Jenyfer's nails pierced his skin as she pulled him so close he could feel her heart beating, and could hear the blood charging through her veins. The heartfire was like lightning shooting through him, potent and powerful and alive. He gasped into her mouth.

'You're thinking,' she accused, her voice breathy and thick.

'If you must know, I'm thinking how much I need to taste you.'

'Please, do.'

He guided her back, covering her body with his so he could kiss her again, before he climbed off the bed, hooking his hands beneath her backside. Jenyfer giggled as he pulled her down the bed, that giggle becoming a moan as he ran his fingers down her body, between her breasts and over her heaving chest, across the flat plain of her belly, lower, before he stopped. He took a moment to look at her – her hair was an inky stain across the pillow, eyes closed tight, lips parted and breath thick, fingers curled against the sheets in anticipation. Opalescent scales winked at him.

Moonlight snuck into the cabin through the porthole, silver merging with the golden lantern glow. Ordes could hear the ship, timbers creaking, settling, the crew, the ocean flicking her watery tongue against the hull.

Jenyfer's thighs shifted apart. He dropped to his knees, running his tongue lightly over the inside of one knee, then the other. She squirmed, impatient. Ordes braced a hand on each thigh and she stilled, heart racing. His mouth trailed fire along the inside of her thigh; he could feel the shift in her pulse as he teased with tongue and teeth. Her fingers dug into his scalp as she tried to pull him closer to the burning heart of her body. She growled in protest.

'Nothing to hold on to, Jen?' he whispered. 'Wish you'd not cut it off now?'

Her complaints slid into a moan as he pressed a gentle kiss against the thrumming core of her.

'What would you prefer? Soft?' he asked, gently stroking, the taste of her exploding on his tongue. 'Or hard?' He pressed an open-mouthed kiss firmly into her, teeth closing over swollen flesh. Jenyfer gasped, spine arching, fingers abandoning his hair to clutch at the bedding.

'Like that?' Ordes asked, repeating the action, earning another gasp.

'Whatever you want,' she managed, voice a hoarse whisper, its earnest rawness sinking inside him. He paused, biting his lip, wanting nothing more than to sate his thirst on her, to push himself into her until the fear and the apprehension melted away.

'Ordes?'

'I don't want to hurt you.'

'You won't hurt me,' Jenyfer said. 'You've never hurt me.' She sat up, hands cupping his face, tilting his head up to hers. Her eyes were dark, half-closed, her smile lazy and lust-filled. She bent her head to catch his lips with hers. 'Let go,' she murmured against his mouth. 'You don't need to be scared. Nothing will change how I feel about you.'

She lay back, bringing him with her. He nestled between her thighs, holding his weight free of her, but she wrapped one leg around his hip, pushing herself against him. When he didn't move, she rocked her hips. 'We don't have to do this.'

He silenced her with a kiss, light at first, and then deeper. She was right – she was always right. For now, he needed to feel. To shake the demon haunting his thoughts, to push everything away, to just focus on the warmth of the woman beneath him.

The ship rocked beneath them gently. Sweat soaked sheets tangled around Ordes' legs. Jen lay with her head on his chest.

'What you did in Malist bothers you, doesn't it?' she asked softly.

'I'm not sure,' Ordes said. 'In Cruithea, Goerika had wanted me to shift my shape. She insisted I could, but I was terrified, not so much at changing what I was, but losing who I was.'

Jenyfer kissed his shoulder. 'It's not unusual, though, is it? Think about it. Your father can change his shape, Jalen can as well. Olwen turns into smoke, and a Korrigan can become something else. And then there is me – whenever I'm in the water, I change, don't I?'

'I was a bird, Jen,' Ordes pointed out, but a smile tugged at his mouth. He held out his hand – his flesh rippled, and feathers flecked his skin before they faded away.

'You could be whatever you wanted,' she said. 'You've got wings – why not claws or sharper teeth? Fur? You could be taller. Bigger.'

He gave her a curious look. 'What are you saying? Are there parts of me I need to change?'

She pretended to consider it, dissolving into laughter when he jabbed a finger into her ribs, before tucking herself against his side and draping her arm over his chest. 'I like you as you are. And to answer your earlier question about the future ... I don't care what we do or where we go when this is all over, Ordes. As long as we're together.'

CHAPTER 28

'You're going out?' Lamorna asked. 'I thought you were having dinner with me this evening.'

'I shall, but later,' Mordred told her. 'While you are at the women's prayer circle, I will be visiting the tavern. I am to share an ale with the Konsel, without my uncle present.'

'They invited you?' Lamorna asked in surprise.

'No, but they will not turn me away,' Mordred said. 'I have attended many meetings now between my uncle and the Konsel. They are hard men, suspicious of me and my motives. The Red Hand will be easier to manipulate. They are all young men, and if there is one thing young men want, it is more power, Lamorna. The Chif and the Konsel – all older men – are the ones who hold power in this town. I will find the cracks in that shield, because there are always cracks, and when I have learnt enough, it will be easy to offer the men of the Red Hand the lion's share of power.'

Lamorna was listening with interest. 'And how will you give it to them?'

Mordred pulled on his shirt, his large fingers stumbling with the buttons. 'I don't have to, not yet. The idea of it will be enough to begin with. Think of a man like a garden – you plant a seed, water it, tend to it, then sit back and watch it grow.'

'I see,' Lamorna said softly. It was then that she realised that he was dressed like any other man in Kernou. 'Where did you get the clothes?' she asked, a little disappointed. She liked his Cruithean clothes. They fit him well, and she could see the shape of him – all of him – in them.

'My uncle insisted,' Mordred said, making a face. 'Do I look ridiculous?'

'No,' Lamorna assured him. 'You look like anyone else, except you are darker than they are, and your hair is different.'

He reached up to run his hand over his long, braided hair. 'Should I cut it?'

'No!' she cried, and then blushed when he raised his eyebrows. 'I like it,' she admitted.

'Well, then,' he said, kissing her. 'I shall keep it, for you. You said you wanted to help me? Well, this is how you do it. At prayer circle, you need to befriend the young women of this town, Lamorna. They will be the ticket to our success. Women, even those who think they have no power, have an extraordinary amount of it.'

'This isn't Cruithea,' Lamorna reminded him curtly. Her stomach was slowly turning to stone.

Mordred nodded. 'Trust me. Make friends with them and—'

'How do I do that?' Lamorna clutched at his arm as panic speared through her. 'Mordred, you don't understand. You make it look so easy. You walked into this place, an outsider – from Cruithea, of all places – and you've got people eating out of your hand. I can't do that. I don't know how! I don't know how to have friends because I have never had any! The idea of … I don't know what I am doing!'

She'd never had friends, not even one. Her own thoughts, her routines, and her habits had been her friends. She'd learnt to rely on herself and the Word for comfort. Only she hadn't realised it. Lamorna had thought she was better than everyone else, that her piousness lifted her above them, but that wasn't the truth.

It was loneliness.

Lamorna had been lonely.

She looked at Mordred imploringly, wringing her hands.

He came and took her face between his large hands and kissed her gently. 'Show them who you are, Lamorna.'

'And who am I?' she whispered.

'Magnetic and cunning. Intelligent and forthright. Strong,' Mordred said, and the stones in her belly gently dissolved, a warmth spreading through her. 'Powerful, as all women are, only you have never realised it. It is time we changed that.'

She nodded. 'Yes, it is.' She took a deep breath. 'Do I tell them about the One God?'

'Not yet,' he said. 'But it will be your job to remind them of all the things they are missing, of all the things you have learnt about power.' He smiled. 'I have something to show you.' He reached into his pocket and removed a folded piece of paper, handing it to her.

Lamorna frowned. 'What is this?'

'My uncle left me alone in his study today – a sign that he is beginning to trust me. So I took the opportunity to have a look around, and I found something interesting,' Mordred told her. He nodded at the paper. 'Read it, Lamorna.'

Curious, she unfolded the paper and read it out loud. '"A messenger will come from distant lands. This messenger is the One God's chosen, and he shall lead the faithful from the lands of their fathers to the lands of old, where they shall find salvation from slavery and oppression. Here, in this place, shall they hear the true Word. This promised land, this paradise, shall be their reward for their devotion."' She looked up at Mordred in shock. 'This … this isn't in the Decalogue!'

'No, not in the version you have all been taught,' Mordred said. 'I told you, the Word has been corrupted. Here is the proof. My uncle has another copy of the Decalogue, hidden.' He kissed her quickly, running his hands over her shoulders. 'Lamorna, those lines are going to be the key to everything. They will bring the Red Hand to my side, and the people of this town to *us*.'

That evening, Lamorna's stomach was full of butterflies with their wings on fire. Anxiety had dug its claws in deep the moment Mordred had left her to join the men in the tavern, and they had not let go. She wished he was with her, but then reminded herself that was not possible. She would have to pretend he was there, and take strength from that.

She could not stop thinking of those lines. Such innocent words. Such powerful ones.

Ulrian was a liar.

Lamorna clenched her fists, bit the inside of her cheek hard enough to taste blood, and forced herself to focus.

Women's prayer circle was always held in a small, nondescript building not far from the main square. It must have been a storehouse of some sort once. To Lamorna, it had always smelt musty, like flour that had sat too long. The door was plain, with no sign adorning it – not like there was on the men's prayer rooms, she realised.

A flush of anger swept through her at that thought. Yet another, subtle way women had been pushed down in this place.

Lamorna squared her shoulders and pushed open the door. When she stepped inside the dimly lit room, all eyes turned to her. She hesitated, then closed the door behind her, coming in and finding herself a seat on the far side of the room. She sat alone, but she didn't mind, for it gave her the opportunity to watch those around her. Opening her battered copy of the Decalogue, she could feel them watching her as she began reading.

Slowly, the heat of stares receded, and Lamorna lifted her head, glancing around the room. The dark-haired woman, Calla, was sitting with a group of young women on the other side of the room. She was not reading the Word, however. She was watching Lamorna. With a sly little smile, like they held a secret between them, Calla lowered her eyes.

Lamorna was now certain Calla had left the note.

Mordred had said she must befriend the young women, but Lamorna did not know how to start. Once, it would not have bothered her. She would have marched up to them, full of false confidence, and suggested they pray together. The thought of doing that now, after all she'd learnt, was terrifying. She swallowed, returning her eyes to the Decalogue, but she did not read a single word. She couldn't, not when those butterflies were burning a hole through her.

Failure coated the back of her throat as she sat, without moving, until the old woman who oversaw the prayer circle announced they were done for the evening. Lamorna shot to her feet and hurried for the door, wanting nothing more than to be out of that stuffy room with its old yeast smell.

Outside, she raced around the corner of the building, gulping at the evening air gratefully. She stood with her hand braced on the outer wall, feeling the rough texture of the stone beneath the pads of her fingers.

'Lamorna?' a voice said, soft and hesitant.

Lamorna jolted, standing up straight, not realising she had been doubled-over, her chest aching, heart pounding, her fingers clutching her copy of the Decalogue so hard she was surprised the spine of the book had not snapped. Calla stood nearby, her friends hanging back. They were all watching Lamorna curiously.

Wiping her face, Lamorna forced a smile. 'It's Calla, isn't it?'

Calla nodded. 'I'm glad you came.'

Lamorna bit back the desire to ask why, to let her suspicions raise their heads, remembering instead what Mordred had asked her to do. So she nodded. 'I have missed being at prayer circle. I'm glad I came.'

Calla exchanged a look with her friends, women with faces Lamorna could not put names to. 'Will you come again next week?'

Lamorna nodded. 'I will.'

The young women left, and Lamorna could not help feeling a strange sort of accomplishment. It was only a small step, but it was a step, and she was proud of it. As she began the walk back to her cottage, the door to the prayer room opened again. Curious, she glanced over her shoulder.

Two of the older women were standing in the open doorway, and although Lamorna could not see their faces clearly, she could feel their eyes. She turned her face away and hurried towards home as those flame-winged butterflies began flapping again.

CHAPTER 29

'Think about it, Arthur. The sun is shining and the weather is glorious,' Jalen said, gesturing at the porthole. 'And Teyath has a Magic Wielding ruler once more. You will be amazing.' He dropped a kiss on Arthur's mouth, then left. Arthur remained in bed, listening to his footsteps echo along the passageway and up the stairs.

Jalen spent his days being a sailor, lending his strength to the crew, who, if they were still awed at the demon of storms in their midst, did not show it. Jalen was treated as any man would be, and Arthur knew that was important to him. Nights were spent together, and Arthur liked those quiet moments, those soft and tender moments, more than anything else.

Then there was Katarin.

'I know you don't like him,' Arthur had said to his sister. 'But I do, so be nice. Please?'

She'd rolled her eyes and muttered, 'Fine.'

Arthur lay staring at the ceiling. He linked his hands behind his head, trying to count how many days he had been aboard this ship, and how long it had been since leaving Cruithea. At least three moons had passed, and he had claimed the Sword of the White Dragon as his. Most of the time, the Sword was locked away in a trunk covered in spells and magic. The idea that its power could impact the human crew terrified Arthur, so he'd asked Merlin to guard it. The trunk was in Arthur's cabin. He could still feel the Sword – could hear it whispering to him – but it appeared no one else could. Occasionally, he'd catch a wistful look on a man's face and his heart would pause, but Kat kept the crew busy.

Arthur unlinked his hands, bringing them in front of his face so he could study them. *Still a scholar's hands*, he thought. His fingers were long and slender, but there were callouses there now, ones he had earned and was proud of.

Ever since he had held the Sword, something had changed. His magic was different. It was still and quiet, as if waiting for something. He had continued his sword practice with Halymere whenever he could, but had not been practising his magic with Melhala or Ethinne. He'd been avoiding them, and they had been patient with him, but now he was wondering if he had made a mistake. Magic was supposed to be intuitive, but Arthur's intuition was telling him his magic had a different reason for being. He froze in the act of climbing from bed. Eseld had said something in his dream, but he hadn't been certain of how to interpret it: that his magic was tied to the Sword now, which Arthur had assumed meant something to do with the Treasure being his. But doubt niggled at the back of his mind.

He found his clothes and dressed quickly, perching on the edge of the bed and looking at his hands again.

'I should probably see if I remember what to do,' he mumbled, unsure of where exactly he should start. He closed his eyes, searching his mind for a time when his magic was strongest. That moment in the forest with Mordred, when he had conjured that shield as his cousin attacked him.

Arthur concentrated on pulling his magic to the surface, on setting it free, but nothing happened. He could feel it, but it felt locked inside of him. He tried again, imagining it growing out of him, like a seedling.

Nothing. Not even a spark of golden light.

Panicked, he tried again, before tearing from the cabin.

It was not Jalen he went searching for, nor Ethinne or Melhala or his sister, but Merlin. If anyone knew what was wrong with his magic, surely it would be Merlin. The Prophet of the Gods was in the galley, sitting down to a breakfast of stewed apples. Thankfully, he was alone when Arthur flung himself through the door, tripping over himself in his haste.

'My magic is gone!' he announced, the words pouring out of him. 'I think. I can still feel it, but it's like it's asleep. The only time it's awake is when I'm—'

'Near the Sword,' Merlin finished, pushing his plate to the side as Arthur hurried towards him. 'Your magic was never yours to begin with.'

Arthur's steps faltered, the blood draining from his face. 'What … what do you mean?'

'It's the magic of the Sword you feel, and the magic of the Sword you have dipped into,' Merlin explained.

'But … my father … what happened with him that day … if that wasn't me, then …' Arthur's voice trailed off. He sat, his knees suddenly weak.

'It was the Sword. Without that moment, you would never have left Kernou and you would never have taken your first steps on the path to being King,' Merlin said. 'It needed to happen. I told you the Treasures were sentient. They have a will and desires all their own, Arthur.'

Arthur froze. 'Magic manipulated me?' he whispered. '*You* manipulated me!'

Merlin's expression was sorrowful. 'I did, and I am not proud of it. But it needed to happen so you would act. I knew what the Sword would make you do.'

'Then leaving Kernou was never really my decision, was it?' Arthur breathed.

'You had already decided Kernou was not your future. You needed a push – the Sword gave you that,' Merlin said. He reached for his food again.

'A push!' Arthur exploded. 'I almost killed two people!' He shook his head, a bitter laugh escaping him. 'My rule begins in violence, then. How does that make me a man fit to be a king?'

'Only you can answer that question,' Merlin said.

Disgust filled Arthur. 'And you want me to bring magic back to the world? To let magic make decisions that will affect everyone?'

'I never said that,' Merlin told him quietly. 'The choice is, as it always has been, yours.'

You needed a push – the Sword gave you that.

Never had Arthur felt more of a tool of destiny than now.

He found Jenyfer sitting on the steps leading to the quarterdeck, her eyes on the sky, dark hair blowing around her. The sunlight caught on the scales that coated her wrists and forearms. Without taking her eyes from the stretch of blue sky above them, she moved over for him. Arthur sat, wondering what she was looking at.

'Ordes,' she said, nodding at the sky.

'What?' Arthur said, glancing up.

'He got up this morning and decided, since he has wings, he may as well learn to use them. He's fallen in the ocean twice,' she added, the corners of her mouth twitching. 'It would probably be easier if all of him was a bird, but he's not keen on that.'

Arthur jumped as a mass of limbs came tumbling from the sky to crash into the sea.

'Three times,' Jenyfer mumbled. 'Not that I'm counting or anything.'

Ordes burst from the water, hovering above the waves he'd created. He was scowling, water streaming from his body. Like Jenyfer's scales, the sunlight caught on Ordes' wings, the black feathers shimmering blue.

'I thought they were white,' Arthur commented.

'They change colour with his mood,' Jenyfer said with a laugh. 'If he gets this right, they'll probably turn bright pink or something.' Her grin faded as she took in Arthur's expression. 'What is it?'

He looked at his hands, flexed his fingers, waiting, but the magic did not come. 'It's not there anymore,' he told her. 'My magic.'

'What do you mean it's not there? Where did it go?' she asked.

He told her in a quiet voice what he had learnt.

'I'm sorry,' Jenyfer said kindly. 'I know that must be a blow, Arthur.'

Arthur nodded, then sighed. 'You know what? I don't think I'm upset about the magic part – it never really felt like me, or like the me I am becoming. I'm more upset that—'

'Merlin manipulated you. Yeah, I can understand that,' Jenyfer said, voice low.

'Magic manipulated me,' Arthur said. 'He knew it would happen, but … I don't know. I don't know what we should do, Jen. I feel like everyone has been lying to us from the moment this began, and as someone who was lied to my whole life, as someone who was manipulated, I'm angry.'

Jenyfer was watching him closely.

'How are we supposed to make a decision about the future of the world when we can't trust what we know, or what we're being told?' Arthur said, dropping his voice.

She sighed and closed her eyes, rubbing at them in irritation. 'I can't believe I am about to say this, but maybe my father was right. We need to start asking the right questions, but of whom, I don't know.'

A shadow draped itself over them, and in a flurry of wings and feathers, Ordes landed on the deck. He put his hands on his hips, wings spread triumphantly, looking from Jenyfer to Arthur. His grin slipped a little; the wings drooped. 'Did anybody see me not fall in the water that time?'

Jenyfer got up and kissed him. 'You did well.'

Ordes' eyebrows lifted. 'You didn't see, did you?'

'No,' she admitted, patting his shoulder. 'But I'm sure you were amazing.'

'What's it like to be good at everything?' Arthur's voice came out dark and bitter, but he didn't have the energy to pretend he was alright. Just when he thought he was beginning to truly understand who he was, everything was taken away from him as quickly as it had been given. Arthur glanced at his hands.

He stretched his fingers, felt the magic he was tied to shift in response, then curled his hands into fists instead. He could feel Ordes and Jenyfer frowning at him, but he didn't say anything, didn't offer up an apology like he usually would. Instead, he stomped his way below deck.

Chapter 30

Katarin couldn't sleep. Her head was so full, she was waiting for her skull to split down the middle and spill her thoughts all over the place.

Things used to be simple.

She had *The Queen* and her crew, and they had their mission. Not a goddess-given one, but a mission nonetheless. A purpose. She was proud of what she had accomplished as Captain of that ship. Never had she considered anything else. She'd *liked* her life as it was.

She could hear Aelle chuckle.

What, you wish you'd never found your brother? Come on, Kat. Who would you mother then?

Kat sighed and smiled.

No, she wouldn't change anything. She'd never once imagined Arthur would appear on her ship, a man grown, hiding a terrified boy inside. She'd known who he was the moment she'd laid eyes on him. He looked like their mother, with his father's colouring.

Ulrian had been gentle to her, once. When Igraine was newly pregnant, Ulrian had shared Katarin's joy, and later, her fear. What Kat had not told anyone was the dreams she had had, ones where her mother, belly swollen, lay in a pool of her own blood while a baby wailed in the background. The dream had persisted, night after night, and Kat didn't dare tell her mother. However, she was a child plagued with terror, with worry and fear, so she told the only other person she could trust.

And where had that gotten her?

Katarin pushed the memories of Ulrian Tregarthen away. Her lantern burned low, but dawn was still hours away. She was out of rum, so she pulled out her pipe from the drawer and tucked it into the pocket of her long coat, before heading out onto the deck.

Iouen was on watch. Kat swallowed. She'd been avoiding him – not because she felt guilty for locking his sister in the hold, but because she didn't have words to reassure him that Olwen was safe. Everything that happened in Malist, and since, was a kaleidoscope of brightly coloured pictures. She could still hear Jenyfer's song when they rescued Isolde – even though the magic in the syhren's voice didn't affect her, the power was undeniable. And what Ordes had done during the battle with the Witchfinders' ships … Katarin closed her eyes briefly, feeling again that horrible emptiness in her belly when the ship shot across the ocean with such speed.

It scared her, if she was being honest. Magic like that, that level of power, as untapped and raw as it was, was the power of the Gods. She could only begin to imagine what it must feel like, what must be going on in Ordes' head. He never wanted power, and now he'd had it thrust at him without being given the chance to refuse it.

Sensing he was no longer alone, Iouen glanced over his shoulder. He met Katarin's eyes, then turned back to watch the shoreline. They weren't far from Kunis. There had been a strong wind behind the ship, pushing her steadily north, her sails full day and night.

Katarin took a deep breath, and made her way to Iouen's side, keeping some distance between them. He didn't move as she leant against the railing and packed her pipe, bringing it to her lips and lighting it with a wave of her hand.

She hesitated, then held it out for Iouen, who, after meeting her eyes once more and seeming to decide it was a peace offering, took it.

'There's something in the water,' he told her, passing the pipe back. His tone was brusque. 'Whatever it is has been following us for hours.'

'Mermaid or syhren?' Kat asked.

'Neither usually come this far north – I think it's too cold for them,' Iouen said. 'I'd guess it's a morgen, or a selkie, but it's difficult to tell in the darkness.'

Kat nodded, gesturing towards the shore where tiny lights winked along the beach. 'Those lights – I didn't think there were any settlements besides Kunis here.' As soon as she finished speaking, the lights winked out, and then flashed back on again. 'What the—'

'Olwen and I used to call them the night mouths,' Iouen said. 'We used to see them all the time. Sometimes they speak, but mostly they appear as a flickering flame.'

'Are they dangerous?' Katarin asked, watching the lights blinking on and off in the darkness.

'Harmless, mostly,' Iouen answered. 'We used to think they were a warning, and maybe they were. If we saw them, our father would often become so drunk he couldn't stand, but he'd still be capable of giving me a flogging.' Iouen sighed. 'I'm glad she killed him. He deserved it. I only wish I'd have done it.' He paused, then, 'Are you going to keep her tied up forever?'

'I know she's your sister, but can you blame me for being suspicious?' Kat asked.

'No,' Iouen said, surprising her. 'But Olwen is on our side. She wouldn't be here otherwise, I can assure you.'

Kat rubbed her cheek. 'I can't trust her, Iouen. The things she said—'

'Are truth, Katarin,' he insisted. 'You didn't grow up in Kunis, in the shadow of the House of Bone. Ereshki wasn't worshipped – she was *loved*.

There are shrines to her all over the town. Every household had one. We never feared the darkness because the darkness was hers. We never feared the faeries that lived alongside us – drawn to the Ossuary, to the magic of the Red Sisters, and drawn to The Teeth – because they understood the darkness like we did. You have no idea how hard I had to work to throw the shadows of that place off me. Not just my father, but everything, and now here we are.' He paused. 'Olwen didn't want to be sent to the House of Bone, Katarin. It wasn't her choice. And when she left, without her … it was worse. She protected me. Father was frightened of her, as much as he was thrilled the Red One had gifted her with magic.'

Kat wasn't sure what to say. The woman locked in her hold was dangerous because she was unknown. Kat chewed her lip. She'd taken a syhren onboard her ship, even though Jenyfer's magic was also dangerous. Maybe it had simply been that Jenyfer didn't have control of herself that stirred some sympathy in Kat and her crew. Jenyfer had been so lost and afraid, and that was what they did – helped women who couldn't help themselves. Olwen was different, though. Kat sighed.

'Arthur is having doubts. Ordes is having doubts. *I* am having doubts. The Old Ones have been meddling in our lives for too long. If Arthur, Ordes, and Jen decide they don't want them around, is Ereshki likely to roll over and accept that? Niniane surely won't, and I can't imagine Melodias will be thrilled, either. Your sister is bound to a banished goddess. Can you see why I might be a little reluctant to believe what she tells us?'

Iouen did not reply.

'Tell me what you know of The Teeth,' Kat asked instead.

Iouen shrugged. 'I know to stay the fuck away from there.'

'Not an option, unfortunately,' Kat mumbled. Silence dropped between them, but instead of being tense, it was strangely companionable. Kat had to admit there was something about Iouen that she liked – he was cheeky and forthright, but there was a vulnerability beneath the smiles, one that she now knew the reason for. Ulrian had been a prick, but at least he hadn't beaten her or her mother.

'Did you know I saw my own funeral once?' Iouen asked matter-of-factly.

'What, like in a dream?'

He shook his head. 'No. A bunch of faeries showed me. I came across them in the trees north of the village – I was exploring, doing what kids do – and there it was. A little faery funeral. The creatures were carrying a coffin, little faces sombre. I even took my hat off in respect as they passed, only it wasn't a faery they were burying, but a tiny, life-like version of me.'

'That's … disturbing,' Kat said.

'That's tame,' Iouen said. 'Wait until you hear the Night Criers. They often sound like children. Sometimes they warn you of danger, sometimes they are the danger, and the problem is you can't tell which is which. A fisherman I knew walked into the ocean and drowned himself because he listened to them. Olwen always liked the faeries more than me. She understood them.' He paused, ran his hand through his hair. 'Captain—'

'Let's get this third Treasure and get out of here, and then I'll think about what to do with your sister,' Katarin said. 'I get that she's your family, but—'

Iouen turned to her, eyes irritated. 'Look, everyone on this ship – Ordes, Jen, Arthur, even your grumpy arse – are like family to me. You're important, and what we're doing is important. If I thought for one moment that Olwen was going to harm any of you, I'd be telling her to leave myself. If you can't trust her, then trust me.'

Katarin wasn't sure what to say.

Iouen glanced over his shoulder. 'My watch is over.'

He left before Kat could say anything. When she turned around, it was to find the storm demon watching her curiously. 'You're good at upsetting people,' he commented.

She scowled. 'Why are you on watch?'

'Why not? I don't need to sleep.'

Katarin narrowed her eyes as he approached her. 'You were gone yesterday – where?'

'I went to get something for Arthur,' Jalen said.

'What?' she demanded.

Jalen glared at her, then turned away. 'Apples,' he said quietly.

Olwen was sitting against the bulkhead, bound hands in her lap. She looked up as Kat came down the ladder, expression wary, deep brown eyes accusatory. Katarin hung her lantern on a peg, taking her time, trying to work out what to say to this woman.

She turned, lowering herself to the floor, feeling the ocean stroke its fingers against the hull of the ship beneath her as *The Excalibur* ploughed through the water.

Olwen stared at her, brown hair falling to brush her shoulders. There was a slight curl to her hair, a piece tickling her cheek. She shook her head irritably, and the curl was pushed away.

'Should I be worried?' the Red Sister said eventually.

Katarin shifted her position, sitting cross-legged. She moved her long-coat aside so her dagger was visible, a reminder to the woman sitting across from her. Someone had given Olwen a change of clothes. The red robes were gone and she was wearing dark pants, a tight-fitting black shirt, and a leather vest. She was slimmer than Katarin first thought, with an oddly starved look about her.

They sat in silence, staring at one another, until eventually, Olwen sighed. 'We're close to Kunis, aren't we?'

Kat nodded.

'I can feel the bastard of a place. Its shadows are long,' Olwen muttered. 'How long until we reach The Teeth?'

'A week, if we're lucky,' Kat said.

'You don't trust me.'

'No,' Kat agreed. 'I don't. I don't know a thing about you, other than you're Iouen's sister, *and* a Red Sister, at that.'

'Not backwards in coming forwards, are you,' Olwen murmured. She shrugged. 'Doesn't matter. I'm here for my brother, and for Arthur's quest. What my role is exactly, I don't know yet.'

'Your goddess didn't tell you?' Kat sneered.

'Did yours?' Olwen shot back. 'She lied to you.'

'Shut up. You don't know what you're talking about,' Kat said.

'Don't I? She lied to you about the Red One, about the Treasures – everything,' Olwen went on.

Kat shook her head. 'Why do you care?'

'I don't, not really. Your mistress has her plans, mine has different ones. Arthur will need to choose which path he wants to follow,' the Red Sister said.

Katarin narrowed her eyes. 'So you're not here to convince him?'

'No.'

Kat fell silent. Irritated, she untied her hair, letting it fall down her back.

'Your hair looks better like that,' Olwen commented. Kat looked at her, startled. 'You can see the colour better. In the sun I imagine it would be rather spectacular. It would be nice to see it.'

'The sun, or my hair?'

'If I had to choose … I'd take your hair,' Olwen said.

Something squirmed in Katarin's belly. She pushed it away. 'I'll get someone to bring you some food.'

'Are you going to untie me?' Olwen asked.

'No.'

'Then how do you expect me to eat?' the Red Sister demanded. Her expression shifted, and a slow smile spread across her face. 'Unless you're going to feed me?'

'Untie yourself.' Katarin scowled and got to her feet. She could feel Olwen's eyes on her long after she returned to her cabin, where she lay and stared at the ceiling until the sun threw itself over the horizon.

Chapter 31

Lamorna lingered in the doorway of the women's prayer circle. It was getting easier to be here, but still, she knew people in town were still talking about her. She took a deep breath and stepped into the room, closing the door behind her. Heads lifted, and the whispers began, but this time, they felt different.

Calla rose from her seat and approached. Lamorna tensed, unable to help it, but when the woman grasped her hands and drew her forward, she felt her eyes widen in surprise.

'You must sit with us,' Calla said, keeping her voice low. She led Lamorna across the room towards her friends, but there was no spare seat. 'Arwen, get up. Let Lamorna sit.'

Arwen flashed an irritated look, but did as Calla ordered. Lamorna sat, her knees weak, taking a moment to rearrange her skirts. She had not worn her cap and could feel Margaret from the fishmonger's watching her. She shook her hair back deliberately.

'Your hair is so lovely,' Calla said, a wistful tone in her voice.

'Calla!' One of the other women, Naidiene, scolded.

'So?' Calla objected. 'It is.'

'Thank you,' Lamorna said politely. She tucked her hair behind her ear, the way Mordred always did. She had thought about wearing her cap to this prayer circle, but had decided at the last moment not to. They were already all talking about her, anyway, so what did it matter?

Part of her wanted to see how far she could push things. That had surprised her more than anything. Once awoken, the part of her that had been rebelling against the Word and the One God since her return made her feel powerful and in control.

She could understand why Jenyfer had fought so hard, had pushed back against the rules, even when the rules of this place tried to consume her.

Lamorna decided then and there that the rules would not consume her.

She was going to write new rules, and perhaps, the women in this prayer circle would help her.

The young women watched Lamorna, a strange eagerness on their faces. She cleared her throat, but before she could say anything, Calla grabbed her hands again.

'You must tell us about him,' she said, lowering her voice. The others leant forward; Lamorna looked at them all, feigning confusion. 'The Chif's nephew,' Calla said. 'What is he like?'

'I do not know him all that well,' Lamorna began.

'That's a lie,' Arwen said with a giggle, blue eyes twinkling. 'Everyone knows he is staying in your home.'

'Yes,' Lamorna answered. 'He was, but—'

'He's so handsome,' Calla cut in. She squeezed Lamorna's hands. 'Has he kissed you?'

'Calla!' one of the women gasped, then, 'Has he?'

Lamorna shook her head furiously. 'No!' She stopped, glancing around the circle of hungry faces, and warmth spread through her. She pushed it away. They were not really interested in her. Were they? She shook her head again. 'We should read the Word. Margaret is looking cross.'

She was. They all glanced over at the older woman, and giggled when Margaret jammed her work-worn hands on her hips and gave them all a nasty look. Lamorna reached for her copy of the Decalogue waiting in her lap, and opened the book, but did not read it. Her eyes moved quickly around the room.

There would be no getting anywhere with people like Margaret, who hadn't liked Lamorna before she left for Cruithea. Who did nothing to hide how much she disapproved of her now.

Beside her, Calla was reciting the Word, but Lamorna thought she sounded bored. Lamorna bit her lip. She had no idea what friends talked about, how they behaved. She had only had Jenyfer, and they had squabbled frequently, but having a sister was not the same as having a friend.

There was an obvious division in the prayer room. The older women positioned themselves together on one side, while the younger women sat together. There was no strict structure to the prayer circle, and, Lamorna realised for the first time, it was not really a circle, but two separate half circles. They were to sit for an hour and read together, taking turns to recite the Word. There was never any discussion about what they had read. No lessons from anyone. Just continued iteration, verse after verse.

They were not supposed to question what they read.

Lamorna had thought about what she would say to these women, if she was able to befriend them. She wanted to tell them they did not have to twist themselves into strange shapes to fit into the world that had been created around them, a world they did not have a say in. She wanted to tell them about the women in Cruithea, who were leaders and warriors as well as mothers and wives. She wanted to tell them that, although that had been taught they could not be both, that the One God does not allow them to be both, it was a lie.

But she wasn't sure where to begin. She had asked Mordred as much as she could about Ereshki, about what the Red One truly wanted for women. Now that she had latched onto the idea of women's freedom, she could not let it go. She would find a way to show these young women they were powerful in their own right, and that they did not need to be afraid.

After the prayers had finished, Lamorna excused herself, barely making it outside before Calla and the others had crowded close to her.

'We will walk with you,' Calla announced. She introduced all her friends, so quickly that Lamorna had to grab hold of their names before they slipped away.

'You want to see the Cruithean,' Penny said, brown eyes twinkling with mischief.

Calla laughed. 'Alright, yes, I do. But Lamorna does not mind, do you Lamorna?'

'Why would I mind?' Lamorna asked, but she did. She did not want Calla or any of these women looking at Mordred. Her body felt tight and hot. She shook her hair back again. She had the fierce desire to lay claim to him, but to do so meant admitting her sins, and she wasn't ready to do that. 'Do you want to know something?' she asked, lowering her voice. She looked around; the older women had come out of the room and were clustered together, talking. 'Not here,' Lamorna added.

Calla nodded and took her arm, the others following as they walked away from the meeting rooms. When they were far enough away from the older women, Lamorna smiled secretively, looking from one face to the next.

'He has not kissed me, but I wish he would,' she confessed, then clapped a hand over her mouth dramatically. 'I shouldn't have said that!'

Naidiene shook her head. 'Men talk about this all the time,' she said knowingly. 'My brother and his friends never shut up about the girls they liked. I wasn't listening on purpose, of course,' she added quickly.

'Will he kiss you, Lamorna, do you think?' Calla asked.

'I don't know,' Lamorna said.

'You could always kiss him,' someone put in.

Lamorna gasped in mock horror and shook her head, but inside, triumph was blooming. This would not be so difficult after all. They walked to her cottage in silence. It made Lamorna feel warm inside, even though part of her knew this was pretence. She was only doing what Mordred had suggested, but she liked the companionship. The wind became stronger as the path turned steep, and as the cottage came into view, Lamorna began to worry. What should she do next?

She hesitated before opening her gate, sweeping her eyes quickly over the garden. It was neat and tidy and flourishing. Someone commented on how pretty it was, and Lamorna smiled. The lavender was flowering, as were the sweet peas and bluebells.

'Would you like to come in?' she found herself offering. 'For tea?'

They nodded, exchanging an excited glance.

'Mordred won't be here,' Lamorna told them regretfully. 'He'll be with the Chif.'

She headed down the path towards the front door, the others following.

'What do they talk about?' Naidiene asked. 'I mean, he's Cruithean. Have they heard the Word in Cruithea, Lamorna?'

Lamorna shook her head, opening the door and inviting them all inside. Her cottage was well-presented. There wasn't much furniture, but she knew there was enough to be acceptable and not seen as greedy or sinful. She led the way into the kitchen, the women crowding around her table. There were not enough seats, so Lamorna and Calla remained standing.

Arwen complimented Lamorna on her cottage, and then asked what it was like in Cruithea. As Lamorna made tea, she told them all about the heathen wilds in the north of Teyath, realising that no one except for her had ever left Kernou. 'It was different,' she said. 'But my aunt was with me, so it wasn't so bad. Mordred became my friend. He looked after me and when I said I wanted to return home to Kernou, he helped me. I could not have made the journey alone,' she added. 'There are dangerous faeries in the mountains.'

'Did you see any?' the women all asked.

Lamorna nodded.

But no one was interested in faeries.

'And then Mordred decided to stay here,' Bronny declared, her smile filled with longing. 'It's terribly romantic.'

Lamorna blushed, fidgeting with a strand of her hair. The women left not long after that, but they returned the following morning, Calla leading the group up the path. Once seated around Lamorna's kitchen table, Penny looked around guilty, and then removed her cap, letting her deep red hair flow free with a grateful sigh. Silence flooded the kitchen.

'What?' Penny demanded. 'I'll put it on before we leave.'

Lamorna poured them all tea, using her aunt's nicest crockery. 'I'm sorry I have no biscuits,' she said, but no one cared.

'Aren't you scared?' Arwen asked quietly, putting honey in her tea.

Lamorna frowned. 'Of what?'

Arwen and Bronny shared a look. 'That he'd take advantage of you,' Arwen said.

'Oh no, Mordred isn't like that,' Lamorna assured them. 'He's actually polite.'

Calla set her tea cup on the bench. 'Then he's better than half the men in this stupid town.'

Some of the others frowned.

'What do you mean?' Lamorna asked innocently.

'You must know,' Calla said. 'Surely your sister told you? About what happened between her and Bryn after they were married.'

'She didn't, and I haven't seen her since …' Lamorna let her voice trail off. She didn't want to talk about Jenyfer.

'Since you were taken beneath the waves,' Naidiene finished. 'Where did you go, Lamorna? Where did that creature take you? It was all anyone could talk about.'

'Oh, it was horrible,' Lamorna cried dramatically, setting her cup down. 'There were faeries and water, and all I wanted was to die! I can barely remember anything, though – it's a feeling more than a memory. A horrible, horrible feeling.'

'But the One God sent you back,' Arwen said with heavy meaning.

Lamorna nodded. When she picked up her tea, her fingers were trembling. 'That is what the Chif said.' She paused, looking around at them all. 'Do you know what happened with Jenyfer and Bryn?'

'The same thing I'd imagine happens all the time,' Calla said. Her voice grew hard. 'My cousin was married last year.'

'And?' Lamorna asked.

'And he did not treat her right,' Calla finished.

'Calla, he did what the One God demanded of him,' Penny said sternly. 'He did nothing wrong.'

'Do you truly believe that, Penny?' Calla snapped. 'Wait until it is you, forced beneath a man while he uses you for his pleasure.'

The women gasped; Lamorna gasped also.

'That is what she told me,' Calla said, shaking her head. 'It's a little different from what we get told, isn't it? All this obeying your husband talk is rubbish. Why do they matter more than us?'

'Calla, you need to be careful,' Arwen warned. Lamorna and the others nodded in agreement.

Calla snorted. 'I'd rather burn than end up with some man I don't care about on top of me like some rutting animal,' she announced crudely. 'You're lucky, Lamorna. If Mordred is as you say, then you should marry him before you end up being forced to marry someone else.'

Lamorna swallowed and dropped her eyes, hiding her smile. She had already decided that she liked Calla, but now, she decided she liked her a lot. Calla was fierce, like Jenyfer. She was bold and not afraid.

The visits continued, and Lamorna's days were suddenly busy, taken up with her new friends, her secret evenings with Mordred, and her chores. Now that she had visitors, it was even more important than usual to make sure her home was presentable, and her garden was neat and tidy.

But she had not yet said the things she truly wanted to say. On the fifth morning of her friends' visitations, Lamorna decided to take a risk. They had shared a cup of tea, and the conversation had turned, as it usually did, to Mordred.

'How dark his skin is.'

'He is so tall! So big!'

'I wonder how big his—'

'You would wonder that.'

Lamorna giggled. She wanted to tell them she knew exactly how big it was and that he knew exactly what to do with it, but she couldn't.

Not yet.

Instead, she sat her cup down and looked at each woman carefully, weighing up her words. 'What do you wish you could change about this place?' she asked, and when no one spoke, she went on. 'I would wish for one thing only – the power to make my own choices, for me and nobody else.'

The others shared an uneasy glance.

Lamorna swallowed, but would not back down now. If they ran from her in terror, then so be it. 'We're trapped here. I never knew it, until I left and saw a different life. We're no better than animals – caged, chained and trapped.' She leant forward and lowered her voice. 'We've been told we must be humble, that we cannot want for anything. That we must never complain … and these are all good traits, of course, but doesn't it make you want to scream sometimes?'

Her words hung in the air, heavy and thick with heresy, until Penny admitted, 'I've never screamed.'

'You should try it,' Lamorna said. 'It's liberating.'

A laugh rippled through her friends.

Lamorna tapped her fingernails on the edge of her cup. 'Men are measured by their achievements, their successes. We are measured by our servitude.'

Arwen frowned. 'Mordred does not mind you speaking like this?'

Lamorna kept her eyes on her cup. She could feel Calla watching her, her friend's gaze burning a hole through her face, not with malice, but a deep interest. 'He's the one who has taught me that I deserve a voice, that I deserve to have dreams and desires of my own.' She met the eyes of each woman in turn, held their gazes, and when she spoke her voice was firm and proud. 'He's allowed me to be myself.'

CHAPTER 32

ounds of jagged rocks rose from the water in a series of curved lines. Some were small, barely large enough for anything other than a few birds to perch on, while some were as large as castles, stretching into the misty air. Waves pounded the rocks relentlessly, and Jenyfer could see where the water had carved itself into the limestone over time.

She'd been on deck since before dawn, unable to tear her eyes from The Teeth. She jumped when Ordes slipped his arm around her middle and pressed a kiss to her cheek. They watched The Teeth in silence, the rising sun splashing the rocks with golden light as the ship came to life around them.

An air of unease hung over *The Excalibur* and her crew. Sailors generally avoided The Teeth – apart from the treachery of the rocks and the force of the waves, there were eldritch dangers lurking where human eyes could not see them. The skeleton of a ship wedged between two shoals was testament to the treachery of this place.

Jenyfer gazed out across the water, leaning her forearms on the railing. She was trying to look casual, calm, but her mind was churning, slipping backwards into what had been, even as *The Excalibur* approached all that would come to be. She did not know what that future would hold, and it was hard to look towards something new when she was slowly falling into the past. Sometimes, she wondered what her life would have been if she'd remained in Kernou. If Lamorna had never been taken for the sea, and Jenyfer had never had to reveal her magic to save her, what might have been? Jenyfer frowned, straightening.

Why *had* Lamorna been taken? She couldn't begin to guess, and, she realised guiltily, she'd not truly thought about it. Had it been a ruse? Tamora had always warned her to be careful, perhaps knowing that the binding spells she'd put on Jenyfer's magic would eventually unravel. Bryn had warned her to be careful, but she hadn't listened to either of them.

Had Ulrian Tregarthen and the Konsel set a trap that Jenyfer had walked straight into?

She supposed she'd never know for certain, but if she could go back, she would demand the answer. Jenyfer sighed and shook her head. Since they had weighed anchor close to The Teeth, she'd become aware of a thrumming in her blood, lullaby-soft, but filled with dark power.

The past could wait, she decided. What would happen when she claimed the Treasure? Her father's magic was in her blood – deadly, beautiful magic – and Jenyfer was aware of how different it felt now. She'd unleashed her song in Lyonesse at Andromache's manipulations. She'd used it in Skulls Rest to save Ordes, and again to save *The Excalibur* and her crew. She'd used it to defend those she loved. Would the Stone change that? Syhren magic was tied up in death and cruelty, and that wasn't who Jenyfer was. She was terrified of losing herself, just as she knew Ordes had been.

He had embraced who he was. It was time for her to do the same.

'I wish I could tell you everything will be alright,' Ordes murmured. Jenyfer leant back against him.

'No wings?'

'Not today.'

She liked them, especially the feathers, but while he had made peace with this new part of his magic, she knew it worried him. Not the wings themselves, but the unpredictability of his magic. Ordes, for all his calm, did not like it when something was outside his control. Jenyfer could understand that.

She sighed lightly. 'I may as well get on with it then.'

'I'm coming with you.'

'You went off to collect yours without me.'

He shook his head. 'This is different. There are dangers here that we can't see, things we don't know. There is no way I am letting you go in there'—he nodded at The Teeth—'alone.'

She pressed a kiss to the underside of his jaw. 'Thank you. I didn't fancy the idea of going in there without you.' Jenyfer turned back to The Teeth. 'As much as I want to swim, I think we should take a boat. We don't know what's in the water,' she added, peering over the railing at the greyness of the ocean. Something shifted in the depths.

'When do you want to leave?' Ordes asked.

'I don't suppose it matters too much,' Jenyfer answered. 'But the sooner, the better. I want to talk to your father before we go. I wonder if he'll tell us anything useful?'

'Those who inhabit The Teeth are unlike any fey creatures you've ever met,' Merlin said. 'While the Small Folk can be dangerous, it's usually for a reason.'

'Like when you forget to leave the milk out. I did that once. It was my job but I forgot, and when I woke, my hair was terribly knotted and there were dead bees in the honey,' Jenyfer said. She was sitting cross-legged on the bed, playing with the tip of her dagger. Ordes stood close to her, arms folded. His father filled the single armchair on the other side of the room, his expression thoughtful, while Arthur lingered near the door, face sullen.

Merlin nodded. 'The fey in The Teeth don't need a reason to harm anyone or to cause mischief. For them, it is sport. There are no rules there, you need to understand that. They do whatever they want, and they don't like humans.'

He met Jenyfer's eyes.

'Do I need to worry?' she asked.

'They will know who you are,' Merlin told her. 'They will know who you belong to – no matter how much they enjoy their games, they won't harm the child of an Old One. Melodias could destroy them, if he wanted.'

Ordes was frowning. 'What else?'

'They're hedonists. They like to drink and fight. They like music and dancing as much as they like torture,' Merlin said. 'These are the fey who willingly gave themselves to the darkness in the days when Medb walked the earth. They are her creatures, loyal to her.'

'And she is the guardian of the Stone?' Jenyfer asked.

'She is,' Merlin replied.

'If she is so terrible, why was it given to her at all?' Arthur asked quietly.

'Because she, like the other guardians, is powerful. The Treasures of the Gods could not be left with just any fey. They needed to be given to those who would be able to resist them, and who had the power to keep them contained,' Merlin explained. 'Medb is known as the Triskele – mother, maiden, and crone all rolled into one. She is as old as this earth, and connected to all parts of it – life, death, rebirth. Her magic is much, much more than the magic of the common fey. She is also cunning and shrewd, and she likes to play games,' he added, glancing at Jenyfer, whose stomach tightened. Her father also liked his games.

She chewed her lip. 'What if Medb won't give the Treasure to me?'

'She will, once you pass her test,' Merlin said. 'And before you ask, I can't tell you what it will be. Wait until before sundown. There is no point going now. Medb won't see you until the sun has sunk and darkness has covered the land.'

As Ordes rowed them over, Jenyfer's stomach sank as the islands of The Teeth grew larger. They were scattered amongst the blanket of fog that shrouded the ocean. Some peaks were small, while others stretched high into the sky. All were dark with mystery and magic. Jenyfer could feel it in the air.

'Which one is Teñvali-enez?' she asked. Merlin had told them where they could find Medb before they left. 'What does that mean, anyway?'

'Island of Shadows,' Ordes answered. 'And I think that might be it.'

Up ahead, a monolith of limestone shot into the sky. The rocks were blasted smooth from water and wind. Jenyfer could not see the top of the mountain through the fog. Faint streaks of gold and peachy pink from the setting sun fought a battle with the thick grey, pushing through in parts to splash against the sides of the rocks.

There was a small inlet near the Island of Shadows, and Ordes guided the boat in, dragging it onto the pebbly shore while Jenyfer climbed out. She turned back the way they had come. Small lights like tiny fires decorated the shoals they had passed. Iouen's night mouths, she guessed. At the water's edge of the nearest shoal, three figures were hunched over, dipping grey-skinned hands into the water.

'Who are they?' Jenyfer asked Ordes.

'The washerwomen,' he told her. 'They wash the shrouds of those about to die.'

Jenyfer swallowed. The faeries were dipping their fingers into red water, lifting bundles of cloth from the water and wringing them out. One met Jenyfer's eyes and smiled, revealing red-stained teeth.

She shuddered, putting her back to the washerwomen and the night mouths. An ear-splitting shriek echoed through the air as night fell in earnest. Jenyfer glanced up at the towering spike of Teñvali-enez; black shapes flapped around its peak. 'How do we—'

She jumped, grabbing Ordes' arm as the rocks nearest them moved. A humanoid shape uncurled itself, standing upright, and Jenyfer realised it was not a human at all, but another faery with skin the colour of an eel. His smile revealed teeth like razors, and his eyes were yellow. He bowed and tipped an imaginary hat, straightening the red waistcoat he wore. He was naked besides that.

'You seek an audience with my Queen,' the creature said, his voice like water over rocks.

'We do,' Ordes said. 'Will you take us to her?'

'Will I? Should I? Perhaps,' the eel-man said. He examined fingernails he did not have.

They waited. Eventually, he sighed dramatically and gestured for them to follow him. The faery led them across the small beach towards the mouth of a cave. Ordes gripped Jenyfer's hand tightly, whispering to her not to let go.

The cave led to a series of tunnels, the darkness so thick and deep that Jenyfer's heart surged, panic crawling up her spine. She could smell old water and moss, fish and seaweed, and inside her chest, alongside the beating of Ordes' heart, was something else. A tugging sensation.

The Treasure. The Singing Stone was on this island. She could feel it, hear it, its song sullen and muffled like it was underwater. Jenyfer didn't know what to expect from her father's Treasure – part of her didn't want anything to do with it. Retrieving it would connect her to him in ways she couldn't predict. Melodias was cold and calculating, and she feared becoming like him. Would being in possession of his Treasure change her magic? Jenyfer had only just begun to feel comfortable with that part of herself. She didn't want something belonging to her father to influence her. While in Lyonesse, she'd worked so darn hard to hold onto herself, to not let that world of water and music weave its way into her blood. The Treasures hadn't changed Arthur or Ordes, at least not in any detrimental way.

Jenyfer held firm to Ordes' hand and promised herself that, no matter what she had to do to collect the Stone, she wouldn't sacrifice who she was.

The eel-man did not speak to them as he led them through the darkness. Jen couldn't see a thing and hoped Ordes, with his fey eyes, could tell if they were about to walk into a wall or tumble off the edge of a cliff. The path through the tunnel was steep. At last, they emerged into a great cavern that reminded Jenyfer of the one where she had practised her songs in Lyonesse. The ceiling was cathedral-like, black stone dripping with moisture. Lanterns glowed along the walls, where more tunnels shot off into the darkness. Like her father's throne room, there was a pool of water in the middle of the cavern, and she wondered how deep it was and where it led. She could smell the ocean faintly, beneath the other scents that saturated the cool air.

The eel-man beckoned them forward. As she was led through the cavern, skirting the edge of that pool of dark water, Jenyfer realised they were being watched. Faeries lounged against the walls, too many to count, their skin as dark as the stone surrounding them, or pale and silver like the underbelly of a fish. Some were green as emeralds, others had tails and furry ears like foxes, partially hidden beneath long flowing hair. Eyes of gold and bright purple glinted in the dim. All were partly dressed in a strange assortment of human clothes, and the majority were human in appearance. She saw tiny things with bat-like wings darting through the air, buzzing over the water like overgrown insects.

Silence followed them as the eel-man walked ahead, his stride strangely solemn. When he stopped, it was before a black, stone dais. He bowed.

'My Queen,' he said. 'I found these outside. They smell fresh enough to eat.'

The Faery Queen of The Teeth leant forward on her throne.

Medb was smaller than Jenyfer had imagined. She was slender, girlish, with long black hair that tumbled over her shoulders, shells and bones woven through it. A water snake poked its head free of her tresses and flicked its forked tongue, before it slid down its mistress' jaw to drape itself over her shoulders. Medb's eyes were dark as the night, her skin pale and tinged with pink along her hairline. When she smiled, black lips revealed elongated fangs.

She ran the tip of one pointed talon across her lips, forked tongue darting out to run across her teeth. Her black velvet gown cascaded down to pool on the stones at her feet.

'Speak,' she commanded in a voice like the wind.

'Medb, the Faery Queen,' Ordes said. After a moment of hesitation, he bowed his head to her, exposing the back of his neck, like he might in supplication to a predator. Jenyfer copied him, heart thundering. He squeezed her hand again, a reassurance, and straightened. When Medb did not respond, he cleared his throat. 'My father told me what you are.'

Medb did not take her eyes from Ordes. A slow smile crawled over those black lips. 'The Merlin is very wise to tell you such pretty, pretty lies.'

'He told me you were maiden, mother, and crone,' Ordes said. 'Was that a lie?'

'He did not tell you the things I know, he did not say, nor did he show.' She shrugged, then climbed from her throne, stalking towards them. Jenyfer had to resist her urge to run, to move away. Medb circled them, pausing to sniff the air around Ordes. He jolted when she ran the tip of her finger from one shoulder blade to the next, her talon scratching over cloth.

'Things with wings …' Medb whispered. Her face shifted, shimmering out of focus, and where a young woman had been was the face of a crone, withered with age. 'Ever burning, ever bright, the flame that burns against the night,' the faery said, turning her attention to Jenyfer. She licked her lips.

'Do you mean the heartfire?' Jenyfer asked.

Medb nodded. 'Down she'll go, down below. Tell her what she needs to know. Tell the truth, don't force her hand. Will she drown this world of sand? When the light leaves your eyes, will she cause the seas to rise?'

'Ordes, what's she talking about?' Jenyfer asked. Dread coiled in her belly.

'Nothing,' he said, shaking his head. 'She's messing with us.'

The faery was still watching Ordes, those black eyes curious. She placed a claw-like hand on his cheek. 'Sinful pride and fealty sworn, a name of a face and vanity reborn,' she muttered. 'You aren't so different, you and he, destined to fall and die, I see.'

Ordes pulled away from the claws stroking his cheek. Medb laughed, while the creatures lounging around her lair snarled.

'Careful, pretty, you'll lose your face. Mindful, then, and know your place.' She turned and gestured at the pool of dark water. 'In the depths, in a cage of bone, one might find the Singing Stone.' She paused, her black eyes finding Jenyfer's. 'You are here for the Stone, Daughter of Bone? Or have you come to learn some truths? I know all about your father's ruse.'

'Just the Stone,' Jenyfer managed, although her mind was suddenly whirling with questions, wondering what this faery could tell her about Melodias, or if she could trust a single thing that came out of Medb's mouth.

'Heartfire, heartfire, burning bright. Will it burn against the night?' Medb whispered.

Jenyfer peered into the darkness of the water until Ordes touched her arm. She shook herself, straightened and turned to face the Queen of The Teeth. 'What do I need to do?'

'You'll need to be at your best, or in the depths, so ends your quest,' Medb answered.

Ordes frowned. 'That doesn't answer the question. What does—'

'Temper, temper running hot, still thinks he's something that he's not,' Medb sang. Ordes clenched his fists. 'The Treasure is yours, only once you play.' She stopped, eyes narrowing as she wrinkled her nose at Ordes. 'This one – he can go away.'

'I'm not leaving,' Ordes said firmly.

Medb shrugged. 'Stay, go, it matters not to me. Born between the worlds, you be.' She tilted her head, studying them curiously again. Jenyfer's muscles liquified as the Faery Queen moved closer and lowered her voice, her black eyes on Ordes. 'Interfere not, the Bow of Mists you've already got. This trial is for the syhren, she – break the rules, and deal with me.'

A shiver raced down Jen's spine at the promise of violence and bloodshed in Medb's tone. 'He won't interfere. I'll do what I have to, to get the Stone.' She swallowed. 'You said play. Play what?'

'Games, of course, what else there be?' Medb replied. 'The Singing Stone is yours to earn. Oh heartfire, heartfire how it burns. I can see it, smell it, taste it, too – the Singing Stone is right for you.' Medb flashed her teeth. 'Far below, the water is black. Don't disturb them, or they'll attack.'

'Who will?' Jenyfer asked, glancing again at the water.

The faery smiled. 'Your kin, in a way. Careful, they like to play.'

Medb strode away, back to her throne.

'She'll test your fears,' Ordes said quietly. 'They're all faeries here.'

Jenyfer nodded. She knew her magic would not harm any of them, but nerves clawed at her as she peered into the pool of dark water. She swallowed and met the Faery Queen's dark gaze.

Medb clapped her hands and glowing balls of light appeared, hovering over the pool. She nodded, and gestured to the water.

CHAPTER 33

Arthur woke with a hammering heart. He had taken a nap, something he had never done before, but his head was so full with the Sword of the White Dragon always talking to him, except in his dreams.

For in his dreams, it was Eseld.

The Fisher Queen had come to him again, her face grave and her voice troubled. She had met him in her cave, with the fire whose warmth Arthur could not feel. Eseld had not held the Grail in her lap this time, nor was she wearing her crown of chipped coral. She did not waste time speaking in riddles, either, but had gotten straight to the point.

'You have to be careful,' she'd said. 'You might not be able to trust the ones you are with. A dream shared is not always a dream.'

Arthur sat up, rubbing the back of his neck.

Ordes and Jenyfer had gone to The Teeth. Anxiety gnawed at his belly. The Stone was Jenyfer's to find and no one could interfere, but what if she needed help? What if something had happened? He knew neither

Jen nor Ordes would leave the other. Arthur had told Jalen, had told Mordred, he did not want to be the sort of king who would not risk himself for others, and he would hold himself to that, no matter what.

Jalen was nowhere to be seen, but recently that was not unusual. Arthur bit back on the spark of worry and left his cabin. Jalen's absence made this easier – if he wasn't around, he couldn't stop Arthur. He did not go above deck, instead delving deeper into the belly of the ship, where he could hear the ocean slapping the hull. It was cold and dark, and he wondered if this was a good idea, but getting to The Teeth was not only important, it was necessary.

There was a lonely door, its outline visible in the watery darkness. It was not locked, which surprised Arthur, but he didn't dwell on it, stepping inside. He felt her eyes on him immediately, and busied himself with lighting the lantern hanging on a peg while he figured out what to say.

When he finally turned to look at the Red Sister, she smiled, a mockery, but he didn't care.

'Your Majesty,' Olwen said. 'I'd bow, but, you know,' she added, indicating the rope around her middle. 'What brings you to my prison, dreamwalker?'

Arthur frowned. 'What did you call me?'

'Dreamwalker,' Olwen said. 'Ah. You didn't know. It makes sense. It's not a common gift, a family trait usually, a gift from the Two in One.'

Arthur set the lantern to the side and crouched before the renegade Red Sister. He wasn't sure he could trust her, but he was willing to take the chance. He settled himself on the floor, sitting cross-legged. He had never heard the term the Two in One before, either, but he put that aside for later. 'Ordes mentioned dreamwalking. What does it mean?'

'You walk in your dreams, don't you? You see things that have happened and things that are yet to happen,' Olwen explained. When his frown deepened, she leant forward as far as her restraints would allow. 'You have the gift, Arthur. I can sense it. The things that happen in your dreams are real. They are not happening in the real world, but often in the world between the worlds, in the space between sleeping and waking, or sometimes, the space between life and death.'

'Between the worlds,' Arthur murmured, then looked up sharply. 'You said a family trait. My father has no magic. That would mean my mother could walk in her dreams.'

'And possibly your grumpy sister,' Olwen said.

And possibly my cousin, Arthur thought, remembering the dream he shared with Mordred when they were still in Cruithea. When he had spoken to his cousin about the vision – the castle, Camlann, the roaring beast with wings – Mordred had not acted like any of it was familiar. But then again, Arthur reasoned, Mordred was an enigma wrapped up in shadows and mystery. He knew nothing about his cousin – what he could do, what he was capable of. The thought sent unease skimming the length of his spine, but also thrilled him.

The magic he thought he'd possessed was gone, only there when the Sword of the White Dragon was in his hands, but dreamwalking was something different. Something that was his. He would hold on to it as tightly as he could.

Olwen was watching him, so Arthur pushed aside the thoughts of dreams and Mordred aside. He would think about magical familial gifts later.

He took a deep breath. 'Olwen, I need your help.'

'Do you, now?' she replied, eyes narrowed as her whole demeanour changed, closed off and suspicious once again. 'With what?'

'I need you to take me to The Teeth,' Arthur said.

Olwen burst out laughing. 'You have got to be joking. Do you even know what lives there?' She raked her earth-brown gaze over him. 'There isn't much of you, but I'm sure they'd find enough to gnaw on, for a while.'

'My friends are there, and I need to help them,' Arthur said, ignoring the threat, even though his skin crawled. He had faced his fears, and they had the Sword. Ordes had retrieved the Bow. Now, with the last Treasure so close, they could not afford to make any mistakes. Those in The Teeth could not be trusted, and Arthur was not going to leave Jenyfer and Ordes there. He could not shake the feeling that something terrible was going to happen. He kept his eyes on Olwen's. 'This is your chance.'

Her eyes became slits. 'My chance for what?'

'To show us we can trust you, that you really are on our side,' Arthur said. 'Can you help me?'

Olwen stared at him for a long time. 'Yes,' she said eventually. 'But you're going to have to get me out of these.' She held up her wrists; Kat's magical rope was bound tightly around not only Olwen's wrists, but every available part of the Red Sister.

Arthur smiled. 'Can't you get yourself out?'

'It's hard to maintain the illusion that I'm willing to cooperate if I'm constantly setting myself free, you know,' she grumbled, but moments later, the rope was gone. 'I wasn't joking about the silk,' she said as she rubbed her wrists. 'Your sister doesn't like me much.'

'She's wary of you,' Arthur said.

'Well, she wouldn't be smart if she wasn't,' Olwen replied. She stood, stretching the muscles in her neck and arms. 'Are you wary of me?'

'Not really,' Arthur answered. 'If you wanted to hurt us, you'd have done so already. So, how do we do this?'

'The Prophet of the Gods will know the moment we're gone,' Olwen told him. 'So will your sister and your demi-god. Are you willing to risk it?'

'Will they follow us?'

Olwen shook her head. 'The storm demon won't, as much as he would like to. He can't get in. Medb has warded the islands so no Old Ones, or ones close enough to being one, can get it. And Merlin could get in if he wanted, but he won't. He'll stop our good captain from following us.'

'How can you be so sure?' Arthur asked.

'Call it a hunch,' Olwen said. 'Right, we need to go, if we're going to go before anyone realises I'm free. Still want to do this?'

Arthur nodded, and she closed her hand over his arm.

Slowly, a red mist rose around them. 'Hold on,' she said, and Arthur was tumbling through red-tinged darkness. It was similar to when he travelled with Jalen, but Olwen's magic was dark and deep and smelt like rust and old blood. He had no idea how blood magic worked and wasn't sure he wanted to know. He closed his eyes and hoped she didn't let him go.

Arthur and Olwen stood on a rocky shore, wind rippling around them. 'Welcome to The Teeth,' she said. 'Teñvali-enez, the Island of Shadows, to be precise. This is Medb's place. All the islands here are inhabited by something or another – selkies, carlings, the washerwomen, the night criers … all such charming creatures. Jenyfer and Ordes would have been taken here, to Medb.'

Arthur stared up at the towering pile of rock. There were no stars to be seen in The Teeth, and he couldn't help but feel that was an omen of sorts. 'Is there a way in?'

'Follow me,' Olwen said.

'How do you know where you're going?' Arthur asked, scrambling over a pile of rocks after her. Olwen moved quickly, oblivious to the darkness, but she slowed her pace so he could catch up. She pointed – up ahead, twenty metres off the ground, was an opening in the rock.

'What's on the other side of the dark hole, I have no idea, but can you see any other way in?' she asked him. Arthur shook his head – he could barely see what she pointed at. The wind pulled at their hair and clothes, the ocean pounding the rocks, sea spray brushing their bodies. Arthur glanced over his shoulder and couldn't see the ship at all.

'Can you climb?' Olwen asked. 'It doesn't look too difficult – there's enough to hold on to.'

'Can't you magic us in?' Arthur asked.

She shook her head. 'Like I said, the islands are all protected. I could break through the barriers, but that would not be looked upon kindly.

Medb would see it as an act of war, no doubt, the cranky bitch,' she muttered.

'Have you met her?' Arthur asked. Katarin and Halymere had given the impression that no one went to The Teeth, and Mordred and his aunt had said something similar when he saw them last. 'Olwen?'

The Red Sister ignored him and started to climb. Arthur took a deep breath and followed.

CHAPTER 34

Nothing stirred beneath the surface of the water.

Medb watched Jenyfer, a grin plastered across her inhuman face.

'You said my kin were down there. Do they have the Stone?' she asked.

Medb shrugged. 'The time for lies is at an end, time for you not to pretend. Be what you were born to be, set the Stone and yourself free.'

Jen glanced at Ordes. His face was pulled into a frown, but he met her eyes and gave her a nod. She had to do it alone, as he had, and as Arthur had.

Jenyfer took a deep breath, and plunged into the pool.

The water was thick and oddly warm, making her wonder if it was water at all. The deeper she went, the thinner it became. It wasn't until her lungs were burning, and she was gripped with a terrible fear that her magic had failed her, that Jenyfer's skin tingled. Her lungs expanded and she sucked the strange dark water into herself.

It was bitter, not the taste of seawater she was used to, but beneath the tang was the comforting bite of salt. As Jenyfer's eyes adjusted to the gloam of Medb's underwater world, she began to make out shapes – rocks, large and dark, covered in slime and moss, and a forest of deep green kelp. Unlike the waters of Avalon, there didn't appear to be anything else down there with her.

When she reached the bottom of the pool, Jenyfer set her feet on the ground, then pulled them back in fright. Sharp rocks spread across the bottom of Medb's pool in place of sand. She hovered there, rubbing the pad of her foot, hoping she wasn't bleeding. Medb had not bothered to tell her what exactly was lurking down here and whether they were hungry.

It was so dark. Jenyfer waited, heart pounding; Ordes' heartbeat was steady, calm, and she focused on that, pushing away the panic she could feel starting to take hold.

She had no idea what she was supposed to do down here or where the Singing Stone could be. Medb had mentioned a cage of bones, but all Jenyfer could see was darkness. She closed her eyes; the water shifted past her, underwater currents. Something touched her ankle. She bit her lip, but did not panic, focusing on the Stone. She had nothing to go on except for that drawing in the mysterious book about the Otherworld.

Faint music floated to her ears. A slow melody in a minor key. Something tugged at her chest, like a drawstring pulled tight. Jenyfer opened her eyes and gasped. A thin thread of light had emerged from her chest, shooting away into the underwater gloaming. Swallowing, she set off, following the light.

Jenyfer swam quickly but cautiously. Rocks emerged from the gloom without warning; she darted around them. She had seen nothing else alive, not yet, but Medb's words echoed through her mind.

Your kin, in a way.

As far as Jenyfer knew, syhrens were created by her father. Whatever Medb was talking about must be something different. A seal-like creature sped past her, followed by another. *Selkies.* She followed them, their fins just visible in the murky water. Soon, there was a glimmer of white in the darkness and a cage of bones took shape. As she approached, heart in her mouth, something swam towards her. Jenyfer stopped. A mermaid, she thought, her mind shifting back to the dead creature in the square in Kernou, her grey skin and fish-like tail.

This creature, however, was not a mermaid, and it was not alone. Three others joined it, and they came closer, moving with terrifying speed. Green skin and scales, huge milky eyes, and when one opened their mouth, Jenyfer saw rows of sharp teeth. Instead of fishtails, the creatures had tails like eels, the bones visible beneath transparent skin. Like Ophine, Jenyfer could not tell if the creatures were male, female, or something in between.

Behind them was the cage.

The creatures looked at her, blinked as one. A voice, as rough as the water beneath the fiercest storm, barrelled into Jenyfer's mind.

She who seeks the Singing Stone, deep within the cage of bone.

Jenyfer nodded.

The creatures moved aside and let her through. The cage was indeed made of bone – she didn't stop to think about what they had belonged to – but when she reached for the door, a hand shot out of the watery darkness, closing with frightening strength around her wrist.

A *human* hand.

Jenyfer pulled her wrist free, wheeling back in fright.

Inside the cage was a man. His white hair floated around his face like a halo. He was naked and gaunt, skin stretched tight over his bones. Jenyfer covered her mouth with her hand as the glowing light from her chest crawled over the man's body, stopping over his heart.

The Singing Stone in its cage of bone.

The Treasure of the Gods, her father's Treasure, was embedded in a human man's chest. Jenyfer could see it straining against his skin, like it was about to burst free. The man met her eyes. How was he alive? Then she realised. The Stone was keeping him here, suspended in this thick, viscous soup, like a babe in its mother's womb.

Jenyfer looked to the faeries desperately.

Sing the Stone free of its cage. Their voices echoed through her head, disjointed and jarring. *This vessel has been waiting an age.*

How long? Jenyfer thought, jolting when her question was answered.

Years and years and years have passed since he gave us this task.

He? Who was he?

And then it hit her.

Her trial, her greatest fear.

Her voice, a weapon. Her voice – death.

If I take it, he'll drown, she thought.

Yes, the creatures hissed in her mind. *We're hungry. So hungry.*

Jenyfer recoiled; the man was watching her with empty eyes. *You're going to eat him?*

Only once it's dead. You cannot save its vacant head.

Arthur had to confront and dispose of a spectre of his father. A shade, not the actual man.

Ordes had shifted his shape, overcoming the fear of losing himself to his magic.

She had to use her power to kill a man.

Here she was, more in control of who she was than ever before. It was cruel to expect her to do this. Was it because she was a syhren? Neither of the others had to kill someone. She had killed to protect them against the Sacellum's ships and the Witchfinders. She would have killed Marsh to stop him from harming Ordes. This was different. This was forcing her to choose – destiny or failure? A new world or the one they had?

Jenyfer shook her head, eyes burning. Was it possible to cry underwater?

Jen? Ordes' voice – she placed her hand over her heart, felt the strength of two heartbeats. *Are you okay?*

No! Quickly, she told him what she had to do, what she was being asked to do, her words tumbling over one another. Surely, there had to be another way? She waited for him to tell her that, to promise they'd find some other way to get the Stone.

His voice returned to her, soft and regretful:

You have to do it.

I can't!

Jenyfer, this does not define you. Ordes' voice was tight, then gentle. *We need that Stone.*

Maybe we don't. Maybe two is enough. Maybe the Fisher Queen will let us have the Grail with two Treasures—

Jenyfer, I'm sorry, Ordes whispered. *I'm so sorry.*

The man in the cage was stroking his chest, the Stone pushing at the prison of his skin and bone, wanting to be free. Jenyfer's throat was tight, but she drew closer to the cage again.

One person. One nameless man. One man to save the world.

The creatures were watching her eagerly, their milk-white eyes and sharp teeth glimmering in the darkness.

Jenyfer closed her eyes.

She was not her father. She was not ruthless and cruel, cold and heartless. Even after all the time spent with him in Lyonesse, with Andromache learning her songs, even with the watery rendering of Bryn she had destroyed with her voice, Jenyfer had held tight to her humanity. The one part of her that her father thought made her weak. Although she had drowned the Sacellum's men, this was different. That had been protection.

This was murder.

Maybe her father was right. She was weak. *He* would do this. He would do what needed to be done. He wouldn't think twice about it. Neither would Katarin or Ordes. Even Arthur, although it would hurt him. They would all do what needed to be done, but here she was, hesitating to use her magic to do this one thing.

Jenyfer could feel her song climbing up the back of her throat. It could feel the Stone and wanted her to do this. The Singing Stone was created with her father's magic, and her magic, her gift from him, was quickly gathering strength.

Andromache had told her she could stop a man's heart with her song. She had taught Jenyfer the words, and though Jenyfer had tried to bury those words deep inside where she would never find them again, they came easily, flooding her mind and her throat with a melody that was hers and hers alone.

She could feel the Stone, could feel the man's will wrapped around it. He was completely bound, a slave to the magic of Melodias' Treasure.

If there was one thing Jenyfer knew, it was what being trapped felt like.

She opened her eyes; somewhere in the man's vacant gaze was something she recognised – the will to be free.

Jenyfer opened her mouth. She had never tried to sing underwater, but it didn't matter. Her song flowed out of her, powerful, melodic, soothing. The man's eyes closed; his hands dropped from his chest as Jenyfer continued to sing, calling the Stone to her.

She watched it explode from the man's chest, his scrawny fingers suddenly grasping for it as it floated towards her. She made herself watch as his eyes widened, clutching at his throat as his blood filled the water.

Her hands closed around the Singing Stone, and a glorious melody rushed through Jenyfer's blood, her bones, her very self, layers of voices tumbling over one another, perfectly harmonised, perfectly pitched, the sound sliding inside her and wrapping itself around her heart. The Stone fit perfectly into her palm, like it was made for her hands.

The creatures pounced, tearing open the cage, their hungry, vicious glee resounding through Jenyfer's mind. With the Stone clasped tightly in one hand, she swam away from the cage of bone and the carnage behind her, cursing Merlin and his prophecy with her entire being.

Arthur followed Olwen through the darkness. He had no idea where they were going, and the back of his neck prickled as he wondered if he'd been a fool to trust a Red Sister. He knew nothing about her, nothing at all.

He swallowed. Up ahead, a slice of light cut sharply through the darkness. Olwen stopped suddenly and Arthur ran into her back. 'Right,' she said. 'Might as well go and say hello.'

Olwen took a deep breath and marched towards the light. Arthur followed, drawn along in her wake, letting her courage in this moment be his. His fingers brushed the dagger at his hip, but as they stepped from the darkness and into the light, he knew any weapon he carried would be useless.

They were in a great cavern, the walls dark stone. Lantern light cast strange shadows, and glowing orbs of dim light floated through the air. Arthur swallowed as the sheer number of fey creatures in that cavern became apparent, lounging around the edge of a large pool of water.

Arthur's heart seized as many sets of unnatural eyes turned to him and Olwen.

Standing on the other side of the pool, eyes on the water, wings spread, was Ordes. Arthur froze. Ordes had always been human to Arthur, even knowing the truth, but in this place, surrounded by faeries, Ordes was obviously not human. The dim light in the cavern cast shadows on his face, accentuating a bone structure that Arthur knew did not belong to a normal man. In this place, Ordes' face was Otherworldly, beautiful, like his mother's was.

'There's Medb.' Olwen closed her hand over Arthur's forearm. Next to Ordes, Medb was small and slight, her long dark hair shifting around her shoulders. She was not watching the water. She was watching them. She laughed, the sound causing Ordes to lift his gaze. His silver eyes widened when he saw Arthur and Olwen. He vanished and reappeared next to Arthur, standing in front of him, as if shielding him from everything in that cavern. Arthur noted that Ordes' wings were not made of feathers this time – they were shadows and mist again, like they had been when he'd returned from Malist with the Bow.

Medb strolled around the pool, the hem of her black gown trailing along the ground after her. The fey in the cavern were all watching, eyes gleaming, sharp teeth sliding free of lips as they grinned.

'The little Once and Future King, what a dark world he'll bring,' Medb sang. 'Bright of heart and sound of mind, what will he choose when in a bind?'

Arthur wasn't sure how to react.

The Queen's eyes shifted to Olwen – she bared her teeth in a menacing snarl. 'Ereshki's pet, a traitor be, blood so red.' Medb held up a clawed-hand. 'Shall we see?'

'Bring it, bitch,' Olwen retorted. Arthur looked at her in alarm. Olwen held up her hands in surrender, but her dark eyes blazed with anger. Arthur waited, breath like sap in his lungs, heavy and thick, but the Queen of The Teeth made no more threats. Her black lips curled, a chilling smile that caused Arthur's heart to skip a beat.

He swallowed and stepped free of Ordes' shadow. They exchanged a look and Ordes motioned to the water, so dark Arthur couldn't see anything beneath the surface. He peered uselessly into the depths, mindful of the creatures watching his every move. Olwen stood behind him, arms folded, her expression a promise of death if anyone should touch them.

Something was moving beneath the water, and moments later, Jenyfer's head broke the surface. She pushed her wet hair back from her face as Ordes reached down to help her, his wings vanishing. Arthur breathed a sigh of relief to see her unhurt.

Without a word, Ordes folded Jenyfer against his chest. Water streamed from her hair and clothes to pool on the stones at her feet. Arthur saw her shoulders shake. Slowly, she pulled away from Ordes, his hand on her waist ready to pull her back at a moment's notice. Her eyes met Arthur's and widened, that sea-storm blue clouded.

Her gaze found Medb, so furious and ferocious that Arthur sucked in a breath.

'How long?' Jenyfer demanded.

'Ages, ages, ages, past,' the faery crooned, unworried by Jenyfer's fury. 'But now it's done, it's come to pass. Treasures three collected be. Come the dawn, we shall be free.' As the words left the Faery Queen's lips, her eyes became feral and dark. The air around her shifted, like it did before a storm. The room full of fey began to prowl, their lips pulled back from their fangs, their eyes slitted, claws raking the air. Tails lashed against rock and fur stood on end. Something howled, the sound racing through the air to plunge into Arthur's chest.

He froze. He knew the feeling that raced through him. They were surrounded by predators, and they were prey.

'Free?' Ordes demanded of Medb, his voice sharp.

Olwen rolled her eyes and cursed under her breath. 'Why does no one *listen* to me? She's got the Stone. We need to go. Now.'

Arthur nodded. He didn't want to stay a moment longer in this place with its malevolent energy. The hair stood up on the back of his neck in warning as a low, rumbling growl echoed through the cavern.

Jenyfer cast the Queen of The Teeth a final look of contempt, grabbed Ordes and dragged him towards the tunnel. Arthur and Olwen followed, the Red Sister blowing a cheeky kiss to Medb, who bared her teeth and hissed at her.

Before Arthur stepped into the darkness of the tunnel, the Queen's voice called to him, soft and loud and powerful as thunder. 'Future King, you've much to fear. Mind the darkness that lurks near. Those you trust have dreams to share. Careful if you lay yours bare.'

He swallowed, recalling Eseld's words. He made to turn back when Olwen shoved him forcefully into the tunnel.

'We need to go,' she insisted.

'But—'

'Now, Arthur! Can't you feel it?' she asked. 'In the air?' Olwen paused, met his eyes. 'Power. That fey back there is not a thing to be trifled with. Sunrise is coming,' Olwen added.

'Come the dawn,' Arthur murmured. A memory of a conversation tugged at his mind, Mordred leaning over the fire. 'She was trapped here?'

'They all were,' Olwen said as she and Arthur hurried through the darkness, emerging into the open air, the water crashing onto the pebbled beach before them. Dawn was a smear of blood on the eastern horizon.

Ordes and Jen were waiting for them. A little boat bobbed on the water. Jenyfer went to climb in, but Olwen shook her head, gesturing furiously at the rising dawn.

'No time. We need to be back on the ship before that sun rises.'

When no one moved, she pulled at her hair in irritation. 'You don't know what she is! We'll be safe on the ship. The Myrddin is there. She won't cross him,' Olwen added.

'Why not?' Ordes asked.

Olwen gave him an incredulous look. 'Do you know nothing? Merlin is the one who locked her in there! Let's go,' she demanded, turning to Arthur. 'Your sister and your grumpy boyfriend scare me less than Medb does.' She put her hand on his arm. 'Take the syhren,' she told Ordes. 'Let's go!' Her tone had shifted from worry to sheer terror. The sun was inching closer to rebirth. From inside the Island of Shadows they heard laughter, deep and menacing and manic. The island began to shake.

Ordes hesitated only a second longer, and then wings exploded from his back. Arthur sucked in a breath – they were glorious in the light, dark grey feathers bleeding to white at the tips, like a storm over the ocean. With his fierce expression illuminated by the dawn, Ordes reminded Arthur of a painting he had once seen in a book belonging to his father. It had been of a stained-glass mosaic, and the inscription had said the picture had filled a window in the Sacellum. He'd been struck by the man, his shining grey eyes and wings, the look of serene determination on his face and between his hands had been a bowl …

Olwen shouted, 'Go!'

Jenyfer wrapped her arms around Ordes' neck. He lifted her into his arms, beat his wings, and they were gone. Arthur had only a moment to watch them, to marvel at the sight, before Olwen closed her hand over his arm, and the world dissolved in red mist and the scent of rust and old blood.

CHAPTER 35

Jenyfer's face was pale when they touched down on the deck of *The Excalibur*, and Ordes wasn't sure if it was the flight – he could hardly believe they hadn't tumbled into the ocean – or what she'd had to do to claim the Stone. Had Merlin known and not given her any warning? Ordes knew his father wasn't supposed to interfere with their quest, but surely he could have bent the rules for outright murder?

The deck had dissolved into chaos. Jalen and Olwen were shouting at one another, and Katarin was shouting at her brother while Arthur tried to assure Jalen he was fine, but if looks could kill, the demi-god's glare would have flayed the skin from Olwen's body. Lightning crackled over Jalen's knuckles, and Olwen's skin steamed with red mist.

'Jen?' Ordes whispered. She took a shuddering breath. Her eyes moved past his face, and he didn't need to wonder whom she was looking for.

'You fucking bastard!' She slipped from Ordes' grip and started pounding her fists against his father's broad chest. 'You bastard! How could you not warn me? How could you?'

Merlin let Jenyfer unleash her rage at him, a ship's mast weathering her storm. Katarin's face was like stone; she did nothing to intervene as Jenyfer let out a yell of pure frustration as her strength began to flag. Only then did Merlin step forward and fold his arms around her, pulling her against him and tucking her head into his chest gently. She seethed and struggled, hissing like a cat, lashing out with feet and hands until the fight slowly left her.

'I'm sorry,' Merlin said softly as Jenyfer slumped in his arms. 'I'm so sorry.'

Jenyfer mumbled something, then, 'Why? Why … *that*?'

'You had to earn it – you had to face your fear, Jenyfer,' Merlin said. 'You need to understand. I'd seen you – all three of you – but I never thought … I never thought I'd *know* any of you, let alone come to care about you.' He met Ordes' eyes. 'And I am grateful for knowing you.'

Jenyfer pushed him away, wiping at her eyes. She levelled him with a hard, angry stare, before she turned away, going to sit on the steps to the quarterdeck. Ordes remained where he was – he wanted nothing more than to sit with her, offer whatever comfort he could, but he was focused on something else.

Katarin simmered with a rage greater than Ordes had ever seen. There was no more shouting. She pointed a finger at Olwen. 'I should have taken Halymere's advice and thrown you overboard.'

'I can swim,' Olwen said with a shrug. 'And they're all fine. Back in one piece. No damage done.'

'No damage done?' Katarin repeated, her voice rising again. Jalen looked like he'd strangle the Red Sister with his bare hands.

'Kat,' Ordes said, faltering as she turned her glower on him.

Olwen sighed and held out her hands, and for a moment, Ordes wasn't sure what Kat would do. Olwen was calm in the face of Kat's anger, all her earlier fear about Medb vanished as if it had never existed.

That was something Ordes was deeply curious about.

'I couldn't be bothered wasting time tying you up again,' Kat snapped.

Olwen's face fell. 'Oh. And here I was excited at the idea. Are you sure? I'll make it worth your time, I promise.'

Kat shook her head, turning away from the Red Sister, and it was Arthur's turn to suffer her anger. 'What the fuck were you thinking?'

'Kat,' Arthur said. 'I made her take me.'

'How am I supposed to keep you safe if you do things like that, Arthur?' she said wearily.

'Protecting me is not your job,' he told her firmly. Katarin opened her mouth then closed it again, throwing her hands in the air and stalking away. The door to her cabin slammed, the sound ringing around the deck.

'It might be best if you stay out of her way for a while,' Arthur told Olwen. Jalen's arms were folded, his expression deadly. He had not looked away from Olwen.

The Red Sister rolled her eyes. 'Should be easy on a ship,' she muttered. 'So, can I go now? I mean, am I free to roam this wide, open ocean?'

Arthur nodded, and Olwen stalked off.

Ordes met Arthur's gaze and then Jenyfer's. Her face was still dark with anger and grief. He turned to his father. 'We need to know what we set free.'

'I'll tell you about her, but first, I need to tell you something else. Long ago, the Old Ones went to war,' Merlin began. They were crowded in Ordes and Jenyfer's cabin. Merlin had claimed the armchair, leaving Jen, Ordes, and Arthur to perch on the bed. Jenyfer sat as far back as she could, legs tucked up to her chest, face still stormy. Ordes shoved his trembling hands in his lap.

Jalen had wanted to be here, but Arthur had managed to convince the tense and pissed-off demi-god that he was fine, he was safe, and nothing was going to harm him in Ordes' cabin. Jalen had left, scowling darkly at everyone.

'Gawain crafted the Sword of the White Dragon from the depths of the earth. Niniane created the Bow from magic and mist. And Melodias' Stone was made from the power of the ocean. The world was at a tipping point, and the Old Ones disagreed on what the future should look like. Battle lines were drawn – Niniane and Gawain on one side. Ereshki and Inanna on the other,' Merlin told them.

'Hang on,' Arthur said. 'Ereshki and Inanna were on the same side?'

Merlin nodded. 'Inanna and Ereshki are one and the same. They are the Two in One – light and darkness, life and death. Balance.'

'We've never heard them called that,' Jenyfer challenged snappily.

'I have,' Arthur murmured, 'from Olwen. But I didn't know what she was talking about.'

Merlin tapped his chin. 'Letting you believe Ereshki was at the heart of all this served a purpose. It is true – this is her doing – but not in the way that you think.'

'Melodias, Ankou, and Morrigna?' Ordes asked. 'What was their role in this war?'

'Fate and Death could not interfere with what was to come,' Merlin explained. 'And Melodias played the same game he is playing now – he waited.'

At the mention of her father, Jenyfer crawled forward, wedging herself between Ordes and the bulkhead. He rested his hand on her leg. Anger still coated her eyes and her skin was bloodless.

'So, who won?' he asked.

'Nobody ever wins a war, Ordes. A truce was called, which lasted until Ereshki took the Treasures. She took them not to gain power over the others, but to prevent this from happening again.' Merlin paused, ran his hand through his hair, glancing at Ordes. 'Before I met your mother, before I washed up on the shores of Avalon, I helped Ereshki hide them.'

For a moment, no one spoke.

'You ... what?' Ordes managed finally. Medb's words, her anger, suddenly made sense, and Voss had hinted he knew Merlin. 'Every time

I think I know you …' Ordes' voice trailed off. 'Did Niniane know where they were? Did any of the Old Ones, besides the Red One?'

'Niniane did not know,' Merlin said. 'She knows what I did, but I made a vow to the Two in One that I would not reveal where they were, not even to those who would seek them. I kept that promise, for all those years.'

Arthur tapped his fingers on his thigh, his expression thoughtful. 'But if Ereshki and Inanna are in this together, why did my aunt banish Ereshki from Cruithea? Why force the Red Sisters into the Dead Woods and banish them from their land?'

'So all this would come to pass,' Merlin answered. 'Inanna and Ereshki agreed to be separated. They agreed to sacrifice themselves so that this world could be healed. Even though the Old Ones had come to a truce, it was fragile, and it would only be a matter of time before old wounds were opened, and the cycle would begin anew. Someone needed to take the blame. Ereshki allowed herself to be the scapegoat.' He looked around at them all. 'You have to understand what it is to be never-ending. Boredom is a terrible burden, as is power. Once already the Old Ones have brought the world to the brink, only to bring it back, shape it how they want it, and then let it all fall again when they couldn't agree. We are now heading towards the third age of gods and men.'

No one spoke, until Ordes cleared his throat. 'Already? The Old Ones have destroyed the world *already*? They have been playing games with the world since it was created, is that what you're saying? The shifter told me that fey and humans had never been given a choice in any of it – that's what he was referring to, isn't it?'

Merlin nodded. 'Ereshki and Inanna wanted things to change. They wanted to break the cycle. Taking the Treasures was a distraction, and it worked, for a while. But the Gods are precarious, and the Gods are greedy. War was brewing again, unknown to mankind, so Ereshki reinvented herself as the One God. She shifted the focus of man away from the Old Ones, and so she removed some of their power. She gave them a reason to unite and to see things clearly.'

'Only they didn't, did they?' Ordes asked.

'No,' Merlin said regretfully.

'What do we do?' Arthur asked. 'We need to know what sort of world we will be forcing people to live in, because they won't have a choice, will they? And you've told us the Old Ones ...' His voice broke off, and he shook his head.

'Balance,' Ordes murmured. 'We need balance.'

'I agree, but without knowing what was, how can we decide what balance looks like?' Arthur argued.

'Before Ereshki stole the Treasures, magic ran wild. The creatures you encountered in The Teeth were everywhere, as well as the more gentle fey, but even they can be dangerous,' Merlin said. 'Once humans acquired magic through their unions with the fey – sometimes by choice, sometimes not – magic became theirs to wield. What no one has told you is that the ancient rulers – Enyon and Eseld – were Magic Wielders; him I didn't like much, but she was always cordial. She liked to fish in the river that once ran across Camlann Plain.'

'You met them?' Arthur breathed.

'I served them,' Merlin said. He met Ordes' gaze. 'Your mother told you what you needed to hear. Some of it was true – I did set myself on the ocean, to die, and ended up in Avalon. But before that, I was advisor to a King and Queen. And I saw magic destroy them.' Merlin looked at his hands. 'Ereshki tried to warn him, but Enyon would not listen. He made a deal with the darkness, and it cost him his sister, his rule, his life, and any vision of the future he might have held.'

'Who did he bargain with?' Jenyfer asked slowly.

Merlin's voice was low. 'Medb.'

Arthur gasped. 'Mordred told me, when I was in Cruithea. I wasn't sure what to believe. Everything he said was designed to rattle me.'

'He told you the truth. After what happened with Enyon, I locked her in The Teeth, but now she's free to do what she does best – make deals and bargains and promises with men who want what they cannot have, who want to be what they are not,' Merlin said. His expression turned grave. 'She will find him. Mordred. Like calls to like. She will sense the darkness in him, and she will use it.'

'Can't you bind her to The Teeth again?' Ordes asked.

'The Stone bound her,' Merlin explained. 'Melodias' Treasure has the power to compel – I used that power to compel Medb and all those fey who had allied themselves with her to stay in there.'

'I shouldn't have taken it,' Jenyfer whispered.

'You needed to take it,' Merlin told her. He looked around at the three of them, saw the fear, the suspicion on their faces. 'I cannot control what I see, or what I saw all those years ago. The only choice I had was what I did with what I was shown – a future borne of the ruins of the past could be a future of balance and harmony, or it could be a future of a repeated past.'

'When the Treasures were stolen and Dinas Emrys fell, what happened to the world? What was it like?' Arthur asked quietly.

'All was darkness for a time,' Merlin answered. 'Confusion. The Old Ones were fighting amongst themselves. The humans were without guidance. Camlann Plain was dying.'

'The curse,' Arthur said.

Merlin nodded. 'Yes. And it was here, in this time, before any decision had been made, that the Old Ones went to war.' He ran his hand over his face, his eyes tired. 'And now, we find ourselves back at the beginning, with a similar set of decisions to be made. But this time, it is not the Old Ones who shall make them, and that may make all the difference.'

CHAPTER 36

Katarin ground her teeth so hard her jaw ached. Frustration coiled beneath her skin, living and breathing, twisting through veins and muscles. She could feel it sinking into her bones. Usually, she'd be able to let it out, go ashore and find someone to argue or fight with, but now that option was lost to her.

So was the other option – talk to Aelle, storm around her cabin muttering and cursing while Aelle sat and waited for her to finish, and listen when she'd offer up some of her sage and always timely advice.

Katarin missed her, more than she had ever missed anything. She'd tried to think of what Aelle would say if she were here. But Katarin didn't think the same way, which was why she relied on her friend so heavily, much more than she had ever realised.

The *fear* she had felt when she realised Arthur had gone to The Teeth, and that Olwen had taken him there. That nail-biting, burning fear that she had had to endure waiting for them to return, powerless in the face of it all. She didn't know how to handle it, so instead of throwing her arms around her brother in utter relief that he was safe, she'd raged at him. At Olwen. At all of them.

Katarin sighed, leaning against the railing and putting her head in her hands. She should apologise, but she wasn't any good at it and was afraid that whatever words came out of her mouth would sound insincere.

Footsteps padded towards her. Ordes leant against the railing next to her, looking out to sea. They didn't speak for a long moment, until he nudged her with his shoulder.

'Were you worried about me, Katarin?' he said playfully. 'I saw your face when we returned. Should I be flattered? I didn't know you cared so much.'

She knew what he was doing – giving her an opening to talk about it, to share what was inside of her without making her openly admit her fears. In that moment, she appreciated Ordes more than she ever had.

'Well, I didn't lose any sleep over you, let's put it that way,' she said lightly.

'But you did lose sleep?'

'I've lost a lot of sleep lately,' she admitted.

'He's tougher than you think,' Ordes said. 'He stood there in that cavern, human and powerless, with a bunch of faeries who could have torn us all to pieces, because he was concerned about Jen and me. He faced that, for us.'

'I know,' she replied. 'I know he's strong. He had to be, to survive in that place with his father for so long and not lose his mind.'

Ordes nodded, turning to rest his back against the railing. 'I'm not sure how to take the new you, if I'm being completely honest. Caring, concerned, mothering. It makes me nervous.'

Katarin elbowed him, but she smiled as she did so. 'Don't get used to it.'

'He didn't mean to scare you,' Ordes said, his tone softening. 'I think Arthur still feels he has something to prove, not to any of us, but to himself. I was surprised to see him and Olwen there. They arrived out of nowhere, and her exchange with the lovely Medb was interesting indeed.'

Kat's eyebrows lifted as her stomach sunk. 'Oh?'

'They knew each other. Medb called her "Ereshki's pet",' Ordes replied. 'So it's safe to assume there is no love lost between Medb and the Red Sisters, which makes sense, I suppose. Ereshki stole the Treasure from Melodias, and then my father forced Medb to guard it for hundreds of years … Medb's probably entitled to be a little pissed off.'

'*Merlin* hid the Treasures? What the fuck, Ordes?' Katarin gripped the railing. 'What game is he playing? I know he's your father, but—'

'I know,' Ordes cut in. 'Do I trust him? I don't know sometimes.'

Katarin chewed her lip. 'Well, I don't trust her. Olwen,' she clarified. 'We don't know a thing about her, other than she's Iouen's sister and Ereshki's pet.' Kat found she liked that particular epithet for the Red Sister. 'I'd like to know exactly why she is here and why Ereshki has chosen this moment, when we're moving towards the Grail, to decide she wants to help us.'

'Then why don't you ask,' Ordes said. 'Here she comes. No matter what you think, Olwen saved our arses in The Teeth. She saved Arthur's arse.'

'Arthur, who wouldn't have been there if it wasn't for her,' Kat hissed under her breath.

'Arthur probably would have found some other way to get himself there,' Ordes said. 'There's something in the water,' he added, motioning at the slick ocean surrounding them.

Katarin squinted. 'I can't see anything.'

'It's a syhren,' Ordes told her quietly. Katarin's heart rate increased. 'I'll let Jen know.'

Olwen strode towards them. Her hair was loose; the wind picked it up and blew it about her face, but she didn't care. She looked like someone who had not seen the sky or fresh air in a long time. Kat bit her lip, curious. When she was a child, the Ossuary was talked about in whispers.

Ordes gave the Red Sister a nod, and left. Katarin sighed, resting her elbows on the railing and staring out to sea. Olwen echoed Kat's sigh, copying her posture. Kat raised her eyebrows, all her questions falling away. Ordes was right – Olwen had brought Arthur back safe and in one piece. If she'd wanted to hurt him, she could have easily done so.

'Can you go and find someone else to annoy?' Kat said.

'Annoying you is fast becoming the highlight of my days,' Olwen replied. She straightened and turned around, gazing around the deck. 'I never knew ships could be so boring. I thought being a pirate was all adventure and waving cutlasses and—'

'If you're bored, I can easily find you something to do,' Katarin cut in. This woman was infuriating.

'I'm good, thanks,' Olwen returned. Her tone grew serious. 'I know you don't want me here, and that's fine, but I'm staying until Arthur tells me otherwise. You may as well use me.'

'Use you? How?'

Olwen's eyes made a slow pass over Katarin's body, from head to toe and back again. The corners of her lips curled. 'In any way you want, but I was thinking for information,' she said.

'You've already told us about Ereshki,' Kat said, mortified to feel her cheeks heat.

'I wasn't referring to her. I was thinking, perhaps, you might be curious what your charming cousin has been up to,' Olwen said.

'You know Mordred?' Kat asked, frowning.

'Not personally, but I know he's messing with things he shouldn't be. Blood magic isn't for men,' Olwen added, her expression darkening.

Katarin felt like someone had knocked the air from her lungs. 'Wait. Mordred has been using blood magic?'

Olwen nodded. 'For some time now. He's a rebel, that one, but he's a rebel who's going to get himself killed. There's a reason Ereshki chooses women to receive the gifts of Her magic, Katarin. Blood is part of our lives – we bleed with the moon, and we bleed giving life. The secrets of blood have never been shared with men before.'

'Then how did he learn?' Katarin pressed. 'Why did they teach him if it is so dangerous?'

Olwen gave her a serious look. 'Because Mordred has a role to play.'

Kat chewed her lip, her thoughts on her cousin. She didn't ask what Olwen meant about roles. She wanted to know one thing. 'What will happen to him?'

'If he uses his common sense, nothing much,' Olwen said. She met Katarin's eyes, and held them. 'But if he doesn't, it will consume him, eventually. He will wish for death in the end.'

Katarin hadn't had a choice in the matter. Iouen had flung open her door and marched in, a bottle of rum under each arm. He waved one at her, a lopsided grin plastered to his face, making her wonder how much rum he'd consumed already.

'We're celebrating,' he said, as people filed in behind him, and suddenly the cabin was so crowded no one could move without tripping over someone else. 'Whoops,' Iouen said, looking around. 'I didn't think I'd told this many people.'

Katarin laughed, despite everything, and accepted the bottle Iouen passed her. As she drank, she looked around, eyes skimming over faces: Jen and Ordes, glued to one another as usual; her brother and his demigod; Tahnet, smiling at Iouen; and Halymere, who gave her a quick smile. These people were her family now, like Iouen had said they were his. The faces of those she had lost from *The Night Queen* dipped into her mind, but Katarin gently moved them aside. She would never forget them – she could never replace them – but they were gone.

It was time to move on, long overdue.

She pushed all thoughts of The Teeth and her cousin from her mind, and in the safe confines of her cabin, Katarin let herself relax. She let her guard down, smiled, laughed, spoke to people, enjoying the moment where she could be a person and nothing else. Not their captain, or someone caught up in the future of the world. Just a person.

She hadn't realised until people started leaving that Iouen had invited his sister to the party. As everyone filed out, Olwen did not. She waited until Iouen had shut the door behind him before she flung herself into the seat that Arthur had vacated. The Red Sister was mighty comfortable now she was no longer tied up below deck. Katarin wasn't sure yet if she had made a mistake, but she had to let Arthur make this decision, and her brother had decided Olwen could be trusted.

Kat sat back, watching the other woman carefully. Olwen was snarly and sharp, like a weapon or a thorn. She was rude, abrupt, and annoying, but there was a spark to her that Katarin couldn't help but admire. Every word that left Olwen's lips was designed to antagonise. Kat hadn't failed to notice the spark that ignited in her belly when the Red Sister taunted her – she liked having someone to bicker with, someone who was as sharp-edged and quick as she was, and if there was one thing Kat was learning, it was that Olwen did not disappoint.

Olwen reached for the bottle of rum, popped the cork and drank straight from the bottle.

'Do you mind?' Kat said.

'Not at all. It's good – not as good as the wine in Malist, but it'll do,' Olwen replied, taking another sip. 'Empty. Got any more?'

Wordlessly, Kat pointed to the cupboard to their left. Olwen got up, helped herself to another bottle, returned to her seat and put her feet up on the desk. Kat followed the line of Olwen's legs with her eyes, moving slowly up her torso, over her breasts, up the column of her throat, until she stopped, her gaze lingering on Olwen's mouth as the Red Sister lifted the bottle to her lips again.

'Are you going to share that?' Kat demanded eventually. Her mouth had gone strangely dry.

Olwen laughed, holding out the bottle. 'You want it, come and get it.'

'This is my cabin,' Kat reminded her, irritated.

Olwen's eyes moved around the room. 'Yes. It must be nice to sleep in an actual bed. Do you know how long it's been since I did that?'

Kat half expected the woman to get up and claim the bed, but Olwen didn't move. She drank more rum, and when she spoke again, her voice was soft.

'In the Ossuary, we had a thin mattress filled with straw and one blanket. Discomfort is not something the Red One wants for us, necessarily, but She also doesn't believe one person should be more comfortable than another.'

'Are you telling me Ereshki wouldn't like my bed?' Kat asked.

Olwen's eyes returned to the bed. 'She'd ask why you need so many pillows.'

'There's two pillows!' Kat protested.

'Exactly – and there is one of you. What does one person need two pillows for?' Olwen mused. 'Unless you're planning on sharing them.'

Katarin folded her arms. 'You're only free because my brother has decided to trust you.'

'I'm free because your chains can't hold me,' Olwen shot back.

'It was a rope.'

'Chains might have been the better choice, though, don't you think?'

Katarin ground her teeth. 'You are the most insufferable person I have ever met.'

Olwen's grin was lazy, relaxed. 'You're paying me compliments way too early in our relationship, Captain.' She paused, cocked her head to the side, studying Katarin with interest. 'Too soon?' She got up and wandered around to Kat's side of the desk, perching there, her arse not far from Katarin's hand. 'Like I said, it's been a while since I slept in an actual bed. The hammock is nice, I suppose, but it's not the same, is it?' She held out the rum, not taking her eyes from Kat's.

Kat took the bottle, mortified to see her fingers tremble against the glass. She sat back in her seat and drained the bottle, wiping her mouth with the back of her hand. She hesitated, then held out the bottle for Olwen again.

The Red Sister took it, her smile shifting to a frown. 'It's empty!'

'I know.'

Kat expected Olwen to fetch another bottle, but the other woman did not move. Her gaze crawled over Kat's face, settling on her mouth.

'You're going to have to share.'

Kat laughed. 'Oh really?'

Olwen leant forward so that her nose brushed Katarin's. The breath hitched in Kat's lungs, and sudden heat speared through her. She bit back on a gasp as Olwen's fingers brushed hers, a teasing touch, but enough to set Katarin's blood on fire.

Slowly, Olwen pulled back. The smug smirk Katarin expected to see was not there. Olwen's brown eyes were black in the lantern-kissed darkness. Katarin could not see her face clearly. She squirmed on her seat; her fingers flexed against Olwen's.

The Red Sister let her gaze travel over Katarin's face, so slowly it was painful for Kat to endure. Olwen's lips curled finally.

'Sweet dreams, Captain,' she said. Then she was gone.

Chapter 37

Arthur and Jalen had not long returned to their cabin after lunch. It was a warm day, and Arthur pushed open the porthole to let the sea breeze in.

'You will have to make hard decisions,' Jalen said. 'Not everyone will support what you want to do. The people have been living under the One God's rule—'

'Ereshki's rule,' Arthur cut in gently, sitting down to remove his boots. He hadn't told Jalen that Merlin had hidden the Treasures, and he wasn't sure why.

Irritation spasmed in Jalen's face. 'People have been living a life where everything is laid out for them. They have forgotten what it's like to think for themselves. You will have to think for them.'

Arthur frowned. 'I'm not sure I want to do that.'

'You might have to,' Jalen pressed. 'Magic back in the world, free once more, will be a difficult thing for them to come to terms with. You will have to lead them on this new path.'

'The things Olwen said about Ereshki …' Arthur began.

Jalen shook his head, his face dark at the mention of Olwen. Neither of them mentioned The Teeth. 'Lies.'

'How can you be sure?' Arthur asked. 'We know that the One God is Ereshki, and we know now that the Sacellum is under the control of the Red Sisters, so where does that leave us? With more questions, yes, but also possible answers, Jalen – answers about what to do once we have the Grail. I need to speak with Olwen again.'

'You can't trust her,' Jalen said, folding his arms. 'Ereshki betrayed the other Old Ones.'

'I'm beginning to think that sentiment depends on who you talk to,' Arthur murmured.

'Niniane won't like this, Arthur.'

Arthur sighed and ran his hand over his face. 'I understand you're loyal to her, so, tell me about her. Tell me why you bound yourself to her and not the others.'

Jalen shook his head. 'I think it's time I told you about me, about who I really am, instead.'

Arthur offered him a smile. 'I know who you are.'

'No, you don't.' Jalen's voice was sharp, regretful. He sat beside Arthur and squeezed his hand – an apology. 'When I lived, Arthur, I lived in the shadows. In darkness. My father had a hard-hand and a sharp tongue. That in itself was not unusual. Life was tough for those of us without magic, like my family. The Magic Wielders around us wanted for nothing – they shared their gifts, but my father did not want their charity. So we froze and we starved, often.'

Jalen did not speak for a long time, and when he did, his voice was low. 'Once I was old enough, I took to the water like my father. One of the men I worked with was a Magic Wielder – he could charm fish into the net.' Jalen laughed, a dark and bitter sound Arthur had never heard from him before. 'I was so jealous of this man, of what he could do, and

I cursed the Old Ones for not giving me their gifts, for seeing me born a mere human in a world full of magic – in a world where I was less.'

Arthur said nothing. Jalen lay back on the bed, so Arthur trailed his fingers through his lover's hair, a comforting gesture, the only thing he was able to offer in that moment.

'Fishing wasn't enough. It was winter, and it was cold. I heard of an old woman who lived in the forest. I heard she paid well for odd jobs. So, curious, I sought her out. She did indeed pay well.'

'What did you do for her?' Arthur asked. He imagined Jalen splitting firewood or hunting for the old woman, returning triumphant with a snared rabbit or a pheasant.

'She was a witch, specialising in charms and curses. I think she was part fey, but at the time, I didn't realise that. Her spells were simple things, but they worked. And sometimes, people refused to pay. They had gotten what they wanted.' Jalen swallowed. 'I told you I learnt to use a blade? She paid me to spill blood for her, and I did it. Those who would not pay for her services met me, and I took their lives in exchange for a witch's gold.'

Arthur sucked in a breath, startled.

'I kept telling myself I would stop, because my family had enough money to survive now. But there was a part of me that liked it, the killing. It was never people from my village – they respected the witch of the woods and always paid. But others would travel for miles for her spellwork,' Jalen said. He did not look at Arthur when he spoke. 'It was when I was away that my sister was violated. I guess our gold and our new comfort had captured the wrong sort of attention. I came home, blood still wet on my blades, and when I found out what had happened to Nessa … you saw the rest.' He glanced up at Arthur with solemn eyes. 'The only regret I had about dying was that my mother and sister would be alone. I cared nothing for myself.'

'Jalen,' Arthur whispered.

'I took the Bag Noz to the Otherworld, and was met by Ankou. As he weighed my darkness against my light on those scales of his, I could see how out of balance my life had become. We all have darkness and light inside us, Arthur, but what was left of my light was completely extinguished. I don't know what he saw in me that day, but Ankou gave me a choice – pass by him to the Pit, where my soul would stay in agony forever as punishment for my wrong-doings, or be reborn and serve him.'

'You chose Ankou,' Arthur said, offering a smile.

'I chose the Pit, Arthur. I chose eternal fire and torture,' Jalen said. Arthur's smile froze on his face. 'But, the God of the Otherworld chose differently. Magic was all I had wanted, and magic was what he gave me. And power!' Jalen sat up suddenly, swinging around so he could face Arthur. 'The feeling of it flowing through me, after being powerless my whole human existence, was glorious! I can't even describe it. In the early days, I delighted in the violent storms I could create. I was still angry, and now I had the means to take it out on the world. My master warned me that if I failed to find balance within myself, he would strip me of the gifts he had given and send me to the Pit. By this stage, I wanted to live. I wanted to remain in the world of magic and gods.'

'What happened?' Arthur breathed. 'Why did you leave him?'

Jalen took Arthur's hands in his, running his thumbs over Arthur's fingers gently. 'Merlin happened. I went with Ankou and the wraith who serves him, the one you met in your dreams of Lyonesse, to Avalon to hear Merlin speak his prophecy. To me, who had only known darkness, Avalon was like a dream. To me, it represented what a true world ruled by magic could be like, and I started thinking, why couldn't Teyath be like this place? A paradise. Enyon and Eseld, the sibling rulers of the mortal realm, had magic at their fingertips, but they did not use it to create something wonderful. Their rule was ending when Merlin had his vision of the future – his vision of you, Arthur. He told me then it was my duty to serve you, that in doing so, I would atone for my sins.'

Jalen released Arthur's hands and climbed off the bed, going to look out the porthole. Arthur wondered if he was seeing Niniane's realm in his mind. 'Leaving Avalon that day was torture. I didn't want to leave Niniane, who was the most glorious creature I had ever laid eyes on, or Merlin, who captivated me with his words. Perhaps Ankou sensed it. I don't know, but breaking my bond with him was easy, like cutting off a limb you no longer needed. It hurt, but beyond the hurt was the promise of something better. When I washed up on Avalon's shores, Niniane was waiting for me, like she knew I would come. She saved me, and I pledged myself to her.'

'Did she send you to Kernou?' Arthur asked. He kept his tone neutral, but his heart was thundering and claws had dug into his stomach. Jalen nodded. 'How did she know I was there?'

'I don't know. Perhaps Merlin told her. But she knew when you were born, you and Jenyfer. Ordes was first, several years before the two of you, created by a goddess and a man made of magic. I met him when he was new to the world, before his father took him from Avalon. But you were children, all of you, so Niniane and I waited. Ereshki had already stolen the Treasures and war had broken out between the Gods long before you existed, Arthur. Things were changing. We could feel magic's grip on the world slipping, but there was nothing we could do except continue to wait until you were ready.'

'And this is what Niniane wants? A world like Avalon?' Arthur asked.

'Don't you see?' Jalen said, coming to grasp Arthur's hands again. 'Teyath could be like Avalon, if you only wish it. Think about it – a world without pain or fear, without darkness. A paradise, Arthur.'

Arthur frowned. Pain and fear … without them, what lessons would humans learn? How would they come to know themselves? How would they learn morals? The value of their lives?

Jalen watched him eagerly.

'I don't know if human beings are meant to live that way,' Arthur said gently. 'I think we need to suffer sometimes. We need to fall into darkness in order to embrace the light, Jalen.'

'It isn't that simple, Arthur,' Jalen argued. 'Some people are incapable of finding that balance within themselves, and that is what leads to pain. That is what leads to fear and corruption and greed. I know.'

Arthur placed his palms against Jalen's cheeks. 'And you are better for it. Without the things you experienced in your life, the darkness you experienced, you would never have been able to appreciate the light, Jalen. I would never have experienced the light, or what it means to be happy or be free. I'm not saying that what you and Niniane desire won't happen – I'm saying I haven't decided yet.'

Jalen nodded, pressing his lips to Arthur's forehead. Arthur gave him a smile he hoped was convincing. He'd known all along what Jalen wanted him to choose – a world of magic, as wondrous as the one Jalen had come from and the one he had come to know. But the more of this world Arthur experienced, the more he learnt, not only of the present but the past, the more unsure he was. He wanted to do what was right, but how could he tell what that was?

Whatever decision he made, it would be because he had chosen it – he, Ordes, and Jen.

Jalen laid down, his arms linked behind his head. He stared at the ceiling.

If Arthur chose a future vastly different to the one Jalen wanted, what would that mean for them?

CHAPTER 38

Jenyfer tucked her knees up to her chest. The water lapped at her toes and she dug them into the sand. *The Excalibur* was just visible in the distance, anchored off the coast near the headland. The Teeth were far north now, and they had seen no sign of Medb and her fey. Around the headland from them was Malist. Jenyfer could feel the city waiting for them, as if it had unfinished business.

The Singing Stone lay in a small pouch around her neck. Even though the Treasure wasn't touching her skin, Jenyfer could feel it, could hear it whisper to her. She would not listen. She didn't want to know what it wanted. After all she had endured to get it, Jenyfer wanted to throw the thing into the sea. But whenever she thought about dropping it over-board, it knew and she was compelled to keep it close. Once they'd done what they needed to do, she'd bury it and never think about it again.

They now had all the Treasures in their possession, and soon they would begin the search for the Grail – only no one knew where it was. Had the location of the magical artefact appeared on the map that had been stolen from them? It certainly hadn't appeared on the paper copy they were left with, so where was it? Jenyfer wasn't even sure what it looked like. Arthur had described what he'd seen in his dreams, but the book of the Otherworld that had appeared on the ship as they were leaving Cruithea didn't contain a drawing of the Grail.

Merlin's prophecy didn't specifically mention the Grail at all, Jenyfer realised.

Ordes pressed a kiss to her shoulder.

'Are you sure we need to find the Grail?' Jenyfer asked.

His eyebrows lifted but before he could speak, she went on.

'We don't know where it is, we don't know what it does, and we don't know how to use it. We've got all the Treasures,' she paused, reaching up to touch the pouch around her neck, 'but *how* does it work from this point?'

'I don't know,' Ordes admitted.

Jenyfer tapped her fingers against her knee, chewing her lip. 'What if we didn't go back?'

'To the ship?'

She nodded. 'What if we, I don't know, swam away from here?'

'Where would we go?' he asked.

Jenyfer sighed and lay back on the sand. The stars were out, bright dots pinned to an indigo blanket. 'I don't know. What about one of these other places? The ones on the map you showed me.'

That moment felt like a lifetime ago.

Ordes' face appeared above her. 'We could,' he said slowly. 'But is that what you really want?'

She reached up and trailed her fingers over his cheek. 'Would you come with me if it was?'

'You know I would,' he answered, catching her hand. He kissed her palm.

'I hate this,' she said after a moment. 'I know we have a choice, but do we really? I thought once I left Kernou I'd never be controlled by something I couldn't control, but all I did was exchange one cage for another.'

'You are in control,' Ordes told her gently. 'If you seriously wanted to walk away from this, then I'd follow you. Because if I had to choose between helping Arthur fulfil some destiny or being with you, then I choose you.'

His hand brushed her cheek, fingers curling behind her ear. 'I just don't know *how* we're supposed to change things. I don't know why it had to be us your father chose for this. Saving the world has never entered my mind.'

'But what about changing it?' Ordes asked her.

'Alright, yes, I always wanted things to change, but to what? I know I said I wanted the freedom to choose my fate, to have a voice, but I still know so little about how the world works. I'm unsure of what my role in all of this is supposed to be. Arthur will be King, and you and me … what will we be?' Jenyfer asked.

Ordes' smile was soft. 'What do you want to be? Because the way I see it, we can be whatever we want. Once this is done, we can go wherever we like, do what we want … unless you truly don't want to do this,' he added seriously.

Jenyfer stared up at the night sky. What did she want? The Singing Stone in its pouch vibrated against her chest. She wanted her freedom. She wanted to be happy, and not have to worry anymore.

Ordes was watching her with the sort of patience only he seemed capable of. He'd never rush her decision, and in a way, that decided it.

'Destiny, fate, or whatever we want to call it, gave me you,' she said. 'So I suppose I need to give it something in return, right?'

'So, we're saving the world?'

Jenyfer nodded. 'But, after it's done, let's go. There'll be nothing to stop us, Ordes.'

His face was shadowed, stars winking above him. He leant down to kiss her, and she melted beneath his lips, as she always did, winding her arms around his neck. The sea brushed her legs, water foaming around her as Ordes kissed her neck, before shifting to rest the weight of his body over her. He found her mouth again, kissing deeply, his hand running down the side of her body, tracing the shape of her.

Jenyfer groaned as he pressed himself against her. She hooked her leg over his hip, pulling him closer. They were dressed, their clothes saturated from the swim to the beach, and she wanted them gone.

Her back arched as Ordes nipped at her throat. Heat raced through her. She tugged at his shirt, making him chuckle.

'Here?'

'Why not?'

'If anyone is on the deck of the ship, they'll probably see my bare arse,' Ordes mumbled against her throat, making her grin.

'Fine. We won't. To preserve your modesty.'

He laughed and dropped a kiss on her mouth, then moved off her. They lay side by side on the wet sand, the ocean climbing over their legs. The water was cool and smooth and Jenyfer's skin tingled, her song crooning away beneath her skin.

The melody shifted into a warning. The notes changed – sharp and staccato, dissonant. She gasped and sat up. The Stone in its pouch thrummed against her chest.

'What is it?' Ordes asked.

'We're not alone,' she whispered. Music slipped into her head. 'The syhren you saw? She's here.' Jenyfer stood, heart pounding as she scanned the dark streak of the ocean spread out before them. 'I know you're there,' she shouted. 'Show yourself.'

The water rippled. A head emerged, silver hair trailing behind her.

Jenyfer narrowed her eyes. 'Andromache,' she hissed. A shiver of fear crawled up her spine as she watched the syhren stand, her hair a wet slick down her back, water pouring from her skin. Andromache's scales glowed in the moonlight. 'What are you doing here?'

'Taking a risk,' the syhren spat, her tone like ice. 'This water is freezing.'

'How did you find me?' Jenyfer asked.

Andromache's lips curled. 'Your father would be proud of what you've done, Jenyfer.'

'My father can rot,' Jenyfer snapped.

The syhren did not react. 'He wants—'

'I don't care what he wants,' Jenyfer said from between clenched teeth.

'—to talk to you, to all three of you,' Andromache finished. There was a hint of urgency in her voice as her eyes swung to Ordes. 'He knows you have the Treasures.'

'Good,' Jenyfer declared. 'I hope betraying me and stealing the map was worth it, then.'

'He—'

'Don't,' Jenyfer warned. 'Don't you dare make excuses for him, Andromache.'

'You need to understand what's at stake, Jenyfer,' the syhren said.

'I think what's at stake right now is you,' Jenyfer shot back. Her eyes slid sideways to Ordes, whose magic was curled around his hands. 'You need to leave.'

Andromache looked at Ordes. The panic on the syhren's face was clear.

'I don't want to hurt you,' Ordes told her, his fingers lengthening into blade-like claws. The syhren paled. 'But I will, if I have to.'

Andromache's beautiful, inhuman face screwed up. 'You don't understand,' she said, turning back to Jenyfer. 'What he will do. He didn't send me, but I'm here for him. To try and stop …' Her voice trailed off.

Jenyfer waited.

'If you reject him, he will offer his power to another,' Andromache said finally. 'I came here to warn you, Jenyfer.'

'Why?'

'Because …' she sighed. 'Because I think he is about to make a mistake.'

Jenyfer's eyebrows lifted. 'He took the map from us because he wanted to use it as leverage. He locked us up, threatened us, and *now* you think he's making a mistake?' She took a step closer to her father's pet. 'What has he done with our map, Andromache? Who did he offer it to?'

'No one,' the syhren said. 'He knows it's too late, that he waited too long. I think he expected the others to show up and beg for his help, but they didn't.'

Jenyfer realised she meant the other Old Ones.

'You've got his Stone!' Andromache said shrilly.

'My Stone,' Jenyfer corrected; her song crooned in agreement.

'And soon, you'll have the Grail. Your father has weathered every storm the Old Ones have thrown at the world by staying out of it, by sitting back and letting them try and kill each other,' the syhren explained. 'But now, he's sick of waiting, sick of this game. If you want him to stand with you, not against you, you need to talk to him. Come to Lyonesse with me – the three of you.'

'Not a chance,' Jenyfer said simply.

The syhren took a step closer. 'Listen to me—'

'Go home, Andromache,' Jenyfer said.

Andromache hung her head, her shoulders slumped. She sighed, gave Jenyfer one last, imploring look, and then was gone with barely a splash.

'What was that about?' Ordes wondered.

'I don't care,' Jenyfer said. She waded into the water. 'Come on. Let's go save the world.'

Chapter 39

The Fisher Queen's cave was dark. Arthur could smell stale water and damp stone. The pebbled earth crunched beneath his feet as he walked, his steps cautious. 'Eseld?' he called. 'I need some light.'

Golden light suddenly roared to life in the darkness, making him shield his eyes. Someone chuckled, and the light dimmed somewhat. Blinking, Arthur waited for his eyes to adjust, and then jumped back in fright.

'Mordred!'

'You don't appear happy to see me, cousin,' Mordred said smoothly. He was sitting on one side of the dead fire, dressed not in his Cruithean warriors' clothes, but the simple garments of a man trying to blend into a fishing village. There was no sign of Eseld. A ball of light hovered over Mordred's head, casting strange shadows on his face.

Arthur shook his head. 'I wasn't expecting to see you, but I think we should talk.'

Mordred gestured at the rocks opposite him. Arthur sat. He could feel the tension in his spine, his shoulders, and tried to make himself relax.

Mordred did not speak. He poked at the cold coals with a stick, and then waved his hand and the flames surged into life. He shrugged. 'For atmosphere, I guess. There is nothing worse than sitting around a dead fire, wouldn't you say?'

Arthur nodded, although sitting around fires was not something he was accustomed to.

'How goes the hunt?' his cousin asked.

'It goes,' Arthur replied, after a moment of hesitation.

'Still don't trust me?'

'It's not about trusting you, Mordred. It's about understanding your motives.' Arthur kept his eyes on the flames.

'What is it you still don't understand?' Mordred asked.

'I don't understand why you went with Lamorna back to Kernou,' Arthur replied. He kept his tone as neutral and free of suspicions as he could and waited, not expecting Mordred to reply.

Mordred's face was shadowed, but his hands where they rested on his thighs flexed. 'There is a passage in the Decalogue that you may not know. It certainly took Lamorna by surprise.'

'Is she alright?' Arthur asked. Jenyfer would want to know.

'Don't you want to know what the Word really says? What your father kept from you?' Mordred asked instead. 'And you can tell Jenyfer her sister is fine. Lamorna does the One God's work.'

'She does Ereshki's work, you mean,' Arthur corrected. 'Does she know?'

Mordred nodded. 'She was not thrilled.'

'I bet,' Arthur mumbled.

'It was not learning the truth of the One God that unsettled her, Arthur. It was learning the extent of your father's lies,' Mordred explained.

Arthur said nothing.

'Don't you want to know what the Word really says?' Mordred pressed. His expression was curious. Without waiting for an answer, he went on. '"A messenger will come from distant lands. This messenger is the One God's chosen, and he shall lead the faithful from the lands of their fathers to the lands of old, where they shall find salvation from slavery and oppression. Here, in this place, shall they hear the true Word. This promised land, this paradise, shall be their reward for their devotion."'

Arthur was silent, letting those words sink in, wondering why he had never seen them before, but not why his father kept them to himself. He already knew the answer to that. 'The messenger is you, I assume?' he asked.

Mordred leant forward, closer to the heatless fire. 'I am preparing the way for you, Arthur. I am doing this for you.'

That's a lie, Arthur thought.

'You should thank me,' Mordred said. 'I will gather the faithful of Kernou for you.'

'How?'

'The truth will set them free,' Mordred said.

'You managed to convince the Konsel to follow you?' Arthur asked incredulously.

'I never said that.'

'Mordred, what have you done?' Arthur asked. Dread coiled in his belly.

'I'm doing what the Red One demands I do,' his cousin snapped. 'I have begun building the new world, Arthur. Your world.'

'Mordred, I haven't decided what the new world will be yet!' Arthur cried.

Mordred's expression darkened. 'Still indecisive, I see. It's quite simple, cousin. The new world will be a world of magic, where magic will rule and where the Old Ones—'

Arthur shook his head. 'That isn't the answer.'

Mordred stared at him, puzzled. 'You're a Magic Wielder – a terrible one – but magic is in your blood. How can you not want a world of magic?'

'Why does it have to be one or the other?' Arthur murmured. 'Why can't it be both?'

Mordred laughed. 'You've learnt nothing. I guess I am not surprised that the Myrddin's King is an indecisive, unknowledgeable little boy.'

Arthur refused to let the insult upset him. He closed his eyes and when he opened them, the fire was out and Mordred was gone. He couldn't remember what he'd wanted from Eseld.

CHAPTER 40

Most of the crew had piled into the galley for dinner. Lanterns hung from the ceiling, throwing warm orange light over everyone. Dinner was vegetables and overcooked meat – the same as it was most nights. Jenyfer had resisted the temptation to cook them a decent meal, but she wasn't about to tell the Doctor she was unhappy with what he'd given them. Katarin, on the other hand, had been quite vocal about *The Excalibur's* lack of fine dining, and sat a few tables away poking at her food with a displeased expression. Arthur sat beside her, his eyes downcast.

Iouen and Tahnet were sitting close. Jenyfer smiled at that. She was happy for them, especially after what Tahnet had told her when they were in Carinya. Happiness, Jenyfer decided, sneaking a glance at Ordes, was something they all needed to grab onto when they could, especially now.

At the table nearest them sat Tristan and Isolde. The two of them were rarely apart, and rarely alone. Katarin didn't trust Tristan – he was free to wander the ship, but under guard. Not far from them sat Carbrey, Kayrus, and a few of *The Excalibur's* old crew. Jenyfer wondered what was going through their minds. She had been as surprised as Arthur that not one man had jumped ship somewhere along the way, that they had dared brave The Teeth, a place where sailors rarely went. They had sat and waited in Malist's harbour while Ordes recovered his Treasure. Iouen had spoken true – the men were bound to this ship, and to whoever was her captain.

Jen glanced at Katarin again. The Captain was in a mood, and not about the food. There was a darkness to Katarin's face that had not abated since their return from The Teeth. Katarin's anger had been palpable. Jenyfer was still figuring out if it was anger at Arthur putting himself in danger, or the sense of helplessness Katarin was feeling – something she would rather die than admit to anyone. But Jenyfer could see it, as she knew others could.

With the Treasures collected, they were at a bit of a standstill. The Singing Stone was in its pouch around Jenyfer's neck; she hadn't taken it off since she'd claimed it, and she found herself touching it more than she liked. She loathed it, but was fascinated by it at the same time. Then, she'd remember the look on the man's face in his underwater prison, the vacant, almost loving way he stroked his chest, and she'd drop her hand away in horror.

Ordes had left the Bow of Mists in their cabin. He wasn't worried about whatever the Bow might be asking of the people onboard this ship, not like Arthur was with the Sword. No one but Ordes could touch the Bow – the Treasure turned to mist whenever Jenyfer tried to close her hand around it.

Three Treasures, and three people who had no idea what to do with them.

Jenyfer pushed her barely touched meal away, shifting her thoughts to something else that had been bothering her.

'I saw Ophine,' she divulged quietly. Ordes raised his eyebrows. 'They were on the shoreline, before we came down to dinner. I'd like to know why.'

'Me too,' Ordes mumbled. He sat back, poking at his dinner with his fork. 'If Ankou has such a role to play in this saga – as the wraith claims – then where is he? Why haven't we seen him?'

'We haven't seen some of the other Old Ones, either,' Jen reminded him. 'The Green Knight, for one. If Arthur has his Treasure, why hasn't he come? And Morrigna—'

'Fate cannot interfere,' Merlin said, plopping into the seat across from Jenyfer and Ordes. 'This seat taken?'

Jenyfer rolled her eyes. 'Fine, no Goddess of Fate. But what about the others? My father hasn't made an appearance, either, and that bothers me – a lot.' She'd thought of nothing but what Andromache had said, and couldn't work out whether the syhren had been genuine or not. She'd certainly appeared frightened, but Andromache was also a master manipulator, which left Jenyfer on edge. If there was truth to what Andromache had said, what was the big decision Melodias was about to make?

Ordes tapped his fingers on the table, something he did when he was thinking. 'You said the Old Ones were at odds before Ereshki took the Treasures. Why? If we're to remake a world with the Grail, shouldn't we know what they were fighting about before all this happened?'

'What does anyone fight about?' Merlin answered. 'Power. Your mother and Gawain had plans for this world, plans that were slipping away. What they had failed to understand was people. Gods do not think like humans. They do not feel their lives passing with each turn of the Wheel.' He sat back, running a hand over his face. 'As mankind spread across this land, things changed. People still worshipped the Old Ones, but their faith slipped as they gained their own power over the landscape, over each other, and over their lives. Niniane and Gawain did not want that to change. Ereshki and Inanna disagreed. So they fought.'

'What did the Two in One want to see happen?' Ordes asked.

'I might not be the best person to answer that,' Merlin said. He turned and beckoned for Ethinne, who sat with Melhala and Halymere. The Priestess stood immediately and came over, but did not sit, not until Merlin invited her to. 'Tell them what you know, what Cruitheans believe, about the Two in One.'

Ethinne's face folded into a slight frown. 'We do not call her that, not anymore.'

'We do,' said a voice at Jenyfer's elbow. She nearly jumped out of her skin to find Olwen sliding into the seat beside her. Ethinne levelled a stare at the Red Sister, who held her eyes, expression determined. 'I know you in Cruithea want to forget that Ereshki exists, but you cannot. Denying her is denying a part of Inanna. We do not forget your Goddess, for she is ours also.'

Ethinne's eyebrows lifted. 'You worship Inanna in the House of Bone?'

Olwen nodded. 'We recognise the importance of the Two in One, Ethinne. It is time for you to do the same.'

The Priestess opened her mouth to argue, but Jenyfer jumped in first. 'Alright, why? Why is it important that Ereshki and Inanna are worshipped together?'

'Because that is how you understand their true purpose, how you understand what the sisters wanted for this world and what they gave up for what Merlin prophesied,' Olwen said. 'A king, and those who will bring us all back into the Light.'

Olwen paused and gave Jenyfer a serious look. 'I don't mean the light you had preached at you in that place – some mythical, mystical place that doesn't exist. I mean the true Light, the opposite of Darkness. But to understand and embrace that Light, you need to first understand and embrace the Darkness.'

Ethinne shook her head. 'No, it is my job as a Priestess of Inanna to protect people from that darkness, to guide them when they come to me and ask for it. We teach people how to embrace the shadows that live inside. We teach them how to accept the undesirable parts of who they are – greed, envy, the damage of pride – for only when they have reconciled all parts of themselves can they be whole.'

Jenyfer leant forward, fascinated, but Olwen chuckled.

'You do the work of Ereshki even though you claim not to,' she said. 'The Red One has no tolerance for deceit or disrespect. Isn't that what you teach the people of Cruithea about Inanna? Respect and truth? Yet, you deny the Two in One their true existence.'

'I …' Ethinne began, then jolted as a hand came to rest on her shoulder. Melhala was glaring at Olwen, but the Red Sister did not shrivel under the force of the Cruithean's mistrust. She simply sat back and folded her arms challengingly.

'That's enough of your lies,' Melhala spat in a tone Jenyfer had never heard her use before. Melhala was possessed of such grace and patience, but the look she was giving Olwen spoke only of violence.

'They're not lies if they're the truth,' Olwen retorted, and Jenyfer groaned inwardly.

'What do you have to say about this?' Melhala demanded of Merlin.

The Prophet of the Gods held up his hands in supplication. 'Ladies, let's not argue. Let's discuss this calmly and rationally.'

Ordes snorted.

Jaw tight, lips a thin line, Melhala levelled a hard stare at Olwen. 'You and your heretical magics have no place on this ship.'

Olwen cocked an eyebrow. 'That's hardly up to you, is it? But I'm not the one questioning my place, am I? I'm not the one wondering why the High Priestess, in her infinite wisdom, sent me here.'

Melhala recoiled, but before she could react, Ethinne stood, talking to her in whispered tones. Face tight with rage, Melhala allowed Ethinne to lead her away, not taking her eyes off Olwen. Before they left the galley, Olwen blew the Cruitheans a cheeky kiss.

'If you want them to listen to anything you say, you're not going about it the right way,' Merlin told Olwen, who scowled. He stood, reaching for Jenyfer's plate. 'If you're not going to eat that …'

'Take it,' she managed, and they watched as Merlin sauntered away. The galley was almost empty. 'Come on,' Jenyfer said softly to Ordes. 'I want to see if Ophine is still out there.'

'Jenyfer,' Olwen said as they stood. 'Be careful who you trust. The God of the Otherworld likes his games as much as any of the Old Ones do.'

Jenyfer stared at her. Olwen should not have the knowledge of them and their quest that she did, yet the Red Sister spoke with a level of intimacy and knowing that only someone close to Jen, Ordes, and Arthur did, someone who had been with them from the start.

It made her wonder how much of this prophecy was Merlin's doing, and how much of it was Ereshki's.

'You're even more skilled at pissing people off than I am,' Katarin said. The galley was empty except for her and the Red Sister, who, at her words, jerked her head free of her hands and looked up. A knowing smile crawled over Olwen's face.

'It's more of a talent than a skill, really,' she said.

Katarin managed a half-laugh. Olwen smiled, stretching her arms above her head luxuriously, as if she hadn't nearly started a fight in *The Excalibur's* galley.

'What did you mean before, about Melhala questioning her place?' Kat asked.

'Eavesdropping, were you?'

'It's my ship.'

Olwen wandered across the galley, perching herself astride the bench Katarin sat at. Her knee bumped Kat's thigh; Katarin could not help the quick intake of breath at the contact.

'I'm not usually a bitch. Well, I am, but I was brought up by an arse-hole and then lived in the Ossuary. What's your excuse?' Olwen asked, drumming her fingers lightly on the table, not far from Kat's hand.

Kat raised her eyebrows. 'Are you calling me a bitch?'

'If the shoe fits,' Olwen said with a shrug. 'I've never been good at compliments.'

'That was a compliment?' Kat asked, smothering a laugh.

'It's whatever you want it to be, Captain,' Olwen said, her voice low. Slowly, she reached out her index finger, and Katarin held her breath. When Olwen's finger touched hers, she jolted, even though she knew it was coming, had watched it happen.

And had let it.

Slowly, Olwen leant forward. Her nose brushed Katarin's neck, her breath touching Kat's skin. Kat's heart froze, then roared to life as one of Olwen's hands slid along the back of her neck.

'What are you doing?' Kat managed.

'It depends,' Olwen replied.

'On?'

'On whether you truly hate me, whether you'd rather not talk to me at all, whether you want me to leave, or whether you'd like me to kiss you.'

Kat swallowed. 'I …'

Olwen pulled back. Their eyes locked. 'I know about Aelle.'

Something inside Katarin snapped. She pushed Olwen away. 'You won't ever—'

'No one can ever replace another person, Katarin,' Olwen said, her tone soft.

Katarin stood, anger flowing like a hot river through her blood, through muscle and bone and sinew. Anger and grief that she thought she had put to bed, had tried to put to bed. 'Get out,' she said icily.

'But I haven't had dessert yet,' Olwen complained. Kat fisted her hands in Olwen's shirt and hauled the Red Sister to her feet. Olwen laughed. 'You'd rather fight? Fine, Katarin. Have it your way.'

Katarin ground her teeth as heat surged through her.

'I'll make it easy for you,' Olwen said. She uncurled Katarin's hands from her clothing and stepped clear of the bench. 'No magic.'

Kat scoffed. 'Easy for me? I could—'

Olwen shook her head, brown curls flying. 'No, you couldn't, and I don't want to hurt you – not like that, anyway.' She smirked. 'You don't know what I can do, do you? You don't know what we learn in the House of Bone.'

'No one knows,' Kat snapped. A tiny trickle of fear moved down her spine as she recalled the way Olwen first materialised on the ship, appearing out of fucking nothing in a plume of blood-red smoke.

Olwen was watching her. 'No magic.'

'Whatever,' Kat snapped, resting her weight on her heels. She rolled her neck, flexed her fingers, curled them into fists, and struck.

Katarin had learnt to fight in tavern brawls. She was good with her fists and whatever else she could use as a weapon, but she quickly realised she was outmatched. Olwen moved like water, fluid and swift. Her eyes never left Katarin's face, reading every movement before they were executed. She blocked each blow, side-stepped each punch. Katarin could not land a single hit.

Olwen did not make contact, though she easily could have. Katarin grit her teeth in utter frustration. She *wanted* this fight. She needed it. She needed somewhere to put the anger, the fear, that swam through her.

'Hit me,' she snapped, throwing another punch, which Olwen easily dodged.

'I don't want to mess up your pretty face,' Olwen shot back. Her hand snapped out, and she caught Katarin's wrist, spinning her around and pulling her back against her chest. 'Only because you won't let me kiss you better.'

Kat freed herself with a growl. As she turned around, fists raised, Olwen crashed against her, pinning her on her back against the table. Her thigh came to rest between Katarin's legs, and her hand twisted in Kat's hair, forcing her head up. Chest heaving, Kat tried to push Olwen away, but the other woman simply smiled and pressed herself closer. Slowly, she reached up with her spare hand, freeing Katarin's hair from its braid.

Kat could barely move as Olwen ran her fingers through her hair, nails scraping her scalp as she arranged the red mane around Kat's shoulders.

'Much better,' Olwen whispered.

Katarin could barely hear her over the thundering of her heart.

Their eyes met. Katarin's fingers, fisted in Olwen's shirt, slackened as Olwen's gaze softened, settling on her mouth. Kat strained forward, a fraction, enough that if she wanted, Olwen could claim her mouth. But the Red Sister did not move.

'What's wrong?' Kat managed.

'You don't really want this,' Olwen said, releasing her abruptly and stepping away.

'Don't tell me what I want,' Kat snapped, angry again and unable to stop it. She sat up, smoothing her hands over her shirt. Her fingers were trembling.

'I can wait,' Olwen said.

Kat took a heaving breath and resorted to attack. 'You'll be waiting a long time.'

The Red Sister smiled. 'I can wait.'

She left Katarin sitting there, eyes burning, her body screaming at the absence of touch.

CHAPTER 41

Ordes left Jenyfer on deck, scanning the shoreline for any sign of the wraith, but Ophine, if she was there, did not allow herself to be seen. He returned to their cabin, his mind running over the strange conversation between Ethinne and Olwen, grabbing hold of the snippets they had learnt about Ereshki and Inanna. Ordes could not help but think the Two in One was at the heart of all this, but he could not prove it.

His father was being his usual, cryptic self. Not interfering. Letting them work it out for themselves.

Ordes sometimes wondered if Merlin put too much faith in his son's intelligence.

The Bow of Mists sang to him from where he had left it, resting on the bed. It was nothing but a graceful curving of silver mist. Slowly, he reached out and touched it. Immediately, the Bow solidified, but he did not pick it up, instead withdrawing his finger and watching as it faded away into nothingness once more.

Why did his mother create a weapon of war? Niniane did not strike him as a warrior, but then, he knew next to nothing about the woman who had birthed him. All he had to go on were his father's words.

He was still staring at the Bow when someone knocked on the door. Ordes saw Arthur's face poke around the door frame. The Once and Future King hesitantly stepped inside at Ordes' invitation.

'You look troubled,' Ordes observed.

'I am,' Arthur answered. He cleared his throat, uncomfortable. 'Jenyfer told me about touch magic, how it works. How you can tell what a person is thinking just by touching them.'

'You want me to use my magic on your boyfriend?' Ordes guessed, eyebrows raised.

Arthur blushed, but nodded.

'Firstly, I'm not sure it would even work on him – if I could touch him, that is. He'd know what I was up to before I had the chance to do anything,' Ordes mused. 'And secondly, why not talk to him?'

'Because he's lying to me,' Arthur said.

'Maybe he doesn't want to worry you?' Ordes suggested.

'It's more than that. He told me he had been given the job of guiding me, that your father told him it was his destiny to serve me. Yet he's distant, distracted. And I get the feeling he doesn't like your father,' Arthur added, a wry smile pulling at his mouth.

Ordes laughed. 'Can you blame him? I don't like my father sometimes, either.' He sighed. 'Look, I don't have much advice for you on this. I wish I could help, but I don't know what to tell you.'

'You and Jen make it look easy,' Arthur commented, but beneath his tone was worry.

Ordes smiled. 'It isn't.'

'Because of the heartfire?'

'Yes and no.'

'But you love her?'

'Yes. I honestly don't know what I'd do without her, but it's like we haven't had time to just be together without all this'—he paused, waving his hand at the air around them—'and that's hard. I want to be with her without having to worry about the fate of the world, you know? I wish I could suspend time for a moment – everything is hurtling towards us so quickly. I think we all need a moment to take a breath.'

'That I can understand,' Arthur said. Then, 'Could you suspend time? I'd like a little bit more of it right now.'

Ordes shook his head. 'I have no idea, and it's not something I want to attempt. I think time works on its own schedule, and we can't control it. No matter how much we wish we could.' The thought sat heavy between them. 'How do you know Jalen is lying to you?'

'I can sense it,' Arthur said. 'He's wound up so tight, I'm worried he's going to snap. In truth, he's been different since you showed me the book on the Otherworld.'

'Ah,' Ordes said. 'Ankou was Jalen's master before my mother, wasn't he? He made Jalen what he is.'

'Yes,' Arthur said. 'He doesn't talk about the God of the Otherworld much, but he did tell me what it was like when he first became a demi-god. He told me about leaving Ankou.'

Ordes chewed his lip. 'Demi-gods are immortal, but with conditions. When Jalen left Ankou, he severed a bond that should have been unbreakable.' Ordes paused, frowning. 'He should have died, Arthur, but my mother took him in.'

Arthur hesitated, and then, in a quiet voice said, 'Jalen wants to see the world like Avalon.'

'Does he?' Ordes tapped his fingers on his thigh. 'My mother wants a world ruled by magic, and Jalen is bound to her now.'

'What are you implying?' Arthur asked.

'My mother is a liar. She's self-serving and does not want to lose her power,' Ordes replied. 'All those times Jalen disappears, I would bet he's being called back to Niniane.'

'But why would he not tell me that?' Arthur asked.

'Would you willingly admit to the man you love that you had no free will? That you had no choice?' Ordes replied. 'That you were a slave to a goddess with a grudge?'

Arthur fell silent.

'Why don't you ask him, Arthur?' Ordes said. 'At least then you can say you tried.'

Iouen flung open the door. His eyes were wide, expression somewhere between panic and excitement. 'You need to come above deck – now!' he demanded and left, his frenzied footsteps racing down the passageway. Ordes frowned, and then realised he could hear more running feet. The ship was alive with activity.

He and Arthur exchanged a look, then hurried out, rushing along the passageway and up the ladder onto a deck crammed with people.

'What's—' Arthur began, then stopped. 'I can smell smoke.'

They pushed their way to the starboard side. Ordes squeezed between Jenyfer and Katarin, who were watching the mainland, their faces tight. Slowly, he turned towards Teyath, and sucked in a breath.

Flames licked the night sky and smoke cloaked the land.

Malist was burning.

'What the fuck?' Ordes whispered.

Olwen's voice rose above the chatter of the crew. 'It's Medb.'

'How do you know?' Arthur demanded. He had not taken his eyes from the city.

'Because there is no way this would be happening otherwise. The Warriors would not allow it,' Olwen added fiercely. She was standing on the quarterdeck, looking out at Malist. Her expression was hard. 'The Red Sisters would not allow it. What the fuck has that psycho done?'

'There are innocent people in there,' Arthur murmured. 'How are those people going to feel about faeries and magic if we do nothing? If they don't see faeries and magic trying to save them?'

'You're right,' Jenyfer said. 'We should help.'

Katarin rubbed her face. 'Normally, I'd say let them all burn, but you're right. You both are. Olwen, how many of your people are in the city?' she asked. 'And would they fight?'

'Are you asking for my help?' Olwen said, lifting an eyebrow.

Katarin ground her teeth, hard.

'Alright, you're not in the mood,' Olwen muttered. She sighed, jumping down from the quarterdeck. The crew moved aside for her. 'Yes they'll help – if they see him,' she added, nodding at Arthur. 'He needs to be there, Katarin.'

Arthur turned to his sister. 'Are you letting me out after curfew?'

Kat scowled, but nodded.

Ordes could feel something tugging at him. The Bow of Mists was calling from where it lay in his cabin. His fingers twitched – he shared a look with Arthur, whose eyes were wide, and he wondered if Arthur could hear a godly Treasure whispering to him, as Ordes could.

Katarin squared her shoulders. 'Right. Let's do this.'

CHAPTER 42

When Lamorna woke, Mordred was not in bed. She found him in the garden, staring out at the ocean. Kernou lay to the east, quiet and unassuming in the dawn. His eyes were heavy and bloodshot – she suspected he had barely slept.

'What is it?' she asked him, wrapping her robe around her tightly. A chilly breeze was blowing in from the sea. It pulled at her hair, creating knots she would have to comb free. The grass was wet with dew and Lamorna's feet were getting cold.

'Tell me, Lamorna,' Mordred began. 'If you had to exchange your sister's life, your aunt's life, for what you believed in, would you do it?'

'I already did, in a way,' she whispered.

'Then you understand,' he said. 'We don't have to like the things we do to know they are right.' He sighed, troubled, and rubbed at the back of his neck. 'I think it is time to put everything to the test. We can't wait for things to change on their own.' He turned to her, holding out his hand, and when she took it, he led her back to the cottage.

She knew what he was going to do. Mordred would call a town meeting. He would declare his uncle was a heretic and a liar. He would ask the people of this town to follow him, to follow *them*, to Dinas Emrys. But Lamorna was worried, and she told him so.

'The Red Hand are behind me – they know what I plan to do this evening, and they will not interfere. Your not-friend Bryn has been most helpful, as I predicted,' Mordred said. 'We have had many interesting chats.'

'What did you promise him?' Lamorna asked. She kept her voice strong, but she was fearful.

'Don't worry. There is something Bryn wants more than your sister, and that is good old-fashioned revenge on the man he believes stole her from him.' Mordred explained. 'He knows Ordes is a Magic Wielder, but his pride stops him from being fearful. It might actually be interesting to watch that moment play out.'

'It is not his pride alone,' Lamorna argued. 'We have always been told that those with magic are less than us, that they are not worthy of the One God's love. That the One God rejected them. Bryn has been hunting faeries, Mordred. That was what he did while I was in Cruithea. To him, a pisky and a Magic Wielder are no different – they are both abominations. He isn't afraid because he doesn't believe he has to be.'

Mordred chuckled. 'The meeting will begin after dark.'

'This town has been living under strict rules, Mordred, for a long time,' she murmured. 'I don't know if offering to hand people all their freedoms at once is going to work.'

He gave her a curious look as he pulled on his boots. 'Then what do you suggest?'

'Me?' she asked in surprise.

He nodded. 'This is your town – these are your people. Tell me what I should do.'

Lamorna chewed the inside of her cheek, thinking furiously. 'Offer them protection from what is to come, even if we don't know what it is yet. People will want to know you will protect them from it.'

'Alright,' Mordred said. 'What else?'

'Show them they do not need to fear you,' Lamorna said. 'Ulrian and the Konsel ruled with fear. People will expect it from you, with you being what you are, but you need to make them see you are not someone to fear. That you will care for them. They are the One God's children. They will expect your love.'

Mordred nodded, stepping past her and moving down the hallway, a tall, dark shadow. She followed him through the front door. She would be at the meeting. As they made their way down the path, he asked, 'Do I tell them the truth about the One God?'

'Not yet,' Lamorna said. 'Tell them the One God speaks to you now – that He has forsaken the Chif because of his greed – and that you know the One God's love. Quote the Word to them, and sound like you mean it, Mordred. I shall tell you which passages will be best. I will write them out for you and give them to you before the meeting. You can use them as you wish.' She frowned. 'Perhaps I should do it now.'

'I know the Decalogue, Lamorna,' Mordred reminded her. 'And I am good at talking to people.'

'You are,' she affirmed. She remembered that night in Cruithea, when he killed that Witchfinder. The people had hung on Mordred's every word.

Mordred kissed her, out in the open, with the sunlight on their faces and the wind in their hair. 'To think, all this time, my uncle had the answer to his prayers right under his nose and he never knew it.'

Lamorna's cheeks heated with pride, but she made her voice stern. 'Do not try and change things too quickly. They will be suspicious.'

'Perhaps you should speak with them,' he suggested.

She shook her head. 'No. I am a woman. I have no voice here, not yet. They are not ready for that.'

'But you have been speaking to the women?' Mordred asked her.

'I have, and I have made progress,' she told him. 'But they are not like me. They did not have someone like you to guide them. It will be slower for them. Maybe. I'm not sure.' She paused, squeezing Mordred's arm gently, thinking about Calla. 'Why is it so important these people follow you?' When he did not answer, she answered for him. 'This is for the Red One, isn't it? The Goddess. This will show her you are worthy and should be rewarded.'

'It's for Arthur,' he said, then sighed. 'My cousin does not agree with me. We are different men, with different ideas, but I want to believe that, deep down, we do share the same desire – for magic to be free in the world, and for people to return to the Old Ways.'

And if that isn't what Arthur wants? What then? Lamorna thought, but she didn't ask.

That evening, Mordred addressed the town. Lamorna saw him briefly before she went inside the tavern, passing him a piece of paper. She did not wait to see if he looked at it. The Red Hand had spread the word, and Lamorna wondered if every person in Kernou was present. She did not join Mordred at the front of the room. She remained seated at the back of the tavern with the other women, trying not to remember the last time she had attended a meeting in this place. Calla sat beside her.

'What is going on?' she whispered. 'All we heard was there was an important meeting. Is someone about to be—'

'You shall see,' Lamorna said quietly.

'But—'

'Sshh,' Lamorna scolded. 'And listen.'

'You all know who I am,' Mordred began, lifting his voice so that people were forced to listen. A murmur rustled through the crowd like wind through the leaves. 'Thank you all for coming. I am glad you are here. The One God thanks you. As you know, my uncle is your Chif. While he trusts the Konsel, he has always put family first. With Arthur no longer here, it falls to me to fill that space. I think of my uncle as a father, and I love him dearly. But,' he said, lowering his voice, his tone sorrowful and regretful, 'I am worried. Deeply worried.'

He paused, waited, and met Lamorna's eyes briefly.

'I have tried to ignore my worries, to not let them take root in my soul, but I cannot stay silent anymore. Ulrian is a proud man – you all know this – and where I am from, pride is not a sin. It is not looked down on. But my people in Cruithea have not yet heard the Word of the One God. They do not know His love as I do, as you all do. Ulrian's pride, I fear, has stopped him from loving you as he should. Pride is a powerful feeling – a drug that poisons the blood and the mind. How often have you asked yourself questions in the darkness that you were afraid to bring into the light? How often have you wondered what my uncle's actions were for, and *who* they were for?' Mordred shook his head sadly. 'I am only new to the Word of the One God, so maybe I can see what you do not.' He looked up, his eyes moving over the crowd. 'Ulrian Tregarthen is my family and I love him, but I cannot stand by while he fails in his duty to you, the people of Kernou.'

The tavern door was flung open. Lamorna twisted in her seat. Ulrian Tregarthen's body filled the doorway.

'What is going on here?' he demanded. 'Mordred? What is the meaning of this?'

Mordred's voice was pained, as if he truly was regretful. 'I was telling the people how you have failed them, Uncle.'

Ulrian's mouth dropped. Rage coloured his cheeks as he swept inside, two of the Konsel behind him. The Chif marched to the front of the tavern, turning to face the crowd. Before he could speak, Mordred went on.

'I can promise you that I will not turn from you. I will take up the mantle of the One God and offer myself as your protector, as the one who stands between you and the darkness. I know the One God's love, but I am afraid you do not truly know it for yourselves. It has been kept from you, squandered by my uncle, who you trusted. The One God does not want you to fear Him – He wants only to love you and lead you into the Light. You do not need to live in fear of what will be, not when you have me. I am willing to take up a blade and fight for you, to protect you against what is to come. I am willing to die for you, as I was willing to die for my people in Cruithea, who are also your people. We are all one people. I believe in my heart that we will all be the One God's children, as it is meant to be.'

The tavern was silent. No one knew what to say, or if they should say anything. Eyes swung between Mordred and Ulrian, who lifted his chin and cleared his throat. 'Yes, we are the One God's children. You all know this, and you all know the One God's love – because I have shared it with you. I have shown you the way of the Light. I—'

'But you have kept the truth from them – you have kept them in the dark,' Mordred cut in. He addressed the crowd again, whispers rising amongst them like waves. 'I will not, for it is through me that you shall know the truth. In two nights, I leave here,' he said. Ulrian looked at Mordred in utter shock. 'I travel to Camlann Plain, to take up the seat of the rulers of old at Dinas Emrys, on the order of the One God. He came to me and told me I must do this. I must begin to prepare for His arrival.'

'His arrival?' someone called out.

Mordred nodded. 'My uncle did not share this with you, but I can assure you, he knows about it. He knows that the One God will soon walk the earth, as the Old Ones once did. What has he done to prepare you for it?' The question hung in the air, thick and slowly growing a life of its own. Lamorna smiled to herself.

'You cannot believe a word he says,' Ulrian cried.

Mordred ignored him. 'You are free to make your own choices. But, knowing that this is what the One God has asked me to do to prepare the way for Him, would you remain here, or would you have the courage to join me on this mission? The One God has promised you a paradise and I will guide you to His promised land.'

A ripple of sound spread through the room. Ulrian looked around wildly.

Mordred cleared his throat, and took up a leather-bound copy of the Decalogue that Lamorna had never seen before. With deliberate slowness, he opened it, and began to read the verse that had shaken the core of Lamorna's world, more than it had already been shaken.

'A messenger will come from distant lands. This messenger is the One God's chosen, and he shall lead the faithful from the lands of their fathers to the lands of old, where they shall find salvation from slavery and oppression. Here, in this place, shall they hear the true Word. This promised land, this paradise, shall be their reward for their devotion.'

As Mordred closed the Decalogue, an eerie silence fell over those assembled. Lamorna held her breath, waiting, praying, that it would be enough. Mordred had not used any of the verses she had given him. She did not care if half of these people lived or died, but Mordred needed them to follow him.

'Do not decide now,' he said smoothly. 'But go home and ask the One God for guidance.'

Slowly, people left the tavern. The Konsel tried to stop them, following them outside, leaving Mordred and the Chif together at the front of the room. Mordred collected the leather-bound copy of the Decalogue. His face was calm, but beneath it, Lamorna could see triumph.

'Where did you get that?' Ulrian raged. He grabbed Mordred by the shirt, pulling him close. 'Where did you get that?'

Mordred chuckled, then, quick as lightning, the Chif was on the ground, clutching his face. Lamorna had not even seen it happen. Blood dripped from Ulrian's nose.

'You cannot bury the truth forever, Uncle,' Mordred said. He glanced at Lamorna, who stood and waited for him to join her. Ulrian muttered to himself as he rose to his feet, his face pale. Lamorna smiled at him, then turned and left, Mordred following her.

Calla and the others were lingering outside, waiting. Lamorna hurried over to them.

'You need to come with us,' she said.

'I don't know …' Penny began. Her gaze flickered to Mordred.

'Please,' Lamorna said, her eyes sweeping over them. 'You must come with us, with Mordred and myself. Come to a better place.'

Penny and Naidiene exchanged a nervous glance. 'What about our families?'

'Who cares?' Calla cut in angrily. 'Your families would see you bound to a man for the sake of it. They would see you chained and imprisoned, nothing more than a slave. The Chif *lied to us*. What more do you need? He lied. We are being offered a chance at something different.'

'But …' Arwen began.

'Think,' Calla hissed. 'This town is wrong. Everything is wrong. I know you see it. I know you feel it.' She turned to Lamorna. 'I will come with you.'

Lamorna nodded. 'Thank you. I will be glad of your company, Calla, but I want you all to come. You will have a new life at Dinas Emrys. You will have choices.'

'But the Word,' Bronny began.

'There will be a new Word,' Lamorna said fiercely. 'The way it was supposed to be.'

Arwen was frowning. 'What does that mean?'

'I don't have time to explain right now,' Lamorna said. 'Come with us. Convince your families to come, and anyone you care for. Pack what you can carry easily. It will be a tough journey.'

They nodded, hurrying away as Mordred approached. 'How did I do?' he asked her.

'You were spectacular,' she declared. 'It will be up to them now.'

The next day passed in a blur. Lamorna was busy with preparations for the journey. Mordred and the Red Hand used her kitchen as a meeting place. She did not know where the Chif and the Konsel were, and she didn't care. Lamorna had packed all the clothing she would take, and wanted to start on the kitchen and the linen.

The men looked up when she entered – some faces folded into frowns at her intrusion, but she gave them her best scowl, the one she had been practising in her imaginary mirror.

'I need to speak with Mordred,' she announced.

The frowns deepened. Mordred said nothing; he watched her, and she knew this was some sort of test of his, to see how she would handle this moment. That irritated her. She drew herself up and marched into the room, coming to stand beside him, eyeing each of the Red Hand one at a time.

'Get out,' she ordered them.

They hesitated, but only for a moment, and then they were gone.

Mordred chuckled and pulled her onto his lap, and they sat in silence.

'My uncle will be lost without his right hand,' Mordred said. 'The Konsel.'

'What do you mean?' Lamorna asked.

He kissed her gently, and told her to be outside the Chif's house tomorrow before sunset.

Tomorrow. The day of the week the Konsel always met with the Chif.

Chapter 43

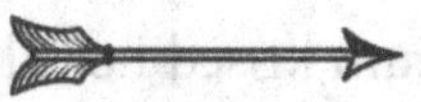

The Excalibur pushed into Malist's harbour, her hull scraping the sea floor. Arthur winced, the sailors around him sucking in their breath. A problem for another time, because right now, there was a fey queen and her horde terrorising a city. Screams rent the air. Flames coated the sky and ash drifted like gently falling snow to coat the deck. It floated on the face of an ocean turned blazing red.

Ordes stood at Arthur's side, his face determined. The Bow of Mists was slung over his shoulder. 'I don't even know how to use this thing,' he mumbled.

Arthur's hand brushed the hilt of the Sword of the White Dragon at his hip. He exchanged a nervous glance with Ordes. 'Me either.' There had been no debate about leaving the Treasure behind this time. He swallowed, wanting to glance over his shoulder, but he knew without having to look that Jalen was not there. The storm demon had been absent since that morning, gone before Arthur had even opened his eyes. Arthur pushed the worry and fear aside, and focused on Malist. Jalen would come.

Katarin was barking orders at *The Excalibur's* human crew. 'Stay here,' she told them, to a chorus of objections. She stamped her foot. 'You're human, all of you. This isn't a scuffle in a tavern in Skulls Rest that we're walking into. Those with magic, with us.' She pointed at Tristan, lingering at the back of the crowd. 'That means you, Witchfinder. We need your magic. Betray us and I'll kill you myself.'

'Not a Witchfinder,' the young man mumbled.

Isolde clutched his arm and whispered something to him. He took her face between his hands and kissed her, then pushed her away gently, joining Katarin.

Jenyfer squeezed between Arthur and Ordes. 'My song won't work on the fey, neither will the Stone.'

'I thought it could compel?' Arthur asked.

'I don't know how to use it yet,' she replied, face troubled. 'I've got other magic, and these,' she added, patting the twin daggers strapped to her hips. Ordes gave her a lingering kiss on the mouth.

Arthur turned away, catching sight of Halymere. The big Cruithean was armed to the teeth, and the glyph between his eyes had been traced over with white. Two lines ran down his cheeks, disappearing into his thick beard. The people of this city might not have any love for Cruithea, or the Inborn, or Magic Wielder's in general, but Halymere was not one to let an injustice like this slip past him. The Inborn were the shield of the world, Arthur remembered, recalling Mordred's words and Jalen's whispered explanation.

Where is he? Arthur's heart pinched.

The Sword of the White Dragon thrummed with magic. He had not drawn the Sword yet, on Merlin's orders, and he had no idea what would happen when he did, or what he would do. Merlin had said the Sword thirsted for war. Arthur did not thirst for war, not at all, but he also could not let this happen.

The gangplank was lowered and Katarin, weapons drawn, led the way onto the jetty. Arthur met Merlin's eyes – he nodded, then vanished in a swirl of mist. Taking a deep breath, Arthur followed Ordes and Jenyfer down the gangplank, Halymere on his heels.

They hurried through the warehouse district, and as they neared the heart of the city, the screams grew louder, like a terrible symphony, a performance staged for their benefit. Flames poured from windows and danced over rooftops. Katarin's face was hard, her steps hastening until she was running, Halymere close behind her. Bodies were strewn across the ground like broken fruit – men, women, even children. To Medb and her followers, it made no difference.

'Spread out,' Katarin called over her shoulder. 'Help whoever you can.'

Fire and ash filled the sky, embers raining down around them. One landed on Arthur's shoulder, and he brushed it away quickly. He could taste smoke and his eyes stung. There was no sign of Medb, but the city dripped with her presence, a lingering darkness. They hurried past people fighting … people. Arthur skidded to a stop. Through the smoke, he could see two men brawling on the other side of the street. One man was doing his best to defend himself, but the other was fighting like a storm, his viciousness breathtaking.

These were ordinary people, not faeries.

'They're compelled,' Ordes said, grabbing Arthur's arm. 'Look at them.'

Vacant eyes and vacant expressions, laying about with whatever they could use as a weapon. Ordes and Arthur hurried on, a sickening feeling in Arthur's stomach. Katarin paused at the end of the street before she drew her cutlass and charged around the corner, Jenyfer, Melhala, and Ethinne following her. Halymere paused, glancing at Arthur, expression torn.

'Go with them,' Arthur called.

He followed Ordes, who led him down a series of side-streets smeared with blood and wreckage, before they arrived at the edge of Malist's main square, an orange sky surrounding them. Arthur heard laughter, then a scream.

The square was full of Medb's puppets, fists and weapons swinging.

'We need to stop this,' Arthur breathed as a woman punched another woman in the face.

Ordes nodded. 'I'll try and find Medb.'

'Be careful,' Arthur said.

His friend managed a grin. 'She can't kill me. I don't think,' Ordes added, but he hesitated.

'Go,' Arthur told him. With a nod, Ordes vanished.

Arthur glanced around as the city continued to dissolve into chaos around him. His fingers curled around the hilt of the Sword and immediately, a voice filled his head.

Draw me.

Arthur hesitated.

Draw me, boy, and become a man.

Arthur hesitated. *If killing things makes me a man, then I'm not sure I want to be one*, he thought.

A woman dragging a small child hurried around the corner, terror stamped on her face. She barrelled into Arthur and jumped away, a thin scream escaping white lips. She thrust the child behind her, eyes wide. Human, and not compelled.

'It's alright,' Arthur told her. 'I'm here to help.'

The moment the words left his lips, he was aware of the futility of them. Before he could say more, a man came running around the corner, rage painted in dull eyes. He saw the woman and rushed at her, his weapon raised.

Draw me. Now!

Arthur didn't hesitate this time. He pulled the woman and the child behind him as he drew the Sword of the White Dragon in a fluid motion. Music swam through his head, beautiful, dark and deep. The Sword sang as his arm moved, the action pulled to existence by instinct and magic.

Let go, the Sword said, and Arthur did. He opened himself to the Treasure of the Gods, feeling magic take hold of his limbs. He danced, he pivoted, he swept his enemies aside. He cut them down like grass as one man became another, then more, Medb's human puppets falling beneath the Sword, her fey soldiers torn to pieces by that magical blade.

When it was over, human and faery lay together, red and green-blue blood mingling on Malist's cobbled street. Arthur blinked. He was on the far side of the square now, the woman and her child nowhere to be seen. Bodies littered the square, left in the Sword's wake. He shuddered as he recalled that beautiful song, the magic that had flared through him, and the thirst, the *hunger*, the godly Treasure had woken in him.

Violence and death.

Arthur vomited, unable to help it. He wiped his mouth with shaking fingers. Sheathing the Sword, he pushed away its whispered protests as he hurried on, following the screaming and the sound of steel on steel. Above the noise was maniacal laughter. Medb.

As he ran, something with wings raced alongside him for a moment, then vanished. He swore he saw a huge cat at the head of a pack of enormous dogs, a giant bird soaring in their wake.

The sounds of battle grew closer.

Arthur spied a woman in grey, blonde curls tumbling around her face on the other side of the street. He blinked. Isolde! She must have snuck off the ship! He drew the Sword and hurried towards her as three fey spied her. They shrieked with amusement as they approached her. Arthur frowned, and quickened his pace, adjusting his grip on the Sword.

'Isolde!' he shouted. 'Get out of here!'

She ignored him, taking a dagger from her pocket and sliding the blade across her palm, not wincing, eyes locked on the fey. Arthur frowned as Isolde pressed her palm to her face. It was a terrible sight, that bloodied handprint on her pale flesh. She closed her eyes, lips shifting, and her body suddenly shook. She dropped to her knees, spine arching, fingers clawing against the stones.

The Sword sung in Arthur's hands, its magic flowing through him. He tore his eyes from Isolde as something rushed at him from the side.

The Sword swung wide, slicing through green flesh with ease. When he turned around, Isolde was gone, and in her place was a large wolf with ashen fur, a bloodied human handprint on its face.

The wolf met his eyes, then lifted its snout and howled. The fey scattered as she struck, fast as lightning, running down the first faery before it had taken two steps. Such was the wolf's strength, one bite of its terrible jaws cleaved the fey's body in two. Blue-black blood splattered across the cobblestones.

Arthur swallowed, leaving the white wolf to tear the limbs from the creature it had pinned on the ground. As Arthur ran towards the nearest screams, the air around him shifted. Ordes appeared, blood splattered across his cheek, his eyes burning with silver fire.

They raced around the next corner to find Jen, Katarin, and Melhala fighting a group of faery creatures. Ethinne worked her magic nearby, vines shooting from the earth to wrap around a man wielding a large stick. A gash ran the length of Katarin's cheek, but she still had her cutlass and the blue light of her magic was curled in her other hand like a rope. Melhala's face and blade glistened with fey blood. Jenyfer gripped her daggers so tightly her knuckles were white.

The great white wolf burst around the corner, jaws dripping with green. The beast hesitated, then leapt on a man rushing towards Melhala, one of Medb's compelled humans.

'That wolf,' Ordes murmured. 'There's old magic there. I can feel it.'

'It's Isolde,' Arthur said. 'I think.'

Ordes' eyes widened but before he could speak, a whirlwind smashed its way across the city, a barrelling storm of smoke and ash. Jen and Melhala raced for cover as the smoke cleared, revealing the Queen of The Teeth. Katarin had not stopped fighting. She pulled her blade free of a man's belly, her magic coiling back around her fingers like a whip, which she unleashed on a faery man with green skin.

Medb smiled, a cruel, vicious curving of bloodless lips, and levelled her dark gaze at Katarin.

'No!' Arthur cried as a stream of black smoke flowed from Medb's fingertips, reaching across the square for Katarin. Arthur's heart plummeted. Even with the Sword, he would not get there in time.

'Katarin!' Arthur screamed.

His sister met his eyes, then shifted her gaze to Medb.

The thick, black smoke was swallowed by a cloud of blood-red mist, and when it cleared, Olwen was crouched on the cobblestones.

Katarin's mouth dropped open.

Olwen held a glistening blade in each hand. Arthur couldn't recall anyone giving the Red Sister a weapon, then realised no one had to. The blades were made of red mist, shifting and swirling like they were alive. Slowly, Olwen straightened. She looked at Medb, and smiled. In the blink of an eye, Olwen was gone again, red mist swirling across the square. Medb snarled and, forgetting Katarin, unleashed a cloud of magic.

Black and red collided, Olwen and the Queen of The Teeth snapping in and out of focus as lightning flashed around them. Arthur stood frozen, watching in terror, unable to help and unable to look away. Medb's dark magic slowly pushed Olwen back across the square, towards Katarin, who lifted both blade and magic, her face determined, eyes hard.

Olwen materialised out of the churning red and black soup, dropping to her knees, a rope of black tight around her throat. She gasped, fingers clawing at Medb's magic as a bolt of lightning lit up the square.

'Enough!'

Medb's unnaturally beautiful face froze.

Then her lips curled and she laughed, releasing her hold on Olwen, who slumped to the ground. 'Here he is at last, come to see what's past. The Myrddin with his arrogant grace, watch while I remove his face.'

Merlin bowed, as if she really was a Queen, but Arthur could see the mockery in the action. So could Medb, and she snarled. One moment she was there, the next she was gone, moving through time and space as quickly as a blink.

It was a dance, a terrible, menacing dance between old foes. People scuttled out of the way, broken and bleeding. The fey of The Teeth fought beside their mistress, but were cut down by Isolde's claws or Halymere's blade. Ordes, Arthur noted, did not kill – he used his magic to defend only.

Arthur glanced about for his sister, finding her on her knees on the edge of the square with Olwen's head resting in her lap. The Red Sister's eyes were closed. Throat tight, Arthur skirted the edge of the square, hurrying over to them, relieved to see Olwen's chest rise and fall with her breathing.

He met Katarin's eyes.

'She saved my life,' Kat whispered.

Arthur nodded, turning his attention to Merlin and Medb, his fingers stroking the hilt of the Sword. It was strangely silent, as if it didn't want to interfere in this particular fight. Medb was forced back, pushed to the edge of the square, feet skidding through blood and ash, swirling smoke catching in the black strands of her hair.

'You can't win,' Merlin said.

The Faery Queen of The Teeth pulled her lips back from her elongated teeth. She cast her feral, black eyes over all of them. 'You who stand inside this space, little do you know your fate. Fresh of face and dark of heart, I'll wait until you come apart.'

Wind tore through the city, wrapping around Medb and turning black. When it cleared, she was gone, her fey swept up with her. The people she had compelled slowly lowered their weapons, confusion writ across their faces.

'I'm going to follow her,' Merlin stated, and before anyone could stop him, he was gone.

Someone screamed as a large cat, huge paws and toothy maw dripping with green blood, came racing into view. It let out a terrible roar and launched itself onto the body of an injured faery who was trying to crawl away. The crack of breaking bone was the only sound Arthur could hear over his furiously beating heart.

The cat yawned, leaving its victim and stalking towards Arthur. He tensed, reaching for the Sword, which was still silent. The cat regarded him through slanted, golden eyes, then shook itself. Suddenly a tall, broad-shouldered man with shaggy brown hair stood before him. He inclined his head.

'Future King,' he rumbled. Blood the colour of leaves was smeared on his chin. He spat into the ashes at his feet. 'That's a taste I haven't missed, I can assure you.'

'Who are you?' Arthur whispered. A cat had turned into a man!

'Voss, the King of the Therians,' the man answered. 'At your service. Maybe,' he added cryptically, running his eyes over Arthur. They settled on the Sword of the White Dragon, and a smile tugged at his lips.

'Voss,' Ordes called, slinging the Bow over his shoulder. 'Didn't expect to see you here.'

'This is my city, and you look like shit,' the shifter grunted. He turned back to Arthur. 'So, it's you or your cousin, is it?'

'Mordred?' Arthur blinked, startled. 'What do you know of him?'

Voss stroked his blood-smeared chin. 'Something you need to understand, Future King, is this – the fey care nothing for prophecies and the words of Merlin, but we do care about our existence. For years, we've lived in the shadows, and now two paths are laid before us. Medb has chosen hers – she will be on her way to your cousin. Her horde will march across Camlann. She won't be bringing war to his doorstep, but an alliance.'

Arthur swallowed. 'Camlann?'

'Your cousin heads to Dinas Emrys, to the castle of the Old Ways,' the shifter said. 'You have a choice to make, cub. Show us a better path. Convince me that what you offer us is truly a better world, because right now, the rallying cry is spreading through the world beneath the world.

The Goddess of Magic has already sent her envoy, and he was rather convincing.'

'Envoy?' Katarin said sharply, overhearing. She froze in the act of helping a scowling Olwen to her feet. 'What envoy?'

'That pet halfling-god she commands,' Voss said. Katarin's face hardened.

Jalen, Arthur realised, his heart sinking. *Jalen had been here!*

The shifter was talking to him. 'Can you match what the Witch of the Mists is offering magical creatures of this land?'

'What did my mother offer you?' Ordes growled.

'Power,' Voss said simply. 'A return to what was. But she's not a fool, Niniane of the Ways. She still needs you,' he added, his eyes returning to Arthur. 'To play her little game. But the question is, will you?'

'What if we offered a world without the Old Ones?' Ordes asked, his voice low and furious. Arthur jolted – they hadn't discussed this, and it was something he had never considered possible. He listened, heart-hammering, as Ordes went on. 'Freedom, Voss, for all fey-kind. Not bound to any master, least of all my mother – I can assure you, if you bend to her, if you allow her to put you on your knees, she will hold you all accountable.'

Voss grew thoughtful, but then his gaze fell on Isolde, human once again. 'Is that allied with you, I wonder?'

'Isolde?' Arthur asked, surprised. 'Yes.'

'Sure of that, are you?' Voss asked.

Isolde was sitting on the ground, huddled in Tristan's arms. Halymere and Melhala were standing nearby; the Inborn was frowning.

'Nonetheless, it isn't just the fey you're going to need to convince. We are one side of a coin, cub. The people of this land should have the right to choose their fate,' Voss said.

'You want to give humans a choice?' Jenyfer asked, suspicion coating her voice. 'Because at the moment, after what happened here, after what

Medb made them do, not one human is going to ally themselves with a fey. It won't matter that we helped them.'

Voss grunted, gesturing at Arthur. 'He's thrown his lot in with you, hasn't he? And if he can, so can others.'

'And what is Arthur supposed to tell them?' Ordes asked. He glanced around. People were sitting, dazed, or leaning on each other. At that moment, a group of women wearing red robes entered the square. Arthur tensed. Red Sisters.

A small smile tugged at Olwen's lips. She was still being supported by Katarin, but on seeing her sisters, she straightened.

There were five Red Sisters. Their hoods covered their faces, but Arthur could feel their eyes on him, on all of them, and he wondered where they had been during the fighting. The woman at the head of the group nodded, and the other four peeled off, moving towards the wounded, but Arthur did not relax. The remaining Red Sister made her way towards them, and as she neared, the shifter, Voss, chuckled.

'Late, as usual, Varna' he said. 'Where are your blasted Warriors? We could have used their swords.'

'They are doing their jobs. We're here when we need to be,' the woman, Varna, said. Her voice was low, gravelly, and it sounded like she didn't use it much. She inclined her head in Arthur's direction, then stepped forward purposefully. 'Use the power of the Word, Future King, to show these people they do not need to fear you or yours.'

Before Arthur could reply, the Red Sister turned to Ordes.

'And you need to show them,' she said. 'Show them what you are.'

'What do you—' Ordes began.

'Your wings,' Jenyfer said, glancing at Olwen, who nodded. 'She means the wings.'

The people lingering in the square were staring at Arthur and those from *The Excalibur* with deep suspicion. Suddenly, he saw what they saw.

Pirates. Fey and Magic Wielders. Shifters. Cruitheans. Whatever Isolde was.

'Ordes, show them,' he said. This was important. He didn't know why, but he could sense this moment needed to happen, when they were bloodied and exhausted, when the One God's city stood as nothing more than a blackened ruin for the history books. These people were confused. They had seen fey kill their friends. They had been compelled with magic to murder their neighbours. And yet, they had seen fey and Magic Wielders fighting to save them. Arthur noticed the woman and her child he had helped.

'Ordes,' he prompted.

Ordes hesitated, and then his wings unfolded from his back in a burst of brilliant white feathers. Arthur caught his breath at the sight, despite having seen them dozens of times before. Around them, people gasped, and the Red Sisters bowed their heads, murmuring in low voices. Sunlight pierced a break in the clouds, pouring into the square, and the white feathers shimmered in its glow.

Silence rang out, until Olwen chuckled softly. 'You're up, Arthur.'

Arthur swallowed and took a deep breath. This wasn't something he was good at, because he'd never been given the chance to speak.

Draw me, the Sword of the White Dragon said. *Show me to the faithful of this city.*

Arthur frowned. The Sword was not singing its battle song. It was not demanding blood be spilt or violence committed. Slowly, he drew the weapon, lifting it high above his head, not knowing why he did so. It was instinctual, but he wasn't sure if those instincts belonged to him or the Sword.

Words poured out of him, powerful, resolute and sure. He did not know their source, only that they flowed into the night air. 'The Word says, "in moments of darkness, look and you shall find me, and I shall be watching over you". Today, you have seen that darkness, and today, you were delivered from despair, for you are the blessed children of the Light. It is into the Light you shall be delivered, and a new world will rise from the ashes of the one left behind, as was promised. A new world will be delivered to you, and it will be a world of harmony and love, where no one shall be persecuted. A world for everyone, no matter who they are, for we are the ones to inherit this earth. Under my guidance as the prophesied King, you shall know happiness.'

The Red Sister who had spoken to Arthur and Ordes stepped forward and addressed the watching crowd. 'Today, you have heard the true Word of the One God, She who has left the world in your hands.'

She?

Not one person listening reacted to what Arthur was sure was a slip of the tongue.

'Return to your homes. Tend to your wounded, and let today be a lesson. There is darkness in the world, but there is also Light,' the Red Sister said. Arthur waited, not breathing, and slowly, the people of Malist turned and limped away, escorted by the Red Sisters.

'You can put the wings away now, pretty boy,' Olwen told Ordes.

'Care to tell me why I made a spectacle of myself?' Ordes asked in a low voice.

'Truth is what we make it,' Olwen managed. Her face was pale, but she wasn't wounded. 'Trust me.' She shared a look with the Red Sister, Varna. The woman nodded.

'What just happened?' Arthur asked blankly, returning the Sword to its scabbard. The words he had spoken swum around his head. They tingled and brushed against him, flowing into every part of him.

'I have no idea,' Katarin said, her voice soft with exhaustion. She tried to pass Olwen over to Halymere, but the Red Sister shook her head in protest. Olwen's steps were heavy, but she kept her feet. Katarin did not argue. 'Let's go back to the ship before something else happens. I don't think I can handle any more surprises.'

They left Malist burning and wounded behind them. A strange, smoky silence hung over the city. Arthur lingered behind, eyes roaming the carnage, settling on the big shifter stood next to Varna. He had his arms folded, a frown on his face.

'Arthur,' Katarin called. He hurried to catch up to her, and they walked in silence, the weight of what had happened beginning to settle on their shoulders.

'Kat,' Arthur said quietly. 'He isn't coming back, is he?'

Katarin gave him a sorrowful look, but beneath it was a deep and unforgiving anger. 'I don't think so, little brother.'

CHAPTER 44

Mordred was not at the Chif's house when Lamorna arrived. She hesitated, wondering if she should go in. It was quiet behind the front door. Footsteps crunched behind her, and she turned to see Mordred and the men of the Red Hand. Lamorna stepped aside without having to be asked, and they swept into the house without her.

Waiting outside, Lamorna heard shouts and the sound of something breaking. It sounded like a fight, but she had never truly seen or heard a fight, so she had nothing to compare it to.

Silence fell, the sounds inside the Chif's house dropping away until there was only her heartbeat and the birds in the trees. Somewhere, a dog howled and she thought she heard the whinny of a horse.

Mordred appeared in the front door. Lamorna jumped, but when he held out his hand for her, she took it, letting him lead her through the darkness and into the formal room.

She did not know what she was expecting, but it was not the men of the Konsel on the floor, with their faces pressed into the lush carpet, held down by the bully boys of the Red Hand. Lamorna met the Chif's eyes. He sat in his chair at the head of the table, a dagger held to his throat by one of the Red Hand.

She swallowed, wondering what exactly was going on.

Mordred placed his hands on her shoulders and put his mouth close to her ear. 'The Konsel has no place in the world we shall build, Lamorna,' he said softly. 'This will be your choice.'

'What choice?' she breathed, while the Chif glared at her. The look he turned on Mordred was one of pure hatred.

'They burn, or they drown,' Mordred said, and she understood. He was going to execute these men, whose faces were kissing the carpet.

And he had given her the power to choose how it happened. He had given her a voice, like he promised.

Lamorna stared at the Konsel, those old men who had helped the Chif rule over the town. Who had helped him oppress and subjugate. Had helped him order the rape of women like her sister, like Calla's cousin – and one day, it would have been Lamorna's turn. The men who had helped spread a false word of a false god.

Men who had bound her hands to the stake and left her to die.

She stared at them, eyes blurring, anger a deep, red flame inside her as she remembered the cold kiss of the water on her bare toes. How unforgiving and hungry it had been. She remembered the musical darkness of Lyonesse and the God of the Seas, asking if she wanted to live.

She did.

So these men would die.

'Drown them,' she said. Her voice was firmer than she expected. Resolute and cold. It didn't feel like hers, but maybe it had always been there, waiting to be called, longing to condemn these men to their deaths. The sound of her voice skittered along her spine and instead of fear, she felt only courage.

The Konsel were paraded through the streets. They did not struggle. They did not fight. The Chif was not with them. He had remained in his house. Not a prisoner – he was free to leave if he wished. But he didn't. Lamorna had expected him to rush out, to tell Mordred to stop, to tell the Red Hand to stop.

He didn't even leave to witness the end of his rule, of the little empire he had built.

The Konsel were taken to the beach. They were made to wait as more stakes were driven into the rocks, joining the one that Lamorna had been bound to. Mordred did it himself. Shirtless, the ocean crashing behind him, he drove those seven stakes into the earth. The afternoon sun blazed overhead, and by the time he finished, it had begun to slip beneath the horizon.

Lamorna had not noticed, but townsfolk had followed them onto the beach. They muttered and whispered, but not one person told Mordred to stop. Not one person told the Red Hand to release the Konsel men, not even their families.

There was no one here with the courage Jenyfer had displayed.

Lamorna watched as the men were tied, one by one, to those eight stakes. She watched, unblinking, unfeeling, as the rope was bound around their hands while the ocean pawed the sand, hungry and waiting.

Once the Konsel were secure, Mordred jumped down from the rocks. The water closed over his ankles, but he ignored it. He did not look at the Konsel, but out at the ocean. Lamorna wondered if he was thinking like she was, of the moment when the ocean would creep up and close over the heads of the men he had bound.

She would stay and watch it happen, Lamorna decided. She wanted to see it, that little moment before they died. Would they feel that same terror she felt, the terror she did not allow herself to show?

Would they cry out in fear?

Or would they die quietly, like the women, the accused witches they had drowned on Ulrian's orders?

Mordred met her eyes, and instead of being frightened by what she could see there – the vicious pleasure in what he was doing – she was proud.

Proud that he had done this. For her.

Someone grabbed her arm and she jumped. Calla, Arwen, and Penny clustered around her as one of the men on the stake suddenly cried out, begging for the One God's mercy. Calla's face was triumphant, as if she had done this, and for a moment, Lamorna wanted to remind her that this was not her victory. But then, perhaps it partially was. Perhaps this victory belonged to all the women who had been wronged in this town.

'This is …' Penny began as the water crept higher, the waves starting to pound the rocks now.

'What needed to happen,' Lamorna said fiercely as the men of the Konsel began to struggle in earnest. 'Justice for what we have gone through in this place.'

'I suppose so,' Penny said softly, but she turned her eyes away from what was happening. Calla did not. She took hold of Lamorna's hand and told her she was going to stay and watch. Lamorna gave Calla's hand a squeeze, pleased she would not be alone to witness this moment.

The watching crowd shuffled up the beach as the tide began to rise higher. The bottom of Lamorna's dress was damp, but she didn't care. She let Calla lead her to higher ground, not taking her eyes from the Konsel.

Mordred turned to face the people of Kernou. 'The invitation I made several nights ago still stands. You are welcome on the journey,' he told them as the sea wrapped around his knees. 'Or you can choose to remain here, in the ruins of a world built on lies.'

The water closed over the Konsel's heads. Calla was smiling.

'It is done,' Mordred said softly. He waded from the sea to join Lamorna and Calla.

Lamorna frowned, feeling a spark of worry. 'Will this make the people turn from you?'

'No,' Mordred said after a pause, and she remembered what he had said about leaders and how people needed them to be strong, to make decisions that were hard but necessary.

'Those who don't come with us?' Lamorna asked.

'Will be nothing but shadows clinging to the wrong side of a world reborn,' Mordred answered.

CHAPTER 45

They'd left Malist a pile of smouldering rubble and were tucked up in the captain's cabin. Katarin sat behind her desk, feet on the table, twirling a dagger between her fingers absently. No one was talking.

What they had experienced, what they had witnessed … she hadn't begun to process any of it, and wasn't sure when she would. She snuck a look at Arthur. Her brother was frowning, his whole body turned in on itself. If she knew where Jalen was, she'd skin him alive, demi-god or not. What fucking game was he playing? What game was Niniane playing?

Kat had a bad feeling she knew the answer, and the betrayal that speared through her was sharper than any weapon.

Jenyfer was pacing the cabin, face stormy, muttering to herself. Her eyes kept returning to Arthur, and Kat could see the worry there. Merlin sat in a chair he had conjured for himself, one that looked suspiciously like Katarin's, while Ordes and Arthur perched on the end of Katarin's bed.

Katarin's thoughts shifted to Olwen. The woman had saved her life, and Katarin wasn't sure how she felt about that. She was grateful to be alive, but Olwen was an unknown ally, and Kat's generally suspicious nature had her wondering when the Red Sister would want something in return. Olwen had been taken below deck, and Katarin had gotten as far as the bottom of the ladder before she'd returned to her cabin. She had no idea what to say to Olwen. 'Thank you' wasn't in her vocabulary, and it wouldn't be enough.

Katarin pushed it aside for the moment, focusing on the woman sitting across from her.

Isolde was slumped in a chair, golden hair tousled, the faintest hint of blue-green smudged around her lips and staining her fingertips.

'You're fey? Why didn't you say so?' Kat demanded.

'Because my kind have been hunted for centuries, long before any Treasures and gods and their petty squabbles,' Isolde returned fiercely. Kat blinked in surprise. Isolde had been nothing but polite, mild-mannered, docile almost. Now, her blue eyes blazed and the remnants of a bloody handprint stained her face. Kat tried not to grin – she could like this Isolde. Tristan sat beside the dishevelled blonde woman, shadows beneath his eyes. He took one of her hands in his.

'You knew?' Ordes asked him; the Witchfinder nodded. 'Her husband?'

Isolde scowled and held out her spare hand. The dim lantern light could not hide the scars banding her wrist like horrible jewellery. 'He kept me chained at first – silver. Not a poison to most fey, but I'm not like most fey. Once he realised what I was, I thought he would kill me, but he didn't. He thought he could use me. Tame the beastly part of me.' She laughed darkly. 'But he didn't understand me. The more he raised his fists – he wore silver rings, you see – the more I vowed to eat the heart from his chest while he still breathed. I would have, and he knew it, which was why he had me declared a witch.'

'You're a shifter?' Ordes asked.

She surprised them all by shaking her head.

'She's a worldling, a skinroamer,' Merlin said. Everyone except Isolde and Tristan frowned at the strange term. Katarin had never heard it before in her life, and had never come across it in Avalon's library.

Isolde nodded. 'Yes.'

'The magic to transform is in her blood,' Merlin explained. 'Unlike a shifter, a skinroamer can wear whatever shape they wish.'

Isolde looked at him. 'Like you can. I can sense it in you.'

Merlin nodded. 'Yes.'

Ordes made a noise, but when Kat looked, his expression was composed.

'Isolde's kind were hunted to near extinction by man. Worldlings are as old as the earth, borne of the earth and the vestiges of Old Magic that was used to fashion the animals and fey things. Somewhere along the way, the magics became muddled, and the worldlings appeared – not quite human, not animal nor fey, but something in between. Shifters came later, when the magic of creation had settled and wasn't as wild or unpredictable,' Merlin explained.

'We were hunted by both human and fey, a thing to be feared because we were a thing misunderstood,' Isolde put in, her tone bitter. She shook back the bloodied curtain of her hair, her face proud. 'And now you know what I am. Will you cut my throat and throw me to the sea?'

'Of course not,' Arthur said quickly. 'But, forgive me for asking, how did a skinroamer end up married to a powerful man of the Sacellum?'

'My family had this idea that perhaps I would be able to influence him. That he would fall in love with me and I could use him to our benefit, maybe start to find us a place in the world again. It was an act of desperation, borne of centuries of being feared. But they didn't know him. They didn't know how cruel he was, how hungry for power. He had them slaughtered once he worked out what I was,' Isolde said.

A stunned silence met her words. Katarin didn't know what to say, though she had some idea of what it must have been like. Her own mother had died in a man's quest for power, as she had nearly died. Isolde had told them her mother had desired her marriage to Mark for material gains, but that was a lie, possibly one Isolde had used to protect herself and anyone from discovering what she was.

Arthur murmured a sorry, his sympathy echoed around the cabin. Kat realised that not one person there had escaped life without being broken by something. She could see the shadow of it in Isolde's face.

'If you have the power to be whatever you wish, why didn't you escape the pyre yourself?' Jenyfer asked Isolde, her tone gentle.

'I had chosen death,' Isolde answered. Tristan's face pinched. 'Even if I escaped, where would I go? Where would be safe? I would have been hunted forever, and what sort of life is that?' She smiled at Tristan. 'He knew what I'd chosen, just as he isn't fearful of what I am. Yet, I did not want that life for him, always on the run, always looking over our shoulders.'

Tristan kissed her cheek, then turned his gaze to Katarin. 'If you want us to leave, we will.'

Arthur shook his head again. 'No. Voss was right, and the words I spoke to those people in Malist were the truth. We need a world of unity, of harmony and balance, where everyone – fey, human, Magic Wielder, or something else entirely – is free to live as they choose.'

'We've got the Treasures,' Jenyfer asked. 'So what do we do now? Find the Grail?'

'First,' Kat began, her face darkening, 'we need to find my charming cousin and talk some sense into him. If Medb is aligning herself with Mordred, and if what that shifter said is true … Mordred was always angry at the world. Angry at the cards he had been dealt. I never expected him to do … this.'

'I've got a feeling it's too late for talking,' Arthur said stonily.

'Mordred!' Arthur yelled. His voice echoed in the space between worlds, the dream space he had claimed as his own, now that he knew what it was. 'Mordred, I know you can hear me.'

Nothing. If Mordred was near, he was not revealing himself.

'And he calls me a coward,' Arthur muttered. He looked around at the blank emptiness. He closed his eyes, concentrating, and the world shifted around him. When he opened his eyes, he was sitting opposite a fire with no heat, Eseld's pale face watching him.

A strange wariness lingered between them. 'Why didn't you tell me I was a dreamwalker?' Arthur demanded. Anger buzzed in his blood. He was sick of people – dead or alive – keeping secrets from him.

Eseld shrugged skeletal shoulders. 'I didn't want you wandering off in the dream space – it's dangerous. Plus, it had been a long time since I had spoken to someone. I … wanted to keep you here, so I could talk with you.'

'So you could manipulate me, as well, you mean?' Arthur accused. The events in Malist sat heavy inside him. He could still hear the screams, even here in this place, the song of the Sword of the White Dragon singing as the blade bit into flesh.

Eseld blinked, unperturbed. 'All I have ever told you, have ever shown you, is the truth, Arthur. What you do with that knowledge is up to you. It always has been. I told your cousin the same thing.'

Arthur's heart seized. 'Mordred was here?'

'He was. He walked into my cave without knowing why he was here.'

'What did you tell him?' Arthur demanded. Mordred could walk in dreams. He needed, now more than ever, to find his cousin.

'The same things I told you,' Eseld said. She was unapologetic, uncaring. Arthur shook his head, laughter bubbling up inside him. Why hadn't he noticed her lack of true concern before? She was dead, and by being here, by guarding the Grail, she was doing exactly what the Old Ones – what Ereshki – had asked her to do. What did it matter who she talked to in this space? What he had taken for sadness in the beginning was apathy. The pity he had shown her, the care … he felt like a fool, caught up in yet another thread in the tapestry of lies the Old Ones had been weaving around him.

He levelled a long, hard look at the Fisher Queen, the once-ruler of Teyath. 'It's time for you to tell me where to find the Grail.'

'There are still things—'

'Eseld, they've used you as much as they've used me,' Arthur cut in, his voice low, dark with loathing. 'Tell me where to find it so I can end this game.'

'For the serpent to become the dragon, it must consume itself and be reborn,' she whispered. 'Are you ready to be reborn, Future King? Are you ready to shed your skin and slip into a new one? Have you grown enough that you will finally fit the role you were destined to play? Or have we all made a mistake?'

Her words sank inside him, and suddenly, he understood what it had all been for. Every step on this blasted journey, every moment of heartache and pain, every moment of bliss, and every fumbled snatch of ecstasy, every muddled thought and every trial he had been through.

For the serpent to become the dragon, it must consume itself and be reborn.

Every moment since leaving Kernou had been about rebirth.

His.

Arthur stood, looking down on the Fisher Queen. He was calm, in control, resolute for the first time since this all began. 'Tell me where to find the Grail.'

'The white dragon shall lead you to the Grail,' Eseld intoned. 'But first, you need to *see* what the future holds.'

Before Arthur could protest, the Fisher Queen clapped her hands, and he was hurtling through time and space, tumbling over and over, until he landed on his knees, the wind knocked from his lungs. He blinked. The sky loomed dark with storm clouds. He slowly lowered his gaze.

The beach he knelt on was wind-whipped and sorrowful.

He knew this place. Kernou. Arthur was on the beach in Kernou. Waves pounded the shoreline behind him.

Slowly, he got to his feet. There were no boats on the water, and the town was eerily quiet. A black bird screeched, wheeling through the sky, drawing his eye to the end of the beach, where strange shapes grew from the rocks.

Arthur frowned, dusting off his hands on his thighs and making his way along the sand. Wind pulled at his hair and blasted his eyes. He shielded his face with his hand. Approaching the shapes, he realised what they were. His stomach leapt into his throat.

Bodies. Bound to stakes. Eight of them.

Their red cloaks flapped in the wind shrieking in from the ocean.

Arthur forced himself closer, made himself look up at the faces of the Konsel, men he had known since childhood. He made himself witness the flesh that had begun to bloat in the sun. As he watched, a crow landed on the body nearest him.

The bird let out a harsh caw, and rammed its beak into an eye socket. As he turned away, Arthur realised he could not recall the names of those eight men, reduced to nothing but a feast for scavengers.

He glanced towards the town.

'Mordred!' he shouted. 'Mordred, what have you done?'

There was no answer.

Chapter 46

'Before we leave, we have one last thing to deal with,' Mordred said. Lamorna looked up from her packing, but she knew without having to ask what he meant.

The Chif.

Ulrian Tregarthen was locked in his house, the Red Hand standing guard at the door.

'There are things I believe you want to tell him,' Mordred said. He picked up a blanket and put it down again. 'Or have you changed your mind?'

'No,' she said quickly, dusting her hands on her skirt. 'I haven't.'

Ulrian was in his formal room when they arrived, the man on the door swinging it wide for them, no questions asked. It made Lamorna smile to think of it – the Red Hand at Mordred's command. How easy it had been. Offer a man more power than he already has, and he would do whatever he could to get it, thinking he needed it, that what he had was not enough.

The Chif gave them a hateful glare when they entered the room. He did not look like he had bathed or changed his clothes since the last time Lamorna had seen him, the day Mordred had left the Konsel for the arms of the sea.

For a long time, no one spoke. Lamorna looked at Ulrian, realising this was one of the only times she had done so without fear of reprisal. There was a tightness to his face, the lines that bracketed his mouth, the streaks of silver in his hair – she wondered if they had always been there. The Chif looked old, tired, and lost.

He said nothing as she sat in one of his hard chairs, spreading her hands in front of her on the table top. She noted her fingernails, how long they had grown. Then, she took a deep breath, and raised her head.

'Why would you taint the Word with lies?'

Ulrian's face tightened further. 'Are they lies when they have kept you all safe?'

Lamorna laughed. 'Safe? You murdered people, Ulrian.'

'Like you and my heathen nephew have murdered people,' he snapped. 'You can look at me however you like, Lamorna Astolat, but you are no different, no better than me. I had my reasons for what I did. I acted on the One God's orders.'

Lamorna shared a look with Mordred. His face was calm, but beneath it, she could see the anger simmering in his eyes. She returned her attention to Ulrian. 'There is something you need to know. The One God, Ulrian Tregarthen, is a woman. An Old One. She is displeased with what you have done.'

He shook his head automatically, and she saw in his face all the things she imagined Mordred must have seen in hers that day he told her the truth. 'No ... this is one of Mordred's lies, designed to draw you in, Lamorna. Like a spider, he has been spinning his web.'

'Did you know that the most intricate spider webs are spun by the females? The ones that are strongest. The ones that can hold the most prey.' She paused, and looked the Chif in the eyes. 'My sister told me that once, when we were small. I think she was trying to frighten me, but now, I'm not frightened. You tried to take away our power – women's power. Why? What ever happened to you to make you hate my sex so much?'

'The One God—' Ulrian began.

Lamorna slammed her hand on the table, the open-palmed slap against the timber echoing around the room. 'It was not the One God who told me to cover my hair or my body. It was you! It was not the One God who made me feel ashamed for forgetting to say nightly prayers as a child – it was you! It was not the One God who forced me to lower my eyes when speaking to a man. It was not the One God who made me less. It was you and men like you – power hungry and filled with hate. The One God speaks to me now, Ulrian. And She sings a different song to the one you had us all dancing to.' She flicked the length of her hair over her shoulder. 'My God tells me I should seek my own happiness.'

Ulrian's dark eyes bored into hers. 'And are you happy?'

'I'm content enough,' she answered. 'For now.'

'With him?' the Chif asked. Mordred didn't say anything, simply watched and let her have this moment.

'He holds no power over me,' Lamorna said.

Ulrian laughed. 'And you think spreading your legs for him will make you feel better, Lamorna? Bring you closer to this … heresy you now worship?'

'Oh, it has.' She laughed, a wild feeling rushing through her chest as Ulrian shrank away from her, like she was a mad and wretched thing. 'Would you like to know what he's taught me about my own body?' she asked, voice low. Ulrian paled. 'I have learnt many things with Mordred, but there is one thing that stands above the rest. There is power in my body, in my hands, my mouth. The sort of power that can make a man do what I want, the sort of power that can put a man on his knees before me. I am finally beginning to understand why someone like you might not want women to know this.' She paused meaningfully, filling her words with all the venom she could muster. 'The women of this town, those who come with us to Dinas Emrys, shall know the truth. I will undo what you have done. I promise you that.'

Ulrian swallowed audibly, the constricted lump making its way down his throat. She hoped he would choke on it.

'I should have had you thrown back to the sea,' he hissed eventually. 'Things that are dead should stay dead.'

'What should we do with him, my love?' Mordred mused. He put his hands on Lamorna's shoulders, his mouth close to her ear, breath curling against her skin.

'I don't know,' she said.

'Let me help you decide.' He withdrew a pouch from the air around him – the Chif made a small noise in the back of his throat at the magic. Mordred ignored him, handing Lamorna the pouch. 'Open it.'

She did.

The shattered glass within gleamed with wickedness.

'I thought you might care to remind him what a great motivator pain can be,' Mordred whispered. Lamorna hesitated, her eyes flickering to the Chif's. 'He gave you your scars, Lamorna.'

'Some scars can't be seen,' she whispered, but Mordred was not listening. He marched over to the Chif and grabbed the man around the upper arm, hauling him to his feet. Ulrian's eyes were wide with the terror of the unknown.

Lamorna stared into the pouch until her eyes blurred.

If she did this, there would be no turning back.

What would you turn back to? the little voice inside her whispered. *What else is left for you, Lamorna? You're in too deep now, girl.*

'I'll let you arrange things as you wish, my love,' Mordred told her.

She wondered what the Chif could truly see when he looked at her. Could he see how changed she was? Could he see the markers of her sins? The ambitions and the dreams she was slowly allowing herself to have? She shook herself. She didn't care what he thought.

His lips curled in a sneer, one last attempt to intimidate her.

Lamorna pushed back her chair and stood, then emptied the glass onto the rug, spreading it out with the toe of her boot. She looked Ulrian Tregarthen in the eyes again, knowing it would be the last time.

'I'll tell you anything,' the Chif implored suddenly, his gaze swinging between Lamorna and Mordred.

'You don't have anything to say that we don't already know, do you?' Mordred said, low and soothing. He shoved the Chif in the lower back, moving him a step closer to Lamorna. Her cruel jewels sparkled in the light sneaking in through the window.

The Chif looked at her pleadingly. 'Lamorna—'

She swallowed tightly, and lifted her chin. 'Kneel.'

Four hundred people abandoned Kernou. Four hundred people stood on the hillside near the stone circle and watched as a bloated moon rose above the ocean. There was a spring tide tonight, the ocean creeping up the beach on a cool wind.

Lamorna held her breath, waiting.

She wanted to see waves as tall as mountains rise and crash into that hateful place. She wanted to see the water sweep Kernou from the map, devouring it, cleansing the land of this place of lies and pain and hatred.

But it didn't happen. The tide was a normal tide, nothing more. She could not help but feel disappointed.

Some people had brought their goats and dogs, and there were even chickens being carried in cages on the back of wagons. Trekking through the darkness in the hours before dawn to the hill behind the town, Lamorna had seen cats with glowing eyes slinking through the shadows and had not been able to tell if they were animal or faery.

People carried their children on their backs or their hips, their little faces dazed. They had been pulled from their beds in the middle of the night, ripped from the world they knew.

Lamorna would give them a new world.

Calla came to stand at Lamorna's side. 'Penny did not come,' she said quietly.

'Oh,' Lamorna whispered. 'Did she—'

'She didn't believe what you told us,' Calla interrupted. 'I tried to convince her.'

Lamorna nodded. 'She has made her choice.'

Calla spoke soft and low. 'There is something you need to know. I don't suppose it matters anymore, not now,' she said. 'Two years ago, Ulrian left my grandmother for the sea. She was a witch.'

Lamorna swallowed. There would be no judgement from her. She had made that mistake once already with Jenyfer, and vowed that this knowledge would not change her friendship with Calla. She found her friend's hand, giving it a squeeze.

Before Lamorna could reply, someone let out a shrill whistle. The high-pitched, anxious whinny of a horse answered, and Pellinore was galloping towards them, as slick as a shadow, the morning sun striking his gleaming coat. Lamorna's heart leapt at the sight of the horse, running straight to Mordred, who stroked his neck. A small crowd gathered around him, marvelling at the animal. Mordred pulled himself onto Pellinore's back, and he was once again a Cruithean, his hair loose and dangling over his shoulders. Pride swelled like a great wave inside Lamorna's chest.

'Come,' Mordred called. He turned his back on Kernou as Pellinore headed towards the peaks of the mountains gilded in moonlight. Lamorna and Calla exchanged a look. Lamorna smiled and held out her hand again. Calla took it, and took their first steps into a new life.

Chapter 47

Arthur woke alone. He blinked, hoping in the split second that his eyes closed that Jalen would appear, lying there with eyes bright, a warm smile on his lips. But the other side of the bed was cool to touch, as empty as the rest of him. The reality of it smashed into Arthur's chest, ripping his wounds apart anew, as it did every morning.

Jalen was gone, and he had taken Arthur's heart with him.

He had not walked in his dreams over the last few nights. He'd felt nothing but bleak despair, an endless pit Arthur had fallen into, and he wasn't sure if he had the strength to climb out.

Was it something he had done or not done? Said or not said? What had driven Jalen to leave and not return? And then there was the other fear – that something had happened to Jalen. There had to be a reason why the demi-god had not returned.

You know the reason, an inner voice whispered. It sounded like Ulrian. Arthur shoved it away, forcing himself to think, to go back over everything, to search for the signs that he had obviously missed. It was all a terrible tangle in his mind, a web that trapped him and wrapped him and then spat him back out.

He needed to get up, face the world, deal with what had happened and turn towards a future he could no longer see, but he didn't know how.

It would be easier to give in to the pain of it, the hurt borne of rejection that he should be familiar with. But it was because of Jalen that he had shaken that particular beast off his back, had grown the courage to see himself differently, to accept who he was and, ultimately, the man he was supposed to be.

Arthur's eyes traced the knots in the timber of the ceiling as the ship shifted beneath him, gentle, usually soothing. Now the soft beat of water against the hull was nothing but a warning knell, one heard too late. He'd let himself be lulled into a false sense of security while onboard this ship. He'd let himself relax.

People had come to see him while he'd been trapped down here in his prison, broken, and wanting nothing more than to scream his pain into the world. He was supposed to be a king, but here he was — a shell of a person, caught up in a never-ending loop of misery and self-pity and the occasional burst of rage, at himself, at Jalen, at the prophecy, the world, *everything*.

He needed … he needed …

Arthur's eyes fell on the Sword of the White Dragon, leaning against the chair near the porthole. If it had eyes, it would have been staring right back at him. The last time he had held it, in Malist, he'd been calm and resolute, filled with courage despite what had been happening around him and to him.

Arthur scrambled upright. The Sword was calling him, as if it needed comfort as well. He was out of bed before he realised it, the Sword in his hands. Magic flowed through him, his fingers tingling. Arthur returned to bed, taking the Sword with him, resting it across his body. He returned to staring at the ceiling, but instead of feeling weighed down and hopeless, he felt calm.

He did not jolt when the door was flung open. Katarin's face was hard, hands on her hips, but when she took in the state of him, the Sword draped across his body like a lover, her shoulders slumped and her expression shifted into softness. She sat on the edge of the bed.

'You need to get up, Arthur,' she said gently.

He said nothing.

'It gets easier,' Katarin said after a while. 'It does. Each time you place one foot in front of the other and continue on your path, the hurt falls away, a tiny bit at a time.'

Arthur did not agree. He couldn't imagine ever waking with a smile again. The Sword hummed in response – it didn't agree.

His sister sighed lightly, leaning over to brush the hair from his forehead, the way Jalen would. Arthur jerked away from her touch. He felt her hurt, heard the sharp intake of breath, but he rolled over, closing his eyes against the brightness of the morning.

'Arthur,' Katarin said. Her voice held an edge, barely contained. 'This is going to sound harsh—'

He barked a tight laugh.

'—but this is about more than you and Jalen and whatever has happened,' she said. 'It's about the people on this ship, the people of Teyath, and the future.'

'What future?' he managed. The Sword did not like that; it grew hot in his hands, but he did not let it go, curling his fingers around the hilt tightly. Let it burn him. He didn't care.

Katarin held his eyes for a long time, her face folded into a frown. 'I'm not good at this shit,' she said eventually. 'But I am good at moving forward, because that is what you have to do. You have to get out of this cabin and get your life back.'

'My life?' Arthur laughed, dark and bitter. 'I have no control over my life, Katarin. I never have had. In Kernou my father controlled me, and now Merlin's fucking prophecy is controlling my every move, my every thought.'

Kat laughed.

'What?' he snarled. Grief was giving way to anger, hot and potent and sliding through him.

'I think that is the first time I've heard you swear, little brother,' Kat said, smiling. 'If you were anybody else, Arthur, I'd say I told you so, but you're not. You're my family. Before anything else, you're my family, and I hate to see you hurting. Believe me when I say none of this is your fault. Jalen—' she stopped as Arthur's face twisted. 'Obviously has his reasons and what they are, I don't know. I'm not even going to try and guess. The only thing I can tell you for certain is this is *not your fault*.'

Arthur rubbed at his eyes, spots dancing in the blackness.

'Sometimes we lose people,' Katarin said, her voice softer. She didn't look at him when she spoke. 'And there is nothing we can do about that, Arthur. The thing is – grief and love are connected. You cannot have one without the other. That's the unfortunate truth, and you can't control it. The only thing you can do is—'

'Move forward,' he whispered.

Even as she nodded, her eyes shifted to the Sword. 'Arthur …'

'What?' he challenged.

'Nothing.' She left him with a worried smile and a kiss to his forehead.

There were so many things Arthur wished he'd been able to say to Jalen, never imagining that he wouldn't have time to do so. So many things he yearned for, had hoped for, once this was all over. He wanted to tell Jalen he liked his cooking. That he liked his hands, the strength in them and that they, like the solid breadth of his shoulders, were where Arthur felt safest. Jalen had been with him from the beginning. From that first kiss, hidden in the warm darkness of that cave on the beach in Kernou, to every kiss since, Arthur had loved him.

It never mattered to him what Jalen was. It only mattered that he was there, a rock that Arthur could cling to in the worst of storms. Now he was floundering in the ocean, waves breaking over his head and the weight of his sodden clothes threatening to pull him under.

Kat had told him he needed to move forward. Arthur knew she was right, but he didn't know where to start, how to untangle the thorny mess that was his head and heart, how to bear the physical pain that sliced through him.

All the pieces of self-doubt that Arthur had shed had come home to roost, like some flock of horrible birds with cruel beaks and razors for talons.

He sighed, shifted the Sword to the side, and sat up.

Those birds had already torn him to shreds.

He may as well get up and try and do what Katarin had suggested – move forward, one step at a time. He wasn't alone. He had friends here. People who cared, who believed in him.

But those people were not Jalen, and it wasn't the same.

Arthur ran his fingers lightly over the side of the bed that Jalen had claimed. It wasn't a large bed – it was better suited to one person than two – but they had made it work.

Leaving the Sword on the bed, he changed his clothes and filled the wash basin from the jug. It was chilled, but he didn't care, splashing his face and the back of his neck, letting the cold settle inside him.

In Malist, Arthur had seen things he'd never expected to see, had done things he never believed he would do. The Sword had spoken words of encouragement, words of battle, and any doubts Arthur had been feeling floated away the first moment he swung that blade. He had felt stronger, powerful. For a heartbeat, he had seen himself as the man he would become. The King he would become.

But that man was not supposed to be alone.

To Arthur, Jalen had always been a part of his dreams of the future. He wasn't sure what that looked like anymore.

His gaze drifted to the Sword, and before he left the cabin Arthur strapped the weapon to his hip, letting the Treasure croon in his ears as he emerged into the brightness of the day.

CHAPTER 48

The journey through the mountains was long and arduous. The wagons had to be abandoned, too big to traverse the rocky ground and narrow pass that wove like a ribbon between towering rocks. People were tired, and fear and exhaustion made for strange bedfellows. The nights were cold, with nothing but thin blankets beneath them, and they huddled together for warmth. There was much muttering and crying. Lamorna wanted to shake them all, take each man and woman and blubbering child by the shoulders and shake them until their brains rattled in their skulls. Couldn't they see they were being offered a better life? A better way? This was what the One God wanted for them.

Instead of growing angry, she kept her head. She had made this journey twice now, and she was not afraid. On the second night, camped in the shadow of the mountains, she left Mordred to his organisational chats with the men of the Red Hand, and went to find Calla.

Calla was sitting wrapped in a blanket. 'I can't sleep,' she said.

Lamorna sat on the rocky ground beside her. There were dozens of small fires lit and people crowded close to them for warmth. Four hundred of them spread through this mountain pass. Lamorna could not remember seeing so many people at once. It seemed like everyone in Kernou had followed them, but she knew they hadn't. Many had chosen to remain.

She wondered how many of these people had come to watch her die that morning on the beach, then pushed the thought aside. It was not their fault. They had been tricked by Ulrian Tregarthen. She was more glad than ever at what she had made him do. The look in his eyes as he knelt on that shattered glass would stay with her forever, a shield if her will ever faltered.

'You need to sleep,' Lamorna declared, gasping as a thought came to her. 'Poppy syrup. It was on the list of herbs and medicines to bring. It will help you sleep. My aunt used to give it to my sister and me when we were small – only a little bit, though.'

'She's a witch, isn't she?' Calla asked. 'That's why she went to Cruithea?'

Lamorna nodded and stood, going to find the elderly man who had been in charge of the Konsel's apothecary. She was surprised he had chosen to come with them, but then recalled something her aunt had once said: the apothecarist was knowledgeable about herbs and medicines, yet forbidden from practising his craft due to the Konsel's rules.

Lamorna found the man sitting with his wife tucked against him. The look they both gave her was a suspicious one, but Lamorna did not let it bother her. She crouched near them and spoke in a low voice. 'I need milk of the poppy.'

The old man raised his eyebrows. 'Sick of this already, Lamorna Astolat?'

She shook her head, wondering what he meant. 'Calla needs to sleep. And I'm sure there are others who are finding sleep difficult to come by.'

The apothecarist's wife nodded. 'I will get it for you,' she said, getting up to rummage in one of their large baskets. Lamorna waited, aware the old apothecarist was watching her.

'I hope you and that man know what you're doing,' he mumbled.

'That man will be your salvation,' Lamorna replied.

'Will he?' the old man mused. 'We shall see.'

'Why did you come then?' Lamorna asked him. She was growing cross and wished the woman would find the poppy milk quickly so she could return to Calla.

'Ignore him,' the woman said, returning to press a small bottle into Lamorna's hands. She was about the same age as Lamorna's aunt, with greying blonde hair tucked beneath her cap. 'One drop in milk, no more.'

'Thank you,' Lamorna told her. She stood, looking down on them. The woman met her eyes and her smile was tight.

'You asked why we came. We came because your Cruithean, if he speaks the truth, speaks of a world we would like to see again,' she said. She settled herself beside her husband again, glancing around. 'You will have a hard time of it, I think. These people will not abandon you simply because, right now, they have nowhere else to go. But you and your Cruithean will need to fulfil your promises.'

'His name is Mordred,' Lamorna reminded her. 'And he will give you what he has promised.'

Lamorna found milk, a mug, and an extra blanket, which she draped over Calla after handing her the concoction. She found others who were not sleeping and gave them milk of the poppy, being careful with the dose, like the apothecarist's wife had said.

When she returned to Mordred, he was not alone. One of the men of the Red Hand was with him, but they were not talking. Lamorna met the man's eyes but said nothing, turning away from him as she wrapped herself in a blanket and laid down. She absently wondered where Bryn was – she had not seen him for a week or more. She did not fall asleep until the man was gone and Mordred lay beside her. His arm curled around her middle and pulled her close.

Over the next few days, they ate little and reserved what water they had been able to carry for drinking only. Lamorna was forcibly reminded of the journey to Cruithea, when all she had wanted was to wash. She could feel the dirt and sweat on her skin. She moved between groups of people, offering reassurance and verses from the Word that she thought would be most fitting in these moments.

'The One God has deserted us,' one woman snapped. 'Why would he do this to us? Why would he send us out into the wilderness like this?'

'The One God tests us,' Lamorna told her. 'Remember what the Word says? "In moments of darkness, look and you shall find me and I shall be watching over you." The One God has set us on this path, and when He returns to the world, we, His most faithful, shall sit at his right-hand side. He will not forsake us. You must have faith.'

So it went on. Mordred held his council each night with the Red Hand, and Lamorna stayed away. Her job during this journey, as she saw it, was to guide the people, to offer comfort, to remind them that the One God loved them. To sing Mordred's praises and speak of the better world that would be waiting for them.

Their paradise.

Their promised land.

On the seventh day of their journey, they emerged from the Nemhain Mountains and stood at the edge of a sea of desolation. The wasteland of Camlann Plain stretched before them, nothing but windswept earth and baking heat. To the north lay the Fey Highlands, beyond which stretched Cruithea and a vast world of trees.

People stared in dismay, and a lump lodged itself in Lamorna's throat. She had seen this place before, so she was not surprised, but she could feel their anger, their fear.

This was not what they had been promised.

Her eyes found Mordred's. He had been leading Pellinore, but now pulled himself onto the horse's back, pushing the animal onto the cracked earth.

'I know what you are thinking,' he called to the people of Kernou. 'This is no paradise. This is no promised land. This is Camlann Plain, a land cursed with bitter barrenness. But my friends, this is a test.' He gestured to the south, where small peaks of the mountain range ran haphazardly into a rise of dusty hills. 'On the other side of those hills is Dinas Emrys. It is there that we will begin to rebuild this world. We will start again, and from this dusty ground we shall prepare the way for the One God's return.' He paused. Pellinore danced beneath him and tossed his head, the black horse impressive in the glaring sunlight.

Lamorna smiled. Mordred was better at theatrics than he thought he was.

'You can turn back,' he called to the crowd. 'You can return to Kernou, or start your life over in some other place, but the gates of Dinas Emrys shall remain open to you.' His eyes moved over the crowd, settling on Lamorna. He held out his hand to her. She lifted her chin and made her way to his side, letting him pull her up behind him.

At that moment, Pellinore reared. People gasped, but Mordred kept his seat and Lamorna kept hers, her arms tight around his middle. As Pellinore's hooves touched the broken earth of Camlann Plain, she thought maybe she enjoyed the theatrics as well.

Dinas Emrys was the biggest building Lamorna had ever seen. The castle stretched into the sky like it had clawed its way free of the parched soil. The stones glinted in the sunlight, and it was surrounded by thick walls, interspaced by rounded towers with small windows.

Lamorna stared at the castle, wondering at the men who built it, wondering *how* they built it. Behind her, she could sense the people's awe and their weariness. It had been a tough journey, especially for the children and the older folk.

Mordred slid down from Pellinore's back and held out his hand for her — she took it, and together, they walked beneath the battlements, the gates of Dinas Emrys wide open for them as if the castle had been expecting them.

Inside the walls, the cobblestones were covered in the dust of ages. It was quiet, eerily so. Lamorna looked around eagerly, taking it all in. People filed in behind them, whispering to each other. Lamorna was surprised to find a town within the walls of the castle – small cottages, the thatch on their roofs thin and brittle with time, and other buildings she assumed were things like shops or trade houses. Blacksmith's tools hung from the awning of one building, covered in cobwebs.

There was another set of walls within the outer ones surrounding the castle that loomed over them. The Keep, she reminded herself. It was called the Keep. Mordred had told her on their journey. He said that was where they would live. Lamorna could not imagine living in such a place. It looked cold and unnatural.

Mordred told the people to wait in the bailey – he would examine the Keep, the Red Hand with him. He did not let go of Lamorna's hand, and she understood she would be going with them.

She would not be afraid of this gloomy, cursed place.

Steps led to the main doors, and as they came closer, she could see the stonework surrounding the doors was carved with intricate patterns of serpents, deer, and other animals, spirals and glyphs like the ones that decorated the brows of the Cruitheans. There were trees and branches, leaves and swords, and a great beast that Lamorna did not have a name for.

'What is that?' she breathed, staring at the creature. It was winged, with a serpentine body, deadly looking claws, and a snout filled with teeth.

'A dragon,' Mordred told her.

'Dragon!' Lamorna wanted to touch the carving, to feel this strange creature bound in stone beneath her fingers, but Mordred pushed open those great doors. A dark hall, the air cool and musty, greeted them. Lamorna peered into the darkness, unable to see anything except their shadows, grown long with the sunlight accompanying them into the castle.

She shivered. Mordred took down a torch from the wall and lit it with a wave of his hand. He gave Lamorna a brief, triumphant smile, and together, they entered the Keep. The men of the Red Hand followed.

At the end of that wide corridor, waiting at the base of a great stone staircase, was Bryn.

Lamorna stifled her gasp, holding tight to Mordred's hand.

'The castle is prepared, as you requested,' Bryn said to Mordred. His eyes touched Lamorna's briefly, before he looked away.

Mordred nodded and thanked him, and Bryn left.

'This is where he has been?' Lamorna whispered.

'I sent him and two others ahead,' Mordred told her. She frowned, wondering when that had happened, and how long Mordred had been planning this exodus. It wasn't that long ago they had decided that Dinas Emrys was where they would go.

There were four levels to the Keep, each containing halls and a dark, curved staircase. Windows were cut into the walls, the stone framework marked here and there with more glyphs and animals. Lamorna did not spy any more dragons. There were lots of bedrooms, more than she could count, and she was startled to find each one still furnished. Every room had a fireplace, left as if it were about to be lit.

'Where did everyone who lived here go?' she asked Mordred.

'They left, a long time ago,' was all he said. They stood in a vast, opulent bedroom, smothered in dust. A sitting area, its armchairs faded but whole, gathered around a table where two goblets sat undisturbed. Another table and chairs waited in silence – Lamorna guessed they were for dining. At the far end of the room loomed a great bed, its four posts towering like sentinels, draped with red curtains frayed and moth-eaten at the edges. A dressing screen stood beside a wardrobe, and as Lamorna's gaze drifted, she caught sight of a mirror, perched atop a dresser, catching the faint light of the room.

She caught a glimpse of her reflection, and stared and stared, realising this was the first time she had ever seen what she truly looked like.

Her hair was loose and flowing over her shoulders, the colour of straw. Her skin was pale, her cheeks flushed with colour, and her eyes an icy blue. Delicately arched brows sat above them, and her nose was small and pert. Her lips the colour of roses, curved like a bow.

She smiled, and her reflection smiled back.

'This will be our room,' Mordred announced. She jumped, dragging her eyes away from her reflection.

Bryn remained in the doorway – he cleared his throat importantly. 'What food we have has been brought to the kitchens,' he said. 'There is a room I think you need to see.'

Lamorna and Mordred followed Bryn through the Keep. Lamorna kept her hand in Mordred's and her eyes on Bryn's back. He led them down a level to another set of heavy doors, carved with a great dragon, wings spread and mouth open. Lamorna had a moment to marvel before Bryn pushed them open. They entered.

A vaulted ceiling stretched high above them. Heavy timber beams, all carved, ran across that ceiling. Lanterns dangled from them on long chains. Braziers sat on stone pillars around the edges of that cavernous room. Mordred clicked his fingers and their flames roared to life, their warm glow mingling with the dusty sunlight easing in through the wide glass windows.

Lamorna gasped. Each window was a picture, a splendid mosaic of colour and shapes. She stared in awe – none of the pictures were familiar to her, but they were beautiful. In one, a man with wings like a bird held a bow and a quiver of arrows. In another, a man with a serene expression held what looked like a bowl. Another featured a woman with flowing black hair and blue eyes. The mosaic woman reminded Lamorna of her sister.

Faded tapestries ran floor to ceiling between each window. They might have once been red, and had dragons and serpents embroidered on them. Three long tables ran down the room, with enough space for hundreds of people. At the end of the room was another table, where Lamorna imagined Kings and Queens might have once dined. For a moment, she could see this room full of life and laughter, music and the scent of food.

Beyond the last table, two thrones sat on a dais; Lamorna knew what they were, although she had never seen one. The timber was dark and the back of the thrones reached high into the air. There was enough light that Lamorna could see the carvings in the woodwork – serpents and other animals. Trees and vines. More dragons.

'Leave us,' Mordred ordered Bryn, his eyes drawn to the thrones. Slowly, he and Lamorna walked the length of the hall, their footsteps echoing off the stones. Mordred ignored the dusty wooden tables. He ignored the tapestries and the pictures in the windows.

He led her towards those thrones and stopped before them.

'Enyon and Eseld, the rulers of this ancient place, once sat here,' he told her.

Lamorna swallowed. 'Mordred, why did the One God – sorry, Ereshki – wish us to come here?'

'This was the heart of the Old Ones' worship, Lamorna,' he said with reverence. 'Enyon and Eseld were Ereshki's most faithful. They saw her worth. She wants us here because this is where we will bring the people back to her.' He flashed Lamorna a smile. 'This is where we will rule.'

'We?'

'Of course. A King needs a Queen, my love,' he said, bringing her hand to his lips and kissing it.

Queen!

Lamorna's heart almost thundered from her chest.

She chose not to remind him that Arthur was supposed to be King.

Chapter 49

The girl clung to her mother's hand. The woman was tall and slender, with creamy brown skin and hair like a living flame. She carried a basket in her other hand. A small dagger was belted at her hip – the girl knew it was not a weapon, but a tool.

It could be a weapon, though, if necessary. The woman knew how to use it.

The girl was only beginning to learn. She liked the feel of the blade in her hand, the purposeful weight of it, and each morning before dawn, she practised with the blade, feinting left and right, the muscles in her tiny arms burning.

The woman and the girl stopped. The trees arched above them, cathedral-like and grand, branches spread wide, leaves turned to catch the last of the sunlight that tickled the canopy. It was cool and dusky beneath the trees. The shrubs were still flowering, their white blooms bright in the gloaming of late afternoon. The path they had taken was uneven and well-worn; after the rains came, it would become soft and boggy, mud clinging stubbornly to the soles of their shoes.

But it was the dry season. The Wheel was turning towards Autumn. Soon the flowers would wither and die, and the game would move in search of warmer places.

Overhead, the branches creaked. Leaves rained down, kissing the girl's head. She pulled one free of her deep red hair and showed it to her mother.

'You should keep it,' her mother said in her gentle voice. 'It is Inanna's gift to you, Morgaine.'

Morgaine tucked the leaf in her pocket, her heart swelling – the Goddess had given *her* a gift.

'Here in these wild places, we can be,' her mother told her, gesturing to the forest that had closed its arms around them

'Be what?' Morgaine asked, all wide-eyed and innocent but filled with a thirst to *know* everything. Her mother smiled, dropping to her knees so she could look searchingly into Morgaine's face.

'Be us, as Inanna wishes. Be with Inanna, as she understands us. The world outside of these forests is cruel, Morgaine. Never forget that.'

Morgaine nodded, solemn. She touched her pocket, where Inanna's gift lay safe and hidden. She wanted to show Mordred, but he would probably try and take it from her. She decided to keep her treasure to herself.

The first fireflies had come out. Morgaine and her mother watched them for a moment, until Igraine sighed, withdrawing her dagger. They were looking for the herbs her mother used in healing. Igraine needed them for the man who had come. The man was not from Cruithea – he was as pale as a snake's belly, paler than Morgaine.

Her mother crouched and gathered the herbs, and when she was done, Igraine held out her hand, and they began the walk back to the village.

'To others, the forest is a foreboding place, but to us, it is home,' Igraine said.

Morgaine did not know what foreboding meant, but she nodded anyway because it sounded like an important word.

'Mama, will the man die?' she asked.

'I don't know. He is sick.'

'If he dies, will he return to Inanna?'

'Perhaps,' Igraine said. 'But I don't think he believes in Inanna.'

Morgaine frowned. If he didn't believe in Inanna, then who? She decided that, if he lived, she would ask him.

Katarin frowned in her sleep and rolled over.

The dream shifted.

She walked deeper.

'Mordred, where are we going?' she demanded crossly.

'It's not far,' her cousin replied, his voice creeping back to her. Morgaine hurried to catch up. She did not like the forest at night, but Mordred was not afraid, so she wouldn't be either.

The trees stretched like arrows into the sky, dark and mysterious.

Foreboding, Morgaine thought. She shivered and clutched at her cousin's arm.

'Scared?' he teased, but let her hold on to him. They were close in age, and sometimes Morgaine wished he was her brother. Then they could be together always.

They walked silently, as children of the forest knew to do. Around them, the trees shifted, trunks creaking gently. A wolf howled in the distance; even Mordred paused at that, but then he kept walking. Wings belonging to things unseen fluttered through the darkness. Spider-silk, stretched between tree trunks, clutched at Morgaine's hair. Irritated, she brushed it away, ignoring the feeling that crept along her spine.

'Where are we going?'

'I want to show you something,' Mordred said. In the darkness, his skin was black. His hair was as long as hers and bound in braids. He was allowed to carry a dagger now. He never put it down.

Up ahead was a clearing. Moonlight speared through the trees.

'Look,' Mordred whispered.

In the clearing were faeries, small and delicate. They were dressed in beautiful gowns and they sparkled. Morgaine could hear music.

'What are they doing?' she asked, watching one faery, a male, bow to one of the females. She took the tiny hand he offered, and he spun her around in time to the mysterious music.

'Dancing,' Mordred said.

'It doesn't look like dancing,' she argued softly.

He shrugged. 'People dance differently in other parts of Teyath. I thought you might like them.'

'I do,' Morgaine said quickly. She smiled, and they watched the faeries dance, silent and still, until suddenly the music stopped and the Small Folk were gone.

'Oh,' Morgaine said wistfully. 'It's over.'

'They'll come back tomorrow night,' Mordred said. 'Raine told me.'

Raine was the leader of the Inborn. Morgaine knew Mordred wanted to be like Raine and his warriors, but he would not be allowed to join for years yet.

Wordlessly, they turned from the clearing and began the walk through the darkness.

'You've been chosen by my mother,' Mordred said suddenly. He picked up a stick.

'No, I've been chosen by Inanna,' Morgaine corrected.

'It's the same thing,' he muttered, angrily swinging his stick at a low-hanging branch.

'You missed,' Morgaine pointed out. Mordred looked like he would like to swing his stick at her instead. 'You're cross because you didn't get picked.'

He said nothing.

'You're a boy, Mordred. The High Priestess cannot be a boy.'

He turned to her then, sullen and broody. 'You won't be any good at it.'

'What would you know?' Morgaine shot back, jamming her hands on her hips.

'One day, Inanna will change her mind,' Mordred growled. 'She'll see that she should not ignore men.'

Morgaine rolled her eyes. 'You're not a man.'

'Not yet,' he muttered.

Silence fell between them, and it was not the pleasant silence like when they were watching the Small Folk dancing.

It was dark and brooding and barbed.

Mordred poked at the ground with his stick.

'I begin my training soon,' Morgaine said.

'You're too young – too stupid,' her cousin snapped.

'I'm not,' she argued, trying to stop her voice from wavering. 'I'm nearly eight.'

'That's too young,' Mordred said firmly. 'You don't know anything, Morgaine.'

'I do,' she protested. Her voice wobbled dangerously. 'I know that Inanna—'

'You know nothing!' Mordred shouted. She took a step back, away from this angry boy who wore her cousin's face but did not sound like him at all.

He turned and ran, leaving her in the darkness with the night creatures and the foreboding trees. Morgaine shivered, and then, she lifted her chin.

She would not be afraid.

She was Inanna's Chosen.

Katarin woke. It was still dark, but she knew there would be no more sleep.

She had not dreamt of Cruithea, of that particular moment, for a long time.

She had not walked in her dreams in years.

Her belly twisted as she recalled the anger, the loss, on her cousin's face.

They had been children, and she had been given the type of destiny Mordred had dreamed of. The type of destiny he had gone out and sought for himself.

With a sigh, Katarin climbed out of bed and dressed. Leaving her feet bare, she ran her hand through her hair as she stepped out onto the deck. Maybe the sea air would calm the racing of her heart.

The sky was a blanket of stars, pinpricks of light on an indigo backdrop. In Cruithea, the stars were rarely able to be seen through the trees and if you were lucky enough to see them, it was only in snatches, a quick glimpse of the vastness of the world through the branches.

Ordes was on watch. He was leaning against the main mast, arms folded, gazing out to sea. Katarin stared at his back for a while, wondering about those glorious wings that had taken form when he'd claimed his Treasure.

She padded across the deck to stand beside him.

'You're brooding,' she said.

He snorted. 'Can't sleep?'

'No,' she said quietly. She hesitated, then said, 'I had a dream. It rattled me so …'

Ordes' eyebrows rose. 'What did you dream about?'

Katarin chewed her lip, keeping her eyes on the faint lights of Teyath in the distance. 'The past, so I guess it was more memory than dream,' she said. 'Ordes, do you ever wish none of this was happening? That, I don't know, things had stayed the way they were?'

'All the fucking time,' he mumbled. 'Well, not all of it. Jenyfer, for starters. Then there's Arthur.'

'Arthur?' Katarin repeated.

Ordes nodded. 'He's a good man. You and I both know the world is in short supply of good men. I don't regret meeting him.' He sighed and rubbed his fingers over his chin. 'I wouldn't change what I know about my parents, either. It's a truth that, had none of this happened, I'd never have known.'

'And your magic?' Katarin asked.

He shrugged. 'Learning to live with it.'

'Yes, I guess being all powerful and part of some great destiny must be a hard thing to learn to live with,' she muttered.

'Both of those things I'd give up in a heartbeat, Kat,' Ordes said. 'Destiny ... sometimes I feel it's bullshit, just another way for something to control me, to take away my choices. And sometimes, I feel it's more than that – that it is important. I wish it wasn't my destiny, you know? But it is, and I can't run away from it,' he added.

All this talk of destiny blended with the fragments of the past Katarin had walked through ... She had held on to this truth tightly, never letting anyone know, not even Aelle. If she never talked about it, never acknowledged it, perhaps it wouldn't be the truth any longer. But she couldn't keep it hidden anymore.

Katarin took a deep breath. 'I've never told you who I really am. Well, who I was once supposed to be, before Ulrian Tregarthen took my mother and myself from our home.' She paused. Ordes watched her, curious. She swallowed, shoving her hands in her pockets where she could curl them into fists and keep them hidden. 'When I was eight years old, I was chosen by Inanna to be the next High Priestess of Cruithea.'

Ordes sucked in a sharp breath. 'I had no idea, Katarin.'

'No one did. I always intended to go back and finish the training I had begun, but by then, Mother was pregnant with Arthur and she was sick. I couldn't leave her,' Katarin explained. 'And then, Ulrian tried to drown me, and your mother ...' She sighed. Inside her pockets, her fingernails bit into her skin. 'That life was lost to me. That destiny, stolen, and even though I could have taken back what was mine, I didn't. I avoided Cruithea for years. I still avoid Cruithea. Whenever I go back there, my aunt reminds me of what, of who, I was supposed to be, and honestly, I can't handle seeing her disappointment.'

'What happened to you was not your fault,' Ordes said. 'Surely she knows that?'

'Maybe, but I know that Inanna has not chosen another, Ordes,' Katarin replied. 'And now I'm dreaming of the past, of the life I used to have, and I don't know why.'

Ordes was silent for a long moment, and then said quietly, 'Do you want to be the High Priestess of Cruithea, Kat?'

'No,' she said firmly. 'I don't.' She flashed him a quick smile. 'I've never told anybody any of that.'

'So why tell me? Why not Arthur?' Ordes asked.

'You were here, I suppose.' She knew why she'd told him – she trusted Ordes, and if there was one person who might be able to listen and not judge, it would be him. She glanced at him quickly. 'Don't read too much into it.'

Ordes chuckled, running a hand through his cropped hair.

'Your hair really is shit.'

'Thanks.'

She turned to go, but his voice caught her.

'You can't control destiny, nor can you outrun it,' Ordes said. 'I'm starting to understand that. So, if it's your destiny to return to Cruithea, when all this is done, then ...'

Katarin shook her head. 'I don't belong there. Not anymore.'

CHAPTER 50

Lamorna had been given the task of seeing people settled. The Red Hand were to help her. She knew those men did not like taking orders from her, but they did as she asked, and over the course of the next few days, the people who had journeyed with them to this place found somewhere warm to sleep. Lamorna went to check on the kitchens. An older woman whom Lamorna did not know had stepped into the role of managing the kitchens and therefore their food stocks.

'You don't remember me, do you?' the woman asked. With greying brown hair worn in a tight knot at the base of her skull, she was short and rounded, about Lamorna's height, and the more she looked at the woman, she realised she did know her.

'You used to come and read the Word with my aunt,' she managed. She stared at the woman. 'Are you a witch like she is?'

The woman chuckled. 'It amazes me, Lamorna. You spent your life with witchcraft right under your nose, with the Old Ways all around you, and you refused to believe. Until now, I see. But perhaps it isn't religion that you believe in, but Mordred.'

Lamorna lifted her chin.

The woman laughed. 'There is nothing wrong with that, girl. He's the reason we're all here, after all. And my name, since you can't remember it, is Maeve.'

Maeve turned away then, and Lamorna left her to her task of organising the kitchens.

She went in search of Mordred, feeling proud at what she had managed to accomplish. She had given Calla and Arwen the job of finding people living quarters. Lamorna suspected Calla delighted in bossing the Red Hand around as much as Lamorna did. She was pleased, and relieved, that most of her new friends had come with them. She liked them all, but it was Calla she was most drawn to.

Lamorna found Mordred standing in the open door to the Keep, surveying the dusty stretch beyond the walls that was Camlann Plain. Lamorna joined him, and they stood in silence for a while. The sun was setting on their fourth day in Dinas Emrys.

'Come,' she told him gently. 'Let me get you some tea.'

They had not taken more than two steps back inside the castle when a voice echoed behind them, low and oddly disjointed.

'Oh this is nice, oh lucky me.'

Lamorna looked over her shoulder and gasped. A woman stood in the open door. Shadows and smoke shifted around her body, her hair long and black as midnight. Her pale skin, flecked with red, glowed in the half-light of the evening.

Not a woman – a faery.

'Who are you?' Mordred demanded. He drew his dagger, the other hand thrust protectively in front of Lamorna.

'Don't you know, he who claims the throne? Free I am at last to roam,' she sang. She laughed, flicking her hair over her shoulder as she stretched luxuriously. Lamorna caught sight of the pointed tip of the woman's ear and when she smiled, her canine teeth were elongated, like an animal. She laughed again, wicked and wild – it made the hair stand up on the back of Lamorna's neck.

'Enyon and Eseld here they sat, side by side, this and that,' the faery said, gesturing to the castle. 'One as bright as light can be, one for the darkness, that one for me.'

'Medb,' Mordred said. He lowered the dagger as Lamorna remembered where she had heard that name.

The Faery Queen smiled, showing off those pointed teeth. 'Medb I am and Medb I be, but tell me who you wish to be. Desires can take the shape of dreams, and dreams can be not what they seems.'

Mordred took a step closer. 'Why are you here? What do you know?'

'I know you seek what you can't find, deep within your darkest mind. Whispers, voices, shadows creak.' Medb paused, her head tipped to one side. 'I can give you what you seek.'

'And what is that?' Mordred asked.

'Power from the world below, more than swords and stones and bows,' Medb sang. 'The Treasures now are in their hands, the Grail is soon to shape the land.'

'Arthur has the Treasures?' Mordred breathed, and the faery nodded happily.

'Treasures three collected be, the Stone is gone and now I'm free. That city of man flames bright as night, ruins all a pretty sight.'

Mordred frowned. 'What's happened to Malist?'

Medb smiled with wicked glee. 'Sacked and burning, burning bright, chaos we rained there in the night.' Her expression darkened. 'Kings and Prophets and things with wings, worldlings, shifters, and all he brings. The one who holds the Sword of Light, shall raise an army for this fight. Wicked does and wicked shall, mind she who'll undo your spell.'

Medb's gaze slid over Lamorna again. A secretive smile tugged at the faery's mouth, and suddenly Lamorna was afraid, so terribly afraid of this creature and the darkness she wore like a cloak. She bit her lip, her mind screaming through the past, trying to remember the rules for dealing with faeries and the Small Folk. She latched onto her aunt's words, assuring her and Jenyfer that unless they were invited inside, faeries could not enter your home.

'Mordred,' she whispered, clutching his arm. 'Don't invite her in!'

'You think those rules apply to me?' Medb said, and stepped across the threshold. Lamorna shuddered and shrank back. 'This castle knows me, you shall see.'

Mordred did not shy away from the creature. 'You are not welcome here, Medb.'

The faery leaned over and sniffed him, running her forked tongue over her teeth. 'Not yet, my pet, not yet not yet. When the scales have tipped for you, you'll know what you need to do.'

She smiled again, clicked her fingers, and was gone in a swirl of dark smoke.

'Come,' Mordred said.

'Will she come back?' Lamorna breathed. Her heart was pounding and her palms were sticky with fear. Mordred did not answer. He was frowning. 'Mordred?'

'Arthur, your sister, and her pirate have found the Treasures of the Gods, Lamorna,' he said, his voice low. 'And if what Medb says is true, Malist has been destroyed and Arthur is gathering an army. Do you understand what that means?'

Her head was spinning. She couldn't remember what he'd said about the Treasures, only that they were important. 'No,' she admitted in a whisper.

'It means the Grail is next,' Mordred said. 'And then everything will change.'

Lamorna ran her fingers over Mordred's chest, tracing the scars there. She hadn't asked where he got them, unsure if she wanted to know. She liked the idea that he had earned them, doing something heroic.

Lamorna smiled. Jenyfer would tell her not to be so stupid.

She loved these quiet mornings with Mordred, when it was the two of them. She liked him best like this – soft and raw, in those moments after he'd come undone. There was a vulnerability to him, and it thrilled her that she was the only one who saw it, who saw him as he truly was. But there was a growing emptiness inside Lamorna that she was finding harder to ignore. She'd hoped that Calla might fill the gap left in Jenyfer's absence, but as much as she cared for her, Calla was not her sister.

'I miss my sister,' Lamorna whispered. 'We didn't always get along – in fact, we argued most of the time – but I miss her. I miss seeing her every morning.'

Mordred kissed her forehead and pulled her closer. 'You have me.'

'I know, but it's not the same,' she said. She lifted her head so she could see his face. 'Can you show me her? Like you did before?'

He looked at her in surprise. 'I didn't think you liked the magic.'

'I don't – it scares me a little – but I want to see Jen.'

Since that faery had arrived with her threats and her sly eyes, Lamorna had wanted to talk to her sister, but had not worked up the courage to ask. They had been busy, but now, with the castle still sleeping, the longing to see Jenyfer crept up and tightened around her throat.

Mordred stared at her, his eyes searching hers, before he smiled. 'As you wish, my love.'

Lamorna climbed out of bed and found her robe, slipping into it. It was red silk, a gift from Mordred. Like his scars, she hadn't asked where the robe had come from, choosing to enjoy the mystery of it instead. She'd never had a piece of clothing that was so nice, and wanted to wear it everywhere, but also liked that only Mordred saw her in it.

She remembered without having to ask what he needed. That night in her cottage in Kernou was branded onto her mind. Lamorna filled the basin on the washstand with water from the jug and carried it over to the bed, placing it carefully on the sheets. Mordred was sitting up, watching her curiously.

'What?' she asked him as she fetched a cloth and climbed onto the bed, careful not to rock the basin and wet the sheets. Mordred didn't reply, reaching under his pillow for the dagger he kept there.

Lamorna shook her head, holding out her hand for the dagger. 'I can do it.'

His eyebrows rose, but he passed over the dagger, hilt first.

She did not look at him as she ran the sharp blade across her palm. Wincing, she bit her lip, careful not to let any blood fall on the sheets as she wiped the blade clean on the cloth and handed it back to Mordred. He was watching her again, his eyes dark in the lantern light, skin black as night and gilded in gold. Shirtless, hair falling over the curve of his muscular shoulders, he looked like a god.

Lamorna shivered, and held her hand over the bowl.

'How much?' she asked him.

'A few drops, that's all,' he said.

As her blood fell onto the face of the water, Mordred whispered those strange words again. Lamorna tried to hold them in her mind, but they slipped away as quickly as they came, as if she wasn't supposed to hear them, to know them.

'That's enough,' he said, and she took her hand back, wrapping the cloth around it and leaning over the bowl, watching eagerly for her sister's face.

First came her sister's eyes, narrowed and dark. She was angry. Slowly, the field of magical vision widened to show Jenyfer's mouth, lips set in a thin, hard line, an anger Lamorna had seen many times before. She was alone, sitting on a bed, the woodwork behind her dark. A cabin on a ship, maybe?

Lamorna wanted to know what made her sister frown like that. This was not enough. She wanted to talk to Jenyfer.

When she told Mordred, his eyebrows lifted. 'Lamorna, I told you already—'

'I don't care how much blood it takes,' she snapped. 'I want to speak to her.'

'She won't be able to see you, only hear you. She'll think she's losing her mind.'

'No she won't,' Lamorna said with certainty. She took up the dagger again. 'Do I just …'

Mordred nodded, his face tight. She watched him this time as she pressed the wound on her palm, feeling the warmth of her blood pool on her fingers. Lamorna did not wince, though her breath caught sharply for a moment. She promptly held her hand over the bowl, and when Mordred finished speaking the strange words, she thought he looked odd, but she didn't say anything. She simply waited, and then—

She gasped in amazement. She could hear the ocean. Could hear the wind as it battered against the ship. She could hear Jenyfer sigh, the sound so dreadfully familiar it made Lamorna's heart ache.

'You don't need to speak aloud,' Mordred told her quietly. The water in the bowl was swirling, slowly coming to a halt. 'She will hear what you say to her if you speak inside your mind.'

Lamorna nodded. She took a deep breath and returned her gaze to the bowl of bloodied water and the image of her sister. *Jenyfer?*

Jenyfer's head snapped up, her eyes wide.

Jenyfer, it's me.

'Lamorna?' Jenyfer whispered. She scrambled off the bed. 'Where … what …'

It's me, Jen. I'm … in your head.

She felt her sister's alarm and rushed to reassure her. *You're not going mad. I'm really here. I can see you, too. On the ship. Where are you?*

Jen shook her head, dark hair flying. *Prove it. Prove you're really my sister.* She paused, chewing her lip. *Tell me something only Lamorna and I would know. A secret*, she added.

Lamorna thought furiously, her mind tumbling backwards over the years, settling on a moment when they were small and playing in the garden while their aunt was inside. *We saw a pisky in the faery brush. You were ten. I was five. It was the first time I saw one, and I was scared, but you grabbed a stick and waved it at the pisky and he disappeared. I called you a hero, and we made a game of it until Aunt Tamora told us to stop because someone might hear us.*

Lamorna held her breath, waiting, leaning over the bowl, watching her sister's face eagerly. Slowly, Jenyfer smiled. *Yes, and then years later, you told me I made the whole thing up.* She dragged a hand through her hair, her expression pained. *Where are you? Are you safe? How are you doing this?*

That last thought was coated with suspicion, and though Jenyfer did not say his name, her sister knew this was Mordred's doing.

I'm not in Kernou anymore. Lamorna felt Jenyfer's surprise. *We left there, Mordred and I, and … some of the people. We travelled through the mountains to …* Lamorna let her mental voice trail off, not sure she should tell Jenyfer where they were. She wasn't sure Mordred would want her to. *But I'm safe.*

Jenyfer nodded. *Aunt Tamora? The Chif?*

She is still in Cruithea. The Chif remained behind, Lamorna said.

Her sister's face folded into a frown.

Lamorna didn't want to mention the Faery Queen and her visit, either. *Jenyfer, is Arthur with you?*

It was the wrong thing to ask. Jenyfer's face froze. *I'm glad you're safe, Lamorna, but I need to go.*

It was a lie. *Can I tell you one more thing?*

Jenyfer nodded, expression wary.

I miss you.

I miss you, too. Lamorna—

Jenyfer's voice and her face vanished. Lamorna's eyes shot to Mordred, disappointed. Then she noticed his breathing was thick and heavy, and there was sweat on his forehead. She could see little beads of it catching the lantern light. They looked like tiny jewels.

'Are you alright?' she asked him. Her hand was still bleeding, so she wrapped the cloth around it, reaching for him with her uninjured hand. 'Mordred?'

'I'm fine,' he said tersely, shifting out of her reach. He got up, taking the bowl of bloodied water away, and Lamorna knew he was lying to her.

CHAPTER 51

'**M**ordred and Lamorna are not in Kernou anymore,' Jenyfer announced.

'How do you know this?' Arthur asked. They were sitting on the steps to the quarterdeck, the wind teasing their hair. Jenyfer shoved hers away, irritation plain on her face as she explained what had happened. Arthur's eyes were wide, his fingers absently stroking the hilt of the Sword of the White Dragon.

'Obviously, Mordred was behind it. Lamorna does not have any magic,' Jenyfer said. 'But what bothers me is why they left. I mean, I'm glad she's safe, but if they're not there, then where are they? And she said some people came with them.'

Arthur chewed his lip, thinking, then gasped, clutching Jenyfer's arm tightly. 'Camlann. They've gone to Camlann.'

'How can you be sure?'

'When we were in Cruithea, I had a dream of that place. Of the castle that Eseld and Enyon ruled from. Mordred was in my dream, and there was a dragon, I think. I told him about it, and he said he had been there, that destiny had made him go to that place,' Arthur said in a rush. 'And then the shifter, Voss, mentioned it after the battle in Malist, remember?'

'But why would Lamorna be there?' Jenyfer asked.

'I think we can assume your sister actually cares for my cousin,' Arthur said.

Jenyfer put her head in her hands. 'I swear, if he does anything to hurt her, I will end him. Lamorna … is easily swayed, and Mordred has charmed her.' She lifted her head, laughing. 'I'd love to know how he did it, to be honest. Lamorna is so pious, so devoted to the One God. She would not give that up, not for a man. Not for anyone.'

'It doesn't mean she's stopped believing in the One God,' Arthur pointed out.

'Do you think she knows? That the One God is Ereshki? Does Mordred know?' Jenyfer asked.

'He knows,' Arthur said. 'He told me.'

'Only on Camlann field will the red dragon yield, and the Once and Future King shall see the land healed,' Jenyfer mumbled. 'Does that mean …'

'That, eventually, we will end up there? Yes,' Arthur answered, his tone sombre.

Jenyfer looked out at the ocean, sparkling in the morning light. 'Lamorna said your father remained in Kernou, but there was something she was not telling me. Do you think …'

Arthur swallowed audibly. His expression was strong, but his words still shook. 'I refuse to believe he is dead. Ulrian Tregarthen would not allow himself to be killed by a Magic Wielder, not even one as powerful as Mordred,' he said bitterly. 'I can feel my father, looking over my shoulder at times, this dark presence that still shadows my life. I don't know if I'll ever be truly free of him.'

Silence slipped between them, until Jenyfer cleared her throat.

'Arthur,' she began gently. 'I'm sorry about Jalen.'

Arthur's face tightened, but he nodded.

Back in her cabin, Jenyfer eased the porthole open, hanging her head free to catch the breeze. The Stone thrummed against her chest and she reached up to touch it. Its power was muted by the pouch Ordes had made her, but she could still feel it.

Since Malist, Arthur carried his Treasure everywhere. Ordes rarely touched the Bow of Mists. It was in their cabin somewhere, but she wasn't sure where. Jenyfer bit her lip, her fingers moving over the Singing Stone as she glanced back out to sea.

Movement in the water below caught her eye. A familiar skeletal face was peering at her.

'Ophine!' Jenyfer hissed. 'Where have you been?'

'I didn't realise you missed me,' the wraith said. They were treading water, their face displeased. 'I hate swimming.'

'Well?' Jenyfer demanded. 'Why are you here? You've been following us all the way down the coast. I've seen you.'

'Only because I wanted you to,' the wraith replied, their tone waspish.

Jenyfer scowled, making Ophine chuckle.

'Alright, calm down. My master wishes to speak with you. He has things to show you, Daughter of the Sea.'

Jenyfer's heart began hammering, the Stone beating along with it. 'When?'

'Tomorrow, when the tides turn. Come ashore,' Ophine said, and then they were gone.

That night, Katarin could not sleep again. She'd spent the day as busy as she could be, hoping it would ease her mind, hoping that when she lay down, exhaustion would pull her under and a dreamless sleep would claim her. But when she closed her eyes, all she saw were trees.

Grumbling, she climbed from bed and dressed, not bothering with her boots, and stumbled out onto the deck. Maybe the fresh air would help. She was surprised to see Halymere on deck, staring out at the ocean. She glanced around; no one else was topside, so she joined him on the quarterdeck. He stood with his hand on the ship's wheel, even though the anchor was lowered and the sails pulled in tight for the night.

'Are you on watch?' she asked him curiously.

He shrugged. 'I only came to ask Iouen a question, and he took it as an opportunity to leave, after telling me how important it was that there was someone on watch.'

Kat laughed. 'I'll go find him.'

Halymere shook his head. 'He's with Tahnet.'

'Oh,' she said. 'Right.'

Need was a deep, dark thing in the pit of her stomach, curling around itself. Katarin caged it there, as she had ever since that night in the galley with Olwen. The Red Sister had stirred something to life, something Kat was not ready to admit she needed.

Touch.

Simple human touch. She yearned for it.

Sighing, she rubbed at her eyes, looking anywhere other than at the Cruithean warrior at her side. He would be able to read her emotions, so she took a deep breath and pushed them away, down into the depths of the ocean inside her, where no one would see them.

But it did no good.

'Kat,' Halymere said softly. 'Whatever it is, let it go. Just for a moment, for one night even, let it all go. Let the weight slide free of your shoulders.'

She flashed him an angry look, then her shoulders slumped as a strange sort of defeat washed over her. 'I don't know how,' she admitted, her voice nothing more than a whisper. He released the ship's wheel and slipped his arm around her instead. She tensed, and then relaxed, leaning into the solid warmth of him.

Halymere was familiar, and when everything was being ripped to pieces and changed around her without her consent, she needed that.

She met his gaze – his eyes were hungry, full of longing, but beneath that was an acceptance that this was the way things would be between them.

'I don't want …' she began.

'I know,' he said, 'but with your permission, I'm going to take you back to your bed, and stay with you to make sure you get a few hours of decent sleep. You look dreadful, by the way.'

'Well,' she said with a wry smile. 'You know how to charm a lady.'

'I'm not charming, and you're not a lady,' he shot back, but he smiled in return. 'Nightmares? Malist?'

Katarin shook her head and sighed, realising how stupid she'd been to think she could hide it from him, who knew her better than anyone on this ship. Who had seen her at her worst, at her most defeated, and who had never judged. 'I'm walking again.'

'Ah,' he said. 'Into places you don't want to go, I assume?'

'Into the past,' she admitted. 'With my mother and Mordred. I keep returning to Cruithea in my dreams, and it's the last place I want to be.'

'Maybe it's where you need to be,' Halymere suggested. At her look, his lips quirked, disappearing into his beard. 'I know you've forsaken our Goddess, but perhaps she has not abandoned you like you think she has.'

Katarin pulled away. She did not want to talk about Inanna or any of the Old Ones. She didn't want to think about the past, of what she had lost and what she had stolen from her. She wanted to sleep.

What had happened in Malist haunted her waking hours – she'd been avoiding Olwen as much as she could. Kat couldn't find the courage to say those two little words. It would be like admitting a failure, owning a weakness she did not want to face. It didn't matter that what had almost happened wasn't her fault – it was Halymere saving her all over again.

'I'm going to bed,' Kat announced, heading for her cabin. When Halymere didn't follow, she glanced at him over her shoulder. 'Are you coming?'

'What about the watch?' Halymere asked.

'Don't worry about it,' Kat said. 'Someone will be up soon, and we're in the middle of nowhere. I think we're safe enough for an hour or two.'

Halymere's footsteps echoed behind her as she padded back to her cabin, where she shed her boots and climbed into bed fully clothed. Moments later, the mattress dipped as Haly climbed in after her. They didn't speak. She lifted her head so he could slide his arm beneath her neck, then lay back down. His other arm draped over her belly. She wove her fingers through his and, within minutes, was asleep.

When Katarin woke, the sun was high. Halymere was curled against her, the bulk of his body a burning brand at her back. She cleared her throat, and when he didn't stir, she drove the point of her elbow into his stomach. He grunted in response.

'You need to go,' she demanded, lifting his arm off her.

Halymere sighed. 'Can I wake up first, Katarin?'

'Out,' she said briskly.

He threw back the covers and climbed out of bed, looking for his boots. 'I know you miss her,' he said bluntly.

Katarin bristled, her defence mechanism springing to life, ready and willing, as it always was. 'Oh, you know, do you?'

'You loved her.'

'Stop it.'

He pulled his shirt on and sat on the edge of the bed, keeping some distance between them. 'Katarin, look at me. Not many people have seen the you behind the mask,' he said. 'Aelle, possibly Arthur, maybe Ordes, and me. You're allowed to break down sometimes.'

She shook her head. 'I can't.'

'You can.' His voice was low, gentle, and soothing. She felt something crack within her, but not break apart. 'Let someone care for you, Kat.'

'That someone is you, I take it?' she snapped.

Halymere looked at her sadly, his face rumpled from sleep, eyes tired. 'Why are you like this? Why push everyone who cares for you away?'

'Because,' she said, not looking at him, blinking furiously, her fists clenched in the blankets. 'If I let you or anyone care for me in any way, I will fall apart, and I don't know if I'll be able to piece myself back together.'

The crack widened. Katarin swallowed and forced herself to focus on her hands, twisting the blanket between stiff fingers.

'It's not a weakness to need someone, Katarin,' Halymere said. She refused to respond, turning her face towards the window, not daring to breathe in case she cried.

'Alright,' he said after a moment. 'But you know where to find me if you change your mind. You don't have to do it all alone.'

He left her with the sounds of the ocean outside the window and a ship coming to life outside her door.

CHAPTER 52

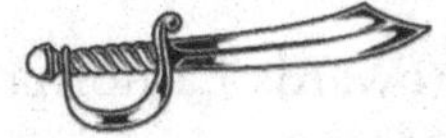

Lamorna smiled to herself as she left her room, her footsteps light. She was truly happy for the first time in, well, she couldn't remember. Happiness had always been tied up in her belief in the One God, in her time spent absorbed in the Word. She had rarely done anything for herself, which made sense. Lamorna had never known herself outside of her faith.

Pausing by one of the large windows, Lamorna glanced out over the brown streak of Camlann Plain. Even that barren, cursed earth could not dampen her mood this morning. She remembered what she had learnt about the One God, about who He truly was. It had consumed her thoughts when Mordred first told her, but then it faded as more pressing matters arose. Now, she was free to think about it. There was something strangely satisfying in knowing that the God she had worshipped wasn't a God at all. That He was a She. Part of her knew she should be angry at being deceived, but it wasn't the Goddess who deceived her – it was men like Ulrian Tregarthen. She smiled, imagining the look on his face once he realised Kernou would be nothing but a relic to the world he had built there. A world that no longer existed.

Lamorna revelled in her newfound sense of self, the knowledge she had gained about her body, her voice, her *agency*. She would pause each morning by the mirror to study her reflection, wondering if others could see all these changes, or if they were hers alone to hold in her heart. In any case, she was glad of what had happened, glad she had followed her aunt from Kernou and into Cruithea, neither of them knowing what would come of it.

Sharp footsteps hurried towards Lamorna. She turned from the window to see Calla, her face pale, hair a mess, eyes wide and haunted.

'What's happened?' Lamorna gasped as her friend practically fell into her arms. She kept a steadying arm around Calla, and led her back down the hall. She led her friend to her rooms, bidding her sit while Lamorna made herbal tea. She added two teaspoons of honey and carried the cup over to Calla, who was staring at the floor, silent and still.

'Calla,' Lamorna said gently. Calla did not reach for the tea, so Lamorna set the cup on the little table and knelt before her, staring up into her friend's face. Tears had left tracks down Calla's cheeks, and suddenly, Lamorna was afraid. Calla was strong and bold, tough like Jenyfer, and Lamorna could not remember the last time she had seen her sister cry.

Calla took a deep breath and wiped at her face with trembling fingers. Lamorna waited, restless with nerves, with fear. The happiness she'd felt that morning fled out the window into the dusty landscape.

'It's Bryn.'

Lamorna went rigid. 'What about him?'

Calla sniffed. 'He has been striking up conversations with me lately, and I didn't see any harm in it. This isn't Kernou — we can *talk* to other people here — so I talked to him. Just small talk, nothing more,' she added hastily, raising her eyes to Lamorna's before dropping them back to her lap.

Lamorna sat back on her heels. 'What happened, Calla?'

'Last night, I was on my way back to my room. It was late. It was dark. Bryn offered to walk with me. I said he could. I'm still a little scared of being alone in these halls, in this castle,' she said.

Something dark clawed its way through Lamorna's belly. She grasped Calla's hands firmly. 'Tell me.'

'When we reached my door, I said goodnight and I thanked him. He did not dare follow me into my room, because he knew Arwen would be there. So instead …' Calla paused, and when she met Lamorna's eyes, Lamorna saw all the things she had seen in her sister's eyes, in Jenyfer's face, when she had gone to visit her after she had been first married to Bryn.

She recalled the fear, the shame, the tension in her sister's shoulders. The way the stormy-blue of her eyes was dull and muted. And the anger behind those eyes, sparks of it that flew out and practically begged to be acknowledged. Begged someone to *see*. Lamorna had not seen then, but she could see now.

'Calla,' she said firmly. 'Whatever happened was not your fault. Do you understand me?'

'How can it not be?' her friend whispered. 'He pushed me against the wall and put his hands on me, and his lips … I can feel them on my neck. He hadn't shaved. His face was rough and scratchy. When I pushed him away, he became angry. He told me I had smiled at him, that I had led him to believe—'

'You led him to believe nothing that was not already in his vile head,' Lamorna seethed. She stood and began to pace. 'I will tell Mordred.'

'No!' Calla gasped. 'I don't want him to think ill of me!'

'He won't,' Lamorna assured her as rage bubbled up inside her. 'I told you before that Mordred was not like the men in Kernou. He *never* forced me to do anything I did not want to do, Calla. He will punish Bryn,' she added.

And if he doesn't, then I will.

Later that day, Lamorna sat in the hall. She had been examining the tapestries that hung limp and sad from the walls, wondering whether it was worth trying to repair their moth-chewed corners or if she should have others made. For hours, she stayed in that room, staring at those walls. She had sent Calla to bed, giving her a dagger and telling her to keep it on her at all times, to use it if ever she needed to.

But a dagger, no matter how sharp, could not erase what had happened.

The door to the hall eased open. Lamorna glanced up as Bryn entered. Her muscles turned to stone, Calla's words swimming around her brain, her distraught face branded on the back of Lamorna's eyelids. She swallowed ash and breathed fire.

'What do you want?' she bit out.

'I was looking for Mordred.'

'He isn't here.'

'I can see that.'

Lamorna waited, but Bryn did not move. She stared at him. He stared back, and she wondered how he felt at this exchange of power between them. He terrified her, but one word from her and Mordred would toss him out into the wilderness. She would see that happen, no matter how long it took.

She smiled, pleased with her resolution. Bryn cleared his throat uncomfortably. He was wearing his Red Hand coat, dark trousers and heavy boots, and still carried the shining dagger the Chif had given him. His hair had grown, and he looked more like the man who used to be friends with Jenyfer.

'Yes?' Lamorna asked.

Bryn shifted his weight from one foot to the other. 'Is she still with the pirate?'

'Jenyfer?' Lamorna feigned surprise. 'Yes, I suppose she is. His name is Ordes, in case you were wondering.'

'I wasn't.' Bryn's voice was brittle around the edges.

A little thrill shot down Lamorna's spine. The tapestries forgotten, she wandered over to the table, positioning herself on its far side. Bryn stood on the other, watching her.

'He's not just a pirate, either. He's a faery and a Magic Wielder. He's powerful, apparently. Mordred said so. Mordred also said they're destined for one another, Jen and Ordes. Some faery thing.' Lamorna paused, watching Bryn's face carefully. 'So even if she had come back to you, who's to say she'd have loved you at all?'

Bryn's face hardened. 'You need to watch your tongue.'

'Do I?' Lamorna mused. Her smile fell and she lowered her voice. 'I know what you did to her.'

'I did what I was supposed to do,' Bryn shot back furiously. There was colour in his cheeks and his eyes had gone as hard as stone.

'You raped her!' Lamorna shouted. She slammed her hand on the table, the reverberation joining the echo of her voice that bounced around the room. 'She's my sister, and you did that to her. I will never forgive you for it!'

'You delivered her down the aisle to me, Lamorna. Or have you forgotten that?' Bryn returned sharply.

'And I hate myself for it,' she hissed. 'But I hate you more. I don't care if hatred is a sin.' She paused and looked him in the eyes, something she had avoided doing since her return to Kernou with Mordred. 'When you die, I'm going to watch. I don't care how it will happen, or when, but I'm going to be there, and I'll watch your life fade away. I'm going to enjoy it.'

'And if it doesn't happen?' Bryn challenged. His fingers fell to stroke the hilt of the dagger at his hip. A reminder.

Lamorna laughed, a horrible, hollow sound. 'You think your blade frightens me? You hide behind it, like you hide behind that red coat of yours. I like the colour red, did you know that?' She paused again, examined her hand. 'I wonder what your blood would look like coating my skin?'

'You've lost your mind,' Bryn snarled.

'No, I've only just found it. Get out!'

Bryn did not move. He stared at her.

'Out!' Lamorna yelled.

He left with a final, hard look at her.

Only once he was gone did she let herself tremble, unable to hold it back any longer. She sank into a chair and put her head in her hands, swallowing her sob.

The door flung open. She looked up in fright, but it was Mordred. He hurried into the room.

'Lamorna, are you alright? I heard shouting.' He rushed to her side. She held out her hands; he gripped them.

'Bryn …'

'Did he hurt you?'

'No,' she said. 'I don't want him here. Send him away, Mordred.'

He frowned. 'Lamorna—'

'I know you think he's useful to you, but you don't understand,' she whispered fiercely. 'Whenever I look at him, I see my sister. I see what he did to her, as clearly as if I were in that room with them. Having to look at myself in the mirror sometimes is bad enough, but having to see him … I can't bear it.'

Mordred did not ask for more information, knowing already what had happened. She did not tell him her role in the whole event – it ate away at her, a deep wound that festered a little bit more whenever she laid eyes on Bryn. Lamorna didn't know what to do with the shame and the guilt that burnt in her belly when she thought of what Jen must have gone through; what all the women married against their will in that horrible place had gone through.

Mordred stroked her cheek.

'Please,' she said. She didn't care that she was begging. She didn't care if he thought she was weak. 'He … Calla's my friend and he tried to …' She let her voice fall away.

'Did he?' Mordred mumbled. His face was hard. 'Is she alright?'

Lamorna shook her head. 'She's frightened.'

'Alright. I'll find him something to do, a long way away from here,' Mordred said. 'But he will return, Lamorna. I'll keep him away from both of you. You won't have to look at him. Will that be enough?'

She nodded. 'I want my aunt.' She wasn't sure where the thought had come from, but now that it was out in the open, it solidified and grabbed hold of her and would not let go.

'She's in Cruithea.'

'I want my aunt, Mordred. She's my family, and I miss her. Can you send for her?' Lamorna asked.

'I don't know if that's a good idea,' Mordred began.

She pulled away from him. 'I see.'

'I only meant she might refuse to come, and I don't want to see you hurt by her rejection,' he explained.

'She'll come,' Lamorna said. 'She will.'

He nodded. 'I'll send for her, if it will make you happy.'

Lamorna kissed him. 'It would. Thank you.'

Chapter 53

When Arthur entered the captain's cabin, Katarin was standing at the window, spine rigid. She glanced over her shoulder, the tightness in her face relaxing when she saw him. She didn't make any comment about the Sword strapped to his hip, but her eyes brushed the Treasure quickly.

'I need to ask you something,' Arthur announced, joining her at the window.

Katarin waited, patient, for once.

'You said our mother was a healer, but was she also a dreamwalker?'

'Where did you hear that?' Kat demanded faintly.

'It doesn't matter,' Arthur replied, his tone leaving no space for argument. 'Was she?'

'Yes,' Kat said. 'There aren't many who can dreamwalk, and in Cruithea, most dreamwalkers become Priestesses of Inanna. But our mother did not choose that path. Healing was her calling.' She stopped and gave Arthur a searching look. 'Are you dreamwalking, Arthur?'

'Are you?' he returned. 'I know you're not sleeping well, and I know dreamwalking runs in family lines.'

Katarin sighed. She grabbed her chair, spun it around and sat, putting her boots up on the ledge. A flick of her hand and the window flew open, the sea breeze waltzing in. 'I was five, maybe six, when I first walked. I walked straight into our mother's dreams. I thought it was a normal dream, but then the next morning she sat me down and spoke to me about it.' Kat shrugged. 'I didn't understand the significance. I was a child.'

'Where do you go in your dreams?' Arthur asked her. He sat on the desk, keeping his eyes on the ocean, one hand resting against the hilt of the Sword.

'The past,' Kat replied, her voice full of shadows. 'My childhood, specifically. I don't know why. You?'

'Eseld told me it was the space between the worlds,' Arthur said. 'It must be where I've been meeting her all this time. I thought she was bringing me to her, but I'm beginning to think I brought her to me.' He rolled his shoulders, felt the tension there. 'Is everything a dreamwalker sees the truth?'

'Mostly,' Katarin answered. 'Sometimes a literal truth, sometimes a figurative one. There are no rules to tell you which is which. Dreamwalkers train to do this, Arthur. I'm completely untrained – I fear my dreams. I always have. Aelle used to help me suppress them. And you? You've stumbled into it.'

He smiled wryly. 'Story of the last six months of my life. Could Ethinne help?'

'She doesn't walk,' Katarin said. 'I think she sees flashes of what is to come, but it isn't her skill.'

'It's funny,' Arthur said after a moment. 'When I first discovered my magic, I was both horrified and elated. Horrified at what I'd done and elated because here was something that was a sure sign I needed to leave

Kernou, that I didn't belong in that world. And then Merlin tells me it was the Sword all along.'

Katarin looked at him. 'What?'

Arthur told her what he had learnt. 'I didn't tell you because I was angry about it, about having it taken from me, but you can't lose what wasn't yours to begin with, can you? But the dreamwalking – that's *mine*, Kat, and I'm not frightened of it. In my dreams, I'm calm, in control. I'm learning how to control the space between sleeping and waking. With the elements, I had to work hard, and I never felt I was succeeding. Magic was always beyond my grasp. The dreamwalking is different,' he added. 'I can do it with ease.'

Katarin nodded. 'It's both a gift and a curse to know what is going to happen. Be careful, Arthur. You're going in blind, and no matter how comfortable you feel, it is dangerous.'

'I'll take care,' he assured her. He stood, looking at his sister, noting the shadows beneath her eyes. 'You should try and sleep some more, Kat. You look like you need it.'

'Thanks,' she responded dryly.

'Kat, can Mordred walk in dreams?'

She was silent for a long time, and he wondered what form her dreams of the past had taken. 'I don't know,' she said eventually. 'But it's possible. Have you seen him?'

'I have,' Arthur said.

'And?'

'And he's angry.'

CHAPTER 54

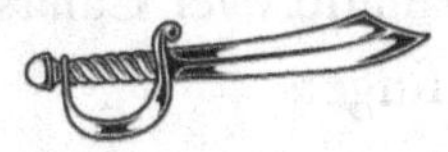

Lamorna was in the Hall with Calla, reviewing a list of food stocks. The other woman had been quiet since she'd told Lamorna about Bryn. Anger had not stopped churning in Lamorna's stomach, and she had made it her personal mission to keep Calla near her as much as possible.

She bit her lip, glancing at Calla as she read aloud from the list.

Calla looked up and met Lamorna's gaze. 'What?'

'Nothing,' Lamorna said, nodding at the list. 'Do we have enough for winter?'

'Not at this rate,' Calla said. 'All the seeds we planted have not taken, Lamorna. This place truly is cursed. We will have to get food from somewhere, or everyone will starve. It snows here,' she added. 'My grandfather told me.'

Lamorna frowned. 'I will speak with Mordred. Perhaps he can send someone to gather food from somewhere.'

Calla nodded, tucking a piece of deep brown hair behind her ear, the way Jenyfer used to do when she was nervous. 'Lamorna,' she began.

The door flew open and Mordred strode in, two heavily armed men on his heels. Behind them was Bryn. He was not wearing his red coat today.

Calla stiffened, and Lamorna's hands curled into fists. She met Mordred's eyes, held them a moment. He bid the men leave and told Bryn he must stay. Calla went to follow the Cruitheans, but Lamorna shook her head, placing her hand over Calla's. She could feel Calla's fear through the tremble in her fingers.

'Wait,' she whispered.

Bryn met Lamorna's eyes – a sneer pulled at his face as he followed Mordred towards the long table where Lamorna and Calla were seated, but he did not spare Calla a glance. Mordred placed a kiss on Lamorna's forehead. Her eyes slid sideways to Bryn, who was watching them.

'Lamorna says you spoke with her a few days ago,' Mordred said to Bryn.

'We talked, yes,' Bryn replied as Mordred beckoned him closer.

'Insult the woman I love again, and I'll make sure you suffer for it,' Mordred said, his voice deadly calm as he approached Bryn.

Bryn laughed, bold and brash. 'You don't really love her. She's—'

Mordred's hand shot out, fingers curling around Bryn's throat. He was taller than Bryn, stronger. His hand tightened. Lamorna did not hide her smile, while Calla gasped.

'She's what?' Mordred asked, still in that exceedingly calm tone.

Bryn didn't dare try and rip Mordred's fingers free.

'Here's what we'll do,' Mordred said. 'You agree not to speak ill of Lamorna – actually, don't even look at her – and I won't enjoy myself by breaking every bone in your miserable body.'

Bryn nodded. His face was pale and he was gasping for air.

Mordred released him and stepped away, taking a seat next to Lamorna. 'Oh, one more thing,' he said. Bryn's features froze. 'The people here are under my protection, Bryn. In Cruithea, if a man touched a woman without her consent, do you know what happened to him? He was flogged. And do you know who wielded the lash?'

Bryn swallowed and shook his head.

'If you even think about touching Calla, or another woman in this or any place without her consent, there will be no whip for you,' Mordred said. 'I will tie you to the battlements with your own intestines and sit back and wait for the crows. They start with the eyes, did you know that?' He paused, watching Bryn closely, like a predator might. His hand rested on the back of Lamorna's neck, warm and comforting. 'Do you understand me?'

Bryn nodded and dared not move.

'Now, I have a job for you,' Mordred told him. 'A way for you to earn your way back into my good graces. As Arthur is hiding away on a ship, it's a little difficult for me to invite my cousin for a chat. Go to Skulls Rest and find me a captain and crew willing to deliver that invitation for me.'

'Skulls Rest?' Bryn echoed.

Mordred's hand stroked Lamorna's neck. She kept her gaze fixed on Bryn, but he didn't return it.

'Are you scared of a few pirates?' Mordred asked.

Bryn shook his head.

'Bring the Captain back to me before he sets sail – I'd like to speak with him first. Do not tell him what his task will be, only that he will be rewarded for it. Can you do that?' Mordred said.

'I can,' Bryn said. 'I won't let you down.'

'No, you won't,' Mordred said.

After Bryn had left, Calla put her head in her hands.

'I thought she'd be pleased,' Mordred whispered, frowning at the woman. 'That is Calla, isn't it?'

Calla's shoulders shook, and for a moment Lamorna thought she was weeping, but when she lifted her head, they could see Calla was laughing silently. Her eyes were bright, her cheeks splashed crimson.

'Thank you,' she breathed, looking first to Lamorna, then Mordred. She stood, clearing her throat, and passed the list to Mordred. 'We're nearly out of food,' she told him.

He frowned. 'The crops? The vegetables?'

'Nothing,' Calla said. Then, 'Would magic help? Or is this land truly cursed?'

Mordred sighed. 'I think we can assume Camlann is indeed cursed.' He rubbed at his cheek. 'I will think of something,' he said. Calla nodded and left. Once the door had closed, Lamorna turned to Mordred. He leant forward and kissed her, scooping her into his lap so he could close his arms around her.

Lamorna frowned. 'Do you really think we can trust Bryn?'

'Not one bit, but I don't think he's brave enough to defy me,' Mordred said. 'Fear is a great motivator. He might have strutted around doing my uncle's bidding and gained a certain degree of power and favour, but I am not my uncle.'

'Thank you,' Lamorna said, kissing his cheek. 'For defending me. For defending Calla.'

Mordred took her hand, lifted it to his lips, and pressed a kiss to her palm. 'Always.'

Lamorna could hear voices – Mordred's, surprised, and rough from sleep, and another. A man's voice. Cross, she crawled out of bed, grabbing her robe and tugging it on. It was the middle of the night! Whoever it was, she would tell them to leave and return when it was light.

Their rooms were cloaked in darkness. Grumbling, Lamorna found the candle and lit it, waiting for the wick to catch before she stomped into the sitting room, shielding the flame with her hands, nasty words on her tongue.

They fell away, however, when she noticed who was standing on the opposite side of the room from Mordred.

'You!' she exclaimed.

The man looked at her and said nothing.

'Think about what I have said,' he told Mordred.

'Wait!' Lamorna cried.

The eyes he turned on her were sad, and in the blink of an eye he was gone, a whirlwind of storm clouds and lightning swirling around the room.

The candle went out, throwing them into darkness once more.

Mordred chuckled. 'Well,' he said.

Lamorna did not bother with the candle. 'That was … that …'

'My cousin's lover, Lamorna. But that's not all he is. Jalen is the demon of storms, a demi-god bound to the Witch of the Mists,' Mordred said. He found her in the darkness and pulled her close.

'And?' she asked faintly.

'And the Goddess of Magic is most interested in what I plan to do next.'

CHAPTER 55

The moon was draped in clouds, the ocean dark and smooth like glass. No waves slapped the sand. Jenyfer folded her arms, peering into the blackness that surrounded them.

'I can't see a thing,' she complained, shifting her weight from one foot to the other.

'What if he doesn't come?' Arthur's voice rose from the darkness somewhere behind her.

Before Jenyfer could respond, there was a light further along the beach. A lantern bobbed along, growing closer. Jenyfer's muscles tensed, her fingertips teasing the dagger at her hip.

'I don't know why humans bother with these things,' a voice said. The lantern winked out. Two orbs of soft, white light materialised above them as the servant of the God of the Otherworld stepped into view. Ophine cast their eyes over them all, their top lip curling back in distaste.

'You brought the faery, I see,' the wraith said. Ordes folded his arms and his wings unfurled from his back. Ophine's eyes widened, before throwing their head back in laughter. She turned to Jenyfer. 'You don't trust me, sister?'

'I'm not sure I should,' Jenyfer said. 'You helped us escape my father, and we're grateful. But you told me Ankou wanted to speak with me, and I've still not had the pleasure. What does he want? And where is he?'

It was then the wraith acknowledged Arthur and the Sword. Ophine inclined their head in his direction. 'The King Who Shall Be.'

Jenyfer glanced over her shoulder. A storm had taken up residence on Arthur's features. Jalen had still not returned, and Jenyfer had the horrible feeling he wasn't going to.

'King. You're still sure of that?' Arthur asked.

'Aren't you?' Ophine asked. 'Ah, I see. The demi-god showed his colours at last.'

Ordes shook his head in warning. Ophine shrugged but stayed silent.

Jenyfer held the book about the Otherworld out for the wraith. She had taken it with them at the last moment, a niggling thought in the back of her mind. 'How did this get on the ship?' she demanded.

Ophine's smile was knowing, but they took the book. 'We thought you might find it interesting.'

'You put it there?' Ordes asked. 'How did you get onboard?'

The wraith merely winked. Arthur drew closer, hand wrapped around the hilt of the Sword. 'I'm tired of games,' he said, levelling a stare at the wraith. 'You wanted us to read it.'

'Not I,' Ophine objected. 'My master did.'

'Why did he not come to us himself?' Jenyfer asked.

Ophine laughed. 'My master does not wander around the human world. He rules the dead, Jenyfer.'

'But he has an interest in the living, doesn't he?' Ordes asked.

The wraith nodded. 'You will come to my master, all of you, tomorrow, when the moon is full,' they said.

'And if we don't?' Arthur asked. His jaw was tight, lips a thin line. Anger was painted clearly on his face, as were all his emotions these days.

Ophine's smile was secretive, smug. 'You will. Tonight was a test, of sorts. You passed.' They turned and moved towards the ocean. Jenyfer followed.

'Wait,' she called.

Ophine halted, spine stiff.

'You're not a wraith, are you?' Jenyfer asked, stepping closer.

Slowly, Ophine turned around. 'No.'

'Then what?' Cautiously, Jenyfer reached out and touched the smattering of scales on the back of Ophine's hand.

'I was the first, did you know? The first one Melodias made.'

'You're a syhren?' Jenyfer whispered.

Ophine's lips curled into a sneer. 'I didn't turn out as expected, and he wasn't happy. I'm not beautiful. I'm a monster, and worse, I'm a monster with no song. None at all. I cannot even hum.'

'What did he do?' Jenyfer asked tightly.

'What do you think he did? What Melodias does with everything that disappoints him – he cast me out. Left me to rot on the banks of the black river, and it was there that my master found me. He took me in, he cared for me, and he gave me a purpose,' Ophine explained.

'I'm sorry,' Jenyfer whispered, aghast.

'I hate him,' Ophine said simply. 'If I can thwart whatever plans the Master of Songs and Death has, I will do it. Whatever it takes. Seeing him fail will be my greatest triumph.'

Jenyfer nodded. 'I can understand that.'

Ophine's smile was tight as they walked into the ocean, the water closing over their legs, their cloak floating on the surface. A wave broke over their head, and they were gone.

None of them slept that night. Jenyfer, Ordes, and Arthur sat on the deck staring out at the water. Moonlight reflected off the ocean, silver and shimmering. Arthur didn't say a word. He did not mention Jalen, or ask any questions about Ophine. Jenyfer guessed that he had nothing to say on the first subject that did not drag his pain even closer to the surface, and maybe Arthur, like all of them, had seen enough of the world that existed beneath the world not to wonder anymore.

A mysterious wraith, the servant of the master of the Otherworld, was one more thing that had been laid out before them. Another test, perhaps. Jenyfer didn't know, and could not even begin to imagine what Ankou wanted from her, or from any of them.

Ophine was waiting on the shore, exactly where they had been the previous night. No one had tried to stop them going ashore, a drastic change since The Teeth and Arthur's sudden arrival there. Jenyfer thought at first that Kat just couldn't be bothered shouting at them, but realised she was wrong. Everything had changed. Since Medb and Malist, the crew were subdued as well. Even though the humans had not joined them in the city, they'd seen the flames and smoke from the ship, had heard what had happened. Medb's attack had altered things for everyone.

'Where's your master?' Arthur asked.

The wraith said nothing as the air beside them shifted and flexed, and suddenly they were not alone.

A man with a skeletal face and hollow eyes stood beside Ophine. He wore a cloak as black as the darkest night and a large, wide-brimmed hat as white as bleached bones. He was tall, towering over all of them, even Ordes, and at his side were two hounds, one white, one black.

Jenyfer took a step back as the God of the Otherworld turned his eyeless gaze on her face. White hair tumbled over his shoulders, shifting in an invisible breeze.

Arthur cleared his throat, but said nothing. No one spoke, and the only sound was the waves lapping gently at the shore.

'Balance,' Ankou whispered suddenly. He clicked his fingers and a set of scales hovered in the air in front of their faces. 'This game that we are all engaged in was set a long time ago. Alliances were made in the darkest hours. Secrets were whispered.'

'What secrets?' Jenyfer asked.

'Those are not important,' Ankou replied, his voice like rattling bones. 'What is important is what you decide to do now.'

Jenyfer pursed her lips. 'How can we trust a thing you say?'

'You can't, just as you can't trust anything any of us say. The Old Ones cannot lie, but they have had aeons of practice at bending the truth, at manipulating language to suit themselves. Remember that,' Ankou told her.

'It's a bit hard to forget it.' Ordes' voice was cold.

Ankou turned his black gaze to him. 'Ah.' He tipped his head to one side, a smile playing on his skeletal face. 'She is not going to be happy with you, my dear sister. Ever did Niniane thirst for power, because power, once obtained, is a difficult thing to let go.'

Ordes took a step closer to the Servant of Death. 'Tell me about her. The truth.'

'I can do better than that,' Ankou whispered. 'I can show you.'

Before anyone could ask what he meant, the world around them shifted, and they were standing in a burning forest. Smoke curled from the earth. Jenyfer shielded her eyes with her hand, glancing around. Arthur's hands were tight around the hilt of his Sword, but he had not drawn it. His eyes were wide. Ankou and Ophine stood beside them.

'I've been here before,' Arthur said in disbelief. 'In this forest, holding the Sword of the White Dragon. Where are we?'

'In a forest that is no more,' Ankou told him. To Ordes he said, 'The truth will show itself in a moment. We have arrived in time. Ah, there she is. Fate has an interesting way of letting herself be known.'

Through the trees walked a woman dressed in a cloak of black feathers. Morrigna, the Goddess of Fate. She carried a sword in one hand, and her dark hair was bound in a series of braids like the ones the Cruitheans wore. She did not turn to look at them, passing right by them, and

Jenyfer realised the Goddess could not see them at all. Morrigna's face was smeared with blood.

Another woman stood between the trees. She was dressed for battle in leather armour. Daggers and an axe dangled from her belt, a sword clasped in one strong hand. Her ashen hair was tipped with red and was bound in a series of braids around her head. Feathers and bones were strung around her neck and around the horns that rose from her braids. She stopped, resting against a tree, and another woman suddenly materialised behind her, dark hair shifting as a swirl of red smoke slipped away into nothing.

She clutched the horned woman's arm. 'Sister. They come. We must fight, or we must flee.'

'We need to end this madness,' the first woman gasped.

The second woman shook her head. 'Niniane will not give up until I am dead.'

'What are we seeing here?' Ordes mumbled.

'War,' Ankou said softly. 'There is nothing you can do but watch. You wanted the truth – let it unfold, and then let it shape you.'

The horned woman rubbed a blood-smeared hand over her face. 'Ever was she one to—'

'It does not matter, Inanna,' the second woman said. She shed her red robes, letting them pool on the ash-cloaked ground like a puddle of blood. 'Let her do what she has come to do.'

'You want me to let her kill you?' Inanna breathed.

Ereshki shook her head. 'I have Seen what is coming, sister. I am not afraid.'

Inanna turned, clutching her sister to her. 'Tell me.'

'On barren field of cursed earth, a veil of green will be rebirthed. An angel's wings shall turn to dust, in the Word you all must trust. By scale and soil and wind and air, the Grail shall sing the world's repair. Three destinies as one will dawn, entangled, so a King is born,' Ereshki intoned, her voice no more than a whisper. She turned her head, and it seemed she was looking straight at them. Jenyfer sucked in a breath and stepped back.

At that moment, something came crashing through the trees, a whirlwind of mist and shadow. Trees toppled like matchsticks, the ground churned to dust and ash, and the last green leaves were torn from the branches. Inanna thrust her sister behind her, lifting her sword as the mist and smoke cleared. The Goddess of Magic was standing before her.

'Fuck me,' Ordes breathed.

There was no white gossamer gown or flowers in Niniane's dark hair. The Goddess wore armour of shining silver, its surface swirling with mist. Gripped in one hand was the Bow of Mists, an arrow notched and pointed directly at her sisters. Niniane's hair was pulled back from her face, her eyes dark and filled with anger. The air around her crackled with power, shifting and swirling with magic, and the expression she had trained on Inanna and Ereshki was one of violence and darkness.

Jenyfer grasped Ordes' hand as his mother smiled and pulled back on the Bow of Mists.

'You can't win this,' she said, her voice echoing across the decimated landscape.

Inanna lifted her sword, fierce determination on her face. 'We shall see.'

Niniane's arrow flew. It was battered away by Inanna's sword. Then chaos exploded as the two Goddesses clashed with magic and sword and Bow. Ereshki screamed a warning as the God of the Earth, his face like thunder, lifted the Sword of the White Dragon. Jenyfer heard Arthur suck in a breath as Gawain charged Ereshki, who vanished in red smoke, only to reappear behind him, sword swinging. He avoided the blow, spinning to meet her, and two became four as the ground shook and the air rang with the strike of steel on steel.

As they watched, Niniane struck Inanna across the face, throwing the Goddess backwards, slamming her into a tree. If she were mortal,

Inanna would be dead. Ereshki tore her gaze from Gawain as Niniane approached Inanna, vicious glee shining in those dark blue eyes.

'Is this what you want?' Ereshki seethed, pointing her sword at Gawain. 'You want her to destroy this world and everything in it? All the things we have made, Gawain. All the things we cherish, those we love. For what? Power? So the world doesn't forget her?' She adjusted her grip on her sword. 'Ever was she selfish, from the very beginning. You know this!'

Gawain paused, but did not lower his weapon.

Inanna had climbed to her feet, but Ereshki shot across the forest floor to stand in front of her sister. She let her sword fall to her feet. 'We surrender,' she told Niniane. Inanna hissed at her and tried to push her away. 'A truce, sister,' Ereshki insisted. 'This has gone on long enough.'

Niniane's eyes narrowed. 'Truce? You?'

'We are destroying the world!' Ereshki said passionately. 'We are destroying our creations.'

'You care more for these humans than you do for your own divinity, sister,' Niniane told her, but she lowered her weapons, the Bow and a glittering sword made of shimmering mist. 'What does it matter if we destroy this place? We can start anew, and get it right this time.'

Ereshki opened her mouth to respond, but the world dissolved around the edges. Jenyfer gasped and sank to her knees, her head spinning. They were back on the beach in the darkness, the God of the Otherworld and his servant standing before her.

Slowly, she got to her feet. Her mouth was full of ash and her eyes burnt with the smoke of a battle long past. Ordes was frozen; she touched his arm, and glanced at Arthur. 'What do we do?' she whispered. 'If we shape a world where magic reigns, *that* might happen again!'

Ankou inclined his head in silent agreement.

'And if we take the other path? My mother will kick our arses,' Ordes muttered.

'Unless you can bring us an army,' Jenyfer said swiftly, gesturing to Ankou.

'An army?' the God mused. 'I see.'

'Do you?' Jenyfer asked. She swallowed and took a step closer to him. 'Because I see a God, a powerful God, content to sit back and watch all of this unfold. To watch people die, betray each other, destroy each other, *again*.'

Ophine made a hissing sound. Jenyfer ignored them, even though her stomach twisted and fear flooded her. Ankou could destroy them all, but she was counting on him being like the other Old Ones – more focused on his own self-interests than any insults she might fling at him.

Ankou's blind eyes stared at her. 'I cannot interfere—'

'Cannot or will not?' Ordes asked. 'My father had a vision. When the battle is waged in the skies, in the seas and on the land, darkness and blood will come for you. Goerika spoke these same words to Arthur. And I don't know if you saw what we saw, but my mother is willing to destroy everything to hold on to her power.'

'There is a battle coming,' Arthur said firmly. 'Mordred has taken the castle at Dinas Emrys, and Medb has left The Teeth, no longer bound by the Stone.'

'And Melodias is about to throw his support behind the false King,' Ankou muttered.

'What?' Jenyfer whispered, her stomach sinking. She should have listened to Andromache that night. Defeat beat at her with heavy hands. 'We need help,' she implored. 'We've got the Red Sisters on our side – I think,' she added. 'And Cruithea, maybe. My father has an army of bloodthirsty syhrens. How are we supposed to stop them? How are we supposed to fight against Medb and her magic, against Mordred and my father, and not get ourselves killed? Against Niniane? You won't have to worry about us remaking the world because we'll be dead before we even get our hands on the Grail.'

'If we die, your dreams of a world held in balance die with us,' Ordes put in.

Ophine shook their head. 'You ask for my master's help but can't find ways to help yourselves? You come making demands—'

'What ways?' Jenyfer shouted. 'We're out of ideas, Ophine.'

Ankou said nothing. Silence draped around them.

Jenyfer sighed. 'Let's go. We'll work something out.'

'Your battle will take place on Samhain,' Ankou said. 'You need an army? I'll give you an army, Jenyfer. But not yet. Not until the tides turn and the veil thins.'

Jenyfer halted. 'What strings are attached?'

'None,' the Servant of Death told her. 'The world is out of balance. I will help tip the scales.'

'Thank you,' Arthur said.

Ankou and Ophine vanished, the latter with a meaningful look at Jenyfer, one she wasn't sure how to interpret.

'I guess,' Arthur said slowly. 'We're going to have to trust him?'

'I guess,' Ordes agreed.

Chapter 56

Wind pulled at Lamorna's clothes. She tried to push her hair out of her face and then gave up, folding her arms around herself instead. Mordred did not care about the wind – he was watching the dead earth that stretched before them.

'What are we doing out here?' she asked crossly. They were standing outside the castle gates.

'Waiting for someone,' he answered. The corners of his lips twitched in a secretive smile.

Lamorna grumbled under her breath, folding her arms and squinting against the wind. She would much prefer to be back in the castle. She did not like the never-ending brown of Camlann Plain.

Mordred kissed her cheek. 'I won't let him hurt you,' he promised.

Lamorna frowned, but before she could ask who he meant, her skin prickled, the way it would sometimes before it stormed. She glanced up, but the sky was clear. It was not long before dawn and the sun was beginning to crawl over the world. Here, the sun came quickly, unlike in Kernou, where it would have to climb over the tallest peaks of the Nemhain Mountains before it touched its golden fingers on the ocean.

Lamorna had no clue who they could possibly be meeting.

The air rippled, and a strange cloud formed not far from them. As they watched, the cloud solidified, until it became a large bubble of water. Lamorna gasped.

'What's happening?' she heard herself ask. There were shapes inside the bubble, large and dark. She narrowed her eyes, trying to make them out – they were moving, growing larger. She gripped Mordred's arm as that bubble of water moved closer. It reminded her of a birth sac. She had seen one once, when she was younger and her aunt was still helping women birth babies. Lamorna had never forgotten what it looked like. A hand pressed against the stretchy exterior of that birth-sac bubble.

She stepped back, preparing herself to run, but the hand punctured the sac, revealing two people.

Her grip tightened on Mordred's arm.

There was something about the strangers' faces, both familiar and not.

Her head was filled with music and her stomach turned over. Lamorna could not pull enough air into her lungs. Her body was light and weighed down at the same time, her muscles turned to liquid, so much so she imagined them oozing from her body and soaking into the ground.

'It's …' she managed, as recognition chimed like a bell in her brain.

The Master of Songs and Death was darkness and thunder. He was shadow and music, cruelty and beauty. Hair like black silk floated behind him, and he was so pale he shone in the eerie stillness of pre-dawn. He walked the length of dead earth towards where Lamorna and Mordred waited. Not a drop of water ran from his black clothes. There was a woman with him, but Lamorna did not look at her. She couldn't take her eyes off Melodias.

He smiled and addressed her. 'How lovely it is to see you again.'

She wanted to run away screaming, but kept her chin lifted and held Melodias' eyes, his music barrelling through her brain. She forced herself to look at the woman, startled to realise she recognised her. Her beautiful face was serene, but beneath it lingered the promise of violence and blood, of death. The woman glided over the ground, her feet not meeting the earth. Her skin was pale as starlight, hair like silver silk falling over her shoulders and down her back. Her dark cloak covered a dress the colour of moonlight.

She was beautiful; they both were. The most beautiful creatures Lamorna had ever seen.

She wanted to weep. A memory tugged at her, but she shoved it away.

Mordred bowed. 'What does the God of the Seas want with me?'

'Yes, I wonder about that myself. Obviously, you got my message,' Melodias said.

Lamorna wanted to ask what message, but she could barely breathe, let alone speak.

Melodias brushed an invisible speck of dust from his black shirt. 'Since the last lot turned out to be such a monumental disappointment, I was hoping you might be better suited to the job,' he said.

'What job?' Mordred asked.

'I can make you a king, Mordred,' Melodias whispered. 'I know that's what you want.'

Lamorna tensed and found her voice. 'Don't make any deals with him,' she hissed to Mordred. Her fingernails dug into his arm.

Melodias chuckled. 'My dear, are you mad at me?' He smiled again. 'I have decided whose side I am on, after years of sitting on the bloody fence – frankly, I'm sick of waiting. So, I'm here to help you.'

'Help me? How?' Mordred demanded. 'I believe your sibling gods want nothing to do with you.'

Melodias rolled his eyes. 'There is no accounting for taste,' he said.

'You said you had something for me,' Mordred said.

'Yes, but it's a little late for that.' The Master of Songs and Death undid the buttons on his shirt and peeled it from his body. His skin was the colour of the underside of a fish, but his flesh was marked with a strange pattern. 'I took this map from my daughter and her charming pirate,' he said casually, then sighed. 'It's useless now, I suppose, considering they have retrieved the Treasures.'

'What good is it to me, then?' Mordred demanded suspiciously.

'You know the prophecy, and no doubt you, like my daughter, believed that the Grail could not be found before the Treasures,' Melodias said smoothly. He clicked his fingers and the lines of ink on his skin floated free. 'I don't suppose any of you have any paper?'

Lamorna stuck her hand in the pocket of her dress, pulling out a piece of paper. She had been intending to use it for a list of supplies they would need when Mordred sent someone to find some. Hesitantly, she unfolded it, then almost dropped it when a map began to form there.

Mordred peered over her shoulder. 'Dinas Emrys is the only place marked.'

'Which I would take as significant,' Melodias said.

Mordred was frowning. 'And this map leads to the Grail?'

'Perhaps,' Melodias told him. 'There would be only two who know, and one of them is already dead. But I can help with that. Andromache, if you please.'

Andromache reached inside the cloak she wore. The air shimmered around her and a sword materialised in her hand. Lamorna could hear its music. Andromache snapped her fingers and the sword floated through the air towards them, pausing in front of Mordred.

'Arthur has one now, doesn't he? So I thought it was only fair. It's a loan, understand? I don't give away my toys. After this whole mess is cleaned up and the world is back to the way it is meant to be, you will return it to me,' Melodias said.

Mordred had not touched the sword. 'What is so special about it?'

'It can kill a god, or as close to a god as a man who isn't a man can be,' Melodias told him. Lamorna looked between him and Mordred, heart pounding. She wanted to drag Mordred away. She wanted to go back to bed and pretend this was not happening, that her nightmares were not here, in the flesh.

'You want me to kill Merlin?' Mordred guessed.

'He is the reason we're in this mess in the first place,' Melodias said. 'But yes, I want you to kill Merlin, after you make him tell you where on that blasted map he hid the Grail.'

'And if I can't find him?' Mordred asked, running his eyes over the map clutched between Lamorna's trembling fingers.

Melodias smiled. 'You will though, won't you? Humans like power, I've learnt, and right now, I am offering you more power than anyone else ever has, Mordred. You will do what needs to be done.'

Mordred still would not touch the sword. 'What's in it for you?'

'Why do people always assume I want something?' Melodias mumbled. 'Nothing, only that, I'd like my daughter returned to me. I miss her, and we didn't part on the best of terms.'

Mordred laughed, startled. 'Is that all? You want Jenyfer?'

'Of course. She's my family and family is so important, is it not?' Melodias said, his voice smooth. He met Lamorna's eyes briefly, then turned back to Mordred. 'She has great potential, and I hate seeing potential go to waste. Are you going to waste yours, Mordred?'

Before Lamorna could stop him, Mordred closed his hand around the hilt of Melodias' sword. She slammed her hands over her ears as music smashed through her mind. Mordred was staring at the sword in wonder, eyes wide, a smile tugging at his lips.

'Andromache will return at the next full moon, and she will remain here, as my envoy,' Melodias said. The syhren looked less than pleased with this decision. Her full lips had become a thin line, her beautiful face tight with annoyance, but she did not argue.

Another supplicant woman, Lamorna thought. Any pity she felt for the syhren vanished when Andromache gave her a cruel smile.

'As your spy,' Mordred growled.

'Yes, that too.' The God of the Seas turned to leave, then paused, glancing over his shoulder. 'It was good to see you again, Lamorna. Are you enjoying your gift?'

She blinked, and it came rushing back, sweeping in like the tide and there was nothing she could do to stop it, not anymore.

Mist swirled on the surface of the lake, its black face as smooth as a mirror, reflecting nothing. Odd shapes twisted and shuddered and moved around each other beneath that water, coming as close as a shadow but never touching.

Lamorna knelt at the edge of the lake, her hand hovering above the glassy surface.

'Careful, my dear. We wouldn't want you to fall in.'

The voice was like silk, a ribbon wrapped around arrogance and coated in steel. Lamorna didn't turn around, but she could feel him standing behind her. The hair along the back of her neck crawled upright, and she shivered as he ran a cold finger along the bare skin of her shoulder, her body tingling as his power caressed her.

Melodias sat beside her. He reached towards the water. One long finger touched the surface, rippling and swirling beneath his skin. A moan echoed through the chilled, damp air, and a ghostly hand broke the surface of the lake, pale fingers grasping his wrist. He smiled, and slowly reached down with his free hand and unwound the fingers. The hand slipped below the water, the moaning turning to a scream that lingered long after it had stopped.

Lamorna stared into the black soup.

'Ankou gave you back, because I asked nicely,' Melodias said.

'Ankou?' Lamorna whispered. She blinked. A man with long white hair. Bones instead of a face. No eyes. She remembered him. Sort of. 'Oh.'

'But what do I do with you?' Melodias mused, tapping his finger against the surface of the water. 'Your sister had me rescue you for a reason. I can't believe it's as simple as she cares for you.'

Lamorna said nothing. She wasn't sure she wanted to speak anymore.

'Are you here to trick me?' Melodias went on. 'Forgive me, but I'm trying to work it out.'

'She saved me?' Lamorna whispered. Or thought she whispered. She wasn't sure.

The world tilted, music thundered through her mind, sinking into her blood, and she was sitting in a chamber filled with sound as a woman sang the most beautiful song Lamorna had ever heard.

'Where am I?' she asked as the notes faded and she was left feeling empty and cold.

The woman was slender, with silver hair that tumbled down her back. Her temple and fingers were graced with scales. She knelt in front of Lamorna, taking hold of her chin and staring at her curiously.

'There's nothing in there,' she said.

'Nothing in where?' Lamorna asked.

'In you,' the woman said. 'No drive. No ambition. No sense of who you actually are. You're empty. A slave. A servant to a god who doesn't exist, not as you know them, anyway.' She stood, looking down on Lamorna with what could have been pity, but was more likely disgust. 'I truly don't know what to do with you,' she declared.

Lamorna tumbled into the throne room, the black lake behind her. She had thought about throwing herself in, but would he let her drown?

Melodias tapped black-scaled fingers against the arm of his throne. It was made of bones. She closed her eyes and thought of the One God, silently reciting the Word.

A sigh cut through her prayers. 'Still, you ask him for help.'

Lamorna opened her eyes.

'You should be asking me,' Melodias crooned. He beckoned, one wave of his hand, and Lamorna was pulled up the steps to kneel on the ground before him. He reached out, cool fingers curling around her cheek. 'I can give you what you want, Lamorna.'

'I don't know what I want,' she whispered. His fingers were wet, like the ocean was slowly trickling from them to caress her instead.

'Don't you?' he said. 'Who tied you to that stake and left you to die?'

'The Chif,' she said, frowning. 'But …'

'Who stood by and did nothing while my ocean reached out to taste your flesh?'

Lamorna swallowed. 'Everyone, except Jenyfer.'

'And what would you give to be back there? To see them all,' he said.

This time she frowned. 'Why would I want to see them? They tried to drown me.'

He laughed, and it was the sweetest music she had ever heard. 'My dear, I don't mean to send you back so they could take advantage of you again. I mean to send you back with the power to control your miserable little life.'

Lamorna opened her mouth, and then closed it.

'Would you like that?' Melodias whispered.

'Yes,' she whispered back.

He smiled and sat back, crossing one long leg over the other. 'Then it shall be yours.'

Lamorna's knees gave out. She sank to the ground, trembling head to toe, pulling great gasps of burning air into her lungs. Mordred dropped to his knees beside her, concerned, but when she looked up, it was Melodias she sought.

He smiled, a familiar, cruel curving of his lips.

She could feel the ocean licking at her feet, the wind in her hair, the rough fibres of the rope where they rubbed on her skin, the stake firm against the line of her body.

The sunlight was swallowed, darkness racing in, mouth open, a beastly thing with teeth and claws that climbed up her spine and wrapped itself around her neck and pulled the words from her lips.

'What did you do to me?'

'I simply gave you what you'd always been missing – the power to believe in yourself,' Melodias crooned. Then he and Andromache were gone.

CHAPTER 57

Ordes scowled, bouncing a ball of lightning from one hand to the other. His features were rigid, silver eyes as hard as granite. Magic rippled over his knuckles as he clenched and unclenched his fists.

'Are you sure you want to do this?' Arthur asked. 'She's your mother.'

Ordes snorted. 'She's no mother of mine, Arthur, and I refuse to be a pawn in her games – in any games – any longer. I have no issues with setting her up. It's nothing more than she deserves. But the question is, do you want to do this?'

'What do I need to do?'

'Find Jalen in your dreams, and tell him …' Ordes paused and chewed on his lip. 'Tell him we have made a decision. Tell him we want a world where magic does not rule, and let him tell my mother. If she truly wants to hold on to her power, she'll pay us a visit.'

'Do we want that?' Jenyfer asked. 'I mean, you saw what I saw, Ordes. She could destroy the lot of us, take the Treasures for herself and—'

'The Fisher Queen won't give her the Grail,' Arthur cut in. 'I'm certain of it. Not if Eseld is bound to Ereshki. Will the threat of losing her power be enough to tempt Niniane, though?'

'Tell Jalen we'll shut off the realms,' Jenyfer said after a moment. 'Avalon will be lost to the world, and Niniane with it. I don't think she wants that. At least, the Goddess in Ankou's vision of the past would not want that.'

Arthur stared at her. 'Can we do that? Lock the Old Ones in their own realms forever?'

Ordes shrugged. 'I don't know, and at this point I don't care if it's possible or not. If it gets her attention, then it's worked.'

With a shaking breath, Arthur lay down. Jenyfer would sing him to sleep, allowing him to walk as far as he needed to find Jalen.

'Ready?' Jen asked. Arthur nodded, and as the first notes of her syhren song washed over him, his eyes slipped closed, and he tumbled into the darkness.

It was not the Fisher Queen's cave Arthur fell into, but the room he had shared with Jalen in Avalon. He was in a soft bed, white curtains shifting in a warm breeze as sunlight crept over the world outside. With a yawn, Arthur stretched his arms above his head, then froze.

He was not alone.

He jumped as a hand smoothed the hair back from his forehead. He knew its weight and warmth.

'You're quieter than usual.' Jalen's voice, soft from sleep.

Arthur swallowed tightly. 'Just tired.'

'Arthur, if something's on your mind, you know you can talk to me,' Jalen said. His fingers moved into Arthur's hair, nails scraping gently against Arthur's scalp.

Arthur sighed and closed his eyes. 'You're not really here.'

'I'm as real as you want me to be,' Jalen said. 'This is your world, this space between sleeping and waking.'

'Did you know what I was?' Arthur asked, rolling onto his side. Jalen nodded. Arthur ran his fingers over the swell of muscle on Jalen's arm, over his shoulder, along the column of his throat. 'Where did you go, Jalen?' he asked. 'When you weren't with us, where were you?'

Jalen stilled. 'I'm a demi-god, Arthur. Bound to my mistress. When she summons me, I have to go.'

'I need you,' Arthur said, realising Ordes had been right. 'Will you come back?'

Jalen's smile was tight. 'Of course. But you don't need me – you've got the Sword of the White Dragon.'

'A sword can't hold me and tell me everything will be alright,' Arthur said. 'It can't remind me that this is important, when all I want is to turn my back on it sometimes.' He sighed, lying back to stare at the gauzy canopy of the bed. 'But I know I can't. I've accepted it, and my role in it, my future.'

Jalen nodded. 'The world will be better for it, Arthur. A return to what was.'

Ice settled slowly along Arthur's spine. 'Perhaps.'

Jalen traced little circles on Arthur's chest, his hand settling over the beating of Arthur's heart. 'You don't know any other world except this one, and it has given you nothing but heartache and pain.'

'It gave me you,' Arthur put in softly.

Jalen brushed his lips over Arthur's. 'Yes.'

'But if it wasn't for the prophecy, I'd never have met you because you wouldn't have been pretending to be a fisherman in Kernou. If it wasn't for what Ereshki chose to do all those years ago, there'd be no need for anyone to make a new world, would there?' Arthur mused. 'I'm not sure how I feel about gods who play with people like they're toys, Jalen.'

Jalen said nothing.

'Why should the world return to that?' Arthur asked. 'Why do we need gods to rule us at all? If I'm to be a king, won't that be my job?'

'Kings need guidance,' Jalen said.

'Wouldn't it be better to have human guidance, though?' Arthur murmured. 'The Old Ones are immortal. They cannot possibly understand human life, human existence, or the way we experience the world. They can't truly understand what it means to be human.'

'People need something to believe in,' Jalen said. 'That's why Ereshki's little plan was so successful, and so damaging to the rest of the Old Ones.'

'But if we return to what was, what would be different? What choices would there be? Believe and be rewarded for it, or don't and be punished?' Arthur argued.

'You misunderstand the Old Ones, Arthur,' Jalen told him, a hint of frustration in his tone. 'They don't want to rule the world.'

'Don't they?' Arthur asked bluntly. 'Melodias surely does, and I think Niniane does.'

'You don't know her,' Jalen replied tightly.

'Jalen, she started a *war* with her fellow gods over power,' Arthur pointed out. 'And we're walking straight into another one. The world does not need a war. It needs peace and unity – balance. I don't want to be the sort of king who commands people to believe in anything. I want to earn people's trust and respect, and I'll only do that by offering them the power of choice and their free will,' he added.

Jalen sighed. 'Arthur, how will you get people to follow you without a show of power?'

'You sound like Mordred,' Arthur mumbled. 'But to answer your question – choice *is* power. Why do you think my father never let me make any choices of my own? Why do you think he worked so hard to take away the power of choice from the people he ruled? I refuse to force anyone to do anything.'

He turned onto his side so he could look his lover – the demi-god, servant to a goddess, *enslaved* to a goddess – in the eye. 'Jen, Ordes, and I will do this ourselves. We were chosen for this. The choice is ours,' he added firmly. After what we saw in The Teeth, after what Jen had to do, after Malist … we don't want things like Medb in the world, free to do as they wish. We don't want people to be scared.'

'There cannot be light without darkness, Arthur,' Jalen argued.

'I know, but there is already enough darkness in the hearts of men, without adding to that,' Arthur responded. 'I know what you want, because it's the same thing Mordred wants. Look at what he is doing, what he has already done, to achieve that.'

Arthur watched Jalen closely, unsure where his loyalties truly lay. Not knowing how to ask the question, he asked a different one instead. 'You've been rallying the fey in Niniane's name?'

Jalen said nothing for a long time; Arthur did not look away from his lover's face, did not so much as blink, until Jalen nodded.

'And it is not the world I want that you've been promising them on her behalf, is it?' Arthur managed.

'No.'

One simple word, and one massive admission.

Arthur sighed and lay back, linking his hands behind his head. 'I guess, there is no other choice then. We must close off the realms.'

'Arthur, wait—'

Arthur closed his eyes, and when he opened them again he was in his bed on *The Excalibur*, Jalen's absence a gaping hole in his heart.

He sat up, rubbing his face, remembering he was not alone in his waking world either.

'Well?' Ordes asked. He was sitting in an armchair in the corner of Arthur's cabin. Arthur blinked. He didn't own an armchair, but he guessed he did now.

'I saw him. And I told him.'

'Then all we need to do now is sit back and wait for my mother to show up.'

CHAPTER 58

unt Morgause was glorious.

Morgaine stared at her in awe. No, she corrected herself. Not aunt. The High Priestess of Cruithea, Inanna's chosen. In these moments of ceremony, that was what she was.

Not Morgaine's aunt.

Not Mordred's mother.

Morgaine sought her cousins' eyes across the flames, but he would not look at her. His chin was lifted, face proud.

This night was not for him, though.

It was for Morgaine.

The High Priestess stood with her palms turned towards the sky. To one side of her stood the Priestess of the Temple. To the other, the leader of the Inborn.

All three were dressed for ceremony. The Temple Priestess, whose name Morgaine could not remember, was a small woman with soft brown skin. She wore her Priestess' robes, the material a deep, ash grey. Her hood was lifted, concealing her features. Morgaine had never seen the Priestess of the Temple before, but she could sense the woman's power.

The leader of the Inborn was a tall man, taller even than the High Priestess. His skin shone in the firelight, his hair braided in tight warriors' braids that dangled down his back. Dark eyes watched Morgaine. He wore his weapons, and his muscular arms were bare, revealing swirling tattoos. The glyph between his eyes was bright and white, freshly etched into his skin.

Morgaine reached up to touch her forehead, wondering whether it hurt when they cut the skin and rubbed the white powder into the broken flesh. If it did, she decided, she would not cry when it was her turn.

The High Priestess wore her long red hair in a series of braids twisted around her head, some left to trickle down her back. Her headdress was made of bones and feathers and deer antlers, and like the leader of the Inborn, her glyph had been freshly done.

Morgause wore a gown that looked like it was made of the forest itself, dark green like the leaves of the trees that sheltered Cruithea from the world. The fabric was embroidered with red and orange and yellow, the colours of the turning season, and Inanna's symbol – the triple spiral – was emblazoned across her chest.

The High Priestess raised her hands to the sky. 'It is time to reveal to you all whom Inanna has chosen to stand as her representative here on earth once I am gone.'

Morgaine swallowed. She did not like the idea of her aunt dying, but death was not to be feared, not for a Cruithean. Death was simply another step on the path Inanna had chosen for them.

Morgaine's head jerked as she heard her name. Her mother's hand was warm and heavy on her shoulder. Morgaine swallowed again, but Igraine guided her around the fire towards the High Priestess.

She met her aunt's eyes and dared not look away, but she desperately wanted to see Mordred's face, to know how he was feeling. She wanted to tell him this changed nothing between them.

He was still her family.

He was still important to her.

As the Priestess of the Temple placed a headdress on Morgaine's small head – a replica of the one the High Priestess wore – she could feel Mordred's gaze.

She wanted to smile, but when she finally looked to him, her cousin had his face turned to the ground, his shoulders slumped as around them people chanted a blessing from Inanna and the drums began to beat.

Her cousin's face was slack with shock. Mordred lowered his weapons, signalling for those behind him to do the same.

Katarin had not laid eyes on her cousin since she was eight years old, when she chanced a look back over her shoulder as her mother led her away, the two of them following Ulrian Tregarthen into the trees.

Mordred had been a sullen boy, his hair brushing his shoulders and woven into braids, his deep brown eyes filled with emotion – worry, for her perhaps. Fear. Loss and regret at the harsh words they had exchanged.

Now, he was tall and strong, with broad shoulders and arms that looked like they could crush her. His eyes were sharp and alert, his hair tightly bound and tied in a knot on top of his head. In one hand he carried an axe, and in the other a bow. A quiver of arrows rested over his shoulder, and there were two daggers at his belt. The glyph on his brow was the sign of fire, and Kat remembered then that had been Mordred's element.

Fire, and anger.

Would he be the same now that he was grown?

She did not move from where she stood on the beach in the Moon's Bite, *The Night Queen*, newly gifted to her by the Goddess of Magic, anchored out to sea. Katarin had told the crew they were not to come ashore, not until she knew what sort of welcome awaited them.

Mordred took a hesitant step forward, then stopped.

Cruitheans feared nothing.

Mordred feared nothing, but at that moment, Katarin knew he feared her.

'I'm no ghost,' she told him. She knew what he saw – a pirate, a fierce woman, nothing like the child he had last glimpsed.

'You're alive?' he whispered. Another step, less hesitant. 'We heard … how?'

'What did you hear?' Kat asked. Her heart pounded painfully at the memory. The water lapping her toes. The fear that had gripped her. Her pleas to Inanna – unanswered. Her punishment for abandoning her duty. She gave the Inborn lingering behind Mordred a challenging stare. Her cousin did not turn from her; he flicked his fingers, and the Inborn slunk back to the treeline.

'Igraine is dead. And you …' Mordred swallowed. 'You should be dead.'

'Should be, but I'm not.'

He was still looking at her with that hesitant awe. 'Where have you been?'

'Avalon,' she replied.

His eyes widened at that. 'For over ten years?'

'Yes. It's because of Niniane that I'm alive, Mordred.'

He said nothing. He did not move closer, and neither did she. Years and years stretched between them. Loss and memory and all that time they should have been able to spend together.

'You're the leader of the Inborn now?' she asked, needing to break the silence.

'Just this moon,' he answered.

Kat nodded. 'Your mother?'

'Will be pleased to see you, Morgaine,' Mordred said. He finally took a step closer.

'That isn't my name anymore,' she said.

He frowned. 'What do you mean?'

'I go by Katarin Le Fey now,' she told him firmly. 'It's the name I chose for myself.'

Something crossed his face, too fleeting for her to read, and his expression became hard. He opened his mouth, but she cut across him harshly.

'Morgaine Tintagel and everything she was and would be is dead.'

Slowly, Mordred shook his head. 'You cannot give up who you are because you feel like it.'

Katarin stared at him. Rage and memory swirled inside her. 'You don't know what you're talking about!'

Mordred took another step towards her. He was close enough now that she could see the tension he carried in his shoulders. 'You were chosen by Inanna, Morgaine. You cannot turn your back on your people, your land, your *duty*,' he said, his voice low.

Katarin laughed. 'I can do whatever I please.'

Mordred grit his teeth. 'Come. I'll take you to my mother.'

Katarin sat up with a gasp, clutching at her chest. She blinked. Trees were stamped behind her eyes, tall and dark and reaching for the sky. She could smell the sweetness of damp earth and decaying leaves, rotting wood and water, wood smoke and wild mint. She could feel spider webs brushing against her skin, while the wind whistled through the trees and the branches creaked.

She could hear drums.

She shook her head then climbed out of bed, hurrying to the window. She'd been dreamwalking again. With shaking fingers, she flung the glass open, pulling the sea air into her lungs.

All she could smell was the forest.

All she could see was her cousin's face, the pain of losing something that would never be his, lingering in her mind so clearly after all those years later, even when she made it clear she did not want it.

Inanna had abandoned her long ago.

'Oh, Mordred,' Katarin whispered. In her mind, she saw the little boy she used to know. 'What have you become?'

And then, the thought, unbidden.

What have I?

Chapter 59

The landscape was flat and bare. No trees sprouted from the ground. No mountains scraped the sky. Arthur turned slowly, frowning as he looked around. Nothing. The cursed barrenness of Camlann Plain had taken over everything.

He bent to touch the ground at his feet. Smooth, like glass. He could not press his fingers into the soil. He stood, brushing his hair from his eyes, then stumbled as the ground beneath him began to tremble.

He ran, not knowing where he was going. Out of the alien sameness around him, a man appeared. As Arthur approached, he could see it was not an ordinary man. Antlers rose from his dark hair, and his eyes were as golden as the sun, with flecks of green floating through them like chips of stone.

The Green Knight.

The Old One did not acknowledge Arthur's presence. Instead, he bent and placed his hands on the earth. A carpet of mossy grass grew beneath his feet, spreading in all directions, the green consuming the lifeless ground around them. He stood, and with a wave of his hands, trees and plants sprang into existence. Arthur realised he was watching the moment a god carved a landscape, the creation of Teyath.

From the earth, the Green Knight called forth the Nemhain Mountains, that great rocky spine that wove its way through the centre of the continent. Then he summoned the rivers and the creeks, and Arthur could smell water, could hear it trickling as it flowed along the beds that had been crafted for it.

Time shifted, and Arthur's stomach shifted with it. The Old One bent to the earth and dug through the soil with his bare hands, slowly, methodically, with a kind of reverence that Arthur recognised.

Arthur peered over the Green Knight's shoulder. There, in a cradle of soil and stone, lay the Sword of the White Dragon. A roar echoed through the air and Arthur glanced up to see a great, winged beast soar overhead, before the world tilted again and he was somewhere else. There was a weight at his hip. He glanced down to see the Sword there. He touched it, felt its magic spark within, then looked up, and sucked in a startled breath.

The White Dragon stood before the God of the Earth, its glorious head lowered. The Green Knight spoke to him, and the beast sank to the ground. Arthur's heart leapt as the Green Knight rested his hand on the dragon's snout and slowly, the beast turned to stone.

'I am sorry,' he heard the Old One whisper. 'You will live again.'

Darkness closed in around them and a furious wind pulled at Arthur's clothes. He closed his eyes, and when he opened them he was sitting in the Fisher Queen's cave. The God of the Earth sat opposite him, and a fire burned in the pit, flames twisting and coiling around themselves like orange and gold serpents.

'Finally!' Arthur said. 'Where have you been?'

The God of the Earth did not smile. His eyes fell to the Sword, strapped to Arthur's hip. Arthur cleared his throat. 'There are things I need to ask you,' he began. When the Old One did not reply, Arthur took it as permission.

'Why did you support Niniane in the war against your siblings?'

'I was misled,' the Green Knight answered simply. 'I am of the earth. I cannot be forgotten. Even if humans forget my name, they do not forget the earth, who provides for them.'

'So why?' Arthur pressed.

'Men had begun to reshape my world – they cut down the forests, dammed the rivers, diverted the creeks – my realm was in pain, crying out for vengeance. I had to act to protect it – to make sure the land would be strong enough to survive all that humans threw at it. But I had failed to understand that while men were changing the land, they were also tending it. The forests were cut down to make way for crops, and as men tilled the soil, I saw care in their actions. I saw worship in the libations they poured into the fields, the love they gave the new land they had crafted.'

Arthur waited. The firelight cast strange shadows on the wall behind the Old One. Antlers became branches, the shape of his head became a mountain and the water that slid down the stones a river.

'It was too late to relent – like men, I am not immune to the sin of pride, Arthur. I wonder, sometimes, that Melodias had it right all this time,' the Old One said.

'And now?'

The world shifted again, and they stood on the barren earth of Camlann Plain. Gawain bent and ran his hand over the dead ground. 'Now, I want to see *life* here again. It's been too long. I want to see green life on this broken earth once more.'

Arthur looked around. Dinas Emrys was visible in the distance, rising from the treeless landscape, a symbol of the past, and a possible future. 'Who cursed this place?'

'A sister's love for her brother was not enough to stop him betraying her and everything they held dear,' the Green Knight said. 'A brother who lost who he was, and couldn't find himself again. A man who let himself be what he was not because he was afraid of being who he was.' Gawain looked up at the cloudless sky. 'To truly break this curse, two must become one, like Eseld and Enyon once were.'

'What does that mean?' Arthur breathed.

The Green Knight's face was sorrowful. 'The spilling of familial blood began this curse. The spilling of familial blood shall help end it.'

Waking alone was no longer the torment it once was, so Arthur lay there a moment, contemplating what he had learnt in his dreamwalk. Perhaps Niniane's alliance was not as strong as she believed it was. There was one person who would know the answer to that question, and he wasn't here to ask.

Not that Jalen would tell the truth, anyway.

He thought about the curse and realised he'd been a fool to believe it would not come back to what Goerika had told him in the temple. He was leading his allies – his friends – into a war, one that he desperately wanted to avoid. But there was no escaping it, not when his family was at the centre of the battlefield.

Lamorna jumped, her hand pressed against her heart. An owl was perched on the window ledge, blinking at her. She frowned. It was morning, not the time for owls. Maybe it was lost but, lost or not, she did not like the way it was staring at her.

She flicked her hand at it. 'Shoo.'

The bird did not move.

'Get out,' she commanded, waving her hands.

The owl took flight, but instead of leaving, it soared into the room, landing on one of the armchairs. Lamorna glared at it. It would leave a mess, no doubt. She was about to toss a cushion at it when there was a flash of light.

She stumbled back, hand over her mouth.

Where there had been an owl sat a man with shoulder-length dark hair and silver eyes. He was wearing a long coat, like a pirate, and carrying a dagger.

'Mordred!' she yelled.

He came racing into the room, stopping dead at the sight of this strange man sitting in their chair. Quickly, he seized Lamorna's arm, pulling her behind him.

The man in the chair chuckled and crossed long legs, putting his dirty boots on the small table. Lamorna peered at him from around Mordred's arm. The man had tattooed fingers, and his eyes, that unnatural colour …

He looked at her and the air around him shimmered. 'She who breathes when she should not,' he said.

The blood drained from her face. 'Get out,' she whispered. 'Whoever you are, get out!'

He laughed, and it sounded like thunder, dark and ominous. Mordred drew his dagger; the blade quickly turned red with heat. He dropped it and when he went to reach for it, it shot across the floor, landing near the silver-eyed man's chair.

'Mordred,' Lamorna said. She was frightened. 'Do something.'

'And what would you have him do? Fight me? He knows he cannot. He knows who I am,' the man said. 'But you do not. I am the Myrddin, Lamorna Astolat.'

She gasped. This was the Prophet of the Gods, the most powerful Magic Wielder in the world? She moved a little closer to Mordred, putting her hand on his back, feeling the tension in his muscles. She suddenly remembered Melodias' sword. Would Mordred go and get it? Would he try to do what the God of the Seas wanted?

'Did Arthur send you?' Mordred demanded. He made no move towards the sword. It was in their bedroom, leaning against the wall casually, like it deserved to be there.

'Arthur has no idea I'm here,' the Myrddin said.

'Then what do you want?' Mordred asked.

The Myrddin glanced around. 'It's been a long time since I sat in this room,' he commented, then his expression shifted. 'You think you're helping, Son of Inanna, but you are not.'

'I'm not here for Inanna,' Mordred said. 'I'm here for—'

'Yes, I know, and you have no idea what She wants, Mordred. None at all. You are interfering in things you have no comprehension of. The rules of this game were written a long time before you ever existed,' the Myrddin said. 'You should have listened to your mother. You should have stayed in Cruithea, under Inanna's care. You should have listened to the Red Sisters. Listen to her when she arrives, and perhaps, it is not too late to undo all the wrong you have done.'

He bent and picked up Mordred's dagger, twirling it between long fingers, watching as it turned blade over hilt and back again. 'Ereshki's love for her sister is the only reason I have not killed you,' he said. 'Because no matter what you think, you still belong to Inanna.' He leant forward, silver eyes pinned to Mordred's face. 'You know nothing, boy. Nothing at all. I've seen a King, I've served a King, and you are no King, Mordred.'

Mordred said nothing, but Lamorna heard his sharp intake of breath.

'I am here to warn you,' the Myrddin said. 'If you raise an army against Arthur, if you try to stop what he will build, it will not end well for you. I have seen the future and I know what is coming, but the future's not set in stone, not yet. You can still change what you have set in motion.'

'What does he mean?' Lamorna whispered, digging the points of her nails into Mordred's back.

The Myrddin's silver eyes met hers briefly, then flickered back to Mordred. He tossed the dagger onto the table. 'He knows what I mean. Stop what you are doing. Call back your envoys.'

Envoys? Lamorna frowned, shooting Mordred a curious look. He ignored her, his attention on the Myrddin.

'Enough of this,' Mordred growled. 'Get out.'

The Myrddin stood and stretched, so casual and calm. In the blink of an eye, he was gone. Lamorna gasped, rushing to the window, watching a brown owl soar away from the castle. She turned, worry thick in her throat. 'Mordred—'

Mordred bent and collected his dagger from the table, and when he straightened, he held a feather in his other hand. He met her eye. 'This changes nothing.'

'But—'

'Arthur is truly against me now.'

'Mordred, maybe—' Lamorna began, but he stormed from the room, slamming the door.

She glanced into their sleeping area. The sword stared back from its place against the wall.

Chapter 60

Arthur sat in Katarin's seat behind the grand timber desk, everyone else gathered on the other side.

'We need people on our side,' his sister announced. She was leaning against the windowsill in her cabin, arms folded. 'I never thought I'd be the one to say this, but we need help.'

'I know,' Arthur said wearily. 'But who do we ask? Teyath is fractured at the edges. Those who follow the Old Ones will want what Mordred wants, won't they? And those who follow Ereshki … there's division whichever way we look at it, especially after what Medb did in Malist. I'm not sure my little speech did anything to sway anyone to our side, not when their homes had just been destroyed and their loved ones murdered or ensorcelled.'

Melhala cleared her throat. 'I'll return to Cruithea, gather those able to fight – those willing to fight.'

'Will they stand against Mordred? He's the High Priestess' son,' Arthur pointed out.

'And you're the King they've been waiting for,' Melhala argued. 'They will follow you.'

'Even when I'm not going to be giving them the world they thought I would?' Arthur said, his voice lifting in frustration. He sighed, wanting to tear his hair out. He had never been so helpless. These people were looking to him for answers, and he had nothing to give them, not even a shred of hope. He could feel Jalen's absence like an open wound and wondered when, or if, it would ever stop hurting. 'I'm sorry. Any help anyone can give us will be welcome.'

Melhala frowned. 'I'll speak to the High Priestess. I'm sure she will agree that your way is best. She wouldn't condone what Mordred is doing, nor would Inanna.'

'Speaking of the Divine, I'll return to the Ossuary,' Olwen said.

'The Red Sisters are at Mordred's side as well, remember,' Jenyfer put in. 'They've taught him blood magic.'

'Not for the reasons you think,' Olwen said, shaking her head. She shared a look with Merlin. 'They are not helping him. They have been trying to guide him'

'The people of Kunis will follow you, Arthur,' Iouen said. Tristan nodded in agreement. 'If the Red One supports you, then they will. Tristan and I will go and bring you as many men as we can.'

'I'm going with you,' Tahnet announced. She glanced at Kat, who nodded reluctantly. 'Isolde as well. Those people are our people. We might be able to help sway them.'

Isolde nodded. 'I'll find my wild kin, if I can,' she said.

'Merlin?' Arthur asked. The Prophet was sitting in the corner, one leg crossed over the other, arms folded, a frown between his silver eyes. 'You're sure Mordred is gathering an army?'

'It has begun, but I can't fight this fight with you,' he said. 'I saw myself elsewhere, surrounded by white light.' He sighed. 'If that's death, then I welcome it. Three hundred years is a long time to be alive.'

No one knew what to say to that, so Arthur went on.

'I don't like the idea of everyone being spread across Teyath, but I'm not sure how else to manage this,' he said. 'Kat is right – we need an army of our own. Ankou has promised—'

'What has he promised you?' Merlin cut in sharply.

'I asked him for an army, and he told me I could have one,' Jenyfer said. 'But the Old Ones lie, so I'm not expecting him to fulfil that promise.'

'Interesting,' Merlin mused.

'Why?' Ordes asked.

'It means the God of the Otherworld has made his choice,' Merlin replied. 'Your mother will not be pleased.'

'I'm going to guess that she's already angry,' Ordes told his father. 'When she shows up, demanding some sort of divine vengeance or whatever, do you think you're capable of calming her down before she kills us?'

'She's likely to lock me up and throw away the key,' Merlin said.

Ordes' answering chuckle was dark. 'What will she do to the rest of us traitors?'

Arthur swallowed and turned away from the words Ordes did not say – it was Jalen's fault Niniane knew anything about their plans. It was Arthur's fault. 'It doesn't matter,' he heard himself say. 'We do what we have decided to do.'

'Right,' Iouen announced. 'My group will head to shore in the morning and start making our way north.'

'I'll travel with you,' Olwen said. 'Then leave you with the good people of Kunis.' She turned to Arthur. 'They're not soldiers, but they will fight for the Red One.'

'I don't want to go into this fighting under the banner of any of the Old Ones,' Arthur said firmly. He glanced at Iouen. 'Don't lie to them. Tell them … tell them Ereshki is on our side, but that we don't do anything in her name. Let them decide for themselves.'

Iouen nodded, but his face was troubled.

Arthur turned to Melhala and Ethinne. 'We're a long way from Cruithea.'

'We'll follow the Nemhain Mountains north. We'll avoid Camlann and your cousin,' Melhala said.

'Be careful,' Ordes told her. 'With Medb free, no doubt other things are also free.'

Melhala nodded. 'We'll manage between the two of us.'

'Right,' Arthur said. He reached for the stack of maps Katarin had rolled up on the table, hunting through them until he found one of Teyath. He chewed his lip, then laughed. 'I'm not a solider. I don't know the first thing about war or strategy, yet here I am planning … what? A battle?'

Kat squeezed his shoulder, then leant over the map, tracing the barren expanse of Camlann Plain. 'Halymere, how do we do this? We will have to gather our forces in one place.'

Halymere shook his head. 'Arthur's vision showed him Camlann, so that is where we need to be.' He glanced at Iouen and then Olwen. 'You will need to bring whoever you can find to Camlann from the east. Melhala, you'll come from the north.'

Arthur nodded, his eyes finding Jenyfer, then Ordes. 'And us?'

'From the west,' Jenyfer said resolutely. Her eyes were on the map. 'We'll come from the west. From Kernou.'

Arthur stared at the map. 'Alright,' he agreed. 'We return to Kernou.'

Kernou. The root cause of all Katarin's problems. She could barely remember her life there, but she remembered clearly the day it was taken from her.

Sighing, she reached up and rubbed at the back of her neck. Tension lingered in her muscles, as it had been since her brother and Merlin had wandered off for a stroll in the Faery Forest, leaving her waiting to see if Arthur would come back. Then it was Ordes and Malist, then the terrible waiting while he and Jenyfer went to The Teeth, and all that had happened since.

Kat wasn't one to avoid trouble. She didn't shy away from it, but right now, staring out at the ocean, at the reflection of the setting sun on the water, she felt old and tired. She needed sleep, but it had been eluding her, when she wasn't actively avoiding it. Sleep meant dreams, and she had been tormented by dreams of trees.

The door to her cabin opened without warning – no knock. Irritated, Katarin turned from the window as Olwen stepped in. Kat swallowed as the Red Sister closed the door, the action filled with purpose. Halymere's words – why do you push everyone away? – had sunk inside her so deeply Katarin could feel them in each beat of her heart. He was right. She didn't let people in. She didn't know how, and now Olwen was looking at her, dark eyes reading her face.

'Do I have a sign on my door that says come on in?' Katarin asked, trying to pull on the mask, to drag up the storm and bluster she had grown so accustomed to. Olwen did not respond. The other woman's expression was carefully composed as she strode across the floor to where Katarin stood. She did not stop at the desk, did not fling herself into a seat. She kept coming, eyes locked on Kat's. Kat took a step back, startled.

She never shied away from anything or anyone, but as the corners of Olwen's lips twitched, her mouth went dry. Memories of the last time they had been alone in this cabin barrelled through her without remorse.

Olwen stopped a mere handspan from Katarin. She was so close that Kat could see each freckle that splattered her nose like a miniature constellation. Kat's heart jumped as Olwen's fingers grazed her cheek, a teasing, testing touch. Their eyes met. Olwen was taller. Kat had never noticed, but now that difference in height had her pushing herself unconsciously onto her toes.

'You've been avoiding me,' Olwen accused softly.

Katarin shook her head. 'I'm the Captain of a ship. I'm busy.'

'Too busy to say hello? To even look at me?' Olwen replied.

'I …'

Olwen smiled. 'I understand. If the shoe was on the other foot, I'd probably be avoiding you as well,' she said. 'I'm terrible at thanking the person who saved my life.'

Katarin swallowed. 'I would have managed.'

'No, I'm not sure you would have,' Olwen said. 'Not because you're not brave and fierce – but because Medb …' Her voice trailed off. 'I wasn't about to let her kill you,' she murmured. Slowly, agonisingly so, she moved closer. Her breath brushed Katarin's mouth and every part of Katarin smouldered, ready to ignite, and she found she couldn't speak.

'I'm leaving soon,' Olwen said, voice husky, low. 'I could die.'

Kat swallowed, feeling the muscles in her thighs clench. 'How is that my problem?'

'I don't know yet,' Olwen replied. 'But I'll be fucked if I'm going to die without knowing what you taste like.' Her tongue flickered out, brushing Katarin's top lip.

Olwen pulled back a fraction, Kat's body screaming at the sudden absence of her.

Their eyes met again. Kat's breathing was thick, her chest heaving as her world narrowed to this moment, to the look in Olwen's dark eyes, to the overwhelming awareness of the current that flowed between them.

'Stop thinking,' Olwen told her. 'You always overthink.'

With a growl, Kat fisted her hands in the front of Olwen's shirt and yanked her close, bringing their mouths together. To shut her up. To wipe that knowing smirk off her face. To … the moment their lips touched, that fire in Katarin's belly roared into life.

Olwen's mouth was so warm, so alive, a blazing torch that burnt and ate at Kat's insides. Her skin tightened – it was painful, echoed in the throbbing between her legs. Their lips met again. Kat wound her fingers in Olwen's hair as Olwen's teeth grazed her lip. She groaned, squeezed between the glass and the warmth of Olwen's body.

'I'm not even sure I like you,' Kat said as Olwen's lips found her throat.

'You kiss me like you do,' was the reply, 'but the real question is, why are we standing here when you have a perfectly good – and ridiculously large – bed over there?'

Kat pushed the other woman away. Olwen's lips were swollen with kisses, her hair tousled. She didn't move, didn't speak. Whatever happened next was up to Katarin, and the power of that choice swept through her. For so long, Kat hadn't chosen anything for herself – she realised that now, after stepping back into the past. Everything in her life had been orchestrated by someone else, for some other purpose. She'd chosen Aelle, and now, she could choose this, even if it was a moment and nothing more. It was her choice.

Olwen smiled and took a step back, then another. With each step she took towards that bed, Katarin followed her. She took Olwen's face in her hands and kissed her until neither of them could breathe. Olwen's thigh was between her legs, pushing against the core of her, her hands pressed in the small of Katarin's back.

It was bliss, the feeling of those hands, the fingers long and strong, Olwen's lips soft, her mouth inviting, welcoming.

'I need to touch you,' Olwen whispered. 'Because, like I said—'

Katarin silenced her with another kiss as Olwen's fingers teased the edge of Katarin's shirt. They slipped beneath the fabric, leaving a trail of fire on Kat's flesh. Kat's breath hitched as those fingers brushed the underside of her breast, butterfly soft, delicate yet purposeful.

Kat sighed and closed her eyes. Her head tipped back involuntarily – wanting – and Olwen's lips walked the length of her throat, stopping beneath her ear. As Olwen's teeth closed gently over Kat's earlobe, she jolted, making the Red Sister chuckle.

'You've touched,' Katarin breathed. 'Now, you can taste.'

She'd barely gotten the words out when Olwen spun her around and pushed her onto the bed. Her hands went to work, fingers moving swiftly, tugging at buttons and cloth, and when her mouth brushed the sensitive skin of Kat's inner thigh, every muscle became as taut as a bowstring.

Olwen left a trail of fire from her knee to the top of Kat's thigh, lingering there between her legs. The desperate, hungry longing that surged through Katarin's blood was reflected in Olwen's face.

'I can't promise you anything,' Kat said.

'I know,' Olwen replied. 'But with your permission, Captain, I'm going to do my best to make you change your mind.'

Their eyes met, held for the space of one heaving breath, and then Olwen's mouth closed over the thrumming, burning heart of Katarin's body. Her back arched off the bed, mouth open as her eyes slipped closed, and she was swept away.

'Why are you here, Olwen?' Kat asked. They were sweat-soaked, lantern light gliding their naked flesh.

'Do you mean in your bed? Because, honestly, I thought you'd have kicked me out by now,' Olwen said cheekily, propping her head on her elbow. Dark brown hair fell to cover half of her face; absently, Katarin reached up and pushed it away, fingers lingering on Olwen's cheek.

'I meant on this ship. Why did you get involved in all of this?'

'The Red One—'

'No mystical shit,' Kat said. 'The truth.'

Olwen sighed. 'One of our Seers had a vision. She told me I needed to be on this ship, that I would find what I was looking for. I thought that meant Iouen – I had vowed to find him again. The Seer told me it was my destiny to be here.'

'Destiny.' Kat snorted half-heartedly.

'Whatever it was, I had days to mull it over. Plan how I would get onboard. I was going to stowaway, but you never brought the ship to the wharf – I didn't really think you would. I thought about rowing out and asking for work – whatever it took. But then you and Jenyfer turned the city upside down, and I was out of options,' Olwen said.

'So you chose to land on my deck in a haze of red smoke instead,' Kat mused.

Olwen grinned. 'Was it impressive?'

Kat laughed. 'Yes, it was actually. And it was terrifying.'

'Oh, the big bad pirate captain was afraid of little old me?' Olwen mocked. Kat pinched her, then pulled her close and kissed her.

'I hope you're not planning on dying,' she said.

'Oh?'

Kat ran the tip of her nose along Olwen's throat. 'I haven't thanked you properly yet.'

'Well, in that case, I'd better come back.'

Kat laughed and kissed her again, her hand shifting to close over Olwen's breast, before moving along the length of her spine, finding the gentle dip of her waist where Katarin had sunk her teeth into Olwen's flesh. She brushed the raised and damaged skin before she sighed and shifted away.

They lay side by side, the ocean stroking the hull of the ship.

'I should get up,' Katarin said eventually.

Olwen stretched. 'Yes, you're a very busy pirate captain who couldn't possibly do whatever she wanted for a while.' She shifted onto her side, propping herself onto her elbow. 'I'll see you before I go, if you can spare the time.'

Katarin gave her a wry smile. 'I'll have to check my schedule,' she quipped. 'Do you think you can find my brother an army?'

'Some of one,' Olwen replied. All the lightness had fled her face and Kat was almost sorry for asking. 'I can't make any promises about Kunis – that will be up to Iouen – but the Red Sisters will come. The Warriors of the Light will come.'

'What about the Sacellum?' Katarin asked, fidgeting with the sheet. 'Will they try to stop us?'

Olwen shook her head. 'The Sacellum has no power,' she said. 'Not anymore. The Witchfinders … will be dealt with.' She hesitated, her lip between her teeth. 'You still doubt the Red One's involvement in this?'

'It's a little hard not to,' Kat argued. 'I've only ever been told that Ereshki was a traitor.' She sighed, sitting up and running her hand over her face. 'But the Old Ones lie.'

'They do,' Olwen confirmed. Her fingertips trailed over the scars on Katarin's back. She didn't ask who hurt her, or how. Perhaps she already knew. 'But I don't lie. So when I say I will do my best – for Arthur, for the Red One – I mean it.'

Katarin nodded.

CHAPTER 61

Ordes glanced up as the sails snapped taut, a furious wind wrapping itself around the ship. Jenyfer shoved her hair out of her eyes as the clouds above transformed from bloated white to dark grey, shot through with deep purple bruises. Lightning bounced around within them. The crew were battling with the ferocity of the wind, Katarin shouting at them to tighten the sails before they lost the mast.

'Here she comes,' Ordes muttered to himself.

'This isn't a normal storm,' Jenyfer shouted, her voice snatched and tossed away as raindrops pelted them.

Ordes didn't take his eyes from the sky as it opened; water fell in sheets and the ocean seethed with unnatural anger. He pushed his damp hair from his forehead. 'I think we can assume my mother took the bait.'

A whirlwind of mist and shadow and storm clouds descended on the deck of *The Excalibur*. When it cleared, the Goddess of Magic was standing there, fists curled. Behind her stood the storm demon.

Jalen would not look at anyone.

Ordes turned his attention to his mother.

For a moment, he could see rage like fire brimming in those blue eyes. She was terrible and beautiful; her power throbbed through the air, like it had in Ankou's vision of the past. Her white gown was as light and insubstantial as smoke. Mist rose from the length of hair, spilling over her shoulders like a dark waterfall. The rain that drenched the world did not touch her.

Her gaze fell on Arthur, who had raced above deck, the Sword strapped to his hip. He stopped dead, face pale, at the sight of Jalen. Niniane's eyes fell to the Sword, before they settled on her son.

Ordes did not cower under the withering glare she sent him. He folded his arms instead, mustering up every ounce of courage he possessed. She could crush him, crush all of them, if she wanted, but she needed them.

'Hello, Mother. No armour? Can we assume you're not here for a fight? You'd need this, though, right?' Ordes clicked his fingers and the Bow of Mists, his mother's Treasure, her weapon of war, was in his hands. He slung it over his shoulder casually.

Ice-blue eyes narrowed.

'You're a long way from Avalon,' Ordes said. 'You told me you couldn't leave.'

'I lied,' she snapped.

'Go home, Niniane,' he said firmly. 'We've got nothing to say to you.'

'You don't understand what you're doing!' she said, taking a step towards him. Ordes sent her a warning look. 'If you let them choose, the humans of this land, you'll be condemning the Old Ones to death! You'll be condemning *me* to death. I'll cease to exist if belief in me, in magic, fades.'

Ordes said nothing.

'I'm your mother!'

'You are many things, but you are not my mother!' Something snapped inside him, that long held anger at her abandonment. His wings burst from his back. Niniane's eyes widened, but her smile was cunning, triumphant.

'Such power, Ordes,' she whispered.

He shrugged the Bow from his shoulder. Rage poured through him, omnipotent and omnipresent. He kept his eyes on Niniane. Calmly, hands steady, Ordes notched an arrow. He could feel everyone looking at him like he had lost his mind.

'You can't kill me,' Niniane said softly.

Before anyone could do anything, Ordes fired the arrow. It sailed towards her in slow motion, and then she was engulfed with shadowy mist. When it cleared, the Warrior Goddess was standing before them, clad in silver armour. 'And there she is,' he said.

'I don't take kindly to—' she began.

'To being a pawn in someone else's game?' Ordes said coldly. He notched another arrow and when he next spoke it was through his teeth. 'You used me. You used all of us. You've done nothing but manipulate and undermine us every step of the way.'

Niniane's face twisted. 'Your father—'

'Yes, my father. The man who helped you do this, but who also cared enough for *me* to take me from you and let me have a life. You're no mother, Niniane. Your machinations and schemes have done nothing but drive the world to the edge of destruction. I will not do a thing to help you,' Ordes bit out. He sent another arrow sailing in her direction, but this time it was the storm demon who deflected it.

Jalen's eyes blazed as he leapt to his mistress' defence. Lightning danced over his knuckles and his chest heaved.

'However much I might like to hurt you, Jalen, Arthur doesn't want that,' Ordes said. Jalen's eyes shifted to Arthur briefly, before swinging back to Ordes. In the blink of an eye, the storm demon was across the deck, his hand around Ordes' throat. The Bow vanished with a thought, and with both hands free, Ordes threw his fists at the demi-god, and received blow after blow in return. He couldn't hear what anyone was shouting over the roaring in his ears, over the thundering of his heart, of Jenyfer's heart, her anger mingling with his own.

Ordes and Jalen were a tempest of lightning and magic, storm clouds and wind.

Jalen was strong, but Ordes was stronger, the magic of both his parents flowing through him. He grabbed Jalen's wrist and twisted it sharp enough to break bones, driving the demi-god to his knees. Ropes of silver magic shot from his hand and wound around Jalen's torso, tightening in Ordes' closed fist. Jalen glared up at him, blue eyes dark. Ordes crouched so they were eye to eye.

'You think you're more powerful than I am?' he said, loud enough for everyone to hear. 'She might be your mistress, she might have a rope around your neck, demi-god, but she made me. Her power is my power.' A strange thread was visible between Jalen and Niniane, thin and transparent. Ordes suddenly understood what he was seeing. His hand shot out, and he closed his fingers around Jalen's throat, while the other grasped the magical thread. Jalen gasped.

'Ordes!' Arthur's voice, tight, broken. 'Don't!'

'What would happen if I ripped you lose?' Ordes asked, voice low, leaning over to place his mouth close to Jalen's ear.

'You'll kill me,' Jalen hissed.

'Not if you get yourself somewhere else before the end,' Ordes whispered. Jalen shook his head. 'If you won't let me do it, find a way to do it yourself, Jalen. You did it before, so do it again. If not for yourself, then for Arthur. Whether you believe it or not, he needs you.'

'I …'

'You've got a choice,' Ordes said quickly. 'Serve her and remain a slave, or take back your free will.' He let Jalen go, pushing the demi-god back across the deck with his magic. Jalen landed in a heap before his Goddess. He slowly got to his feet and stepped away.

Niniane narrowed her eyes at him, then turned her fury on her son. She didn't attempt to strike him, with fist or weapon or magic, but when she spoke, her voice rang with power, a command. 'Kneel!'

Ordes watched those around him slowly lower their weapons and sink to their knees.

Everyone except him.

'You can't control me,' he told her.

'The future of the world is at stake!' Niniane's voice rose.

'I know!' Ordes shouted. Thunder rumbled overhead. 'But the decision is not yours, Niniane, however much you wish it was. It wasn't then, and it isn't now.'

Niniane laughed, a dreadful, horrible laugh. 'She got to you. I don't know how, but Ereshki got to you. She's filled your head with the same poison she filled Enyon and Eseld's heads with. She's a blight on this world. A parasite who does not have the strength to be what she was made to be – a goddess, a divine power. She should demand the world bow to her, to all of us.'

'Niniane, enough.' Merlin's voice rang out across the deck. Ordes turned to watch his father approach. People were slowly getting to their feet. Jenyfer's face was a mask of fury as she glared at the Goddess of Magic. Ordes knew, if she could, she'd sing his mother into her grave.

'Fashionably late, as always,' he told his father.

Merlin gave him a crooked smile and approached Niniane, coming to stand in front of her, his hands held out as if in surrender. 'I told them the truth, my love.'

She stared at him. The air around her shifted with her breath, magic rippling across the ship. 'Traitor!' she hissed.

'They deserved to know,' Merlin said, calm in the face of the Goddess' rage. 'I like seeing the real you,' he told her. 'Full of fury and vengeance, like you were when we first met. Do you remember that day?'

Niniane's fists were curled.

Merlin simply smiled. 'You were the most glorious creature I had ever seen.'

Ordes watched in disbelief as his father held out his arms. Niniane glared at him, and then stepped into them, turning dark eyes on Ordes over his father's shoulder, before her face relaxed and her body shimmered. The armour vanished, and she was once again wearing her shimmering, white gown.

'Go home,' Merlin told her gently. She mumbled something no one could hear. Ordes watched them, unable to believe what he was witnessing, unsure of what power his father held over her.

With a sigh, Niniane stepped away from Merlin. Jalen lingered behind her, his eyes downcast. There were no marks on his throat, nothing to reveal what Ordes had done to him.

And nothing on his face to reveal what words had passed between them.

'Say your goodbyes, demi-god,' Niniane ordered, and then she was gone.

Arthur stood on the opposite side of his cabin from Jalen. There were so many things he needed to say, but the words refused to form, turning to dust in his mouth. He wanted to lower his eyes, to cry, but he didn't. He kept his chin lifted and his voice, when he finally spoke, was firm.

'Have you been spying on us this whole time?' he asked bluntly. 'Did you tell her everything? Every conversation? Every moment shared?'

'Yes,' Jalen breathed.

'Why?'

Jalen's eyes burnt – anger, pain, resentment. 'Because I have to! If she asks me a question, I have to answer. You don't understand what it means to be bound to the Goddess of Magic. I cannot lie to her. I tried, but it was like my insides were being ripped from my body and she knew, Arthur, she knew.'

'So was that all it was to you? You and me? All part of the role you had to play?' Arthur said. When Jalen didn't respond, when he turned his eyes to the floor, Arthur swallowed and made himself speak. 'Was any of it real?'

'Yes, Arthur. Gods yes. I love you,' Jalen said. He took a step forward and Arthur wanted so badly to close the gap between them, but he didn't move.

'You lied to me. Whether intentional or not, you didn't tell me the truth. What happened to believing in me? To trusting me?' Arthur asked. He kept his hands in his pockets, fists curled tight, his emotions swirling around his head. Love, hurt, anger, pride … all coalescing in one great thunderstorm that he wasn't sure how long he could hold back.

He was not the same man Jalen knew in Kernou.

He was not the man who would beg, not anymore.

'I gave her my allegiance,' Jalen said sorrowfully. He dragged his hand through his hair. Arthur's heart pinched, but he pushed it away.

'In exchange for what?' Arthur shouted, anger roaring through him. Jalen flinched. 'For being able to get close to me? For making me trust you enough that I would share *everything* with you? I thought you'd given your allegiance to me? Or was that another lie, so long as your Goddess got what she wanted?'

'I'll find a way to make this up to you.' Jalen's voice broke. 'I'll find a way.'

'Even if you could, this isn't about me any more, Jalen. This isn't about us. It's about everyone on this ship. All these people who have chosen to support me. It's about Jen and Ordes,' Arthur said. 'It's about the people of this world and what the future will look like for them.'

'You don't want her as your enemy. She could crush you all, except perhaps her son. That little display up there was a mere performance. She's the Goddess of Magic! You don't understand her power,' Jalen said, the words rushing out of him, panicked, tight and breathless, as if it hurt to say them. 'You don't want her against you.'

'And if it comes to it? Will you stand with her?' Arthur asked.

Jalen laughed, dark and bitter. 'I won't have a choice. Sometimes I know I made a mistake leaving Ankou, but I can't go back and change it. I can't. When Merlin spoke his prophecy, all those years ago, I latched onto the idea of a king who would see the world as it once was – wondrous and terrible and better than the future we faced. But Ankou did not share my vision. When I broke our bond, I had minutes until I would die. I made it to Avalon, half dead. Before she returned my life to me, Niniane made me swear myself to her,' Jalen said. 'But she wanted what I wanted – magic and power back in the world, the Old Ones reigning once more. That was the life I knew, the world I knew. So I gave her what was left of me.'

'Things can't ever return to what they were, Jalen,' Arthur said, even though his heart ached at the look on his face – regret and sorrow. 'I thought you understood that.'

Jalen sighed and looked at the floor.

'You can't stay here. Those people up there can't trust you. I can't trust you,' Arthur said. He kept his voice strong, controlled, but all he wanted was to fall to his knees and sob like a child. He made himself speak. 'She sent you to manipulate me.'

'She sent me to guide you.'

'You tried to influence my choices, Jalen, ever since I found out who I was destined to be. You tried to get me to choose the world *you* wanted, the world Niniane wants,' Arthur said. 'That's manipulation. There is no other word for it, and I can't believe I didn't ...' He shook his head. 'Katarin will kill you if you stay here.'

'I know. I welcome it. Let her flay the skin from my body, over and over, until there's nothing left of me. When I don't die, tell her to wait, then do it again. Or you can do it yourself. I'd deserve nothing less,' Jalen added.

Arthur made a choking sound. 'I don't want that! But I don't want you here at the moment, either. I can't have you here. Don't you see? Niniane is the reason we've made the choice we have – Niniane and all those who want to control others through magic. It can't be like that again, Jalen. The world deserves better than that.' Arthur paused, rubbing at his eyes.

Jalen took a step closer, his face broken. 'She can cast me into the sea to die a true death before I do anything to hurt you, Arthur,' he said, his face shifting as the words left his lips.

'It's too late for that,' Arthur said. He nodded at the door. 'You need to go.'

Jalen moved towards the door, taking another piece of Arthur's heart with him. He did not look at Arthur when he spoke, his voice low, fractured and bleeding.

'I know you don't believe it right now, but I do love you. For the man you are, right now. For the man you will be. No matter what happens, you are the right person for this,' Jalen said softly. 'Merlin got that part right, at least.'

He put his hand on the doorknob. Arthur's heart seized.

He saw Jalen's shoulders shake as he took a deep breath.

'The future you want, Arthur – make sure you get it.'

CHAPTER 62

Lamorna had not yet seen the new arrivals from Cruithea, but she had heard about them. Only a handful of people had arrived, but Mordred was pleased – he was smiling when he finally came to bed. She was too tired to ask many questions, like when he had invited them. She took a moment to smile to herself as the mattress dipped with the weight of him and he curled his body against hers.

She'd never imagined she would end up sharing a bed with a man. The Sisters in the Sacellum only had thin beds with thin mattresses. That had been the life she had imagined for herself – one of servitude and prayer, of plain food and hours spent devoted to the Word. Now, that imagined life truly was like a dream that belonged to another young woman in another village somewhere in Teyath.

As Mordred's arm closed around her middle, Lamorna closed her eyes and let sleep pull her under. The strangeness of the castle no longer bothered her. All these people living here beneath the same roof no longer bothered her. She had Mordred, and she had Calla and the others. She had purpose once again.

When she woke, Mordred was gone, but only recently. The mattress was still coated in his warmth. Lamorna dressed and washed her face, tying her hair in a simple knot at the base of her neck. It was longer than it had ever been, and it annoyed her some days. She checked her reflection in the mirror, taking a moment to marvel at herself.

She had decided she liked her eyes best of all. She liked the blue of them – not as blue as the sky or the stormy blue-grey of the ocean, like Jenyfer's were, but a sharp pale blue. She liked her eyelashes – they were longer than she had imagined. Lamorna stepped back, so she could see more of herself. The soft grey dress she wore accentuated the shape of her. Slowly, Lamorna ran her hands over her hips. She'd never seen her body look like this before, her curves fluid, graceful. Beautiful. And her face. Her cheekbones were higher than she'd ever realised, her brows delicately arched, her nose pert, and her lips bee-stung and plump. Mordred had told her her lips were made to be kissed, and looking at them now, she decided he was right. She lifted her finger to her lips, tracing the bow-like shape of them, not taking her eyes from her reflection.

Satisfied, she wandered down to the kitchen for a few slices of dark bread. There had been baskets of fresh vegetables and fruit on one of the benches. The Cruitheans had brought the food, someone told her. She smiled. Mordred had said he would fix their food problem and he had. Maeve placed a mug in front of her.

'The goats are finally giving milk,' she said, and turned back to overseeing the younger of her staff. They were carrying sacks, one between two of them, to the store rooms at the far end of the kitchen. Lamorna drank the milk, grateful to have something to soften the bread, then went back up the stairs in search of Mordred. He would be in the Hall, she decided. It was where he usually was first thing in the morning.

The castle was busy – people rushed about, some carrying bedding to be aired and cleaned, others baskets of clothes for washing. They had discovered an underground spring, and the men had uncovered a well in the castle grounds.

Lamorna paused by one of the windows, looking out over the vast brown of Camlann Plain. It was so lifeless, so still, out there on the plain. Nothing moved. Nothing was green. The cursed soil stretched on forever. She knew people were apprehensive, but that they were also making the best of things. Raised garden beds were being constructed, and would fill the courtyard at the rear of the castle. Soil would be brought in from elsewhere and hopefully, whatever they planted there would grow.

Turning from the window and the achingly blue sky, Lamorna continued through the castle. It was always dark in these halls. Lanterns were lit along the walls, wax building up and dripping to the stones below. They had done their best to make this castle habitable, but there was still a long way to go to make it feel like a home. She wondered whether it ever would. It was too big, too grey, and too cold.

Two members of the Red Hand guarded the door to the Hall. Lamorna could not remember their names, and didn't care to remember. They did not look at her, but one pushed the heavy oak doors open. She lifted her chin and swept in, her footsteps echoing off the stone, and stopped.

Mordred was not alone. There was a man with him, a Cruithean by the way he was dressed. Something about him tugged at Lamorna's memory.

She frowned. The man was sitting close to Mordred, much closer than anyone else did except for her. She cleared her throat. Mordred looked up, saw her, and smiled.

'I don't believe I introduced you last time, Lamorna,' he said, his voice like silk. He did not rise to greet her, like he usually would. 'This is Alden, a … friend.'

Alden tipped his head in Lamorna's direction. He was lean, his body not as muscular as Mordred's, and his hair was long and black, falling like spilled ink over his shoulders. His skin was dark as shadows.

'Alden was one of my Inborn,' Mordred said.

'I still am,' Alden interrupted. He lay his hand on Mordred's arm, and Lamorna sucked in a breath, suddenly remembering.

Alden smiled at her. 'The last time we met, we were both wearing nothing but what we were born in,' he said, his eyes lingering on her body, suggesting he remembered that night clearly.

Heat scorched Lamorna's cheeks. She could barely remember Fire Night, could barely remember the man sitting on Mordred's bed.

'What are you doing here?' she asked, coming further into the room. There were drums in her head. She pushed them away, hesitated and then boldly announced, 'You're in my seat, Alden.'

He laughed. Lamorna wondered if she had overstepped, but Mordred looked amused. Alden vacated the seat, pushing the chair in for her as she sat.

'Thank you,' she said in her most polite voice. She turned to Mordred. 'I saw all the fresh food in the kitchens.'

'A gift from Cruithea,' Mordred said.

'Sort of,' Alden chimed in. He was now sitting across from Lamorna, brown eyes walking her face.

'Oh?' she said lightly. Inside, her heart was tight as she remembered the way Mordred and Alden had kissed one another on Fire Night.

'Alden has brought you a gift also,' Mordred said.

Lamorna raised her eyebrows.

'You were right – she came because you asked,' he said, and Lamorna leapt up.

'Where is she?' she breathed. Tamora had come!

Alden smiled, then turned to Mordred. 'Family is important, is it not?' he paused, reaching across the table to touch Mordred's hand again. Lamorna bristled inside, but said nothing. 'Your mother has come also, Mordred.'

Mordred's eyes narrowed. 'The High Priestess is here? Why didn't you say that last night?'

'We arrived so late. Your mother wished to rest. She was given a suitable room, don't worry,' Alden said, his voice soft. 'I will get her for you.'

Mordred nodded, and when Alden had gone, Lamorna squeezed his hand. 'You do not wish to see her?'

'I do,' he murmured. They sat in silence, Lamorna trying not to bounce in her seat. She wanted to see her aunt, but knew she needed to wait. She did not ask Mordred if he wanted her to stay while he met with his mother. She could sense he needed her. He had not let go of her hand. She wove her fingers through his and squeezed in reassurance.

The doors to the hall opened and Alden entered, closely followed by the High Priestess of Cruithea and Tamora. Lamorna beamed at her aunt. She jumped to her feet and rushed around the long table, taking her aunt's hands, not caring anymore that Morgause was there, or that she had left Mordred's side.

'I am so happy to see you!' she gushed.

Her aunt looked at her, eyes combing her exposed hair, her face, the dress. 'Lamorna,' Tamora breathed at last, and folded her in her arms. Lamorna took her hand, aware of all the questions in her aunt's eyes, and led her to a seat at the table. She resumed her place next to Mordred, and at last, raised her eyes to Morgause. Mordred had not said a word to his mother.

Morgause stood tall, back straight, her eyes on her son. She was dressed in dark brown trousers and a fitted shirt. Weapons dangled from her belt, her bare arms showing off the swirling ink of her warrior tattoos, so like her son's. Lamorna frowned. To her, Morgause was pale, her breathing laboured, deep shadows beneath her eyes.

The High Priestess' eyes found Lamorna. 'This isn't for her ears.'

'Whatever you need to tell me, you can say in front of Lamorna,' Mordred said.

Morgause's eyes narrowed, but then she sighed. 'Very well. It has been made clear to me that you have no intention of returning to Cruithea. You still have friends there, Mordred.'

'My friends are here,' he said.

'Come home,' she said.

Mordred frowned. 'Why are you here, mother?'

'Your place is in Cruithea—'

Mordred slammed his hand on the table. Lamorna and Tamora jumped. 'Cruithea? Cruithea has given me nothing,' he snarled, his expression dark and bitter. 'You have given me nothing. Why should I return to a world where I am nothing? Inanna does not care for me – she never has, and the fact you still believe she cares for you makes me wonder.'

Morgause did not reply.

'What's wrong with you?' Mordred demanded suspiciously. 'Usually you'd fight me if I said something you consider heresy.'

The High Priestess turned her attention to Lamorna. She smiled sadly. 'Had I have known that first night you and your aunt stumbled into the forest that it would be you to lead my son on this path, I'd have slit your throat,' she said, so matter-of-factly that Lamorna's blood ran cold, her fingers lifting to her throat unconsciously. Beside her, Tamora paled.

Mordred scowled at his mother. 'Lamorna did not do this. Leaving was my decision, just as coming here to this place was my decision. I'll ask again – why have you come?'

'I'm dying,' Morgause answered, so calm, so regal, that Lamorna gasped on her behalf, despite what she had said. Instinctively, Lamorna knew the High Priestess of Cruithea would not harm her, not now.

Mordred's face had frozen. 'How long?'

'Not long. Weeks, maybe, if I'm lucky.' She nodded at Tamora. 'My healer did not want me to make the journey here, fearing it would make my condition worse, but I needed to see you, Mordred,' Morgause said.

'Mother—'

Her expression became sorrowful. 'I needed to see what you had become, so I could see where I had failed.'

Tamora touched Lamorna's arm. 'Come,' she said. Lamorna glanced at Mordred, but his eyes were on his mother, his face a thundercloud of swirling emotion. Lamorna let her aunt guide her to her feet, and as they left the hall, Morgause sank into a seat.

Lamorna took her aunt to her room. 'We believe this was Eseld's room, the old Queen of this place,' she said importantly as she opened the door and led Tamora inside.

'It has a lovely view,' Lamorna continued, going to the window in the sitting area and gesturing at the world outside. The Nemhain Mountains were visible in the distance, their tallest peaks scraping the cloudless sky. She sighed. 'It never rains here,' she said, taking a seat in one of the soft armchairs, nodding at the other.

Tamora sat, eyes wide, her face tight. Lamorna did not mention the grey that streaked her aunt's hair or the shadows under her eyes.

'Oh,' Lamorna said instead, jumping up. 'I'll send for some tea.'

'Lamorna,' her aunt said wearily.

'It's no bother,' Lamorna said.

Tamora's voice became sharp. 'Lamorna. Sit down.'

Lamorna did, frowning. Then, she smiled. 'I am so happy you're here!'

Tamora rubbed at her temples, her expression conflicted. 'What are you doing, Lamorna?'

'What do you mean?'

'Here, in this cursed place. What are you doing *here*? Why did you leave Kernou?'

'Why, for Mordred, of course,' Lamorna said simply.

'What has *happened* to you?' her aunt whispered, aghast.

'Nothing has happened to me,' Lamorna argued. She frowned. 'I thought you might be happy to see me, Aunt Tamora. I thought you would be pleased I—'

'Pleased? I'm confused, my girl!' Tamora said. She sighed and leant forward, eyes pinned to Lamorna's face. 'While I am pleased that you are alive and seemingly safe, I am confused as to *why* you are here at all! And please, don't tell me it was for Mordred. I am not an idiot. I know he's sharing your bed and I know he has been since you were in Cruithea,' she paused, shaking her head. 'I thought I was doing the right thing in bringing you there.'

'You did,' Lamorna said. 'Tamora, everything is going to be fine. I mean, yes, the castle is not overly cosy, and there is work to be done, but Mordred is—'

Tamora sat back and closed her eyes briefly. 'Goddess save me,' she muttered. She fixed Lamorna in a piercing gaze. 'What about the One God? Have you lost your faith?'

'Why do you care?' Lamorna shot back. She sighed, and then told her aunt what she had learnt about the One God. Tamora's eyes were wide. She opened her mouth, but Lamorna went on before her aunt could speak. 'The Chif was not pleased, of course. But, I have decided it does not matter. I have not lost my faith – I have had my eyes opened and, for the first time in my life, I see things clearly.'

'I'm terribly certain you do not, Lamorna,' her aunt said. 'Ever were you one to follow and not question,' she muttered under her breath, but Lamorna heard. She stood, angry now, and returned to look out the window.

'I shouldn't be surprised,' she said eventually. 'You always cared more for Jenyfer than me. She's fine, by the way. Out on that ship. Her, that pirate she loves, and Arthur Tregarthen. They found the Treasures of the Gods, in case you're interested. Medb told us, after her and her ghastly fey sacked Malist. The city is destroyed. Pity. I always wanted to go there.' She turned back to her aunt. Tamora's mouth was hanging open, eyes wide, her skin pale beneath her bright orange mane. 'So,' Lamorna said. 'There you have it.'

Her aunt put her head in her hands as Lamorna turned back to the view.

Chapter 63

Arthur found himself alone in the galley. He had no idea what time it was. His head ached. His heart hurt, and beneath the pain was an emptiness he wasn't sure would ever go away.

Someone cleared their throat. Ordes strolled into the room. The other man hesitated, and then took a seat opposite Arthur.

'I wanted to apologise,' Ordes said.

'For what?'

'For putting my hands around Jalen's throat.'

Arthur swallowed as his muscles tightened painfully. 'It's alright.'

'He's as much a victim of my mother's lies as the rest of us,' Ordes said. His voice softened with reassurance. 'I don't believe he'd have left you if he had any other choice, Arthur.'

Arthur nodded, but he wasn't sure he believed that, not fully. 'You tried to kill your mother,' he said, mouth dry.

Ordes shrugged and sat back. 'I knew I couldn't. But I wanted her to know how much I utterly despise her existence.' He sighed and snapped his fingers – a bottle of rum and two glasses appeared on the table between them. Ordes poured two drinks and slid one to Arthur. The glass was cool to touch, and Arthur wrapped both hands around it, enjoying the chill.

Ordes smiled and raised his glass in a toast. 'To us, I guess. You're destined for great things. And I'm … well, I'm whatever I am. It no longer worries me. I no longer need an answer to those questions.'

Arthur clinked his glass with Ordes' and drank, then held out the glass for a top-up.

'When Jenyfer left me, I spent two months at the bottom of one of these things,' Ordes said. He examined the bottle of rum, then filled Arthur's glass. 'I didn't know what to do without her. I didn't see the point in anything. I didn't understand it, at the time. It was the heartfire. You're stronger than you think. I know you're hurting, Arthur, but you haven't curled into a ball in the corner. You're still here, making choices, being a leader. It takes a level of strength to pick yourself up and keep going.'

Something stirred to life in Arthur's mind, a distant memory of a moment he had forgotten, a thread of the fabric that had been his life in Kernou. 'I'd seen you before I met you.'

'In a dream-dream or a real-dream?' Ordes asked, eyebrows raised.

'In a book,' Arthur said, his eyes running over Ordes' face, comparing the shadows of memory to the man sitting across from him. 'The more I think about it, the more I realise I'm right. There was a book in my father's study, a beautifully bound copy of the Word, and in it were pictures painted in glorious detail. I used to sneak a look at them. I wasn't supposed to touch that particular copy – my father told me it had been scribed by the One God Himself. Herself,' he corrected.

'What has this got to do with me?' Ordes drummed his fingers on the side of his glass.

Arthur smiled, excited. 'Ordes, after all we have learnt, is it really such a stretch to believe there would be a picture of you in a book written by Ereshki's hand?'

Ordes stared at him, then shook his head. 'But how would she have known—'

'The figure in the painting was winged and holding a bowl … the Grail, perhaps,' Arthur said. He leant forward. 'What if, and hear me out, what if she knew of you before you existed?'

'How would she?' Ordes said, frowning.

'She's a goddess,' Arthur pointed out. 'And your father—'

Ordes scowled. 'If he's still lying to us, I swear I'll shoot him instead of my mother.'

Arthur shook his head and sat back, chewing his lip thoughtfully. 'Okay, let's say, for the sake of argument, Ereshki saw you herself. It would make sense, wouldn't it? You heard what she told Inanna in that vision, or whatever it was, that Ankou showed us. "An angel's wings shall turn to dust".'

'I'm no angel,' Ordes said with a bitter laugh.

'We don't *know* that,' Arthur argued. The two men looked at one another. Ordes' gaze dropped to his hands as he stared at the symbols inked onto his knuckles. Gently, he ran his thumb over the symbol Arthur had learnt meant love.

'Were you or Jen in that book?' Ordes asked slowly.

'Why would we be?' Arthur replied. 'We're not the ones who will carry the weight of the worlds, Ordes.'

'No, but you're the one who will—'

'No, I'm the one who will *find* the Grail, remember. We all wield it together, but you are the one who will carry it,' Arthur said. 'The one who stands between the worlds shall bear the weight of them both. What else could that mean, except that, for some reason, *you* will carry the Grail.'

Ordes said nothing. Eventually, he took a deep breath. 'Let's say you're right, and a goddess knew to draw a picture of me in a book – how does my father's prophecy fit into the Word?'

Arthur frowned. 'I don't know. I'd never heard the prophecy before all this happened. But Olwen said the Word I knew was not the one that Ereshki wrote, that it had been altered, corrupted, by man.'

'Any idea where we would find a copy of the original Word?' Ordes asked.

'That might be a question for our Red Sister before she leaves,' Arthur mumbled.

Ordes stood. 'Then maybe it's time we had another chat about religion.'

Olwen had been expecting them. The Red Sister was sitting on the steps leading to the quarterdeck. Ordes had collected Jenyfer along the way, and the three of them stood before Olwen. The night sky was a blanket of stars. Arthur glanced up briefly, trying to pick out some of the constellations he knew, but this was not the sky he was familiar with. They were still a long way from Kernou.

Olwen's dark eyes moved from Arthur's face to Jenyfer's, settling on Ordes'.

'Carbrey,' Ordes called – the sailor was on watch, but Ordes did not look at him. He stared at Olwen and the Red Sister continued to stare back. 'Can we have the deck for a moment?'

It wasn't until the old man climbed down the ladder into the darkness below that Olwen spoke, her voice low, soft, and ringing with a strange power.

'On barren field of cursed earth, a veil of green will be rebirthed. An angel's wings shall turn to dust, in the Word you all must trust. By scale and soil and wind and air, the Grail shall sing the world's repair. Three destinies as one will dawn, entangled,' she intoned, her eyes moving over them one at a time, settling on Arthur. 'So a King is born.'

They stared at her, dumbfounded.

Olwen's smile was smug. 'Within the Red One's Word are the answers you seek,' she said, her eyes finding Arthur again. 'Answers you already know.'

Ordes shared a glance with the others. 'We've heard that rhyme before.'

'Where?' Olwen demanded.

Arthur shook his head. 'It's … too hard to explain right now, but let's say someone showed us what has already happened. How do you know those words?'

'Because they are in the Word,' Olwen told them.

'But they're not,' Jenyfer objected.

'Not in the version you know,' Olwen said. She reached behind her, retrieving an item covered in thick, red cloth. She rested it in her lap and slowly unwound the cloth. It was a book, bound in dark leather, the edges of the pages gilded in gold. There was no title splashed across the front in gold lettering, nothing to signify what it could possibly be. Olwen ran her fingers over the cover gently. 'I took this from the Sacellum, before all the shit went down, and have been waiting for the perfect moment to give it to you. This is that moment,' she said. She stared at the book for a moment, then held it out for Arthur to take. 'The answers you seek.'

Arthur took the book carefully. He did not open it. It was bound in leather that looked black, but could have been blood-red. The leather was cracked with age beneath his fingers. He traced the spine of the book.

'That is believed to be the oldest copy of the Word in existence,' Olwen told them. 'Whatever you do, don't drop the fucking thing overboard,' she added, narrowing her eyes in warning.

Arthur barked a laugh. 'I won't.'

Olwen stood to go. 'That's all the help I can give you – that's all the help the Red One has said I am to give you. It is up to the three of you to work out what She wanted you to do with this knowledge.'

Jenyfer frowned. 'Wait. Those words – Merlin's prophecy, rewritten – there was a line missing from your version. "A song shall sing the Red Ones home, forever entombed in the House of Bone." Why isn't that there? And what does it mean?'

Olwen's voice was low. 'What do you think it means?'

'Before we knew the truth, I would have said it meant that I was supposed to use my voice to trap the Red Ones in the Ossuary,' Jenyfer said. 'But now …'

'It isn't to be taken literally,' Olwen said. 'And it's actually Red One, not Red Ones. It is beyond me why Merlin didn't tell you that.'

Ordes muttered something savage under his breath. Olwen flashed a grin, before she grew serious again. 'The Red One will leave this world and therefore her house, the House of Bone, shall be her tomb, not ours. We have always been free to make our choices, Jenyfer. She does not ask for our lives, only our belief in Her.'

Jenyfer exhaled, her whole body going slack. Ordes slipped his arm around her, pulling her close. 'So I won't be singing you and your Sisters to your death?' she asked Olwen.

Olwen grinned. 'You sound disappointed.'

'No,' Jenyfer said, shaking her head. 'I'm relieved.'

Arthur didn't like this, but they needed help. With Mordred holed up at Dinas Emrys, Medb who knew where, and now Niniane furious with them, they needed an army of their own more than ever. They had dropped anchor off the southern coast. The Vale was the nearest town, but it was not The Vale they were headed to.

They had taken four boats over, leaving them high up the beach. Katarin walked ahead of Arthur. She had been unusually quiet. He wondered if he needed to ask her if she was okay, but she was likely to lie and tell him everything was fine.

Everyone had been telling him everything was fine, as if they did not want to burden him with anything more than he was already carrying. But he needed it – he *wanted* the extra burden, as a distraction more than anything else, especially now with their group breaking off onto separate paths.

Further ahead of him walked Melhala and Ethinne, Halymere close behind them. Olwen and Iouen followed, talking in low voices. Tristan and Isolde walked hand in hand, with Katarin and Jen sandwiched between them and Arthur. Somewhere above them was Ordes; a shadow passed over them briefly, and then was gone.

When they cleared the trees, Ordes was waiting for them, grey feathered wings folded against his body. The Nemhain Mountains stood behind him, clouds wrapped around their peaks. They weren't far from the Faery Forest – Arthur wondered where the dryad who had guarded the Sword was now that she was no longer bound to the Treasure.

Olwen strode into the clearing and dumped her pack on the ground, turning and waiting for the rest of them to catch up. 'Well,' she said. 'No need to put this off, I guess.'

The Red Sister drew her dagger and ran the blade over her palm. She closed her eyes and as each droplet of her blood fell, the earth shuddered. Arthur blinked, as those around him gasped in shock.

Four horses stood before Olwen. Four living, breathing horses.

Iouen cocked his head to the side, casting a critical eye over them. 'Do you think they could be less … red, Olwen? Nothing screams magic like a blood-red horse.'

Olwen scowled at him and waved her hand at the horses. They shimmered and turned reddish-brown. 'Better?'

Iouen screwed up his face. 'Still a little—'

'Fuck off, Iouen, or walk,' Olwen snapped. He grinned at her, approaching his blood-horse and running his hand over it. Satisfied, he tangled his hands in the mane and pulled himself onto its back. He held out his hand to Tahnet, and pulled her up behind him. Jenyfer passed up a pack, which Tahnet slipped over her shoulder.

Olwen turned to Melhala and Ethinne. The Cruitheans were watching her. Melhala's eyes narrowed in suspicion, her arms folded.

'It's a long way to Cruithea,' Olwen said.

Melhala said nothing. Ethinne whispered to her, and Melhala sighed and nodded.

Ethinne was the one to approach Olwen. The Priestess and the Red Sister stared at one another, chosen daughters of the Sister Goddesses everyone had thought were at war with one another.

Merlin had called Inanna and Ereshki the Two in One, and now, Arthur could see it – Ethinne, bright as the sun, and Olwen, dark and powerful. So different, yet so similar.

Ethinne smiled. 'If you are willing, Olwen, we would appreciate your help.'

'Are you sure Inanna will approve of my heretical magic?' she asked, echoing Melhala's earlier words. Ethinne smiled.

'It is, after all, for the greater good. I don't think even Inanna would argue with that, not if what we have learnt is true,' she said.

Olwen glanced at Melhala, who gave her a brisk nod, and soon, two more magical horses stood before them. 'Right, if no one else wants me to bleed for them, we'll get moving,' she said. Arthur nodded, and the Red Sister pulled herself onto her horse, while Tristan and Isolde did the same. The Witchfinder and the skinroamer smiled at each other, and Arthur was struck once more at how love didn't care what someone was, whether they were friend or foe, familiar or not. Love *was*.

Until it wasn't.

He looked away from Tristan and Isolde to watch Olwen and Katarin exchange a long look. Arthur watched his sister's cheeks colour, but she smiled.

'Be careful,' he said as Melhala and Ethinne climbed onto their horses. 'Don't risk yourselves, please. Please don't—'

'We all risk no more than anyone else does,' Melhala cut in. 'We will bring you an army, Arthur.'

'And what an army it will be,' Halymere called.

'Well, we can't promise an army,' Iouen said. 'But we'll bring you who or what we can find.'

'Have you looked at the book yet?' Olwen asked. Arthur shook his head. She shifted her eyes to Ordes. 'You won't like what I'm about to say because I know how humble and modest you are. And powerful. Let's not forget that. Please don't hurt me.'

Katarin laughed. Ordes rolled his eyes.

'Once you read the book, you'll understand,' Olwen went on, her grin fading. She nudged her horse in the ribs; the magical beast moved closer to Ordes, who reached out to pet it. 'All those places who have turned or have begun their turning to the One God – get your pretty face and your pretty wings out there, Ordes. Show those to the faithful, like you did in Malist. Let them see who and what you are.' She looked around at them all. 'Can any of you draw?'

Ordes raised his hand and his eyebrows.

Olwen laughed. 'Then I'm sure you'll love drawing pictures of yourself.'

Arthur frowned, then gasped as it clicked into place. 'Oh!'

'I don't—' Katarin began.

'She wants us to redistribute the Word – the true Word,' Arthur said, glancing at Olwen.

The Red Sister nodded. She shared another look with Katarin, and then, with much laughter at her brother's riding style, led her party north-east. Melhala and Ethinne left not long after, headed due north.

'I'm confused,' Arthur announced, sneaking a look at his sister. Katarin was watching Olwen's retreating back. 'I didn't think you liked her.'

'I thought she liked Halymere,' Jenyfer commented, while Kat mumbled something under her breath.

Ordes slung his arm around Katarin's shoulder good-naturedly. 'I'm betting the good Captain won't kiss and tell.'

'Fuck off,' Kat said, jabbing her elbow into his ribs, but she was smiling as she ordered them all back to the ship.

CHAPTER 64

Lamorna did not enter the room where the High Priestess lay dying. She waited outside the door. Mordred had not closed it behind him, not fully, so she could hear the conversation. She wondered if had he done that on purpose. He rarely talked about emotions, about how he was feeling, but he wore them on his face, clear for her to see. Maybe this was his way of letting her into that deep part of him, that part where grief lived and breathed like it did in her. When Tamora had come to him after dinner, to tell him Morgause was near the end and was asking for her son, she had to tell Mordred twice before the truth sunk in.

He had not asked for Lamorna to come, but she was not going to let him go alone.

For a long time, neither Mordred nor his mother spoke, but when Morgause cleared her throat, Lamorna jumped.

The High Priestess' voice was strained. 'I need you to find Morgaine.'

Mordred hesitated before answering. Lamorna could hear the frown in his voice, and his tone was dark and bitter. 'Even now, in your last hour, you're going to deny me what I have always wanted. For what? Tradition? A goddess that no longer cares for our people?'

'Our people?' Morgause repeated. 'The people you turned your back on. What happened to "you shall have me as your shield, you shall have me as your weapon against that which hides in the darkness", Mordred?'

The pledge of the Inborn. Lamorna bit her lip, remembering the first time she had ever heard that pledge, spoken from Mordred's lips as he fed the Witchfinder's blood to the earth. She remembered the words the Cruitheans spoke afterwards – the prayer that had rattled her bones and dug into her soul, words that had burrowed inside her and begun the first of the questions she would ask herself while in Cruithea.

She pressed her ear a little closer to the door, jumping back as Mordred's voice sliced the air, whip-sharp and filled with pain.

'I'm doing this for them!' Mordred shouted. Lamorna had never heard him raise his voice like that. He was always so calm and controlled. It was one of the things she liked the most about him.

'Arthur—'

'Won't be building the world you think he will, Mother,' Mordred cut in. 'He isn't the saviour of anything. His choices will see our people – and all those who wield magic – without power at all. The Cruithea you have built will cease to exist,' he added. 'So help me. Help me save us, save the Old Ways. Send for the Inborn, the Priestesses of Inanna. Send for—'

'No,' Morgause said.

Silence. Lamorna, heart in her throat, risked a peek into the room. Mordred was sitting back in his chair, his face drawn. He sighed, then slumped forward, his head falling into his hands. 'You have so little faith in me?' he said, his voice muffled.

'Mordred,' Morgause said, reaching out to rest a pale, limp hand on his head. 'This isn't who you are.'

'You don't know who I am,' he told her, but his voice was softer.

Morgause let her hand drop with a sigh. 'You think Ereshki will reward you? You don't know what you are playing with.'

Mordred sat up. 'Did you truly think you could protect the world from darkness by banishing her?' he asked. 'You can't. Darkness is in all of us. I'm choosing to embrace mine. Don't you see? This is my sacrifice, Mother. I *am* the shield. I *am* the weapon. By choice.'

Lamorna covered her mouth with her hand to hide her gasp. Suddenly, she was angry at the One God, Ereshki – whoever she or he was. She turned from Morgause's room and slipped away down the hall. It was dark and quiet. Lamorna usually took a torch with her, but this time she embraced the darkness surrounding her, like Mordred said he was.

There was darkness in everyone. She could not deny that, as she could not deny the darkness in herself. Had that darkness always been there, or had meeting Mordred changed her in ways she didn't realise?

Lamorna was deep in thought as she rounded the corner to the hallway to her and Mordred's room. With her eyes cast to the floor, she did not realise she was no longer alone, and ran straight into someone. With a gasp, she stepped back.

Alden.

She narrowed her eyes. 'What are you doing outside our door?'

His eyes dropped briefly and then lifted to her face, his expression smooth. 'I was looking for Mordred. He told me to seek him out,' Alden added. Jealousy burnt like a wildfire in Lamorna's chest. She shook her hair back and folded her arms.

'He is with his mother.' Lamorna pushed past him, heading for her door.

Alden's voice rose behind her. 'Is the High Priestess …'

Lamorna froze, fingers curled around the doorknob. Mordred must have told him the other night, she realised, when he did not come to bed until late. She swallowed, glancing over her shoulder.

'Not yet.'

Alden nodded. 'Mordred cares for her, even though he pretends he does not.'

'You think I don't know that?' Lamorna bristled.

Alden's smile was brief. 'We are not competing, Lamorna,' he said.

'Aren't we?' she said, pushing open her door and stepping inside before he could say anything else.

Lamorna lit the candles, then changed her clothes and washed her face. She considered going in search of her aunt or Calla, but Mordred might come back while she was gone, and she wanted to be here for him, so she sat in their little sitting room and waited.

By the time he returned, the candles had burned down to nothing, and it was dark and grim. She jumped up as the door opened. He said nothing, but from his face, she knew. She held out her arms and Mordred crossed the room to pull her close, holding her so tightly it hurt.

'I'm sorry,' she whispered.

She sensed him nod, before his lips touched her hair.

'I never knew my mother,' Lamorna said, stroking the soft skin at the back of his neck. 'She died having me. You're lucky, Mordred.'

'Lucky I got to watch her die?' he managed.

'Lucky you got to know her at all.'

Two nights later, Mordred lit his mother's funeral pyre. Lamorna's eyes watered from the smoke and her skin was slowly sucked dry, but she stood with her spine straight and her hand in Mordred's as they watched his mother burn.

Crowded around them were the people from Kernou and those from Cruithea who had joined them in the ruined castle Lamorna was now calling home. Across the pyre, she saw her aunt. Tamora's eyes were wet. The Cruitheans stood with their heads bowed, as was proper. The people from Kernou were unsettled watching this moment play out.

In Kernou, they did not burn people, except those declared heretics and witches. But in Cruithea, Lamorna knew it was different. Mordred had told her what would happen, and it had been she who had organised the wood they would need to build Morgause's funeral pyre, sending the men out to scavenge the cursed land for any dead wood. She had ordered them to cut down the skeletal trees if they had to. Now the High Priestess of Cruithea had a pyre worthy of who she was.

She had not liked Lamorna, and Lamorna had not liked her. But she was Mordred's mother, and therefore, she was important. Lamorna was oddly proud of the way the fire raged and ate at the wood she had demanded the men find.

Beside her, Mordred stood tall, proud. Firelight cut lines of red and gold across his skin. He cleared his throat, and lifted his voice so everyone could hear him.

'Tonight, we return my mother, the High Priestess of Cruithea, Inanna's Chosen, to the earth. We burn her body so that it may become food for the soil that will nourish us in this place. We send her spirit to the Old Ones, so that they can honour her. And we stand vigil as she burns, so that we will remember her.' He paused, his eyes moving over the assembled crowd. There was no sorrow in his voice, only strength.

'It is time you all learned the truth,' Mordred said. 'The truth about why I have brought you to this place, far from your home.' He paused – all eyes were on him, dark and shadowed in the firelight. Sparks shot into the sky and danced back towards the earth, like fireflies. Lamorna thought it was rather beautiful. Perhaps Mordred was right and his mother's ashes would help fertilise this barren ground. Mordred squeezed her hand as he took a deep breath.

'The One God is not the God you all know,' he said. Faces pulled into frowns. 'Once, the Old Ones walked the earth and were worshipped at shrines across the land. Gawain, the Green Knight, the God of the Earth. Melodias, who rules the seas. Morrigna, the Goddess of Fate, she whose hand shapes our lives – even yours, who have turned from her.

Niniane of the Mists, who gave magic to the world. And in Cruithea, we worshipped the sisters, the Two in One – Inanna and Ereshki, light and dark, life and death. My mother, in her wisdom, banished Ereshki, and we no longer acknowledged her existence. But there cannot be light without darkness. The power of a goddess cannot be contained by the will of man, even the will of a High Priestess.'

He swallowed. Alden stood on his other side, and Lamorna saw a look pass between them, one that shot to the heart of her and made her blood boil. She pushed it away, to deal with later. Mordred addressed the crowd again.

'Years before, when Eseld and Enyon, those ancient rulers of our land, lived in this castle that stands behind us, where you all now reside, Ereshki had begun to spin a web that would soon catch the will of men, and would lead them away from her sibling gods and into her keeping,' Mordred said. He swallowed again and his words slipped away. His hand trembled in Lamorna's. He looked at her, eyes dark, and she smiled, turning to face the crowd, raising her voice and taking up his mantle.

'Ereshki, the Red One, the Goddess, showed another face to the people of this land,' she said. People were watching her, listening. Encouraged, she went on. 'The One God, the God we all know and love and whose Word rules over our lives, is not who we believe Him to be.' Lamorna could see Calla across the pyre, her face shadowed, dark hair billowing around her shoulders. Lingering at the back of the crowd was a man, someone she had not seen before. There was something oddly familiar about him, something she could not put her finger on in the flame-kissed darkness, unsure if it was the way his hair reminded her of Arthur as she had seen him last, or the way his eyes looked a little like Mordred's. She blinked, and he was gone.

Lamorna would feel people watching her, so she cleared her throat and went on. 'When Mordred first told me the truth, I did not believe it. I could not believe that the God we loved was not a god at all, but a goddess of the Old Ways, reinvented, reimagined, Her story retold. The One God is Ereshki, the sister of Inanna, and She loves us dearly.'

The only sound was the crackling of the pyre as the timbers slowly gave way to the flame, as fire consumed the body of the High Priestess and a swarm of fireflies swirled through the air around them.

'It can't be true!' someone called.

Lamorna shook her head. 'Does it truly matter who She is? She loves us, and She has brought us to this place. She has set us on this holy path. If I can believe this, if I can accept this, me, who loved the One God with all my heart, you can as well.'

Mordred had recovered himself. He flashed Lamorna a smile, and when he spoke, his voice was low, powerful and strong. 'Ereshki wants only to love you, as she has always done. Here, in this place, we will worship her. We will heal this land. We will give ourselves to the Red One.'

A murmur spread through the watching crowd, the sound like the bees in the hive in the garden outside Lamorna's cottage in Kernou. She spared them a brief thought, wondering if they were still there, or if they had spread their tiny wings and flown from that place, much like she had.

'There will be those who want to stop us, who will want to push Ereshki into the darkness,' Mordred said with sorrow. 'Those, like my mother, who believe that She is a blight on the world. But I ask you, who already know Her, if they come for us and Her children, will you stand by me?'

It was a bold statement, and Lamorna was not sure it was a wise one. People were whispering. They were confused. She swallowed, and put on her most pious voice. Somehow, through that action, through the words that flowed from her lips, something began to knit itself back together inside her, something she hadn't realised had been broken.

'The Word says, "love those who do not know, and it is through that love that you shall show others the Light"',' Lamorna called. 'We all know those words. We have spent our lives living in the Light. It is our duty to bring that Light to the rest of Teyath. This has not changed. This is Ereshki's wish for us, as it was the One God's.'

She scanned the faces before her, the words sinking inside her, branding her anew. Her aunt was looking at her like she had lost her mind, and perhaps, for a moment, she had. But Lamorna was as sure as she had ever been that this was her path, the one that the One God had sent her. The one Ulrian Tregarthen had set her on when he sent her to Cruithea. She would be a weapon against the darkness. She would be the Light, and she would not falter.

She would be Ereshki's soldier, as she had always been.

Slowly, people drifted away with much whispering, many backwards glances. Confusion hung in the air, as was expected. There would be many questions and she would answer them.

Morgause continued to burn, the flames bright against the darkness of the night around them. For a moment, Lamorna thought she saw that man again, but there was nothing but swirling embers on the other side of the pyre. Lamorna, Mordred, and Alden stood and watched the fire. She did not even mind that Alden was there, not now. As the High Priestess was returned to the earth, something in Lamorna was returned to herself.

Faith.

CHAPTER 65

Katarin had left Ordes to manage the ship, or maybe it had been Merlin who had taken up the Captain's role again. She had retreated to her cabin and hurried to the window, throwing the glass panels wide, and then she had sat and watched the coast of Teyath grow smaller as *The Excalibur* picked up speed.

She was angry. Ordes had been right. Niniane had used them. She had used all of them, and it left Katarin wondering if the Goddess cared for her at all, whether she had rescued a terrified girl on the beach that day because she wanted to use her.

If Katarin never saw the Goddess of Magic again, it would be too soon.

Katarin snatched up the bottle of rum and a glass. She turned her chair around and put her feet up on the window sill. The sun was slowly sinking, the ship was making her way westward towards the Bay of Calledun and Kernou, a place Katarin had not returned to since a faery had saved her life and taken her to Avalon.

Katarin threw back a glass of rum and poured another.

Arthur and Jalen.

Mordred.

It was too much.

She closed her eyes. Behind her lids, a forest was imprinted there. She could smell rich soil after rain, could see the whorls of mist gathering at the bases of tree trunks that stretched into the sky, and could feel the brush of leaves against her skin. Katarin opened her eyes, rubbing at them irritably, and fixed her gaze on the ocean, on the bend and flex of the water left behind in *The Excalibur's* wake. Sea birds swooped low, screeching, before they shot back into the sky.

Someone knocked at the door. Katarin jumped, almost dropping the rum. Scowling, she glanced over her shoulder to watch Merlin step into the cabin.

'What do I owe this pleasure?' Katarin said. She waved the bottle of rum at him. 'Drink?'

'No, thanks,' Merlin said. He sat on the other side of the desk, and for a moment, she considered not turning her chair around, but she could feel those silver eyes on her face.

'What are you doing here?' Kat asked bluntly, shifting her chair back to its usual position. She wasn't in the mood for games. If she had the time, she'd find that demi-god and rip his head from his shoulders. She should have put more trust in her instincts. Now, because she didn't, because of her weakness, her brother was hurting and the Goddess of Magic wanted their heads. She pushed that particular betrayal away, taking a swig of her rum.

Merlin reached across the table and snatched the bottle from her. He examined it and then set it back down, eyes twinkling. 'What is it with the drinking?'

'What?'

'You're as bad as my son. A bit of conflict and you both hit the bottle.'

Katarin blinked. 'Do you want me to smash that bottle against your smug head? I don't care that you're the Prophet of the Gods. I don't care that you're all powerful. Speak to me like that again, and I'll open your throat and see if you can actually die.'

Merlin chuckled, relaxing in his seat and folding his arms casually. 'I was worried you'd softened on us, Katarin Le Fey.'

She picked up a letter opener and spun it between her fingers, glaring at him. 'Is there a purpose to this visit?'

Merlin's expression became serious. 'It's time for you to stop hiding who you really are.'

Kat raised her eyebrows. 'That's rich, coming from you. You're the biggest liar I know. You don't have the right to lecture me about—'

'The High Priestess of Cruithea is dead, Katarin,' Merlin cut in gently.

For the third time in a week, Katarin felt like someone had punched her in the guts. She took a shuddering breath. 'I don't believe you.'

He said nothing.

She swallowed the fire that was slowly creeping up her throat, blinking away the hot rush of tears. But she could not stop the regret from sinking quickly into the depths of her stomach as she recalled all the times she'd avoided her aunt because she was terrified of a simple conversation. Now, she'd never hear Morgause's voice again. 'What? When?'

'Not long ago,' Merlin told her.

'How do you know?'

His silver eyes burnt, and a warm ocean breeze suddenly swept through the cabin, even though the window was closed. 'I saw it. And I saw you, Katarin – not as you are now, but as you will be. I saw you standing on a field of brilliant green. I saw you walking beneath the trees. I saw you—'

'Stop,' Katarin demanded. Her voice shook.

'Cruithea will need you in the years to come,' Merlin said.

'Cruithea doesn't need me. It's never needed me,' Katarin declared. She took another mouthful of rum. Her fingers were trembling. 'How did she die?'

'Illness, from what I could see. Mordred held the funeral rites for her at Dinas Emrys. She must have gone to see him, but now, she has been returned to Inanna,' Merlin said gently. 'Reclaim who you are, Katarin.' He stood, and the look he gave her was kind. 'I understand more than you know about how you feel, but sometimes, we need to let things play out as fate would have them.' He turned to go, and before he opened the door, he glanced at her over his shoulder. 'Sleep well, Morgaine.'

There was something in the way he said the name that caused her stomach to tighten and her heart to race. Kat closed her eyes. The sounds of her thundering heart and the ocean outside her window slipped away, and she saw not the glittering of the golden light on the water, but trees stretching into the sky. She saw fleshy fungi explode to life and a ground carpeted in tiny white flowers, their petals unfolding before her. She saw a tangle of roots cloaked in the deep green of spongy moss.

Through the forest of her mind walked a woman. A pair of antlers rose from the nest of her deep brown hair and in one hand she carried a sword, her face half smeared in blood. Behind her walked another, her face hidden in shadow, red robe brushing the forest floor.

Life, and death.

Inanna, and Ereshki.

The Two in One.

Katarin's eyes flew open. She gasped, but no matter how much she blinked, or how she focused on the slapping of waves against the hull, the image of the Goddess she had ignored since she was a child tied to a stake with the sea kissing her toes, would not fade.

Chapter 66

From the darkness, a fire raged. Arthur stood at the back of a crowd of people, watching as the pyre burnt and a body was returned to the earth. He wondered if he had dreamwalked into Cruithea, for he knew of nowhere else where flame consumed the flesh of the dead. Not counting those his father and the Konsel had burnt before their time.

But it wasn't Cruithea. The night sky above Arthur was a blanket of stars, clear and brilliant against their indigo backdrop. There were no trees to obscure the view and for a moment, he just watched the sky, entranced by those tiny pricks of light and they way they seemed to twinkle.

Arthur rubbed the toe of his boot on the ground, bending to place his hand on hard, rocky earth. Not one blade of grass brushed his fingers.

Camlann Plain, then.

Standing, Arthur peered over the heads of those gathered before him. An orange glow, soft and strangely comforting, drew him forward. Arthur made his way towards the pyre, edging between bodies, their faces a blur, as if he was not to know who they were. They stood four or five deep from the pyre, whose heat Arthur could feel even in a dream.

He stopped. On the other side of the pyre was his cousin. Mordred's face was partially shadowed, licked with fire, and clear. Whatever had brought him to this moment, he was supposed to see Mordred. His cousin's mouth moved, but Arthur could not hear the words. When Mordred stopped, his eyes falling to the pyre and the body being consumed by flames, another face swam into focus. Lamorna. She stood beside Mordred, her hair uncovered and flowing over her shoulders. With the blackness of night at her back and the firelight framing her face, Arthur was reminded of the strange vision he had seen while in Cruithea. It was not difficult to imagine, seeing her like this, that a bloodied sword would be at home in her hand.

Lamorna was speaking, but Arthur could not hear her voice, either.

Grief was draped over Mordred like a blanket, and suddenly, Arthur understood.

The High Priestess of Cruithea, his aunt, was dead.

He closed his eyes, and when he opened them again, he was back where he began, at the edge of the crowd, watching as embers filled the night sky. He was not alone. There was a man beside him, watching as Morgause's body burnt.

A man, with hair the same colour as Arthur's and eyes like Mordred's. He turned to look at Arthur – not through him, like the others had, but *at* him.

'You can see me?' Arthur whispered. He took a step towards the man, and the world shredded as Arthur was thrust into the darkness.

Arthur was sitting by the porthole in his cabin, the remains of his dream-walk scattered through his brain. The ocean was calm tonight, the sky free of clouds, and for a moment, he saw flames reflected on the face of the water and a swirl of embers spread across the sky.

The door to his cabin opened and when he turned around, Katarin was there, a bottle of rum in one hand and two glasses in the other. 'I need to tell you something.'

'Aunt Morgause is dead,' Arthur mumbled.

'Did Merlin tell you?' Kat demanded, plonking the bottle and glasses down on the small table. She poured them both a drink, holding out a glass for Arthur. After he took it, she perched on the end of his bed. The Sword of the White Dragon lay on top of the bed clothes. Katarin didn't mention it.

'Merlin told you, I'm assuming?' Arthur asked.

Kat nodded.

'What happens now? She was the High Priestess of Cruithea,' Arthur said, taking a seat next to his sister.

Katarin stared into her glass, drained it, and then sighed. 'When I was a child, I was chosen by Inanna to be the next High Priestess of Cruithea,' she said. 'And then my life was pulled out from under me, and I never went back there for long enough to find out if I was still Inanna's Chosen. According to Ethinne, I am.'

'Kat,' Arthur whispered.

Kat shrugged. 'I don't want to think about it now. I just thought you should know and,' she indicated the rum, 'I thought we could …'

Arthur got up and collected the bottle, refilling his sister's glass. If she wasn't ready to talk about Cruithea, he was not going to push her, not now. Instead, he thought about the strange man he'd seen in his dreamwalk, and the odd familiarity of him. 'Did our mother have other siblings?'

Katarin glanced at him in surprise. 'Two brothers.'

'I've got uncles?' Arthur smiled and finished his drink, refilling it and shuffling back on the bed so he could sit cross-legged. Katarin copied him, sitting opposite, the bottle balanced between them. Her face was soft.

'I didn't mention them before because I honestly didn't know what to say. I don't even know if they're alive, Arthur. You have questions and I don't know if I have the answers, but I'll try. Morgause was the oldest, then our mother, then Agravaine, and Gaheris.' She smiled. 'Gaheris is, *was* I guess, the High Priestess' spy master. He used to bring me gifts from faraway places when I was little. He was Aunt Morgause's eyes and ears in Teyath, and he only returned to Cruithea to share news or information that could not be trusted with a messenger bird.'

'Morgause told me she had spies, but I didn't actually think about what that truly meant,' Arthur said. 'Is he a Magic Wielder?'

'Gaheris is an air elemental – handy, for a spy. He can get inside people's heads, but that isn't what made him a good spy, Arthur. He's charming and capable of walking in more than one world,' Katarin explained. 'At first glance, to a man in a tavern in Carinya or a shop in Malist, Gaheris is just a man. Not a Cruithean and not a Magic Wielder.' She paused to refill her glass. 'He would know she's dead, and he'd be on his way back to Cruithea.'

Arthur chewed his lip. 'Kat, I saw her funeral.'

Katarin's eyes widened. 'You did?'

'Just tonight. I wasn't sure at first what I was seeing, but now it makes sense. I saw a burning pyre and I saw Mordred and Lamorna, and … a man,' Arthur said quietly. 'The thing is, everyone else in my dreamwalk didn't know I was there, but he did. He looked at me.'

Katarin was frowning.

'I can't explain it,' Arthur said. 'But there was something so familiar about him. He was tall and broad, with hair like mine and eyes like Mordred's.'

Kat's glance was sharp. 'The dream space can't always be trusted, Arthur.'

Arthur nodded. 'I know.'

They sat in silence for a while, the ship shifting gently beneath them.

'The other brother,' Arthur prompted. 'Agravaine.'

'I never met him. Morgause banished him from Cruithea before I was born,' Kat said with a shrug. 'No one ever spoke of him again.'

'What did he do?' Arthur asked.

'I asked our aunt once, when I was older and bolder and perhaps more stupid.' Kat grinned. 'She said he wanted what was not his. That was all she told me.' She yawned suddenly, and climbed off the bed.

'Kat,' Arthur began. 'Do you want to be High Priestess?'

'The thing is,' his sister said, 'it isn't really a choice I can make, Arthur. I am beginning to truly understand how you, Ordes, and Jenyfer are feeling. Can I fight it? Ethinne and Halymere would say no, because this is Inanna's choice.'

'But what do *you* want, Katarin?' Arthur asked. 'Because it is a choice – your choice, and I don't think anyone will begrudge you that, regardless of what you decide.'

She sighed, running her hand over her face. 'At the moment, I don't know what I want.'

Chapter 67

Whenever Jenyfer closed her eyes, she saw Kernou and the sweeping stretch of coastline that was the Bay of Calledun, one of the views she was most familiar with in the world. The salty sea breeze tugging at her unbound hair, blowing it around her face as she stood in their clifftop garden; the sand between her toes and lacey foam kissing her skin as she held her dress above her ankles and stood in the ocean, where she was not supposed to be.

She saw the sea birds that hovered over the boundary between the ocean and the land, wings spread, feathers brushed with sunlight as they floated high on the updrafts, suspended between here and now. Below them, blue-green waves caressed the sand, the water infused with flecks of white as the ocean breathed, folding like curtains upon a pale golden shore.

She saw silvery-black clouds and an ocean that boiled and writhed beneath the storm.

And she saw the sacrificial stake, where they had tied her sister, like they had tied countless others. The cross of the One God looming over the town square, like it had loomed over her life. Lamorna, on her knees, eyes closed, lips moving as she recited the Word.

Jenyfer saw a world of pain. A world that was familiar, and a world that she had escaped from, but that was now pulling her back, like she knew it would, as surely as the tide would rise and fall and leave small treasures on the beach for children to find. Only Kernou was no treasure.

Her life had once been insular, confined to a small town and the domestic routine of her cottage. Her world had been filled with her aunt's voice, Lamorna's constant quoting of the Word, and Bryn. Once, he had been the bright spark in Jenyfer's existence. Now the memory of what he had done to her, what he had become, had tainted all other memories of him. She could barely recall the boy he'd been or the young man he'd become before she had dragged him beneath a wave of lies and he'd surfaced as something else entirely. The Konsel had hurt him, Jenyfer remembered. She'd seen the marks on his skin, but unlike Katarin, who'd used her hurt to fuel her ferocious fire, Bryn had let his pull him further into the Chif's darkness.

Unless he'd already been there and Jenyfer had never known it. She'd spent her life afraid, but realised she'd never known true fear until she'd been forced to marry Bryn, and he'd held her down and done what he wanted. His duty, he'd said, but Jenyfer knew it was more than that.

Now that she knew what love looked like, what it felt like, she could see it in hindsight. Bryn had loved her. He'd just chosen the worst possible way to show her. He'd chosen violent possession over gentleness. He'd chosen his wants over her needs.

He'd chosen himself.

Kernou was not a place that taught anyone how to love. Bryn's transformation was proof of that. Jenyfer wondered where he was, whether he'd gone with Mordred and Lamorna. Her sister had not mentioned him, but the man Bryn had become would have been drawn to someone like Mordred and his power.

The sun made a slow journey into their cabin through the porthole. The air was thick and stuffy. Jenyfer untangled herself from Ordes and sat up. His hand came to rest on her back.

'You okay?'

'Fine. I need some fresh air,' she added, and before she could climb out of bed, the porthole had magically opened. She gave Ordes a wry smile. 'That's cheating.'

He shrugged, and she lay down again, curling against him, his lips pressing against her hair. 'You were talking in your sleep.'

'I was?'

'You were talking about Kernou. Jen, if you don't want to go there, you don't have to. Stay on the ship. Arthur and I can go,' Ordes said.

'I need to see it, so I can face it, put the whole place behind me. Not pretend it never existed, but put it in a little box, lock it, and throw away the bloody key,' Jenyfer answered with a sigh.

'And if we see Bryn?'

She took a deep breath. 'Sometimes, it's like it all happened yesterday. Other times, it seemed like it wasn't me at all, but some other young woman in that horrible place. The memory of him and what he did will never leave me, but it's fading. You did that,' she added, lifting her head so she could see Ordes face. 'Thank you.'

He smiled, bending his head so he could kiss her. His fingers found their way into her hair. She groaned as they pressed against her scalp. Ordes' eyebrows lifted. 'To think I can get such a sound out of you with just my fingers. I wonder what other sounds I can get you to make.'

Jenyfer laughed. 'Want me to sing for you, Ordes?'

'Only if my name is in the lyrics,' he murmured against her mouth.

'While they are nice fingers, they're not my favourite part of you,' she whispered, pulling back so she could run the tip of her index finger over his lips. 'These are my favourite parts.'

'Oh, really?' he chuckled, rolling them over so he was half on top of her. Slowly, with a wicked grin, Ordes undid the buttons on her shirt, exposing her breasts. Breath heavy with anticipation, the heat of his gaze burning a hole through her chest, Jenyfer bit her lip.

'Are you absolutely certain you don't prefer these?' Teasingly, Ordes dragged his fingers over her skin, the calluses on his palm lightly scraping her flesh, coaxing goosebumps to life. He traced around her nipple, eyes pinned to her face, reading each flicker of emotion there, each heaving breath as he touched her.

He could play her like an instrument, and in these moments, nothing existed except him and the burning in her heart, the all-consuming flame that Jenyfer thought would burn and blaze until she was nothing but ashes.

Ordes closed his lips around her nipple. She gasped, her fingers weaving into his hair.

'Not quite singing, but I'll take it,' he murmured smugly against her flesh. His hand slid down her side, over the curve of her hip, curling around her upper thigh, fingers pressing against her skin – a promise.

'Do you remember the first night you touched me?' Jenyfer whispered. Her question drew a groan from the back of his throat.

'How can I forget?'

'I don't think you understand how important that moment was,' she managed. Ordes lifted his head. She met his eyes, saw the question there. 'You showed me that I could trust you,' Jenyfer whispered. 'You could have done whatever you wanted, but you didn't, and it made me want you even more because you made me feel safe.'

He swallowed tightly, before he leant forward and kissed her, gently, so sweetly she was crying when he pulled away. Whatever song he had wanted her to sing, Jenyfer was certain it wasn't this one. Ordes ran his fingers lightly down her cheek, his forehead pressed against hers. They stayed that way, sharing breath, Jenyfer's chest burning, until he kissed her again, one hand cradling her head, the other moving down her body, slowly, excruciatingly so, until he could stroke between her legs.

He was so gentle, so tender, it left her a burning, writhing mess beneath him, but he didn't stop, fingers teasing that painfully sensitive spot at the apex of her thighs, over and over, until she was hovering on the edge of release, burning up inside …

Ordes stopped, withdrawing, and she was left wanting, panting. He moved between her thighs, kissing her deeply, and hooked her leg around his hip.

'I love you,' he whispered against her mouth, then drove inside her in one thrust, so deep that the world exploded. The movement of his hips drew her deeper, over the edge, until she was drowning in heat, on fire from the inside out, her heart tearing apart and knitting back together.

His name fell from her lips, over and over, a litany, a song, until all she could manage was a whisper as the world faded to black.

Ordes' fingers were in her hair, stroking the tangled length of it from her forehead. Jenyfer couldn't move. She had no idea what time it was, what day it was, *where* she was.

It didn't matter.

Nothing mattered anymore.

She blinked, and slowly, the world swam back into focus. The ship rocked beneath them, lullaby soft, wanting to pull her under again.

Ordes' hand trailed lazily down her body and back up again. She caught his fingers, kissed them, then pulled his arm around her. His head tucked against hers, the warmth of him comforting. They didn't speak. Jenyfer wasn't sure what was left to say. She only knew that this was where she belonged, in his arms, and nothing would ever make her give him up.

CHAPTER 68

Lamorna wanted to look away, but could not. Her eyes were glued to the scene unfolding before her. Two men with skin as dark as night, sweat gleaming on the swell of sculpted muscle. Fingers dug into flesh, teeth into a throat.

She wanted them to put their hands on her. Maybe. She wasn't sure. There was something deep and primal about this moment, and her insides squirmed. She should not be watching, but she needed to watch.

She needed to know.

You thought he actually cared about you, a voice whispered. She shook her head. *You're a fool, Lamorna. Nothing but a fool. Look at what you've done. Look at what you're doing.*

A pause. She watched Alden sink to his knees before Mordred. Her Mordred. Not his. She went to get up, to tell him to get out, but she could not move. Then jealousy, *fear,* rushed in like a beastly thing with teeth and claws to climb up her spine and wrap itself around her neck and squeeze.

Mordred's eyes locked on hers.

He smiled.

If you don't have him, Lamorna, what do you have? the little voice whispered.

With a gasp, Lamorna woke. She flung her arm out – the other side of the bed held Mordred's lingering warmth, and she breathed a sigh of relief, the dream tumbling around her mind so quickly she thought she might vomit.

Mordred hadn't spoken much since his mother's death. Lamorna had not pushed him. She had given him the time to grieve, and she had guarded the door to their room ferociously. It gave her a strange sense of pleasure to be able to tell some of the men who had come with them from Kernou that they were to go away. But when he wasn't with her, he was with Alden, and Lamorna didn't like that. When she had passed Alden in the hall yesterday, he had smiled at her, a secretive smile that she'd wanted to smash off his face. She had lifted her chin and ignored him, and had gone to visit her aunt instead. Lamorna did not want her to leave, so she would not.

Tamora was not happy, though, so Lamorna relented and allowed her to send word to Keraine. If having that horrid woman present would make Tamora smile again, then Lamorna would push her own thoughts aside and let Keraine come.

Blinking slowly, Lamorna rolled over, letting the morning sink inside her. With each blink, she saw it again – Mordred and Alden together, and it made her bunch her fists in the bedclothes and bite her lip.

How late did he come to your bed, Lamorna? That voice again. She scowled, about to tell it to shut up, when she realised there were other voices. Real ones, not the ones in her head, coming from the sitting room. Curious, she leant over the edge of the bed, fumbling around on the floor for her robe. She flung it around her and slipped out of bed. A quick glance at the mirror revealed her pale face and wild hair.

Mordred was in the sitting room. He was shirtless and barefoot, which meant he hadn't gone anywhere yet. His hair was loose around the breadth of his shoulders. He was pacing, agitated and tense. She could see it in his rigid spine and his short, sharp steps across the worn rug.

'I didn't send for you,' he said, his voice low, brittle.

'I am here because the Red One deemed it so,' a female voice answered. 'Do not presume you know what the Goddess wants, Mordred. Ereshki wishes for me to be here, so here I am.'

Ereshki!

Lamorna took a deep breath, stepped into view, then stopped.

A woman was sitting in one of the armchairs. She was small, child-like, and wore a rich, red cloak. There was dust on her boots, and Lamorna bit back on her annoyance, thinking about the rug beneath the woman's feet. Mordred turned and held out his hand. Lamorna hurried to his side, her eyes on the mystery woman in red.

'Lamorna, this is Elaine,' he said. 'A Red Sister from the House of Bone.'

Elaine removed her hood, and Lamorna was startled at how young she was. Her dark brown hair was cropped short, and her face was youthful – Lamorna thought she was too young to have travelled all the way from the Dead Woods to Dinas Emrys alone. Lamorna wasn't very old, either – she was only twenty-one. Yet, some days, when she thought about everything that had happened, all that had changed, she felt ancient and tired.

She was shocked to realise the Red Sister was blind. Her eyes were large in her thin, brown face, and were completely white.

'I see in other ways,' the Red Sister said.

'I'm sorry,' Lamorna gasped, suddenly conscious of her nakedness beneath the robe. 'I didn't mean to stare.'

Elaine smiled. She had a nice smile, Lamorna decided. There was something serene and comforting about it, but the look she gave Mordred was not serene. It was irate and exasperated.

'You have been meddling where you should not,' she said. Mordred ground his teeth, but he said nothing. His grip on Lamorna's hand tightened, making her wince. Elaine stood. 'You walk where you should not, and you have a sword in your possession that you should not.'

'Why are you here?' Mordred bit out. Lamorna frowned, not understanding his rudeness. She went to scold him, but he spoke again. 'Have you come to chastise me or help me, Elaine?' There was an edge to his voice Lamorna didn't usually hear.

'Both, I think,' Elaine said. 'Wake the beast who slumbers deep. Draw the serpent from his sleep.'

Mordred stared at her. Lamorna held her breath, not releasing it until he nodded. He left them to finish dressing. Alone with the strange blind woman, Lamorna swallowed and remembered her manners, wondering what Elaine meant about beasts and serpents.

'Would you like—'

'I have Seen what he will become,' Elaine said, her voice low. 'Just as I have Seen you, who breathes when she should not.'

Lamorna's hands began to shake, her fingers clenching the fabric of her robe. 'What … what does that mean?'

'Dead Girl,' the Red Sister whispered. 'You do my mistress' work, as does your sister.' She took a step towards Lamorna, who stepped back quickly, terrified of this strange woman and her strange words. The voices in her head were screaming at her to get away, but there was nowhere to run to, no escape to be had. Elaine came closer until she was standing within the reach of Lamorna's hands, and suddenly, Lamorna was no longer in the cold and draughty castle. She was in the darkness, with the water and the music that never ended. She was suspended somewhere between life and death, her lungs full of water, her body full of air.

'Do you wish to live?' The voice was like rattling bones.

Gasping, Lamorna clutched at her throat. Elaine smiled, and stepped away as the voices in Lamorna's head laughed. *Took you long enough, Dead Girl.*

It was dark beneath the castle. Lamorna held her torch high, following Mordred.

Dead! How could I be dead? I breathe. My heart beats. How?

'Do you know where you're going?' she asked. 'Mordred?'

He did not respond. Lamorna sighed.

Ankou gave her back her life. Why?

'Mordred, where are we going?' she asked, stumbling a little. She cursed, lifting the hem of her dress clear of her feet. 'Mordred?'

Deep, endless nothing – no breath, no pulse, no life.

Nothing.

Dead. She was *dead*.

'It isn't far now, Lamorna,' Mordred said, his voice bouncing back to her in the darkness.

Grumbling, Lamorna hurried to catch up to him. A cool breeze wafted to them, teasing the flame of her torch. It smelt of damp and earth, and something else she could not put her finger on. She wondered how far beneath the castle they were, how deep these tunnels went. She was about to ask when Mordred stopped so suddenly she ran into his back. He reached behind for her hand.

'Mordred, what are we doing down here?' Lamorna demanded. Her voice echoed back to her, disjointed and strange.

'We're here,' was all he said.

The tunnel opened into a great cavern, as tall as the castle and twice as wide. Lamorna gaped, craning her neck to look up. A tiny slice of light snuck into the darkness from high above their heads.

'What is this place?' she whispered.

'Home to something important,' Mordred answered. He clicked his fingers and all around them, torches flared to life, brackets mounted along the stone walls. It was oddly silent in the cavern, but Lamorna thought she could hear something breathing, the slow and steady breath of sleep.

In the fire-kissed darkness, Mordred's eyes were completely black. His jaw was tight. He held out his hand for her.

'Come.'

She let him lead her across the cavern to whatever he had spotted. Annoyed, Lamorna pushed the hair off her face.

'There,' Mordred whispered. A great lump of stone sat nearby. It was huge, towering above her head and stretching to all corners of Lamorna's vision. She heard Mordred swallow.

'It's a rock,' she said.

He shook his head. 'It's a dragon, Lamorna.'

She gasped. 'A dragon?' She took a step forward. 'It doesn't look like a dragon. Is it dead?' *Like me*, she wanted to add, but didn't.

'Sleeping. As it has been for a long time,' Mordred answered.

Lamorna frowned. 'What are you going to do to it?'

'I'm going to wake it up,' he said.

'Why?'

'Because it's a weapon, Lamorna. It is the key to defeating our enemies.'

She frowned again. 'But—'

Mordred wasn't listening. He approached the dragon-shaped rock, then stopped.

'What's wrong?' she asked.

'Nothing is wrong,' he said, but there was a tightness to his voice she had never heard before. He didn't move, as still as the sleeping beast before him, his spine rigid, his body gilded by torchlight.

He's afraid, Lamorna realised. It shocked her. Mordred was scared of nothing.

'Go on,' she said quietly. 'This is what you wanted, isn't it? Power? It's right there, Mordred. Reach out and take it.'

Still, he didn't move.

'Don't you know how to—'

'I know how,' he snapped. She heard the echoing hiss of his dagger as he pulled it free.

But he did nothing more.

'You need blood? I'll give you mine,' Lamorna offered, withdrawing the dagger she carried at her hip. She set her torch down and ran the blade across the skin of her palm. How did a dead girl bleed? She approached Mordred, blood pooled in her outstretched palm. 'Here.'

Mordred shot her a quick look – of gratitude, perhaps, she couldn't be certain – and dipped two fingers into the blood. In the near darkness, it looked black, not red. With his fingers coated in her blood, Mordred approached the stone.

'Stand back,' he ordered.

She nodded, moving back to retrieve her torch. If a dragon was about to be woken up, she wanted to watch it happen. Mordred placed his bloodied fingers on stone; what part of the dragon it was supposed to be, Lamorna wasn't sure, but she waited, and waited.

'Nothing—' she began, then gasped as a great stone eye opened. Mordred stumbled back, but Lamorna edged closer, drawn towards that eye. She could see her reflection in it. Slowly, the dragon shifted. The stone fell away, tumbling to the ground like a skin the beast no longer needed.

Lamorna did not look away, watching as the dragon shook itself like a dog might. Pieces of stone rained down on them, though none fell on her. She was vaguely aware of Mordred somewhere behind her and did not know when she had drawn ahead of him. She tipped her head to one side.

'I've never had a pet,' she mused.

'This isn't a pet,' Mordred snapped. 'It's a powerful magical being, Lamorna, not some cat you can pull onto your lap.'

'Well, of course not,' she said, a smile tugging at her lips. The dragon blinked its great eye. It was watching her, she realised. Listening to them talk about it, and she had the sense it could understand everything they said. That golden eye blinked again. 'Does it have a name? Should we give it a name? What should we call it? Oh, is it male? Or female? How do you tell?'

'Lamorna,' Mordred said painfully, as if he couldn't be bothered with her questions. She shrugged. Now the dragon was awake and looking at her, she couldn't be bothered with him either. She moved closer still, lifting her torch so she could take in the great scales, like a fish but not, the long neck covered in knobs and spikes. *Where are the wings?* she wondered, and as if it knew her thoughts, the dragon moved. Suddenly, the cavern was filled with a pair of giant leathery wings.

'Oh!' Lamorna breathed. The dragon was red, or maybe it was the torchlight, she wasn't sure. The dragon lowered its head towards her. She heard Mordred shuffle back a step, but she did not move. Like that day in Cruithea with the colpach, Lamorna wasn't sure she wanted to, wasn't sure she could.

But this was different, she realised. Then, she had been frightened, but now there was no fear living in her belly, only curiosity. The dragon lowered its head and snorted; her hair lifted, the air from its nostrils warm and dry. She giggled. Her torch flame flickered dangerously, but held. She lifted it higher, so she could see the dragon better. It no longer mattered that she was Dead.

'Hello,' she whispered. 'Do you have a name?'

The dragon tossed its head.

'I think you should have a name, and if you can't tell me what it is, I will think of something,' she said. 'Something powerful and strong. Something that suits you.'

The dragon turned its great head towards her again. Slowly, it lowered its snout. Lamorna reached out her hand.

'Lamorna!' Mordred warned, but she ignored him.

The dragon's snout moved closer. It was so big. She knew that inside that snout were rows of sharp teeth. She knew it could swallow her whole, or maybe it would roast her and then swallow her.

But she didn't care about that.

The dragon did not take its eye off her. Lamorna moved closer. Mordred called out to her again, but she barely heard him. All she could hear was her dead girl's heart, the steady beating of it. Could the dragon hear it?

'I'm not afraid of you,' she said. 'And you do not need to be afraid of me.'

The dragon made a sound. She thought it sounded pleased.

Lamorna stretched out her hand.

She forgot how to breathe. She could hear Mordred talking, but could not make out the words.

She waited, waited, until, finally, the dragon gently, so gently for something so large and powerful, nudged its snout against her bloodied palm.

'Hello,' Lamorna said.

CHAPTER 69

Arthur blinked, shielding his eyes from the blinding white light that surrounded him. It faded, and as his eyes adjusted, he saw he was standing on the edge of a yawning chasm. Cautiously, he peered over – nothing but blackness.

A roar ripped through the air, the sound rumbling through the ground. Arthur stumbled back, away from the edge.

Deep laughter swooped in as the echo of that roar slipped away.

'Do you hear that?'

Arthur looked up sharply. Mordred was standing on the opposite side of that chasm, bathed in rich red light. Dreamwalking, as Arthur was. Mordred was looking up, searching the blackness above them.

'What was that?' Arthur breathed.

'Destiny,' his cousin answered.

Arthur stared at him sadly. 'Mordred, whatever you're doing, whatever you're planning, please stop.'

'Why should I? The people of this land deserve a king with the courage to take the power being offered to him.'

Arthur flexed his fingers – the Sword had not followed him into this space between the worlds. 'A strong leader does not take away people's choices. He does not kill those who disagree with him. I saw what you did in Kernou, to the Konsel, and that isn't the way. This land sits on the edge of a knife, Mordred. Teyath deserves a just king. It deserves guidance – the people of this land deserve—'

'You put a lot of faith in people, cousin,' Mordred mused.

'Why shouldn't I?' Arthur asked.

Mordred chuckled. 'And what will you do when those people turn on you? When they pick up their pitch-forks and their daggers and come for the Promised King who could not keep his word? People need someone to tell them what to do, Arthur. Those people in Kernou, your father's flock, would not know what to do with the freedom to choose.'

'Because they've never been given a choice,' Arthur argued.

'Well, now they will,' Mordred said. 'I shall give them one – you or me.'

'Mordred—'

'Power is not something someone gives you, Arthur. It is not a gift. Power is something you take. You still don't understand that,' Mordred said.

'Mordred, wait.' Arthur took a step towards the edge of that chasm.

'I've waited long enough. If you're not with me, cousin, you're against me. If you do not support a world of magic, you are against me.' Mordred shook his head. 'Never meet your heroes.'

'You're making a mistake,' Arthur insisted, but it was futile. He could tell by the look on his cousin's face that Mordred was set on his path, just as Arthur was. 'I don't want to be your enemy.'

'It might be too late for that,' Mordred replied.

Then he was gone, and Arthur was left in the darkness at the edge of that chasm. He sank to the ground. The weight of something suddenly draped itself across his lap.

He glanced down to see the Sword of the White Dragon.

'What just happened?' he asked aloud, but he already knew.

War, the Sword sang. *We shall taste it once more.*

Arthur shook his head. 'No. There has to be another way.'

Darkness and blood will come for you, the Sword whispered. *When the battle is waged in the skies, in the seas and on the land, darkness and blood will come for you.*

Arthur tumbled through darkness tinged with red, and when he met with Eseld this time, it was not in her cave nor in the space he had seen Mordred, but on the vast emptiness of Camlann Plain.

Arthur stared at her, anger crawling through him. He had done everything that had been asked of him. He had followed prophecies and the whims of gods. He had faced his father and collected the Sword. They had collected the Treasures. They had been pawns in a game he no longer wanted to play.

'Tell me where the Grail is, Eseld,' he commanded.

She levelled a stare at him, lifeless eyes boring into his. 'Forever to be cast in stone, resting where once lay skin and bone. The Grail, it sings to those who hear, as darkness and blood draw ever near.'

'Another riddle?' Arthur cried. He grit his teeth.

'When the White Dragon defeats the Red, when the serpent's skin is shed, when the cursed earth is healed, only then will I be revealed.' Eseld's dead lips curled into a smile, and then, the Fisher Queen, the Guardian of the Grail, was gone.

Arthur screamed into the darkness.

'When you think of this world, of the future you want to build, of everyone in it, tell me what you see,' Merlin asked him. He and Arthur sat in the shadow of the only tree they had seen for miles. It had been a tough trek inland from the coast north of the Redcana Forest. The landscape around them was dusty and dry. Arthur swallowed, remembering his dreamwalk, remembering Mordred, and then Eseld. He scratched moodily at the ground with the toe of his boot.

Camlann Plain lay to the north. If he went there, would he be able to make Mordred see sense?

The Sword whispered to him. *You cannot stop the trajectory of this path, no matter how much you wish it.*

Merlin repeated his question, adding, 'Tell me who you see.'

'People,' Arthur said sullenly. He didn't have to think about it.

'Exactly. People,' Merlin said. 'Where others might see Cruitheans and faeries, a syhren and Magic Wielders, you see people. You don't separate them because of what they are. Your willingness, your innate nature to include everyone, is what makes you different, Arthur. It's why I saw you all those years ago when I dreamed of the future.'

Merlin paused, leaning back against the trunk of the scraggly tree. 'I've been thinking,' he said. 'How attached are you to your name?'

'My name?'

'Your family name,' Merlin corrected.

Everything inside Arthur stilled. His father's face flashed into his mind, as sharp and icy as the winter wind. He swallowed.

'Legends aren't born, Arthur. They are made, and from this moment, you get to choose how you will be remembered. When people hear the name Tregarthen, certain images come to mind. It's a name associated with fear and, yes, with power, but is that what you want? For people to fear you based on the name you carry?'

Arthur swallowed. 'No. But what should I pick?'

'You carry the Sword of the White Dragon. And tomorrow, you will wake the white dragon from its slumber.' Merlin tapped his fingers on his thigh, then smiled. 'Pendragon.'

A shiver passed through Arthur at the sound of that name. 'Pendragon,' he repeated, rolling the word around his mouth. His body tingled. 'I like it.'

'It is the name you were destined to carry. It is a name people will remember. It is the name of the man who will lift the world from darkness and restore balance.' Merlin paused. 'It is the name of a King.'

They camped that night out in the open, night falling on them like a chilled blanket. As the sun rose, Merlin led them to where the Nemhain Mountains met the earth. In the shadow of the peaks was a pile of rocks, large boulders bigger than houses.

'Sleeping as if cast in stone, waiting to once more be flesh and fire and bone,' Merlin said, gesturing to the rocks dramatically. When no one moved, he put his hands on his hips.

'They're rocks,' Katarin commented, folding her arms. 'You've dragged us across a desert for a pile of rocks.'

'Look again,' Merlin commanded.

Katarin muttered under her breath but did as she was told; they all did, and slowly, the more he looked, the more Arthur saw. The sweeping curve of a magnificent spine. The graceful arc of a pair of wings, folded close to a body. Thick, powerful legs ending in claws as long as a man was tall, and the elegant neck tucked in close to a great, scaled body.

'I see it,' Arthur said softly. The Sword hummed in agreement.

'I see rocks,' Ordes said.

Jenyfer laid her hand on his arm. 'No, I see it.'

'Dragons are creatures of the elements,' Merlin told them. 'They breathe fire, rest in the earth, can fly through the air, and swim the seas.' He paused, his eyes sweeping over their faces. 'Some people believed dragons had to be dominated, defeated,' he said. Merlin approached the stones and rested his hand on what Arthur thought was part of a snout. 'This dragon will know you, Arthur, for what you are. It will recognise you – they can read minds, you know. They can read a person's intent. If it trusts you, it will tell you its name.'

Merlin beckoned Arthur closer.

'And if it doesn't trust me?'

'We'd best hope Ordes is at his cheerful best,' Merlin said. 'He's still not a morning person, is he? We shall require a shield, son, if you don't mind,' Merlin continued as Ordes narrowed his eyes.

Ordes grit his teeth. 'Fine.' He drew his hands together at his chest. Silver light grew between his palms. That light became a ball. Ordes sent it floating through the air. He clicked his fingers, and it unfolded, the light spreading out then down like a net to encircle them, a barrier between the group and the sleeping dragon.

Arthur reached out and touched it. It tingled with magic.

'You can step through it,' Ordes told him.

At a nod from Merlin, Arthur took a deep breath, and passed through the wall of light. His flesh felt like it was being pricked by thousands of tiny knives. He wished Jalen were here to see this, his heart pinching a moment, before he pulled it together and focused on what he had to do.

Merlin's voice came from behind him. 'Rest your hand on the stone, hold the Sword with the other, but do not draw it from its sheath,' he warned.

'I know,' Arthur muttered. He wrapped his fingers around the hilt of the sword at his hip. Magic shot through him like a current, running from his fingers, along his arm, over his chest and down his other arm. He flexed the fingers of his empty hand, grasping at air. The magic flowing through him wanted to touch the stones. In his mind, he could hear a voice, deep and ancient. Not the voice of the Sword – something else.

Touch the stone.

He did.

The world shrank away, and Arthur was hurtled through time and space, flying back, flying forward, tumbling over and over, his consciousness shredded, his bones screaming. On and on he went, flung about like a leaf in the fiercest of storms. Stars whirled overhead, a fire raged around him, smoke and ash raining down to coat the earth. He saw a castle, a ruin, then not a ruin. He saw what had been and what would be.

He saw a white dragon fighting with a red dragon.

He saw blood and darkness.

He saw a woman with horns on her head, a bloodied sword in one hand, another woman by her side, her red cloak brushing the ground. Inanna and Ereshki. The Two in One.

He saw a crown, felt its weight on his head.

He saw the entrance to a tomb, strange symbols carved in the stone …

He was flung back into his body, gasping and trembling. He ripped his hand from the stone and stepped back, releasing his grip on the Sword of the White Dragon.

'It didn't work,' he called. The stones before him had not shifted.

Wait, the voice in his mind said. *Wait, King Who Shall Be.*

Arthur could hear nothing but the pounding of his heart.

Something rippled across the world. The hair on his arms lifted and his heart froze, then beat again, slow, deliberate, an echo of a rhythm that did not belong to him.

The stones shivered, and a great glassy eye opened.

CHAPTER 70

He was floating in the womb of the primordial sea, from where all life began. He was floating on a bed of crystalline foam at the edge of the earth. He was floating beneath a sea of stars, watching the moon ride across the sky, his soul borne within the turning of the tide and the soundless break of waves on a distant shore.

He was floating in darkness.

He was floating.

ACKNOWLEDGMENTS

I would like to acknowledge that *On this Broken Earth* was conceptualised and written on the lands of the Widjabul people. I acknowledge and pay my respect to the traditional custodians, past, present and emerging, of the Bundjalung nation, and their continuous connection to the landscape and the rivers of this ancient place. Always was, always will be Aboriginal land.

Writing a book is a solitary event. You sit alone, typing away, no one except the fictional people in your head to guide you and somehow, a story emerges. Publishing a book, however, is a joint production. I have somehow managed to curate a team filled with the most amazing people, and I'm still not sure what I've done to deserve you all.

To my alpha team - you guys saved parts of this book. I might not have told you that, but it's the truth. Your keen eye was exactly what I needed but beyond that, your knowledge of my world and my characters and the journey that they are on is better than mine sometimes!

My beta and my ARC team - thank you for giving up your time and stepping in to read this beast of a book for me.

To the team at Authors Own Publishing - I am so terribly grateful to have found you and to have been on this journey with you from the beginning. Henry, thank you for eliminating all my language crimes, and Danikka, thank you for all your work and for your support. Fran, my wonderful cover designer – once again you have come up with the most glorious cover for my book. I truly appreciate you! Rachael, my cartographer – your art and your skill brought my world to life and I am still in awe of my map. And to Jessie at Book Blurb Magic – thank you, once again, for helping knock my blurb into shape.

My readers – you make this worth it.

And lastly, to my family, for giving me the space to live in my head. I love you guys.

ABOUT THE AUTHOR

KATE SCHUMACHER is the author of *Shadow of Fire* and *Heart of Flame* (The Fires of Aileryan series). The Grail Cycle is a reimagining of Arthurian legend. *The Call of the Sea*, the first book in this series, was published in 2023, and the second book, *A Song of Magic* was published in 2024. *On this Broken Earth* is the third book in the series.

Kate writes worlds you can get lost in, where you will find fierce female characters who don't need saving, and men who support them. Worlds where you will find flawed, reluctant heroes, myth and folklore, power-hungry villains, complicated alliances and a cast of relatable characters.

Kate's writing is influenced by history, sociology, philosophy and mythology, and by politics. She writes multiple point of view stories with individual plot lines that interweave at different points throughout the narrative. Kate never intends this - her characters are just bossy and rude and all have things to say.

She lives in Australia, with her partner, two children and three very spoiled cats.

Follow her on social media @kate.schumacher.writer or visit her website: www.kateschumacherauthor.com for more information about her published books, her worlds, and her new works.